WRO

J.S. Lark is a coffee, chocolate and red wine lover, and a late-night writer of compelling, passionate, and emotionally charged fiction.

Jane's books may contain love, hate, violence, death, passion, a little swearing, but they always have an ending you are never going to forget …

🐦 @JaneLark
f J.S. Lark
www.janelark.co.uk

D1344000

Also by J.S. Lark

After You Fell

The Twins

J.S. Lark

One More Chapter
a division of HarperCollins*Publishers*
The News Building
1 London Bridge Street
London SE1 9GF

www.harpercollins.co.uk

HarperCollins*Publishers*
1st Floor, Watermarque Building, Ringsend Road
Dublin 4, Ireland

This paperback edition 2020

1

First published in Great Britain in ebook format by
HarperCollins*Publishers* 2020

A catalogue record for this book
is available from the British Library

ISBN: 978-0-00-836617-9

This is a work of fiction. Every reasonable attempt to verify the
facts against available documentation has been made.

Set in Birka by Palimpsest Book Production Ltd,
Falkirk, Stirlingshire

Printed and bound by
CPI Group (UK) Ltd, Croydon CR0 4YY

This book is dedicated to my daughter.
You keep me smiling, you believe in me and constantly
encourage me, even when my confidence completely fails.
Thank you for the cheerleading.

Chapter 1

2019

Lucy's arms fold into a tight knot across her chest, holding herself as tightly as the seatbelt. Holding in the anger.

I'm glad she's angry with them. I want her on my side. I need her with me.

I let off the accelerator, press the clutch pedal and drop a gear, then push the accelerator pedal to the floor, hitting the revs hard to get the car over the top of the pass between the peaks of the hills. As if getting over the hill will mean we can escape the past. But I can't change the past, only the future.

Dark shining speckles appear on the windscreen. The drops of rain seem to come from nowhere. I turn the wipers on. The rubber blades screech across the windscreen, back and forth, forming an eerie soundtrack to the uncomfortable atmosphere in the car. The rain is not very heavy, but it's seriously cold outside, and the raindrops are likely to freeze as soon as they hit the ground, layering ice on top of ice.

'You're lucky you don't have a sister.' I say to Lucy, my voice trying to instil some calm. I want to cool this battle off before she speaks to Jonny. But my nerves hum as if a swarm of bees are flying through my blood. I am not calm. I won't let her win. It's not fair. She can't have everything.

Memories run through my head, clips from a film of us, when we were young. From the days when we used to finish each other's sentences and know every thought in each other's heads. I see us doing everything for the first time together. But those days have been destroyed by all the lies and disloyalties since. We had been like two bodies with one mind until she had torn us apart. It's her fault. She says it's mine, but it isn't. It is *hers*. She is evil.

'It's Dad I don't understand. I can't believe he did that,' Lucy says.

'I know. But it wasn't his fault.'

My foot touches the brake as the car begins the descent on the other side of the hill. When it's clear, I can see for miles from this part of the road in the moonlight, across the scenic undulation of the Lake District, the glistening bodies of water sometimes as calm and still as mirrors, the woods and the barren tops of more hills and mountains with white Herdwick sheep dotted across them. But it's pitch-black beyond the beam of the headlights tonight. All I can see are the spots of rain, the windscreen wipers sweeping them away, and beyond that, about fifteen feet along the road to its boundaries, there's a drystone wall and a drop on the other side of the road, where the steep hillside is shrouded in woodland.

I press the brake pedal again before a corner and navigate the turn in the centre of the road. I am probably driving too fast, but I want to get Lucy home quickly, to speak to her father, and I can't see any headlights coming towards us.

I take another turn too fast. Lucy's arms unfold, and one hand reaches forward, to press on the dashboard and steady herself.

The car swerves on the next bend and the back of the car slips out a little. Ice. I'd seen a gritter truck earlier but in this weather, this high up in the hills, the rain will freeze on the ground regardless.

I press the brake pedal to slow down, but this time there's no bite. It doesn't grip anything. Just goes down and up in an indifferent pumping action.

Tree trunks dart past in the beam of the headlights.

Another bend approaches, my foot pumps the brake pedal three times, trying to make it catch. The braking system doesn't respond.

There are lights in the distance. Another car on the road.

'The brakes won't work, Lucy.' I'm worried now. It's not normal.

Through the corner of my left eye I see her look at me.

I steer around another bend, my foot pushing on the brake pedal trying to make it respond with brute force. In my mind's-eye, I travel on down the road trying to remember a farmgate or walking track, where I can steer off the road and slow the car down. All I can remember is the continuous unforgiving drystone wall on the left, and the steep drop down through the wood to the lake.

'I can't stop the car, Lucy.' She's watching my fingers clinging onto the steering wheel. I am not in control of the car. I'm just holding on.

At least I know the road; at least I remember the turns. My foot is still pushing on the impotent brake pedal. Useless thing!

Glaringly bright white headlights face us. Dead on. Blinding me. One hand lifts off the wheel to shade my eyes as the light floods the car. 'Lucy!' Panic pierces through my voice. Every single muscle in my body locks stiff with fear. I am not in control.

Lucy leans over, reaching out and grabbing for the steering wheel, and turning us towards the trees, fighting the inevitable as if there's a chance she'll save us.

As we fly off the edge of the road into the woods, the first impact is instant and hard. It smashes the windscreen and judders through my body like the force of an explosion as the airbag bursts from its casing and presses me back against the seat.

Lucy's scream rips through the car.

We are on the most frightening rollercoaster, racing downwards. Tumbling over and over through the bracken. Cracking branches. Bouncing from tree trunk to tree trunk. The car is no more than a pinball dropping down towards the lake. My head and body are thrown one way then the other, jolted, pulled, and caught by the seatbelt. Every strike against the metal of the car's carcass is agony. The dents gather, crushing us in, narrowing the space we have.

Lucy screams every time we hit something. The roof above her side is crushed right down.

We are going to die.

That's all I can think.

We are going to die.

Chapter 2

2018

Eight months earlier

I walk to the door to answer the insistent knocking and throw a smile over my shoulder for Lucy to catch.

She's sitting at the breakfast bar. She smiles back as her glass of wine lifts to her lips.

We're having a mother-daughter night in – wine, nibbles, and a good natter. Jonny is working late in the café, undertaking a deep clean with Marie. I had not volunteered to help, a night with my daughter is much more fun.

I should have closed the blinds, though, so whoever is knocking couldn't see us inside. They'd have moved on to sell elsewhere. The repeated knocks tell us that the person isn't going away. No matter how much charm they put on when I open the door, I'm not going to buy anything. I'd never buy from someone who doesn't know that someone not answering their door is likely to mean they don't want to be interrupted.

I twist the lock, push the handle down, and open the door.

'Hell— Oh.' Time slides into graphic slow motion, moving a millisecond at a time ... Her. She's here. But she can't be here ... I blink to clear her from my eyes. But she's still standing on my doorstep.

My own blue eyes look back at me.

She can't be here. 'Susan?'

'Hello. Long time no see,' she says.

'Why are you here? How are you here?' *Go away.* A coldness, ice or stone, spreads through my body running through my arteries into the narrowest blood vessels. Medusa is at my door. I can't move.

'Are you going to let me in? I know it's a surprise but I thought, when I found you, it was better to just show up.'

I hold the door firmly with only a foot-wide gap, not letting her in.

The ice cracks and my heart leaps into a running race.

My thoughts scramble around in a cluttered attic, looking for memories I've lost. How? But I lost those memories for a good reason. There are others ... Some break out, forcing their way through prison bars, smashing open the padlocks that have restrained them for years. I had pushed them all out of the way. But her. I've never remembered what happened to her. All I know is that it's tied up with horrible things that my mind doesn't want to remember and that I never thought I would see her again.

'Who is it?' The tone in Lucy's voice implies she's sensed the imbalance in the atmosphere. 'Mum?' Lucy's voice draws closer. 'Are you ...?' Her voice drains away like water whirling down through a plughole.

The Twins

I look over my shoulder at her, to explain, but she is looking beyond me, her eyes breaching the pathetic wall I've tried to build with my body, and she can see.

I want to run and find chairs, mattresses, and everything I have to set up a blockade in front of the open door and the hell on earth beyond.

'Mum?' Lucy's gaze moves from Susan to me.

What do I say?

'You look just like my mum,' Lucy says across my shoulder. Then she looks at me. 'I didn't know you had any family.'

My mind is spinning through all the years we were together and all the years I have had to myself.

'Mum?' Lucy pushes for an explanation, standing so close her breath touches my ear and brushes the loose strands of hair that have escaped my ponytail.

'This is my twin sister, Susan.' I don't move, keeping my body as a barrier between them.

'You have a twin sister?' Lucy's voice lifts, her eyes widening, and her mouth stays open.

You'll catch flies I used to say to her when she was young.

'Let her in, Mum.' Lucy's beautiful, long, slender fingers settle on my shoulder, implying I should move out of the way.

Lucy doesn't understand, and I can't explain. I have not spoken about this since the day I left hospital with every bad memory firmly locked away. Jonny remembers things about when I last saw Susan. But he knows I can't and won't face them. A monster screams in the dark where those memories are. I want to push her away, I want to slam and lock the door. The only thing I know about Susan now is she can let that monster out.

Why is she here?

Lucy's fingers squeeze my shoulder gently, urging me to step back. I do. Letting Lucy pull down the blockade.

'Sarah.' She steps in, her eyes and her voice saying something more than my name.

Shivers run up and down my spine. Wary, defensive heckles rising. It is strange hearing her say *Sarah* in my voice.

Her eyes are on Lucy, looking at Lucy's eyes.

'This is Lucy,' I say, 'my daughter. Mine and Jonny's daughter.'

'You're married, I know.'

How does she know that I married Jonny?

'You two are so alike,' Lucy says.

'We are identical,' Susan replies.

We are not identical. We appear the same. Clones of one another. But we are not the same; Susan is evil. I can't even say how I know that now, but I know. It's a feeling in me. I just know she is the reason I ran. She is the reason I can't remember. She is my living and breathing past that was so bad I have erased it from my memory.

'Come and sit down,' Lucy encourages, her hand lifting in the direction of the breakfast bar where our wineglasses are left, half full, waiting for us to return to them.

The image of me, an identical me from height to weight, walks across the large open-plan space that is my home and immediately makes it not a home. How can it be a home when it's no longer safe?

'Sit down,' Lucy urges again, pulling out the barstool beside the one she has been using. 'Would you like some wine?'

The Twins

With anyone else I would be proud of Lucy's warm welcome. I am proud of the way she is kind and thoughtful towards others because she is my daughter and she has grown into a wonderful woman. But this is Susan she's welcoming, and I can't tell Lucy why we should be pushing her back out the door.

Her hair is long, and it's cut to almost exactly the same length as mine. It lies across her shoulders, the waves and curls in exactly the same places as mine. I'd forgotten how alike we are. It had been normal then. It's strange now. We haven't seen each other for more than three decades, so how can we still be so alike?

I climb up onto the barstool on the opposite side of the breakfast bar from her as Lucy takes another wine glass out of a cupboard on the other side of the kitchen.

Susan has the same deep-set wrinkle as me between her eyebrows at the top of her nose, marking a frequent frown line. We have aged alike.

No. We are not alike. Susan is evil, and I have been living a normal life for years. I am not like her. But I don't know how to be me with her here. She has made me we again. Us. Twins. One entity not two individuals. When we were young it meant everything she or I did was done by us. Nothing was her fault nor mine. It was always ours.

I don't want to be involved in anything she is now; she can't be here to do anything good.

'Mum, you're staring,' Lucy says in the voice I would have used if I'd said the same thing to her when she was a child. She picks up the wine bottle, fills the glass in her other hand, draining the bottle, and hands the glass to Susan.

'Thanks. It's lovely to meet you,' Susan says to her.

'And you,' Lucy answers. 'How do I not know about you?'

'I think you should leave, Susan,' I say. She hasn't taken a sip from the glass. But I have found my voice. I get up off the barstool and lift a hand, directing her towards the door.

'Be fair, give me a chance,' Susan says, watching me and not moving.

When we were younger, I'd known everything she thought, everything she was about to say. Everything she liked and everything she hated. I don't know anything about her now and I don't want to.

'Mum. I want to talk to Susan.' Lucy is always argumentative when she's had a drink. She loves debate. She loves to challenge a point of view when she's had a glass or two.

'No, you don't,' I answer.

Susan sips some wine from the glass in her hand.

I want to push her off the barstool and out of my house.

Chapter 3

The acidic white wine tingles on my tongue, not really wetting my dry mouth. I fight the bitter look that wants to set on my face as I swallow and spread my smile, aiming it at Lucy. Then I look at her. At Sarah. I hadn't known what I would find in this secret little idyll in the Lake District. But now I know for certain that she has stolen what was supposed to be mine. All of it. 'I know it's a shock. I'll go if you want me to. Give you some time to get used to the idea.' I don't move at all, though. I want to stay. I want to watch and listen.

Her eyes – my eyes – watch me. Suspicion hovering. She must have known I would find her eventually. We're identical twins; it is impossible for us to lose each other forever. Twins are connected by invisible threads.

She doesn't answer me. My eyes turn back to Lucy as the glass slips slightly in my sweaty palm.

'Let her stay,' Lucy pleads. Without waiting for Sarah's answer, she looks at me. 'Tell me about yourself. Why are you here?'

I see echoes of us in her expression and she is slim like us. She moves like us too, that is the strangest thing. I have seen

11

her before. I've watched them all from a hiding place among the trees in the wood by the café. It is not the same as being close. Now I can see that Lucy's large eyes are exactly the same as ours, from their shape and the long dark eyelashes to the irises, a mix of pale powder-blues, like water-colour paintings with flecks of grey, and deeper.

She is a beautiful. Like us. She's the child I dream of. I want to touch her, to stroke her hair, and press a hand to her cheek to feel her warmth and confirm her reality.

Sarah has been lucky. She has taken the luck that was mine first.

'I don't know what to tell you. There is too much to say. I have no idea where to begin.'

Sarah walks away from us, to the fridge. Dismissing my presence.

She shouldn't turn her back on me. I'm Susan. I'm the evil one now, and luck can change.

'Begin at the beginning,' Lucy says, as across the room Sarah removes another bottle of wine from the fridge.

Lucy tucks her hair behind one ear. The movement draws my attention to something that catches in the light. There is an auburn tint in her brown her. Mum's hair had an auburn tint like that. We inherited our dark brown hair and blue eyes from the father we never met. But Mum's brown hair had a natural red tint that you could only see when her hair caught the light in a certain way. That gene skipped our generation but here it is in Lucy.

The base of the glass bottle bumps down on the cold slate top of the breakfast bar.

I take another sip of wine and swallow it. 'Maybe your mother should tell the story.'

Sarah looks at me but doesn't answer as she pours herself more wine. She's defensive. Protective. Distrustful.

She should be.

'If I had wanted to tell you the story of my past, you'd already know it,' she says to Lucy offering her the new bottle of wine.

This is not the reunion I pictured in my head. But that's why I hesitated and watched them from the woods for two weeks, because I've been working out how to respond to them no matter how they react. I put my glass down.

If she wants me to crawl on my knees, begging to be welcomed into her family, I won't do it. She has Jonny and she has a daughter. This was supposed to be mine. She has everything, while I have nothing. She should want to share this with me. She should want to make amends. Instead, she's run away and hidden here.

So, let's get the truth out into the open. 'When we were kids we were inseparable ...' I begin.

Chapter 4

1982

We drift back from school, in no hurry, meandering through the streets, alleyways, and parks of the Old Town in Swindon. Latchkey twins. There is nothing to rush home for. Our house is usually empty. It is just a house not a home, with a door and windows, a sofa and beds, and a cooker that Mum doesn't know how to use.

We walk along the muddy routes through the woods in Lawns Park, then sit on the kerb of the street a block away from ours and throw little stones down the drain playing a target game. Drain darts. The slot in the centre is worth one hundred points and the slots going outwards descend in points from that. When we are bored of that we sneak into Mrs Edwards' garden and pull the flower heads off her roses, then scatter the petals like confetti across her perfectly trimmed green lawn.

'Here comes the bride, all fat and wide.' I throw pale pink petals into the air. The eddy of a warm summer breeze catches them and sends them spinning like sycamore seeds over and around Sarah.

'Who do you want to be?' she says. 'Romulus or Remus?'

We had found the story of the twins Romulus and Remus in a book in the school library today. A book about myths and legends.

The twin babies had been lost and found by wolves.

When they were grown-up, they'd built cities. One of them had built Rome.

But because Rome was a better city, one twin had killed the other and taken Rome. The evil one had killed the other.

We are the only twins in our primary school. Identical twins are special people. We're better than others. Rare humans. We are as rare as pearls. Uncle Martin used to tell us, 'Rare as pearls you two.'

Uncle Michael used to say, 'Which is the evil one? There's always one evil twin.' Uncle Michael had left but his favourite phrase hangs around our house. 'Always one good, one bad,' he'd used to tease. Mum says it when one of us does something wrong, but she never knows which of us did it.

'Tell them which one of you is evil,' Uncle Michael used to say in front of his friends.

'Me. Me. I am. I am,' we had argued to make him laugh.

We had liked Uncle Michael's deep laugh. He had pretended he was Father Christmas one day. We knew he wasn't because Mum had told us Father Christmas was 'bollocks'. But we liked Uncle Michael's laugh.

Uncle Michael had disappeared, like all of Mum's boyfriends. They appear and disappear as quickly as the coins Uncle Stuart used to tuck behind his ears. That had been the only magic trick he knew.

The Twins

'I will be Romulus,' Sarah says. She snarls and lifts her hands, curling her fingers over like claws. 'We're wolf cubs.'

Our laughter blends, merging into the same sound. The same laugh. Everything about us is the same.

I love having someone the same as me. Even Mum can't tell the difference between us, because there is no difference. No one can tell us apart.

Sarah howls.

I snarl, then howl back at her.

We laugh again.

Chapter 5

Uncle Harry smokes a lot of cigarettes. Mum says he's like a chimney, puffing away, 'fag after fag'. The house smells horrible when Uncle Harry is here and our bedroom fills with smoke, like a winter fog.

We hate him and the smelly cigarettes he rolls up between his fingers and thumbs.

We want to get rid of him.

We hate the way he speaks to us. He calls us names, he calls us brats, and tells Mum to ignore us.

'We aren't brats, we're wolf cubs.' That's what we tell him. Then he swipes out a hand at us and we run before he can hit us.

Susan told me to throw away the lump of black squishy stuff that he breaks up into his cigarettes. I did that. He turned the sofa cushions upside down and then the sofa upside down, shouted, and threw things at Mum. He thought she'd taken it, or smoked it. But he didn't go away.

Susan told me to cut the toe bits off his socks. She has the best ideas. Mum's boyfriends hate it when they get up in the morning and find their socks and have nothing to cover their toes. We have used that trick four times. Mum's boyfriends leave because of that trick.

Uncle Harry hadn't left.

Now, Susan's dared me to cut his hair when he's asleep.

It is 7am. We creep across the landing together, tiptoeing over the carpet. Susan is in front of me. Criss-crosses of threads show in the carpet in places. I don't step on the threads. We play games with them. We play the snakes-are-in-the-carpet game.

My fingers tighten on the kitchen scissors so they don't slip out of my hand. The oily sweat on my palm is making it difficult to hold the plastic handles and one handle is broken so there is only a bit of the other handle to hold. I need to be quick and quiet. I can't let the scissors slip out of my fingers.

Susan pushes down the door handle that hangs loose because a screw had fallen out.

Mum and Uncle Harry aren't awake. They never wake early. When we go to school they are always in bed.

But they come home late. We hear them banging the door shut, laughing, shouting, or fighting as they move around the house. Then Mum's bed squeaks and creaks.

We cover our heads with our pillows so we can sleep.

Susan pushes the door so it swings wide, then moves out of the way. I tiptoe on, sneaking into Mum's room.

Mum's room has shadows like cobwebs all over it; they are made by the early daylight shining through the net curtains.

Uncle Harry has a long fringe that he loves. He hates it if anyone messes his hair up. His friends rub his hair to make him angry.

The Twins

His fingers touch his hair all the time, pulling his fringe forward and moving it back over his eye in the way he likes.

I am going to cut his fringe off.

A nervous laugh tries to push its way out through my lips. I press them tightly closed so it can't escape. He will hate it. He is going to be so angry.

Susan waits by the open door behind me as I sneak across the room, a stalking wolf cub.

We have looked at every book with wolves in it in the school library. We love wolves. We draw pictures of wolves at school and sometimes we stand out in the garden together, or open our bedroom window, and howl at the moon.

Uncle Harry is lying on his side with his mouth open. He makes a lot of noises when he is asleep, but it's not quite snoring. It's like whispered snores and sometimes his mouth opens and closes like a fish's.

His fringe is flopping to one side in a weird way, hanging at a strange angle because of the sticky styling gel he puts in his hair.

I creep closer, the broken bits of the scissors' plastic handles pressing into my fingers.

I reach out, my fingers shaking, take hold of the ends of the strands of hair with my left hand and raise the scissors in my right hand. The hair is light as feathers, but it is stiff and sticky with all the gloopy gel he uses on it.

The sharp blades of the scissors slice through the first strands. Snip. Snip. I don't cut in a straight line.

Snip.

Snip.

Ten-centimetre-long strands drop onto the pillow in clumps beside his open mouth.

'Take it,' Susan whispers from the doorway, her voice claiming the pieces of hair as our trophy.

I pick up some of the hair from his pillow and rush out of the room, my footsteps heavy and the floor creaking.

Susan pulls the door closed behind me; that creaks too and it bumps against the frame.

Our gazes and our smiles collide and our hands press over our mouths trying to keep our giggles from travelling into Mum's room. Susan's eyes dance with laughter. In the shadowy area of the landing, where there's no window to let in any sunlight, the black pupils in her large eyes are wide and there's a wicked cartoon-glint in them. I must have the same glint in my eyes.

'Fucking kids! Where the fuck are you? Fucking brats!' Uncle Harry's yells boom out of Mum's bedroom. His feet hit the floor the sound thumps through the ceiling, bouncing around the walls.

I look at Sarah. It's half an hour since she cut his hair. We're still smiling.

I imagine his fingers lifting when he woke up, trying to comb through a fringe that's not there. We win. He will go, and he won't come back.

Mum's bedroom door bangs into the wall upstairs. Her door hits the wall in her bedroom when it's opened too fast and too wide. There's a dent of broken plaster where the handle hits every time she or one of our uncles is angry.

'Fucking kids! Where are you? Get here!' His yells and his footsteps bang their way onto the stairs, his hand rattling the loose struts in the bannister.

Sarah's smile lifts to a grin that dents into dimples in her cheeks. There's a gleam in her eyes. She is the daredevil. She loves danger. I have ideas, but she has courage.

Uncle Harry bursts into the living room, smashing the door out of his way, whirling like the Tasmanian Devil. Large, naked, and as violently red as a chilli pepper.

He dives towards Sarah. 'Ah!' Sarah screams as his big hands reach out and she leaps over the arm of the sofa, out of his grasp.

'Ah!' I squeal, ducking and turning away from a grabbing hand. I run towards the front door ahead of Sarah, still screaming. The latch is fiddly and I have to push down the lock, turn the small knob as well as the handle. I twist and push and pull as Sarah screams behind me.

When I run out, cold raindrops hit my hair. Large drops of cold rain soak through my nightdress, pounding down like little hammers. They drench me in a rush.

I turn, looking back for Sarah. She's still in the house running around the living room, leaping on and off the furniture. She's on the wrong side of the room to get out; Uncle Harry is between her and the door.

Uncle Harry snarls, grunts, and shouts as he tries to catch her, spit erupting from his mouth in a revolting spray.

Sarah's screams follow her around the chairs and the sofa.

Rain drips from my hair. 'Come on. Come on.' I urge her to run across the sofa to join me outside. Her eyes are focused on me, reaching out to me.

'Ah—'

Her scream breaks and becomes the cracked cry of being caught as his fingers grab the top of her arm, pulling her back and throwing her from the sofa to the floor. Her head bounces on the carpet.

My breath pulls all the way down to the soles of my feet.

I want to move but every muscle feels as if it is twisted, wrung out like a flannel. I'm scared. Uncle Harry is a giant. He's like Popeye. She kicks and hits. He sits on top of her, straddling her hips, trapping her. 'Fucking kids. I'll teach you to fuck with me.' One hand circles her neck as his other hand curls into a fist.

My hair drips out the milliseconds.

She thumps his thick arms, but her fists bounce back.

His fist hits Sarah's cheek so hard I hear a crack in the moment that I step back through the door, running to help. Too late. Too late to stop him.

Blood sprays from her mouth over his forearm and splatters on the carpet.

She screams again as the second punch hits her cheek.

A sharp pain bursts through my head. I feel everything she feels. I jump on his back, my arm wrapping around his neck. 'Get off her!'

He hits and hits her as I hit him. But my fists don't make a difference. 'Stop! Stop it!' Tears merge with the rain that's still dripping from my wet hair.

His elbow thrusts back and hits my ribs, knocking the air out of me.

'Stop! Harry! Stop!' Mum yells from the stairs.

I press my teeth into the skin on his shoulder, biting as

hard as I can, biting like a wolf. I puncture his skin and bitter tasting blood fills my mouth.

'What is happening in here?' Another man's deep voice rumbles through the room. Another man's large hand pulls on my shoulder and his arm wraps around my waist, pulling, ripping my teeth from Uncle's Harry's shoulder.

Sirens wail outside.

The room fills up with people. There are six men in here. I scream and kick as the man keeps hold of me, keeping me away from Uncle Harry, with an arm around my middle.

'Let me go! Let me go!' I need to help Sarah.

The sirens wail louder.

Three of the men drag Uncle Harry off Sarah, holding his head and arms. His chest heaves like I imagine a dragon's lungs would if it was going to breathe fire.

'Come on, love. Come away,' a woman says to me as the man lets my feet touch the floor. I've seen her before. She lives on our street, over the road.

I don't move. I can't. My muscles have all locked up again. I can see Sarah. A man in a green suit is leaning over her, pointing the light from a thin torch into her eyes. Her skin is white and her body is limp, lifeless, lying on the floor like a blood-stained ragdoll.

The man's arm lets go of me, but the woman wraps me up in both arms and one of her hands presses my cheek against the cushion of her large breasts. Her soft cotton T-shirt smells of flowery soap, and her breath carries the scent of mint. 'It's all right. It's all right, dear,' she says over and over as she rubs a hand across my wet hair.

I must be making her wet. The thin nighty I have worn since I was five is soaked. It's clinging to my skin. The hems of these nightdresses reach to just above our knees. They had been down to our ankles when we were five. I am naked beneath it, with all these people in the room, and it is loose because the elastic in the neck and sleeves has stretched.

Sarah.

I push the woman away. Sarah hasn't moved. The hem of her nighty is at her waist because she's been kicking.

'It's all right dear. It's all right.' The woman tries to hold me again.

I step away from her, my arms outstretched trying to keep all the adults away. It isn't all right. Sarah isn't moving, her face is a mass of scarlet blood and bright red lumps, and she hasn't pulled her nighty down.

'Sarah. Sarah.' I kneel beside her, trying to wake her up. The man's hand surrounds my arm and he pulls me back up onto my feet. 'She's all right.'

'She isn't. Let me go!' I try to pull my arm free. He just holds me tighter.

Chapter 6

2018

The front door opens.

Susan and Lucy turn and look the same moment I do. Jonny pulls his key out of the lock as he steps in.

My heart bursts with relief in an explosion of adrenalin. 'Jonny!' He will tell Susan to get out. I slide off the barstool deserting the glass I've been nursing while Susan tells her tales of us and hurry to the door.

I need to hold him. I need reality to kick back in. I need it to be just me and him. I wrap my arms around his middle and press my cheek against the cold leather of his coat as he reaches to hang his keys up by the door. I look up to greet the warm lips that press onto mine. His short, dark beard tickles my chin. The scent he wears lingers in the stubble and the smell fills my nostrils as I breathe in when he pulls away.

His eyes look over my shoulder and then he moves, disengaging from me mentally and physically. He's seen Susan. His eyebrows lift, increasing the thin wrinkles in his forehead, as his eyes widen.

I turn around, facing her with my arms lifting, to hold him behind me. To protect him. Keep him. I don't want her to come near. I want him to throw verbal stones over my head, over my wall, aiming them all to be a perfect hit on her.

Susan has left the breakfast bar too. She walks towards us, looking beyond me at him, smiling, with my smile. 'Hello, Jonny.'

He walks around my barrier. There is no hesitation on his part either. He walks as quickly towards her as she does towards him.

He will tell her to go.

'Susan.' His voice carries surprise not anger, and he holds out a hand, offering it, not throwing it at her.

What is he doing? Panic wants me to run between them, push his hand down and shove her away. He knows what talking to her will do to my sanity.

'Hi.' Her hand slides into his and her fingers embrace his hand. They do not shake hands, just hold on to one another. 'It's been a long time,' she says with the deeper pitch of warm emotions pressing through her voice.

'Susan has been telling me about when Mum was a child and she was hit by a man,' Lucy says as she walks across the room with her wine glass cupped in her hand, the stem dangling between her fingers.

When Susan releases his hand, there is a reddish tint to his skin visible even through the tan left over from the fortnight we spent on holiday in Egypt a month ago.

He knows I hate her. *He knows*. He shouldn't want to shake her hand. He should tell her to get out.

His eyes glance at me, questioning, as his hand retreats into his back pocket. 'Well ...'

Say it. Agree with me. Tell her to go. I transport the words to him through my eyes.

He looks at Susan. 'Why are you here? Where have you been?' Again, there's no anger in his voice. It is not a challenge. He makes it sound as if her presence is pleasantly surprising.

I want to know how she found me. What she wants from me. From us. What has she come here to do?

She looks at Jonny. No. It's not just looking; she's watching him, absorbing details about him.

'Are you stay—'

'Susan has finished her glass of wine. She probably wants to go home now.' I think Jonny was about to ask her to stay. How can he think I would want that? She is not staying in our home.

She glances backwards, looking at the breakfast bar.

My gaze follows hers.

There's a mouthful of wine left in her glass.

When her gaze turns back it clashes with mine and she smiles, feigning friendliness and innocence. I know there's nothing innocent about her presence here. There can't be. She is Susan.

'I'll call a taxi,' she says.

'I'll give you a lift if you want.' Jonny offers. 'It's hard to get a cab this late on a Saturday night. They'll all be out in town. It's pub-turning-out time. Where are you staying?'

Why is he being nice to her?

'I'm renting a room in Keswick.'

29

'Why?' My voice is sharp. A knife blade that jabs. I don't trust her. How can I?

Her gaze comes back to me. 'Because I want to be near you.'

'You've been near me, now you can go. You don't need to stay near here.' Jonny's and Lucy's eyes stare at me, their expressions uncomfortable.

I don't care if they disagree. I don't want her near me.

I stare at Sarah. *Go away.*

'Mum,' Lucy complains, the hand that holds her glass lowering. She learned that tone of voice from me when she was a child. I'd used her name like that to tell her stop doing something.

'I don't need to stay near here, no, but I want to,' I say to Sarah, then look at Jonny. 'Thank you for offering, but I'm happy to ring a taxi. I'll walk back to the main road. It can pick me up at the bus stop; it's not far, and it won't be long to wait by the time I get there. The driver will probably be there by the time I am.' I knew this first meeting would be hard. There can't be any trust between us and there must be fear. But there should be fear. I just need some glue to stick me to this family so she can't push me away. I glance at Lucy. Maybe she is the glue.

'If you're sure?' Jonny says.

Lucy reaches out with her free hand, lifts my coat off the hook and passes it to me. Her other hand is still holding her glass.

Sarah moves closer to Jonny and loops an arm around his. *Mine*, the movement says.

Everything used to be *ours* long ago. Everything was *ours* until she decided to make Jonny *hers*. Then instead of *us* she became a *me*.

I would have shared. I shared everything with her.

I smile at Lucy as I slide one arm then the other into the sleeves of my coat. Lucy smiles, her blue eyes watching me as Sarah and Jonny watch me too.

Lucy likes me already, and she doesn't like her mother's rudeness. I like Lucy too. I see myself in her. She is intrigued by me. I have been telling her stories that her mother has never told. 'Shall I give you my phone number?' I ask Sarah.

She doesn't move, or even acknowledge that I spoke. She isn't going to take it. She is not going to get rid of me just by ignoring me.

'Give it to me.' Lucy pulls her phone out from the back pocket of her jeans.

Jonny unravels his arm from Sarah's then wraps it around Sarah's shoulders.

I speak out the numbers in groups of three. Lucy types them into her phone with her thumb.

'Ring me,' I say. 'So, I have your number.'

She smiles as her thumb touches the phone; a moment later my phone rings and vibrates in my coat pocket. She ends the call.

I look at the image of myself with Jonny, seeing what could have been. 'I'll say goodbye then.' We are an *us*. She has tried to forget it. But I have never forgotten. No matter how many miles, walls, or years there are between us, I will never forget. We are connected by things that cannot be bound by time or distance.

Jonny smiles. He looks the same to me as he did when I last saw him. I don't see the impacts of age in his face. I see the young man who stole my heart from inside my chest within the first hour that I'd met him.

What is he thinking? I wish I could tell. How much does he know? There's no sign that he knows anything.

I want to ask him a hundred questions. I want explanations. I want to be able to understand. Why was I left behind?

'Goodbye,' I say, even though I am not ready to go. I want something from them. I need words. An apology. But the emotions overwhelming my heart want revenge too. Something in return for all the years I have suffered while she has had this.

Sarah's facial expression is stiff. She is nervous of me. She will be constantly wondering what I'll say and do next. Good. I waited years to find her. It is her turn to wait, to wonder , to suffer.

'Goodbye,' I say it again, expressing the words to all of them, looking from Sarah to Jonny and Lucy.

I don't know if I will say anything yet. I want to see what this is first. Then I'll decide. It's more fun to wait anyway. She will live in dread and I will reap some vengeance and play with her mind.

Lucy walks around me, turns the handle and opens the door. 'Goodnight, Auntie Susan. I'll call you tomorrow.'

We share another smile as I walk out into the bright night and look up at the large half-moon and the stars that are scattered across the sky in their thousands out here where there are no cities to pollute the sky with electric light.

Chapter 7

'Goodbye for now,' Jonny closes the door on Susan.

'For now?' I say as soon as the door has shut. 'You know I don't want to see her, why were you asking if she'd stay?' The side of my fist thumps his leather jacket.

His hands lift palm outwards, calling a truce. 'I've done nothing wrong. Why did she come here? Did she say?' The cadence of his voice lifts and falls in a relaxed response.

I want him to be angry.

'She didn't get as far as telling us, and now Mum's thrown her out before she can. Why didn't you tell me about her?' Lucy's blue eyes focus their accusations on me as she takes a sip from the glass she's held on to.

'For a good reason that I don't want to talk about, which is why I haven't talked about her. Isn't it obvious there's a good reason? Why else would I not mention my twin sister? Why were you being nice to her? She's evil,' My words are launched at them both but I look at Jonny. 'How could you betray me?'

'Mum. She's an aunt I didn't even know I had. Why wouldn't I be nice to her?' Lucy throws back as Jonny turns away and pulls the zipper down on his jacket. 'You said you didn't have any family left.'

'She's not family,' I plead. 'Not anymore. She's a disaster. If she rings you, don't trust her, Lucy.'

Her eyes look at Jonny as he hangs up his coat. She always looks to Jonny to confirm or deny my judgements. Our arguments have a pause button. They suspend like a sports match waiting for a video assistant referee's judgement. Jonny doesn't take part in arguments; he hates conflict. He only reacts to the extremes. But he presides over mine and Lucy's arguments and calls who wins each point. It's a habit for her to look at him for the final ruling. I think today he is going to agree with her when he should agree with me.

My heart is trying to burst from my chest with the energy I'm expending trying to make Lucy understand. Jonny should know without me having to say a word; he remembers what I ran from in London. I don't, but it's so bad my brain has closed it off and he never talks about it.

I feel like slapping common sense into them both.

Lucy takes hold of my hand as if at last she understands how upset this is making me. 'I don't understand,' she says, though. 'Why didn't you say you have a sister? Why not just say you and your sister weren't speaking?'

'It's just families, Luce.' Jonny says, walking around us towards the kitchen. Dismissing the discussion and avoiding the conflict, true to type. 'They are always complex. I don't talk to my dad and your mum doesn't speak about her sister. But ...' Before he reaches the kitchen, he stops, does a one-eighty, and looks at me. 'People can change, Sarah. And she's put the effort into finding you. I think you should give her a chance. She's had a lot of time to regret her past and things have obviously changed. She had a hard time too.'

'What happened, Dad?' Lucy lets go of my hand and leaps on his words like a cat, then, as he turns back, she stalks Jonny across the room, ready to pounce on his impression of a fleeing rat.

You don't have an aunt, I want to scream. She doesn't count. Sisters don't do the things she's done. You have us. We love you. Why do you care about anything else? I follow them. 'Dad and I are your family. You don't need anyone else.' My tone is harder, refusing to let any more emotion leak out from where it has all been buried decades ago.

'Dad, tell me.' Lucy chases Jonny down in the kitchen because it's Jonny who's saying what she wants to hear. He disappears around the corner of the L-shaped open-plan living and kitchen space. She disappears too.

I hear a cupboard open and close. I walk towards the sofa not the kitchen.

'Is she really evil?' Conspiratorial excitement lowers Lucy's voice. 'People say there's always one evil twin.'

When I reach the middle of the living room I can see around the corner into the kitchen. Jonny has a wine glass in his fingers and he is heading for the bottle of wine I had opened.

'Come on,' he says to Lucy. 'Let's sit down and discuss this.' His eyes reach to me as he puts the glass on the black breakfast bar. 'I don't think you should worry.' He unscrews the cap on the bottle as he talks. 'And I don't think you should make her go away.' The wine makes a glugging sound as he pours it.

After he's filled his glass, Lucy holds out her glass for a top up, then he refills the glass with my red lipstick on the rim.

'If she's moved here,' he continues as he puts the bottle down and picks up his and my glass, 'I assume she really wants a reunion. It may be time to forgive and forget.' He looks at me as he brings my glass over, holding it out like a peace offering.

The glass Susan used is left on the black slate. It hits me in the face like a punch. She's been here, in my house. Talking to Lucy and drinking wine as if nothing happened in the past. But it did. There is a period I really don't remember but the rest I have fought hard to forget.

'No.' I accept the glass but not his desire for peace. The room sways, reeling around like a Waltzer carriage at the fair.

Jonny's hand catches my elbow. 'Are you okay?'

'No. I need to sit down; my legs are hollow. But I will be fine if she never comes here again.' Yesterday she could have been anywhere. She could have been dead ...

Jonny keeps hold of my elbow as I turn to the sofa. My arm slips out of his hold when I sit down, cupping the bowl of the wine glass in both hands.

Jonny stays on his feet, looking down at me. Referee, judge, or jury? 'I know this is strange, Sarah, but it isn't necessarily bad. I don't think you should shut her out. Getting to know her again might help you to get over the past.'

I feel as if I'm being lectured to. But he saw the shipwreck I was then. He picked that young woman up and stood her back on her feet. He hears my nightmares, when the memories leak and creep out from the broken part of my mind.

'What happened in the past?' Lucy sits down on the sofa, twisting sideward, her thigh, knee and calf sliding up onto the leather, so she can watch me. She drinks a mouthful of wine.

Memories escape. I need thick metal safety-deposit boxes with complex locks that can't be broken to hide all the memories in. I need a panic room. I don't want to remember.

Jonny sits on the arm of the sofa next to me and his hand pulls one of my hands away from the glass. His hazel eyes look right into mine with a look that has always hypnotized me. 'It's okay. Breathe slowly. Whatever happens, I am here. It's okay. But I think this could be good for you. I think letting go of the past would be good for you.'

A glass clinks down onto the glass top of the coffee table. 'You keep talking about it but you won't tell me what it is,' Lucy complains, her confusion disfiguring her forehead, defacing her beauty with cruel lines that will become wrinkles when she is older. 'What happened in the past?' she presses again.

'I can't.' I drink some of the wine, wanting the alcohol content in my blood to go all the way up to 14% to match the wine so it will calm my nerves.

'Just accept that Mum doesn't want to talk about the past,' Jonny says, his fingers tightening around my hand. 'What we need to do is think about the future.' He taps the back of my hand on his thigh, then rubs my hand back and forth slowly, twice, stroking my hand on the denim of his jeans. 'Are you going to give her a chance to be forgiven? Or not?'

The rim of the glass presses against my lower lip for a moment, before I move it away. 'I don't think I can.' I don't want to. My head shakes back and forth. 'No.'

'She's never done anything to me,' Lucy rules, with eyes that are as assertive as Jonny's. 'If I want to talk to her I don't need your permission. And if you won't tell me why you won't talk to her, I don't have any reason not to talk to her. Do I?'

'The fact that you're my daughter should be reason enough. You should be loyal to me whether you know why or not.'

Jonny's hand lets mine slip free. 'I'm not going to question your decision. This has taken me by surprise too. But I keep thinking about how many years have passed, and Lucy is right, she doesn't need to be caught up in what's become history. Let her do what she wants to do.'

'And if your dad showed up here and apologised for beating the life out of you when you were a child, would you let her talk to him?' My words charge at him, an angry bull storming through a china shop.

His glass lifts and he drinks a large mouthful; he swallows and it pulls on his Adam's apple.

His expression curls the corners of his lips down when the glass moves away, as if he's eaten sour lemons. 'I don't know what I'd do. But I don't think I would ignore him straight away,' his voice hisses at me like a snake. 'I would want an apology. I would want to see regret, and then I would want him to plead for forgiveness.' He stands up and turns, taking his phone out of his back pocket.

Chapter 8

'Thanks.' I lean over and place the cash, the fare rounded up to the nearest pound, into the taxi driver's open palm that reaches between the front seats. 'Keep the change.' My phone vibrates in my coat pocket as I sit back and turn to get out of the car.

I push the door shut and take my phone out of my pocket as I walk along the pavement to reach the path to the flats.

'Hello, love,' a man's voice calls. 'Have you settled yourself in?'

It's the white van man who lives in Flat 24. Alan. He had seen me carrying in my one box of belongings and offered to help as if I had half a dozen boxes to move. I declined his help, but it had taken ten minutes to persuade him to leave me alone.

He slides the side door of his white van shut with a metallic sounding slam then walks towards me, filling up the pavement and blocking my way into the flats unless I walk around him and cross the grass. But he'll think it's strange if I try to avoid him so determinedly and I don't want to seem odd. As he comes closer my hackles rise, even though I know his interest is innocent. At six foot and a few inches more, with shoulders and biceps I imagine have been worked hard in a gym, he is intimidating.

'Hello, yes, all settled in,' I answer, walking towards him with an intent that says I want to get home, hoping he will move. I have my phone in my hand; I could pretend someone has rung me.

'Well, if you need someone to show you around town, I'm your man.'

'Thanks, but I have family here.'

'Oh. Who?' He turns, moving out of my way, and then walks beside me as I carry on towards the door into the flats.

'My sister.'

'Nice. She a local? Did you grow up around here? I don't remember you from school. Will I know her?'

'No.' I turn onto the path that leads up to the front door of the flats. He stays with me, matching me step for step. 'We didn't grow up here. And if you know her, you'd know it because we're identical twins.'

'Then I haven't seen her around. I'd remember her.'

'She doesn't live in Keswick.'

'Oh.'

'They live near Hawkshead.'

'Not far then.'

'No.'

'Did you come up here to move closer to her?'

'Yes.'

'That's nice. All my family live here. I'm a born and bred Cumbrian.'

As we reach the door into the flats, his hand lifts and his forefinger presses keys on the number pad to let us in. The lock clicks as it releases, and he pushes the door wide, holding it open for me in a gesture of kindness that I am unused to.

'Thanks,' I say as I walk in ahead of him.

'You're welcome, love.' He passes me, moving ahead of me a little to open the door into the stairwell too.

'Thanks,' I say it again.

'If she lives out of town,' he says, returning the conversation to Sarah as we climb the stairs side by side. 'She might not know about the best places to find some nightlife in Keswick, away from the tourists. So there's still a good reason for you to take me up on the offer of a drink.'

I glance sideways at him.

'It can be on me, my treat,' he adds.

'Thank you, but no.' I am never going to take him up on the offer of a drink.

We reach the short landing of the first floor where the stairs turn back on themselves to progress up again. 'Goodnight,' I say. My flat is on this floor. His flat is on the floor above.

I put my hand on the door handle to push the heavy fire-door open before he can take command of it.

'You can't knock a man for trying, love,' he says as I open the door.

It depends how forcefully they try. But he hasn't been rude or pushy. I smile in answer, then slip through the door to escape.

I look back to double check he isn't following as the door

slowly shuts, controlled by the mechanism above it that prevents it from slamming. He is not there.

I glance down at my phone as I take my keys out of my pocket and walk to my front door.

The text is from a number I don't know.

Hi Susan, it was good to see you.

It begins. I touch my phone, using my thumbprint to unlock it and read on.

We need to talk. I have to tell you something. It's important. Can I meet you tomorrow some time? Don't say anything to Sarah or Lucy. It would only upset things. I can pick you up if you like. We can go for a drink or a walk. Whatever suits you. Let me know. Jonny.

A smile parts my lips as I slip the key into the door's lock.

When I'm inside and the door is closed, I reply, the phone's screen glowing in the dark room.

Okay. Meet me at 10.30 in the lakeside area?
I'll wait outside the theatre.

I touch the arrow to send the message to him.

I lean back against the door, staring at the phone's screen, hoping he'll reply immediately.

Nothing.

The phone's screen turns black as the phone shuts itself off.

Oh well, he's messaged. That's something to hold on to, and tomorrow I will see him alone. I throw the phone on my bed, turn the light on, and take off my coat.

The phone vibrates. My heartbeat leaps into a quicker pace as I pick it up, looking at the screen.

Okay.

That's all his reply says. I picture him in her company, answering quickly and shoving his phone back into a pocket or putting it down, acting as if no text was sent. It makes me smile again, because I walked back into their lives today and I already have a secret to keep with Jonny. I don't know what he'll say tomorrow, but sorry would be a good start.

The day is warmer than I expected it to be. So warm that I had to take off my coat, but actually it is handy to have it in front of me to hold in my arms like a defensive shield. I don't have any more reason to trust Jonny than I have to trust Sarah, but I want to see him. I came all this way to see him, not her.

Tourists pass me, walking past the theatre towards the lake. A lot of them have dogs with them, and a lot of them are like me, over-dressed in raincoats, and some are in their waterproof trousers too. It was meant to rain but the black clouds have blown over and gorgeous spring sunshine reaches through the vivid green leaves of the trees that line the street, forming a picturesque avenue. The scene is so beautiful it's inspired someone on the other side of the street to stop and sketch it.

The man's pad is leaning on the fence as he works with quick pencil strokes, glancing up and down.

I look towards the carpark. I expect Jonny to park there and walk to the theatre. I look at my phone again; he is now ten minutes late and he hasn't messaged. At what point do I decide he is not going to make me wait any longer and walk away?

'Hello.' The call comes from a way away and it could be directed at anyone, but even from a distance I remember his voice.

I lift my hand and wave at the tall figure striding towards me, a figure that pulls at my heart with memories I should have forgotten a long time ago. I walk towards him slowly. My heart and head want me to run. They expect a welcoming hug when I reach him. But he is my sister's husband now. My hands stay firmly pressed into my coat pockets.

His speedy walk suddenly halts into an awkward standstill when we meet in the paved area beside the theatre. There is an awkward period of silence too that is probably only a second but feels longer. 'Thank you for agreeing to meet.' After he has spoken, his hands lift and hold my shoulders as he leans in, his lips pursing. I turn my head. He was angling for my cheek, but I make sure his kiss lands firmly on my lips.

'Shall we walk down to the lake?' I say, stepping back. I need to be in motion, to use up the adrenalin sprinting in my blood.

'Yes.' His hands slide into the front pockets of his jeans as we start walking. He is just wearing black jeans and a burgundy jumper; he had come in the car and had known what the weather was like. 'Sorry to be so cloak and dagger.'

I glance at him. In profile he is exactly the same; the wrinkles of fifty years of life don't show. 'What is it you want to tell me, and why can't I tell Sarah and Lucy?' There's no point in letting him dress this up. I would much rather whatever he wants to say is straight out in the open.

'I'm sorry,' he begins as he walks with a slow pace, looking at me. 'We didn't just leave you, if you think that. We looked for you.'

Really? My heart jumps into a stronger pulse. But even if that's true, they had not come back.

'I'm glad you look well. I've worried about you—'

'It's been thirty years. You can't have worried that much. You would have found me.'

He looks ahead and releases a long breath. 'I admit I stopped looking a while after we moved here. I was busy with the café.'

Excuses. Excuses. 'Is that what you brought me here to tell me? That you're sorry you left me behind. Does Sarah not know that, or would she hate you to say it?'

'No.' His eyes are back on me. 'Sarah doesn't remember anything about that time, Susan. That's what I need to talk to you about. She had a breakdown. She was badly beaten and when she came off the drugs she just emotionally collapsed. Her mind couldn't cope.'

And you think mine did?

'She wiped the years you spent in London out of her mind and she's never mentioned them since. She doesn't remember

45

things, Susan, and I don't want her to. That's why we couldn't find you, because she didn't remember where you were living.'

We reach the area of the path that turns at the edge of the lake, where the wooden piers reach out into the water for the ferries to dock alongside. There are old fashioned rowing boats drawn up on the gravel beach at the bottom of a tall wall and huts cluster around the space above the lakeside, selling postcards, gifts, tickets for the ferry, grain for the ducks, and ice creams.

'Didn't want to remember, you mean.'

'No. Honestly, Susan, she remembers nothing about that time, and I want it to remain erased. She's seen a few different psychiatrists – when we first moved up, and more when we had Lucy. She's learned to cope with what happened in your childhood, but she's never recalled what happened in London, and she was upset yesterday because you became a part of the monsters in her head.'

He doesn't know. He doesn't know what happened in London. If she's never told him then he can't know. The anger I have been dealing with for years, the anger the psychiatrists have been working on with me for years, flares up in a red mist that hovers. But I have learned to control how I react. 'So you dragged me out here to meet you to tell me you're sorry you left me there, but that I should deal with my own memories because you want to protect Sarah? I'm not a monster, Jonny. I'm her sister.' My voice is measured, the words slow and precise, not shouted, spoken.

'How bad was it? When did you get away? How did you get away? I called the police at the time, but I had hardly any 'details from Susan. You were in Vauxhall, that's all I knew.'

'Thanks for caring.'

'We did care, Susan. But we couldn't do anything more than we did. Do you want a cup of coffee or tea? We can get a takeaway and sit down on one of the seats along there?'

'Why?' I don't stop walking. I lead us on past the hut selling drinks and snacks.

'Because I thought having told you that, you might want to tell your story to me. I do want to know. Perhaps I can help Sarah see things from your si—'

'No.' I stop walking, turn to him, and look into his hazel eyes. They are a gold colour in the sunlight reaching through the trees. When his eyes catch the light, it's just the light-brown, straw-like colours I see. 'No thank you, Jonny. I don't talk about it either.' I turn my back on him and walk away.

I know now that their life is all fake. It's a farce that they have created here. Built on lies and pretence.

I glance back. He isn't following. He's turned to queue at the café hut. I don't turn back; I carry on and break into a run. I will run for now. But in reality, he has given me stones to throw. I am not going to run for long. I will regroup, think about what it means, and then I will plan.

Chapter 9

1982

They won't let me see Sarah.

A black female police officer called Julie has herded me out of the house and into the backseat of her police car, as if I'm a lost lamb not a wolf cub. She's sitting with me so I can't escape.

I'm cold. Even though the rain has stopped and it's not that cold outside she has wrapped me up like a human parcel in a crinkling silver sheet.

'I want to see Sarah.' I keep telling her.

'Let's let the doctors and nurses do their job first, sweetheart.'

Three black-clad policemen push Uncle Harry along the path from the house. All he's wearing are his faded jeans. He doesn't even have shoes on. His hands are trapped in handcuffs behind his back and they push his head down as they reach the police car in front of us, then shove him into the back of the car so hard I see him fall.

One of the policemen sits in the back with him. The other

two go to the front of the car, open the doors, and get in.

Sarah isn't out of the house yet. The ambulance is parked in front of that police car.

I look back at the open door of our house. It's just the ambulance people, Mum, and Sarah in there now. The police had chased all our neighbours out.

The police car in front flashes an indicator light, then pulls out and drives off, taking Uncle Harry away.

A man knocks on the window beside Julie. He holds up a bright-red mug as if he's toasting the policewoman.

Julie winds down the window a little. 'Yes?'

'I brought her some hot chocolate. I saw her shaking. Poor kid.' He lifts the cup in a toast again.

Any other, no, *every* other day, these people who have come out to stare close their curtains so they don't have to see us sitting on the kerb until it's dark, or so we can't see into their houses and interrupt their lives.

Julie winds the window down further. 'Thank you. That's kind of you.' She holds out a hand to take the mug by its handle then passes the mug to me.

My hands squeeze around the warm china as I take it. It smells sweet not just chocolatey.

Julie winds the window up.

The man in the green uniform comes out of the house, the ambulance man. He has a bag. He puts it down on the grass then turns back and lifts a set of wheels over the doorstep. It's the wheels of the wheelchair that the woman had taken inside about ten minutes ago. The ambulance woman in a green uniform is holding the wheelchair's handles.

'Is that Sarah?' I ask Julie. There is a wrapped mummy-like figure in the chair in a bundle of white blankets. It must be Sarah but I can't see her face.

The man picks up his bag and walks on ahead to the ambulance.

'Sarah!' I shout, trying to make her hear me through the closed windows. She isn't moving. 'Is she dead?' I ask Julie. I don't wait for a reply, I discard the mug of chocolate on the floor, knocking it over and filling the car with the sweet, sickly smell of hot chocolate and reach for the door handle, pulling the latch to let myself out. It won't open. 'Sarah! Sarah! Mum!'

Mum is there. She is locking the front door.

'I want to get out.' I turn and look at Julie.

'Jus—'

'Sarah!' Julie isn't going to let me out. I tug at the door handle. It bruises my hand.

If Sarah is dead, I would know it. Wouldn't I? 'Sarah!' She can't hear me.

'She'll be all right.' Julie's hand is on mine, squeezing my fingers and trying to stop me pulling the door latch. Her voice is gentle but insistent. 'Sarah needs to go to hospital and I'm going to find somewhere for you to stay until she's well. It won't be for long.' Julie's voice is like the one people use when they pet a puppy. There, there. Pat, pat.

I'm not a puppy. 'I want to see Sarah.' I keep pulling at the handle as if it will work with more effort. They steer Sarah's wheelchair up a ramp into the ambulance a few metres in front.

Mum climbs the steps beside the ramp and sits in the ambulance.

'I want to go too.' I look at Julie. 'Why can't I go?'

'Sarah needs some special care in hospital. She'll be fine, but she needs to see the doctors and you need to go somewhere where you can change into some dry clothes and be warm and safe.'

'But I want to stay with Sarah!' I lash out, knocking Julie's hand away. 'I want to see Sarah!' I don't want to be separated. 'She'll want me.'

The driver's door of the police car opens. 'What's going on in here?'

I stretch a leg out to climb through the gap between the seats. But the policeman's hand comes out like the lollypop lady's and he stops me like she stops the traffic.

'Calm down, Susan. Your mother told me to tell you that she'll be in touch with you as soon as she can, and she'll let you know when your sister is on the mend. But for now the best thing you can do for your sister and your mother is behave and do as you're told so you're not a worry to them.' He nods at me at the end of his sentence as the ambulance's doors are closed.

They've left me. Mum has left me.

The ambulance people walk around to their cab.

The spilt chocolate is sticky and hot on my feet.

The policeman drops into the front seat. He pulls his seatbelt across and clicks it into place. Julie reaches across me to pull a seatbelt around me as the ambulance drives away. My eyes follow it.

There's no point fighting anymore. I can't get to Sarah. I have to wait. To wait and hope they will take me to her.

Chapter 10

The room is strange and dark but the duvet is warm and the mattress and pillow are soft. The bed smells clean, of sweet fruit and flowers. It smells a little like the tinned peaches that the school dinner ladies serve for dessert sometimes.

I like the smell.

I want to share the smell with Sarah. I try to share it through my thoughts, but I don't know if my thoughts reach her. I can't hear her thoughts. I hope it's because she's asleep.

I want to be at the hospital. I told the police I would behave and sit quietly with her. I'd escape from the house and go by myself if I knew where the hospital is. If I knew where I am too. I'm in foster care in someone else's home but I have no idea where this house is. I have my own room; no one would see me escape but I don't know where to go. I'm lying here instead, trying to make my thoughts reach her.

I've never had my own bed before. It's horrible. The room is too quiet. I miss hearing Sarah's breaths and feeling the warmth of her body lying next to me

The woman has older children. One of the boys has given up this room for me to sleep here. He is sharing now.

I spent hours in a police station before they'd brought me here, my legs swinging in the oversized chair as the radio played in a corner of the office. I wore Julie's coat all day while I'd waited. It was a leather coat with a silky red lining. She rides a motorbike into work. It was her motorcycle coat.

My lip is bruised and sore because I've bitten it for hours and the skin is torn. But the pain makes me feel better because I want to feel what Sarah is feeling.

The police bought me a whole bucket of KFC chicken and fries for lunch, and after lunch I had a Mars bar. Then a man from social services came to collect me. He and Julie brought me here. They gave me some new clothes in a bag, including a nightie. I'm wearing the new nightie. The woman here threw my old one in a metal bin with a snappy lid.

Has Sarah been given a new nightie too?

I had a bath here, with bubbles, and she left me alone, 'to soak,' she said. I've never had a bath on my own before. I've never lain down in the water and let it soak me up until my skin shrivelled into little creases before. Mum doesn't make us wash, and when we do have a bath we get in it together. But the woman here said a bath would feel nice and help me relax.

I close my eyes, trying to look through Sarah's eyes and see the things Sarah is seeing. I should be able to feel her breaths on my cheek. They are the music that I fall asleep to every night.

Tears catch in my eyelashes, trickle onto my cheeks, and run sideways into my hair, wetting the pillow. I rub the tears off my cheeks with the top of the duvet cover. My breaths become short, sharp, noisy sounds. I don't want to cry but I'm scared. My mind can see all the blood on Sarah's face and in her hair.

The door opens and light spills in from the landing. 'Susan, are you okay? Can I do anything? Would you like me to sit with you?'

'No. I just want my sister.'

Chapter 11

'Where's Susan?' My voice is weak. It's hard to talk. Pain is throbbing in my jaw, lips and teeth and around my eyes. Uncle Harry's big fist had set fireworks off in my head and they are still exploding; every pulse of pain sets more flashes off, lighting up my brain. My whole body aches. It feels as if every brick in the house fell on top of me, not one man.

The doctors say I have concussion and they need to monitor me.

'Safe,' Mum says, answering my question with the word she has spoken ten times. Impatience and annoyance give her voice a sharp sound. She hasn't looked up from the crumpled magazine she found in the waiting room. The pages flick over. She doesn't care. She is angry at us for 'causing this mess'. She is angry because we made Uncle Harry angry and 'put social services on her back.'

It's late, and dark outside. I was asleep, but the nurses wake me every hour to shine a little torch into my eyes, take my temperature, and blow up an armband that squeezes and pinches my arm.

Someone has drawn the curtains over the windows since

I last woke. They have pulled across the curtains between the beds too so I can't see the other children. But the lamps above some of the beds are on and the light shining through the thin yellow cotton with giraffe patterns turns the other children and their mums into shadow puppets.

The voices of other mothers travel through and around the curtains. They speak in soft, concerned, caring voices. Whispering, 'how do you feel,' 'do you want anything', 'I love you'.

Without Susan to be my other voice, there's a devil and an angel in my head. They talk at me like they do in Tom and Jerry cartoons. I imagine them sitting on my shoulders. The little devil speaks like Susan, telling me we shouldn't care about Mum being so useless and loveless. We don't need her. We don't need anyone else. We are wolves. Wolf cubs don't need mums. Wolves howl; they don't whisper *I love you*. The angel speaks my thoughts and feelings. She says, *I need Mum today. It's okay to need her. Mums should worry and fuss when their child is hurt. Every other mum in this ward is worried about their child.*

Our mum let Susan go. We don't even know where she is. Mum said, 'I don't need to know. She's with social services so she's safe.' But I think all these other mothers would know. No, they would not have let her go.

My stomach rumbles and growls. I'm not hungry. My tummy has turned somersaults all day, while the large black and white clock on the wall ticks away each minute. I want Susan to walk into the ward every time the clock ticks onto the next minute.

Where is she sleeping? I can't imagine it. I've asked the nurses, but they just say, 'Ask your mum.' Don't they see that mum doesn't care?

A policeman told me Uncle Harry won't come to our house again. But he won. He cut us in half. All I did was cut his hair.

'Why can't Susan sleep here, Mum?' If Susan and I are together, I won't care about the pain.

'Because she's safer where she is. I told you. You don't need to worry about her.'

But I am worried. Why aren't you?

I sit up, my head thumping as if Uncle Harry's fist is inside my skull, and slide off the bed. The hard tiled floor is cold under my bare feet. The hospital gown I'm wearing catches on the bed and pulls open at the back.

'Get back into bed,' Mum complains.

'No. I'm going to find her.'

'You're not. You won't be able to. She's in a foster home tonight and I don't even know where it is.'

'What's going on? Are you all right, Sarah?' A nurse in a pale blue uniform and tabard covered in pink cats walks over to me. She'd been looking at the notes at the end of a bed on the other side of the room. 'Can I help? Do you need the toilet? I can walk with you.'

'No. I want my sister.'

She looks at Mum, as if Mum will give me an answer.

'She's in foster care because I had to come in here.' She looks at the nurse. 'I told her, her sister is safe.'

The nurse makes a little sighing sound. It's not an angry

sigh like Mum makes when she's annoyed, it's a nice sigh. Her sigh says she cares. It sounds as gentle as one of the other mums saying *I love you.* 'Well then, Sarah, I would say the quickest way to bring your sister home is to climb back into bed and get some sleep so your body can heal quickly. Did you know all the healing magic in your body happens when you're sleeping? If you're feeling well enough tomorrow, you can go home and then you'll see your sister. I'm sure she's missing you too.'

'I know she's missing me.'

'Then get back into bed and go to sleep so you can both get back home tomorrow.'

I nod at the nurse with the kind voice, agreeing, but the room becomes a blur of giraffe curtains and soft lights. The tears trickle from my eyes onto my cheeks. I sniff them back and swallow but they roll down my cheeks and drip from my chin.

'Here.' The nurse walks around me and pulls a tissue out from a box on the cabinet next to my bed. She holds the tissue out towards me. I take it and use it to wipe my cheeks.

'If your sister is in a foster home then your mum is right, she's safe,' the nurse says, as she leans over me. 'Come on, back into bed.' She lifts the sheet and blanket.

I climb up onto the bed and slide down to lie on the sheet.

'And straight to sleep,' the nurse says as she draws the top sheet and blanket over me. When she straightens up she looks at the watch on her wrist. 'I have to wake you again in thirty minutes to do your observations; you want to get as much sleep as you can in between.'

The Twins

The soles of the nurse's trainers squeak on the floor as she walks back over to the boy's bed on the other side of the room.

I look at the clock and watch the third thin red hand tick, the one that moves the fastest. The one that counts the seconds. How many places has that got to move around the clock before I see Susan again?

A page of the magazine Mum is looking at turns over.

Chapter 12

I'm dressed in clothes that Mum brought in this morning. All the other children's mums stayed the night here, sleeping, some snoring, in the chairs beside the beds. But Mum said she couldn't sleep in a chair and she went home.

I think she went to the pub. She always goes to the pub. She could have gone to fetch Susan. She came back at 11am this morning and she didn't bring Susan.

The nurse at the desk by the ward's door told Mum off for being late. They want to discharge me. They didn't know I could hear but I'd been to the toilet so I was close to the desk and I heard.

A man from social services had come in with a policewoman to speak to her but they had gone away because Mum wasn't here. They've come back now. The nurse rang them. Mum is not allowed to take me home unless they agree, the nurse told Mum. 'Your daughter will be taken into care if you do not act responsibly.' The nurse spoke in the voice our teacher uses when Susan and I do something wrong.

I can't wait to tell Susan that Mum was told off. I start to smile every time I think about it, but I can't smile because my face hurts.

I went back to the toilet so they wouldn't see me and guess that I'd heard. I stood in there for a few minutes, staring at the strange bruised face in the mirror, a rainbow of purple, blue, red, black and yellow on her cheeks and chin, on our face.

'You'll feel better in a week or two,' a nurse had said to me last night after Mum had gone, when she'd come to look in my eyes. She had seen the tears on my cheeks. I think she thought I was crying because it hurt. She didn't know I was crying for Susan. I liked her, the nurse. I like all the nurses. But I want Susan here with the nice nurses. She would have had fun here if she had slept in a chair.

I asked the policewoman and the social services man if I can see Susan. The man just said, 'We'll see what we can do when I've talked to your mum.'

They're talking to Mum now.

I'm sitting on the hospital bed, my feet crossed and my legs swinging. Waiting. Watching through the window into the small room near the nurses' desk, where they are. I can see Mum through a long narrow window in the door.

She was crying and then shouting at them. I think, when she comes out of the room, she will be angry with me. I don't care as long as she says the right things so they let Susan come back to us.

It feels as if they've stolen Susan. Child thieves. Child catchers. Like dog wardens, rounding up stray dogs, stray wolves. In my mind I see Susan in a kennel somewhere.

My legs keep swinging. I stare at Mum through the window and try to send Susan a message in my mind. *I'm going to find you.*

It's ages before Mum comes out of the room.

Nurses in brown uniforms are handing out sandwiches for lunch.

The social services man holds the door open for Mum as she walks out. He talks over her head to the policewoman.

Mum looks at me. She doesn't smile.

I slide off the bed and run to her. it's only a few steps. My legs don't hurt, but my head hurts when I run.

'Sarah, no running,' a nurse calls.

'Mum. Are we going to get Susan?' I hold her hand. I'm holding on because I want to control her, like a ventriloquist puppet, make her say yes and take me to Sarah.

'Yes,' the man behind her answers. 'We're all going to collect Susan now.'

I look at Mum, not him. 'Thank you.' *Thank you for saying the right things.*

We are sitting in the back of the police car, silent, our hands clasped tightly on the black leather in between us. Sarah and I don't need words; we just know things about each other. We just know how much we need each other. That we can never be separated. I knew she would make them come for me as soon as she could. I waited as patiently as I could this morning, ignoring the conversation of the family I was with, just waiting for Sarah so we could be us again.

Her face is covered in vivid mingling colours, as though

someone painted her face and let the colours run into one another.

We hate Uncle Harry. It's the first time we've hated anyone. We don't like most of our uncles, but we've never hated them so much that it hurts like a fist clasped in our stomachs.

The car pulls up outside our house. The policewoman gets out of the car and holds the door so we can climb out from the back. The man who came to collect me with Sarah and Mum leads the way to the door, and after Mum has unlocked it the man and the policewoman step into the house behind us.

'The housing association have changed the locks,' Mum says, as she closes the door, shutting the man and the policewoman in the house with us.

'Good,' the man says. He looks at us. 'So then, girls. You will be safe here with your mother.'

We nod. Our palms are hot and sticky; we have been holding onto each other for an hour now. We won't ever let each other go.

The policewoman's eyes look all over the place, as if she expects to find something specific. But it's just our house with bits and pieces everywhere. Dirty plates and mugs in the kitchen. Our sofa with the big dip in one seat where we broke the springs because we jumped on it like a trampoline. Our small TV. Our curtains hanging on a bit of string. But there's one thing that's different: a brick-red stain in the middle of the beige carpet. Sarah's blood. The carpet has not been cleaned properly.

The policewoman's eyes catch me staring at her. She stops looking around and smiles, with a smile that shines in her eyes. She wants us to like her. That's what her smile says. I've seen some of our uncles smile like that.

'You have my number, Jackie,' the man says to Mum. 'If you need me, call. But I'll be back tomorrow.' He glances at the policewoman and they share a look that we don't understand. But Mum nods agreement.

'And call 999 if there's any trouble,' the policewoman says as if she thinks there will be trouble. We don't have a phone, though. The nearest phone box is at the end of the road.

'Goodbye, then.' The man looks from Mum to us. 'I'll see you tomorrow, girls.'

We don't answer; we just watch as he turns to the door and the policewoman follows him. Mum stands behind them as he opens the door, and then they both leave. She shuts the door then turns around and looks at Sarah.

We expect her to shout. She doesn't. 'Sit down on the sofa,' she says. 'You need to look after yourself.'

We sit down together. Close. Pressed together.

'Do you want a drink?'

We shake our heads.

'I was talking to Sarah, Susan.' Sarah's bruises mean Mum knows who is who. She turns away. 'Social services left some food for you. Do you want a bag of crisps? Or chocolate might be easier to eat.'

'Chocolate,' I say for us.

'I was speaking to Sarah.'

I want Sarah to look like me again. I don't like her looking different. We are still one person, even though we look different. Us. Sarah and Susan, not Sarah *or* Susan. I don't like Mum looking at us differently. We are the same.

Chapter 13

2018

'The man from social services, Dave, came back every day for three weeks to sit on the sofa and drink a cup of tea, asking us what we had done at school that day, and watching Mum. She would lean against the wall of the archway into the kitchen drinking her tea and suffering his presence.

There were no uncles in those three weeks.

But two days after Dave said he would visit just once a week, Mum went out when we were in bed and came back with Uncle William.' I laugh in a self-mocking tone. It is not a humorous laugh; it's a dismissive laugh that belittles our past.

'No.' Lucy's blue eyes pop out of her head on long stalks as she leans across the café's dark wood table, nursing a cup of hot chocolate between her hands. She lives in Keswick, not far from the flat I rent. I'd sent her a message and asked her if she wanted to meet. She'd messaged back with a smiling face and a yes.

She had asked me to continue my story as soon as we'd sat down at the table. It was interrupted twice by the server asking us what we wanted and then bringing our drinks.

'I didn't know any of that happened in Mum's childhood,' Lucy says. 'Why did you fall out if you were so close?'

'I'll get to it,' I smile. 'But you want to know it all, don't you?' I can't wait until she tells her mum I've promised to tell her everything.

'You're as bad as Mum. You sound like her, you know? I mean your voice sounds just like hers.'

'I know.'

She leans back in her chair. 'Dad told her she should trust you.'

'Did he?' My heart leaps at the thought of Jonny saying something on my behalf.

'Yes. You should go to the café and see her there. She won't be able to whip herself up into a temper there. That's what I do when I know she'll be upset about something: tell her in public.'

She makes me smile, this beautiful woman who could be my daughter as easily as she is Sarah's. There's a little jitter of excitement in my chest when I breathe in. This is everything I've wanted it to be. I want to walk right into the middle of their lives. Their café is as at the heart of it as much as their daughter is.

'Your mother and I were different after that incident with Uncle Harry ...' I say, continuing my story. It makes me laugh inside knowing that Sarah hasn't told her any of these things. She's washed her past away so she can turn herself into someone else. I don't believe she can't remember. I think she deliberately doesn't remember.

Chapter 14

1983

Uncle Harry's violence changed Sarah and me, but it didn't make us afraid. It made us tougher. It made us stronger. We could cope with anything and survive. We learned to attack before we are hurt. We are often in trouble at school for fighting, but the children we fight with are the bullies.

Mum likes violence now too. She fights with Uncle William. She hits him and he hits her back. I've seen her slap him and he pinches her arm and wraps his hand around her neck and squeezes. She's nicer to him after they've had a fight. He's never nice to her.

We haven't tried to get rid of him. He ignores us and we stay out of the house, avoiding him.

When Dave from social services visits, Uncle William goes out, and Mum says we mustn't mention him to Dave.

We haven't.

But today Mum has a bruise around her eye and Dave can see it's from a punch. We didn't see it happen, but we know

Uncle William hit her. It's blood-red not dark purple, like Sarah's bruises from Uncle Harry.

'Go upstairs for a minute, girls,' Dave says. 'I want to speak to your mum.'

As we walk upstairs, Dave shuts the living room door. Sarah is first. She looks back at me, and we agree silently that we won't go to our room, that we will sit at the top of the stairs and listen.

'What happened, Jackie?' The walls are thin; we can hear his voice easily even though he's shut the door.

'Nothing. Do you want tea?'

'Nothing is not an acceptable answer. You know that. If you stick with "nothing" I will have to call the police and take the girls. Yes, I'd like tea, but while we drink it you can tell me what happened.'

Mum sighs loudly in her dramatic, attention-seeking way. From the position of the sound I think she has turned away from him to make the tea.

They don't talk while the water runs into the kettle; the kettle clicks and gradually increases in heating sounds to a steaming boil.

I imagine Dave sitting at the other end of the sofa from the big dip, where he always sits. He is patient. Dave can sit quietly for ages waiting to hear what you will say. It's like the who-blinks-first game. Who speaks first loses. He always wins when we play that game, because we forget we aren't supposed to speak first.

'Thank you.' Mum must have handed him the mug of tea.

The sofa creaks, which means Mum has sat on the arm at

the dip end. When she sits there, she turns sideways and puts her feet in the dip.

'So ...' Dave pokes at her. 'Was it a man?'

I smile at Sarah. Her hand wraps around my hand, and she pulls my hand onto her lap, squeezing it.

'Yes,' Mum answers.

'Is he here often?' There's another period of silence. 'Remember, this is about the girls too.'

'I know.'

'How much time does he spend here? I can, and will, check what you say with your neighbours.'

'He lives with me.'

'Has he hit you before?'

There's another silence.

I look at Sarah. *Should we go down and tell him?*

'Yes,' Mum says. The word is said quietly but it's quick and angry. Just like the way she slaps us.

Sarah's lips pull up into a smile as mine do the same. This will be goodbye Uncle William.

Dave sighs. He sighs when he's thinking about something, when he's working out what he thinks about what you said.

'Then what are you going to do? I can't leave the girls here if you let him stay.'

Sarah's fingers lace us together.

If we go anywhere we will go together, even if we have to run away.

'He wouldn't go if I ask him. He won't leave.'

'Have you asked him?'

'Twice. The second time he gave me this black eye.'

'The rental agreement for the house is in your name. I can ask the police to remove him and you can get a solicitor to help you with a court order that would stop him coming back.'

'He'd still come back. He's been in prison, he was fed and warm, and he had a roof over his head. He doesn't care what the police threaten him with. He'll come back.'

'Then do you want me to contact a refuge and see if they have space for you and the girls?'

'A refuge?'

'If you want to keep the girls with you, that's your only option.'

There's another gap in the conversation. I imagine Dave sipping his tea.

The grating sound of the wheel of a cigarette lighter spins. I picture Mum sucking through the end of a skinny, hand-rolled cigarette.

'Jackie ...' Dave pushes.

'Yes. Okay then.'

'All right. I'll need to go back to the office to make the call.'

Everything will move quickly now. Like it did when Uncle Harry hit Sarah. We will be taken away. Dave makes things happen. He makes promises and he keeps them. He promised we would never see Uncle Harry again and we haven't.

The front door thumps shut behind him and the letterbox rattles, telling us he's gone outside. We stand and walk downstairs.

The living room door opens. 'I suppose you two were listening and you're happy about it.' Mum stands there holding

74

the door with the cigarette hanging between her lips, sending up a thin spiralling smoke signal, asking for pity.

'What's a refuge?' Sarah asks.

The cigarette lifts in Mum's lips. It glows the colour of fire at the end as she sucks on it. Then her fingers take it out of her mouth. 'Somewhere women go to hide,' she says. 'You better pack what you want to take. There's some bags under the sink.'

We left the house an hour later with Dave and five old supermarket shopping bags full of what would become all we had. We got into a taxi, that Dave paid for, and it drove us away from the place where we were born. It drove us out of Swindon and all the way to Gloucester.

Chapter 15

2018

The old-fashioned bell that dangles above the café door chimes, welcoming another customer with its merry jingle.

I'm cleaning off a table, wiping over the pine top, having moved the used crockery onto the tray. I glance over my shoulder, the instinct to respond and present a welcoming smile kicking in.

'Hello,' Jonny calls in a tone that questions as much as greets before I see her too.

An adrenal surge urges fight or flight. But appeasement is the third part of a human's instinctive defence mechanism ... That's what Jonny wants me to do. To wave a white flag and talk to her. But he doesn't know all the details. He can't understand what he's asking me to do. I may not remember everything, but I remember enough to know she's trouble.

'Hello,' Susan answers Jonny, looking at him. She hasn't looked at me yet. His eyes direct hers to me.

I'm frozen into stone, caught in her Medusa stare again. Is it really only me who can see the snakes she has in her hair?

'What are you doing here?' I ask.

'That's not a very nice welcome.' Her voice is jovial. Happy. Everything in her body language and her voice suggests she is not a threat and pleased to be here.

Is she pleased to be with me, though, or pleased to torment me? Is it all pretence?

Was she happy in the years we were apart? The question flies into my mind and lands sharply and heavily like the point of a dart. Like thinking of her dead. I'm not sure I can imagine her really miserable and be happy myself. But I don't want her to make me miserable either.

She looks at Jonny again. 'I saw your advert for a part-time waitress in the window. Any chance?'

He looks at me again, directing her eyes back to me, smiling in a way that makes a statement.

She'd assumed Jonny was the one to ask. He is the one wearing a striped blue and white shirt while I'm wearing a sleeveless, loose summer dress over a T-shirt and black leggings but we're equal partners in this café. The lease and loan that set this place on its feet are in both names.

'I'd suggest you two talk a bit more before you make any commitments. You need to be sure you can endure each other's company. Shall I make you some coffee and you can sit down for a few minutes?' His gaze holds mine, looking for anything I might say through silence. Susan is probably still able to read those sorts of interactions too.

Susan. It's still weird to hear that name aloud, or in my head. I had banished it.

We only have four customers. The Easter holidays are over

and it will be a month before the Summer tourists arrive. In the height of summer the café is full nearly every hour of every day. But today, the people scattered around the tables are regulars from the village. People who just want to get out of their houses for an hour. They are looking, though; it's not every day someone's clone turns up.

'We'll sit outside,' I say, untying the bow securing the pinafore that's wrapped around my middle. I don't want the regulars, or even Jonny, to hear this conversation. 'Come on,' I say to her, leading the way and throwing my apron at Jonny.

I pass her and open the door.

The bell rings again.

I hold the door, letting her walk out first then follow her, as Jonny goes behind the counter to make the coffee himself. He smiles at Marie who is making up a sandwich order. She raises her eyebrows at him, and I see his skin redden.

The door swings shut behind us as if it is closing on the life I have today and leaving me in the past.

'What are you doing here?' I turn to one of the tables in the shade of the awning and pull out a chair from a small round two-seater table.

'Finding you.'

'Why?' The metal seat is cold.

'Because you're my sister,' she says as she pulls out the chair on the other side of the table and sits down facing me. 'My twin sister.'

I wait for more. Expect more. Nothing more is said. 'That doesn't mean anything special anymore. It's just genetics.'

The lake water laps at the pebbles on the narrow shoreline

in front of the café. The gentle sound and the calls of the birds in the wood behind the café deny the intensity that crackles across the table like a forest fire.

'It means something to me, and I came because I want you to admit that it still means something to you. Don't worry, I won't say anything to Jonny. I've accepted everything as it is.' Her elbows rest on the table and she leans in to make the conversation more intimate, my blue eyes staring back at me, promising to tell the truth, the pupils glowing with what looks like a real desire to be forgiven. Her posture is subtly threatening though.

'Are you waving a white flag or a skull and cross bones?'

It's strange looking at her. She is the me I see in pictures. And the me I see in the memories of my childhood. She's like a shadow of me. The evil half of me. Not a separate person.

'I'm sorry.' She says without prompting. I see a very good impression of sincerity in her eyes.

Crocodile. I don't trust her. Why would she come here and say sorry to me now?

'I'm not.' I lean back in the chair, moving as far away from her as I can without getting up and walking away.

'I want us to be close again. I want to forget everything too.'

'And if I don't want us to be close ...?' I sound like Lucy at her most belligerent. But I have a good reason to be confrontational. Why should I trust her Trojan horse of an apology?

She sighs in the dramatic way that mum used to and her eyes glisten with a sheen of moisture that implies sadness. 'Then I'll go away.'

'Is that a promise?' Does she feel as strange as I do, looking at her exact resemblance. We still look absolutely identical, weight, height, hairstyle, everything.

'If you want it to be?'

'I do.' She was always a good liar; I suddenly remember that. What is she really thinking? Years ago, I always thought I knew what was in her head.

'Then I promise to go if you want me to,' she answers. 'If you promise to try to get to know me again for six months before you decide.' Her ransom demand is thrown across the table like the perfect poker hand, with an indifferent expression.

Six months.

Is she lying?

My fingers pick a packet of mayonnaise out of the condiment holder on the table and I squeeze it in the middle, squishing the sauce inside the plastic.

'Six months,' she repeats. 'We need to spend time together to get to know each other.'

'Why?' I ask again, remembering Lucy as a child of five. Every question was followed with three more whys. Why? Why? Why? 'What is the point?'

'You have a husband and a daughter. I don't have anyone. I want my sister back.'

I don't answer.

The café's doorbell rings.

'Here you are,' Jonny comes out carrying a mug of coffee in either hand.

He smiles at me, a smile just for me, his hazel eyes offering understanding and support.

I love you. The words slip through my thoughts. When Susan has gone I will hug him and say the words aloud. 'Thank you,' I say as he puts a mug of foamy cappuccino down in front of me.

'Thank you,' Susan says when he puts the other mug down in front of her.

It's like a perfect echo. Our faces are the same, our bodies are the same, and our voices are the same.

'Do you want to talk about the past?' She asks as Jonny walks away.

I lean forward to drink the coffee. 'No.' I'm looking at the heart Jonny has drawn with milk foam on the top of my coffee, not at her. I lift the mug and sip the coffee, breaking the heart.

'Then tell me about your life. Tell me what Lucy was like while she was growing up.'

I don't want her to know about Lucy. I just want her to leave us alone. Me, Jonny, and Lucy.

'I like going to watch films at the cinema,' she says. 'We were never able to go as children, were we? Did you go with Lucy when she was growing up?'

'Sometimes. She didn't like the noise from the surround sound until she was about ten. How did you find us?'

'Through the café. Someone mentioned Jonny's name on Twitter, with a link to the café information. They recommended it. They'd come here every day on their holiday. Neither of you are on social media. There isn't even a proper webpage for the café. It was just a Google link.'

I know. It's deliberate. My hands embrace the warm coffee

mug. I look at her, telling her to take our lack of online presence as a hint. But I know now that she had never really been able to read my thoughts.

'Do you remember leaving London?' she asks.

I shake my head. 'I know we lived there. I met Jonny there. But I don't know what happened. I don't want to.' A shiver of distaste trembles through my shoulders as my mind shakes, warning of an earthquake and a Tsunami if I touch those memories. I look down, shaking my head again, seeking comfort in the warmth from the coffee cup. 'I just know that it was a horrible time.' I look back up at her. 'And it was your fault. You always got us into trouble, Susan. Did you stay there?'

She stares at me, not responding for ages, then she says, 'For a while.'

'But you've been somewhere else since ...'

'Obviously.'

I can still spot her tells, even if I can't read what's in her brain. She's omitting important things. She's looking at me too directly. Hiding behind a solid mirror that she's cast across her eyes. I don't want to remember the things that will be behind that mirror anyway. But if I can spot her tells, she can see mine too. She is just choosing to ignore my leaking body language telling her to go away.

'Where was somewhere else?' I ask.

'I don't want to recall that. I haven't had the happily-ever-after ending you have. You should think yourself lucky.'

'I do. Is that why you're here? To muscle in on my happiness?'

Her body jerks back slightly. It's a tiny movement that no one else would probably have noticed. But I notice because I know her better than anyone else. I am her.

The years between us break apart, disappearing, exploding in a dynamite blast. She is in my head, another me. I know her mannerisms, her body language. I can read so many things through the way she moves and looks at me. That is what I had thought was our special sixth sense when we were children.

'Yes,' she admits. 'I want to be happy. I've never had a chance to be really happy.' Her gaze holds mine for a moment, then drops, and she drinks from her coffee. Which is strange because the action does not seem the right movement, it doesn't match her words. If she thinks I can make her happy, why not look at me when she says that.

I drink too. But I don't take my eyes off her. 'Are you asking for pity?'

Her gaze rushes back to me. 'No. I've never needed pity.' There's an accusation in her eyes, something that I am being accused of. Words hover on her tongue but she is hanging onto them behind her lips.

'I said we won't speak about it. I won't say anything, if you don't,' she says.

If she is speaking about things that happened in London, I have nothing I can remember to speak about anyway. But if she is speaking about the years before London, then there are things I don't want Lucy to know. I nod, agreeing. 'I won't say anything about the past. Your secrets are my secrets.'

Chapter 16

1985

'Girls! Girls!' The copper's shouts punch through the air with a pitch that says, *stay where you are*.

Susan looks at me, smiles, and then she says, 'Run.'

She laughs as we launch into the race. Our legs pump hard, our trainers with the holes in the seams of the canvas pounding on the pavement.

We have a head-start of a few metres on PC Merry. Uncle Charlie calls PC Merry the laughable policeman. The copper doesn't know we know him. He doesn't know us. But he knows Uncle Charlie.

'Girls! Stop!'

He should know we aren't going to stop. If we stop we'll be in trouble for not being in school. That's all he thinks we've done – skipped school. But that's not all that we've done.

We run across the uneven pavements of Cirencester town centre then dodge into an alley between the shops, the muscles in our legs burning.

Susan stops. As she breathes, her breaths pull at the buttons

85

of her blouse. 'Put the stuff in this bin,' she orders lifting the blue lid of an industrial recycling bin. It's packed with cardboard. She tips goodies out from the sleeves of her cardigan and unloads the pockets of her skirt.

I pull the stolen goods out of my pockets and throw them in.

'Come on.' Susan lets the bin lid fall with a plastic clatter, clasps my wrist and pulls me on.

There's a bench at the end of the alley, a bench that we can climb onto and use to get over the fence into the park beyond.

I hear PC Merry coming, his shoes slapping rhythmically on the pavement. In a couple of minutes, he will reach the end of the alley and see us.

Susan lets go of me and climbs. I climb too. She flops over the top of the fence, falling onto the grass on the other side. I tumble over a moment behind her.

We stay still, huddled together on the ground, listening and waiting. If he looks over the fence and doesn't look down he won't see us but if we start running he will.

His footsteps run into the alley and along it, getting closer and closer, then he runs past us, out of the far end of the alley and into another street.

I look at Susan and press a hand over my mouth to stop a laugh erupting.

'Do you want a cigarette?' Susan pulls a packet out from her skirt pocket.

I do laugh, quietly, because she'd dared to keep a packet. I'm usually the daredevil. I had been the one who had pulled the packets off the shelves in the shop. But she told me to. It was easy, though; Mr Jankowski is always leaving the shop unattended. He goes out the back to talk to his wife and we take advantage.

Uncle Charlie says, 'If people give you an opportunity then it's only polite you take it.'

He makes us laugh and he likes making us laugh. He says things just because he knows we will laugh.

Susan unravels the plastic, opens the packet, pulls out the foil, and throws it aside then takes out two cigarettes. She holds them in her lips, puts the packet back in her pocket and pulls out a pink plastic lighter that had been in the cardboard holder near the till. She lights both cigarettes, sucking on the filter ends as she holds them in the lighter's flame. Then she holds a cigarette out for me to take.

'Thanks.'

We sit with our backs against the fence, our legs stretched out and crossed at the ankles, and blow smoke circles up towards the blue sky. The nicotine slides from my lungs into my blood.

We can't go home for a while. We have to hide until the end of the school day.

We never go to school. We don't fit in there. We can read and write. One of our primary school teachers said we were exceptionally bright. We don't need to know anything else from teachers. We taught ourselves how to steal and we are good at that.

The head teacher told Mum we're feral.

We looked that word up. It means wild. Untamed.

We like being called feral. It reminds us of when we used to imagine that we were wolf cubs.

The day is hot, and the grass is dry, so we don't get up. There's nowhere else to go to anyway.

We strip off our cardigans, pull the hems of our grey school-uniform skirts to the top of our thighs and turn our faces up to the sun, like sunflowers. We close our eyes and let the sunshine warm us from the outside to the inside, letting the sun tan the skin on our faces, arms, and legs.

We open our eyes as a cold shadow sweeps across our legs, as if the sun has been covered over by a cloud.

'Hello. What are you two up to?' Three boys are looking down at us, their shadows stretching over us. The tallest and best looking was the one who'd spoken. He has amazing gold eyes.

'Nothing that's any of your business,' I say. We are tall, for our age, but if we stand up these boys will tower over us by inches. They look like teenagers.

They make us wary, but we aren't afraid. We aren't afraid of anyone. My heartbeat is racing, though, like it was before when PC Merry was chasing us.

'I saw you had cigarettes. Let us have one.' It's not a request; it's an order made by a ginger-haired boy.

It would be better if we were on our feet. We would be less vulnerable, more able to fight. But if we get up they will think we feel threatened. In an unspoken agreement we stay in our casual position on the floor, neither of us moving a muscle. But I feel awkward just sitting here.

'Go on then ...' The tallest and the best looking holds out a hand towards Susan, asking verbally and physically, not telling.

'What are you going to give me in exchange?' Susan asks him. She's smiling at him. Flirting. Mocking the size and the threat of him.

'I'll pay you back for it later.' He smiles. He has a charmer's smile. Uncle Charlie smiles like that when he's sober.

I like a smile like that. It says, *like me. I can make you laugh*.

Susan takes the cigarette packet out from her skirt, opens it, and takes out one cigarette. She holds it out to him. 'Here you are.' When he bends down reaching for it, she pulls it back smiling.

He nearly loses his balance and tumbles on top of her, but his black friend with short black hair grabs the back of his T-shirt.

I think he'll be angry. I see his anger bursting open in my mind. He isn't. He laughs. 'Bitch.' The insult is said in the lightest, least offensive way possible. He holds out a hand, his palm open and facing up. Offering to help Susan stand, not asking for the cigarette. 'If you give me one, we can sit in the playground and share it.'

'What about us?' His black friend protests.

'You'll have to convince her to give you one yourselves.'

Susan reaches out and holds his hand. He pulls her to her feet, leaving me alone on the grass.

His mates don't offer me a hand but then I don't have the cigarettes. There's a hoard of goodies in the rubbish bin on the other side of the fence, though. There are more cigarette packets and some chocolate bars.

I don't tell them. I don't want to share with them. I can get up on my own.

Susan walks off, still holding the boy's hand. She doesn't even know his name. But he's a charmer.

Are we like Mum? Because ... I fancy him too. If she hadn't taken his hand I would have reached out. Smiles like that boy's are like the music of a snake charmer. He is the Pied Piper for girls.

I glance down at the watch Uncle Charlie picked out from a bargain bin in the newsagent and stuffed into his coat, then gave to me. In the time it had taken the long second hand to tick over one minute we had learned to fancy boys.

Just looking at him had made my stomach tumble over in a roly-poly. I held my breath when he held out his hand, my heart leaping around on a pogo stick because I knew something momentous was going to happen. It had happened to Susan.

The ginger-haired boy's eyes are leery. He's watching me in a way that makes an unpleasant tingle run up my back.

'You got any cigarettes?' he says.

'No.' I don't like him. He's ugly and rude. He's not even trying to be charming to persuade me to give him a cigarette. He would try to bully me into giving him a cigarette if I had any.

'Are you coming with us, or are you just going to sit there?' The black kid's eyebrows lift as he asks me. Then he holds out a hand.

I scrabble up without accepting his hand. Probably flashing the crotch of my knickers because my skirt is pulled so high. I pull the hem down, wrap my cardigan around my waist and tie it at the front, then pick Susan's cardigan up off the grass.

'Why are you in the park?' I ask the black boy, my eyes on Susan and the tallest boy, walking ahead, talking to each other, still holding hands. She doesn't seem to care that I'm not behind her.

Why did he pick Susan to hold hands with? Just because she has the cigarettes. That's the only difference between us today.

How can anyone pick between her and me? We are the same. I've never thought about boys before. But how will boys choose one identical twin? By a packet of cigarettes.

***

I spend my afternoon sitting on one of the eight sections of the witches-hat roundabout, with the black and the ginger boys in the sections either side of me, watching Susan kiss the tall boy sprawled across a section of the roundabout. The other boys and I just sit there smoking. They talk, while I listen.

I learn their names. Jonny is the tallest one, the black guy is called Wayne and the ginger creepy one is called Jay.

'Shall we get something to eat?' Susan is looking at Jonny and only talking to Jonny, who is reaching for another cigarette.

Jonny's other hand slides down from a position where it had been on her chest over the top of her school blouse.

I look at my watch. It's nearly five.

'I have money for a burger.' Susan says. Stolen money.

Jonny sits up, his long legs dangling over the side of the roundabout as he takes another cigarette from our packet and uses our lighter to light it.

His gaze catches mine.

I think he's looking for the differences. There aren't any. If I met him and she wasn't there, I could pretend to be her, and he wouldn't know.

'I don't have any money.' Jonny says to Susan his gaze moving off me to her. Then he looks at his mates. 'Do you?'

Shaking heads are his answer.

'We have enough money for everyone.' Susan says.

She's going to give them our money.

'Sarah has it.'

We took the money from Uncle Charlie's wallet this morning when he and Mum were in bed. We took it to buy cigarettes but then Mr Jankowski hadn't been behind the counter so we'd just taken what we wanted.

The notes are still folded and hidden in my skirt pocket.

Jonny, Wayne, and Jay look at me.

What will they do if I refuse to pay for them?

'You'll have to earn your burgers,' I say, taking control, my chin tipping up as I look them in the eyes, one at a time, desperately trying to think of a good, grown-up dare.

I will ask them to steal something else for us.

Chapter 17

2018

A laugh, a sharp, high sound, pulls my attention across the room to the café's counter where the selection of cakes, salads, and pastries are displayed in the chiller cabinet. Marie is placing the freshly baked scones that have been flooding the café with a delicious smell for the last ten minutes onto the cream-tea plates. Jonny is standing beside her. But Susan is there too, this side of the counter, looking over at Jonny. The laughter came from Susan.

Her hands are on her hips in a posture that makes her breasts more prominent. They push against the white blouse she is wearing, stretching the buttons at the front so there is a flash of bright scarlet bra. Although, her bra is clearly visible through the white cotton anyway. Sometimes she looks more like a striper than a waitress.

I can always tell the two of us apart, now, when I catch sight of us in the mirrors we have on the walls to make the café seem bigger because she wears in-your-face clothes. There's always something prominent about what she's wearing. It's sexual. Slutty. And it's Jonny's face she shoves herself in.

Other than that, though, generally, she wears her hair in a pony-tail, while mine is down and that is the only way strangers know which waitress has arrived at their table – the owner or the summer-temp – and sometimes, despite her choice of clothes, when she wears her hair down regulars ask her questions about my life.

Even Jonny mistakes her for me when he's not concentrating and just turns to ask something quickly. Until he remembers what I wore to work.

I have thought about cutting my hair short, just so there will always be something that easily distinguishes me, but that feels like giving in to her. I don't want short hair, so I'm not going to let her force me into cutting it. I like it like this.

The problem is that she likes her hair the same way, and she likes many of the things that I like. Including Jonny.

She said she wanted to get to know me again, but she spends more time at the counter or in the office talking to Jonny than she does out here serving the tables with me. With her breasts trying to pop her blouse buttons open.

I want to say something but it sounds childish. I'm not going to let her force me into feeling like a vulnerable, possessive child. I don't want to let her know she has the power to make me jealous, or to doubt Jonny. I don't doubt him. I've never fretted over Jonny's faithfulness. He's a good man.

But her …

I don't trust her.

She makes me feel as if I'm lying to myself when I say I

trust Jonny. Because I am afraid our relationship isn't strong enough to withstand Susan the bulldozer.

Yes, it is. Jonny loves me.

I pick up the tray I've filled with dirty china and cutlery and carry it over to her.

My movement draws her eyes away from Jonny.

'Here, you can take this into the kitchen and get the dishwasher going; we're running low on china,' I say.

A frown creases her brow, deepening the single wrinkle in the middle of her forehead above her nose. The frown fans out from there in slender lines.

I smile. *Go on. Get lost.* What has she been up to for all those intervening years?

Behind her back, Jonny's dark eyebrows lift, asking me why? He knows we're not running low on clean china.

When she turns away, I poke my tongue out at her back. She has succeeded in making me a child again. I hate her. I have only agreed to her working here for six months on the grounds that at the end of those six months she'll leave the Lake District and leave me alone. And then there's the old adage, keep your friends close but your enemies closer.

Jonny's lips twist in a lopsided smile and he shakes his head a little, his eyes laughing at me but in a way that cautions too.

See. We are close. We can have long conversations across the café without words. We are as close as twins. We are us, me and Jonny.

I send him a smile, letting my inner laughter and love flow into my eyes for him to see. I adore him ten million more times than I hate Susan.

Marie catches my gaze, but she quickly looks away.

Behind me the bell above the door rings announcing more customers.

I turn around but in the same moment Marie walks around the counter to great them and direct them to a table. She must have seen them approaching through window.

A hand rests at my waist. There's breath on my neck. His lips press against the hollow of my neck where it turns to my shoulder and his hand taps my side.

'You can be a bitch sometimes, sweetheart,' Jonny whispers against my ear as he pulls away.

I turn my head and our gazes clash. 'Sometimes, people deserve bitchiness,' I answer, smiling again.

'We're practising forgiveness,' he reminds me in a light voice that half jokes but the other half of the lilt in his tone tells off my jealous child.

He might be on the forgiveness page with Susan but I am working through a different book called temporary tolerance.

The bell rings again, announcing the arrival of another customer. I toss Jonny a less sincere smile, pull the pad and pen out of my apron, and go to take the order.

Chapter 18

1985

I shift my bottom, trying to sit in a slightly different position on the metal bicycle rack. I've been sitting here for hours, and in my stoned state the discomfort is an increasing noise in my head. Any moment I will keel over like a boat out of water or fall like a felled tree.

Jonny passes the joint to me. As I take the skinny stub of white roll-up, our fingers brush.

He smiles an uneven smile at me, his lips listing to the left. The smile lifts to his charmer's eyes.

He bought the cannabis, tobacco, and papers. The dependence on our theft has reduced because Jonny has a job working in the kitchen of a café for the summer.

It's been warm for the last fortnight. We've spent every long day out in the park making the best of the light evenings, mostly with Wayne and Jay because Jonny is working. But Jonny always comes here straight after work.

I spend every minute of every day waiting for the moment when Jonny walks over the grass to join us. My heartbeat jolts harder at the first glimpse of him and my insides wobble. I know Susan feels the same but I don't think she knows that I feel it too. She doesn't seem to know what I think anymore. Or she doesn't care.

He is holding her now, with his back against the corrugated iron side of the bicycle store and his legs splayed. Susan is standing between his legs, leaning against him. His arms wrap around her middle.

She turns her head, looking up as he bends. Their lips touch.

Wayne and Jay ignore them. But I watch, and occasionally his eyes turn to me, saying, *why are you staring, Sarah?*

Because I like you too. He must know it. But if Susan doesn't, maybe he doesn't either. I haven't told her. It's the first secret I've kept from her. I haven't told her because I think it will annoy her. I don't understand where a boy fits in between us. Does she like him more than me? What would she do if I tell her I like him too? What would she say if I tell her it hurts me to watch her kissing him?

He is dividing us. Bit by bit. It has progressed from seconds to minutes, then from minutes to hours. Even when they are apart we think of him and not each other. Sometimes they go off together in the evening. They get something from the shop or something from his house. There's always a reason why she doesn't want me to go with her. 'No, we don't need anyone else to come.' 'Jonny is coming with me, you don't need to, Sarah.' It always takes them longer than it should. Susan and I aren't *us* anymore. It's her and him.

I am jealous. Envious. When she leaves me with Jay and

Wayne, she turns me into the incredible hulk – green and vicious with anger. I hate her sometimes now. I don't want to be left behind. I don't like her doing things that I haven't done. We used to do everything together. I want to be with Jonny too.

'Hurry up, have a good drag, then give me the joint,' Jay says.

I draw a deep breath through the joint, the heat from the burning tobacco and the drug burns my lips as the poison from the cannabis scatters through my brain. My body is a ragdoll's.

I don't know where I fit in anymore. I don't have a place.

'You okay?' Jonny is watching me.

My eyes might have rolled up for a moment; the world turned black.

'I just need to sit on the floor,' I say. My head is spinning. I take another drag from the joint and pass it to Jay, then slide down the metal rack. My bottom hits the hard tarmac.

I close my eyes as the cannabis brushes over me. It's like that, like a sweep of feeling. It makes me float.

I like lying on the grass in the darkest place I can find and looking at the moon and the stars when I'm stoned.

We often stay out all night now it's warm. We run home at sunrise, sleep for a couple of hours and leave again before anyone from social services or the police are likely to come around and force us to go to school. Mum had a letter from the school's solicitor. They are taking her to court. They said they will fine her or lock her up in prison if we don't go to school.

We don't go. She can't make us.

She tries to get Uncle Charlie to make us go but he is out at work in the morning and he can't make us go.

So we live on the streets nearly all day and night.

Something touches my head, ruffling my hair. I open my eyes and look up.

Jonny is touching me. I see him through a haze that's like looking through water.

'Don't have any more, Sarah.'

I don't answer. I can't answer. I can't make my lips or my tongue move.

Susan reaches out to take the last of the joint from Jay.

My head tumbles back and bumps against the metal. I let my head rest there, on the cold metal pillow, as my thoughts swim in the water that is all around me.

The others' conversation drifts in single, isolated words, and the sounds sail off on the mild evening air. I don't know how late it is. It's probably only nine o'clock and I am drunk and stoned out of my head.

A smile slides my lips over my teeth.

Chapter 19

There is something on my thigh. A heavy touch that is holding roughly. It hurts.

It's not just on my thigh. It's pressing on me and into me too. Searching inside me.

The intrusion goes away.

I open my eyes. The dark sky is spotted with stars but there's a black silhouette of someone in front of the sky. I'm not lying on the grass; I'm on hard, uncomfortable tarmac, half under the canopy of the bicycle shed and half out of it. The moon is as thin as a sickle tonight.

I try to move, to get up. My body is heavy, and my legs are tangled in something from my knees down. The figure is frightening. I try to speak, but my numb lips and tongue don't let the sound escape. My body won't obey my brain.

The tarmac scratches the skin on my back and bottom. My shorts and knickers are around my knees. Air strokes over my stomach and the top of my thighs, whispering, *you're naked*.

Why are my knickers and shorts at my knees? Did I go to the loo and I couldn't pull them up, or did I fall? I try harder to get up, to sit up, so I can pull up my clothes. My arms and legs won't do that. I'm like a fish flapping around out of water. Like a mermaid with my legs tied into a fin.

Vomit lurches up into my throat. I swallow the bitter bile back and lie down, giving up the fight against my body. The stars are sparkling, like fairy lights.

A jangle draws my gaze to the human silhouette.

It's Jay. His hair catches the moonlight and instead of looking ginger, he appears blond.

He is fiddling around at his waist. Undoing the button and the zip of his jeans. His loose belt buckle jangles like bells.

Jay's hand presses down on the tarmac near my shoulder, and his other hand pushes down his jeans and underwear.

His breath smells of garlic.

Jay's hand presses hard on my thigh as he looks down at me. He is looking at me naked. I can't do anything to stop him. His penis has its own jutting silhouette. Men's penises dangle normally. I've seen our uncles'. It shouldn't be pointy; it isn't right. That's a sex shape.

'No.' My lips and tongue try to say the word. I don't like him looking at me or touching me. 'No.' I can't say the word loud enough.

His weight comes down on my thighs and there's a feeling inside me again, as if something is pushing into me. His penis. It's a horrible sensation. Invading and uncomfortable. I don't want to be touched. 'No.' The word is too slurry. He doesn't understand me. 'No.' It's a merging of sound, he can't hear it.

His hips lift and push down, bumping and rubbing against me. The skin of my bottom scratches on the tarmac. I hate the feeling of the hair at his groin, and the feeling of whatever he is doing inside me with his penis.

'No.' I can't make the word clear or loud enough. 'No.' My hand lifts to push him away but my arm has no strength. 'No.'

His head is down, looking at me naked. Looking at us naked from the waist down and looking at his penis pushing in and pulling out of me.

I don't want this.

It's sex.

I have seen Mum do this. I have seen uncles on top of her, and her on top of them.

I haven't chosen this.

'No.'

I wish my mind and body could move but they are too flooded with drink and drugs. I want to move. To stop this. It's horrible. I want him to stop and I want to get up. 'No.'

'Fuck.' he swears in a breathless whisper that sounds as if he is in agony too. Then his body pulses into mine with heavier and harder strokes. He is punching at me, like he's hitting a punching bag. 'Fuck.'

A bruised feeling throbs out from my stomach and runs into my thighs as my bottom scrapes repeatedly on the tarmac. 'No.' My voice is desperate and breathless with pain now because I know he doesn't care that I want him to stop.

'Move, Sarah. Fucking give me something back.'

If I could I would knee him in the balls. I can see my knee lifting in my head but in reality my body won't move.

This feels the same as when Uncle Harry hit me. Hard,

heavy, angry strikes that I can't stop. 'No. No.' My refusal is a cry for help that sobs out like a little child's as tears roll from the corners of my eyes. 'Please, get off me.' In my head the words are as clear as the moon in the sky, but in the air they are a blur of consonants and they don't make sense. They don't tell him. He still moves. Invading. Hurting. Raping.

Where is Susan? Where is she? Why is this happening? 'Ahh!' The sound is the scream of a wounded animal. Of pain and betrayal. Of loss. Nothing will be the same after this. 'Help me!'

Jay grunts and stills, his body pressing deep into me.

'Help!' The sound escapes into the dark as a wail. I am moving. My legs are moving, my thighs pushing, trying to get him off.

'What the fuck!' The shouted words don't come from Jay and the pressure of him lifts away in an instant.

'Fuck off,' Jay shouts, but he isn't near me now.

'Sarah?'

Jonny?

'You fucking cunt!' Shock and disgust punch through the low keys of Jonny's words. His silhouette kicks Jay's in the side, shoving him further away from me as Jay pulls up his jeans.

I try to sit up, swaying, unable to take my body weight on my arms, then fall on my side. Childish sobs of weakness echo around the bicycle shed, and I taste the salty tears on my lips.

'You fucking wanker.' Jonny kicks out at Jay again, knocking him down onto the tarmac further away and then Jonny drops onto one knee next to me. His hand touches my hair.

I can't see Susan. I don't hear her. 'Susan?'

'She's gone home already.' Jonny's voice is gentle. 'We thought you'd gone home too. I'll get you there. Don't worry.' He looks over his shoulder to where Jay's shadow is moving. He's dressing in the moonlight; I see him zip up his jeans.

'Fucking bastard,' Jonny punches the words at him.

'Fuck off. She wanted it.' Jay's belt jangles as he buckles it up. He isn't sorry he did it.

'She's off her head. She couldn't decide if she wanted to go for a piss, you dick. And I heard her telling you no, from the other side of the fucking playground.'

'It's all right for you, though.'

'Fuck off.' Jonny is no longer looking at him; he's pulling at my knickers, trying to pull them up.

Jay spits onto the ground near one of Jonny's trainers then he turns and walks away from the bicycle shed, away from me.

'Thank you.' My words lack strength, I have no breath to speak. My heart has raced away with my breath. Running. Trying to make me run away. I can't run, but I can hold on to Jonny. 'Thank you.'

'I'll get you to your feet. Then you can lean on the bicycle rack and I'll help you dress.'

'Sorry.'

'You don't need to be sorry. It's that bastard who should be saying sorry to you. I'm sorry we left you.' He wraps an arm under my arm and pulls me up onto my feet then leans me back.

My legs are shaky; they feel like twigs that will break at any moment. But they don't break; they keep me standing as I half sit and half lean on the bicycle rack. Jonny bends down and pulls my knickers and shorts up my thighs. Then he wraps my arms around his shoulders so I can stand and he pulls them right up.

While he zips up my shorts and slots the button into place, he stands in front of me as if he's trying to stop Jay from seeing me, or anyone else from knowing what happened to me. He knows. I don't want him to know.

'I feel sick.' I lean sideways and I am sick. It splatters on the tarmac, smelling of a mix of bile and cider. We'd drunk vodka too.

'Come on, you little drunk.' The gentleness in his voice cares. It's a tone of voice I don't usually hear when people speak to me.

He pulls my arm around him and holds it over his shoulders.

Other people's mums had spoken with voices like Jonny's in the hospital years ago.

Jonny wraps his other arm around my waist.

I brush the side of my hand across my cheeks, wiping away the tears and sniff back the ones running from my nose. I can't cry when I get home; I will have to be as tough as rubber. That's what Uncle Charlie says. 'Tough as rubber, you girls. Bounce back. Pretend it never happened.'

It did happen. I was raped. We only became teenagers a couple of weeks ago, on our thirteenth birthday; now I've lost my virginity. He was meant to be our friend.

As the tears drip off the edge of my chin, I can't catch my breath.

'That shouldn't have happened, Sarah. I'm sorry.' I stumble and lurch from step to step as Jonny walks.

Our house is twenty minutes away from the park. It takes us longer because I can't walk in a straight line and he isn't sober. But he is warm and strong, and the kindness in his voice is soothing. 'Not much further.'

I can't get the door key out of my pocket.

Jonny's palm presses against my chest, pushing me back against the wall beside the door, pinning me upright, his thumb touching one of my breasts that are loose beneath my T-shirt. His other hand delves into my pocket, pulls the key out, and puts it in the lock.

'I feel sick,' I tell him.

'Are you going to be sick?'

I nod, then throw up, missing his shoulder and his trainer by two centimetres.

'Shit, Sarah. I'm watching how much you drink in future. When I leave you here, don't you dare choke on vomit.'

The edge of the front door falls back from behind my shoulder, opening to let us in.

He takes the key out of the lock and his arm comes around me again, taking hold of me to help me up the step into the house.

'I'll leave you on the sofa and get the basin from the sink.'

The curtains are thin. The moonlight penetrates the fabric, lighting up the room and making it obvious how run down our world is. Everything is old and messy. There are empty crisp packets on the floor, overflowing ashtrays, beer cans.

If he thinks anything about the state of our home, he doesn't say it.

I don't think he's been here with Susan.

I half fall onto the sofa.

Jonny bangs around in the kitchen, opening and closing cupboards, making too much noise. He'll wake Mum and Uncle Charlie. 'Jonny,' I whisper in a harsh voice, telling him to stop it as I put a finger to my lips in an awkward movement.

He is back beside me, squatting down, putting the basin and a glass of water on the floor beside the sofa.

I tumble onto my side, lying down, and looking at his eyes. They are just white and dark in the moonlight.

His hand strokes over my hair as he stands in the same way that his hand touches Susan's hair. 'Take care of yourself and drink some of the water if you can.'

I nod. My breath must smell of sick.

'I'll leave your key here.' He puts it on the arm of the sofa. Then he walks away. The letterbox rattles as he shuts the door behind him.

The drugs and drink in my brain drag me into darkness, pulling me down into sleep, pulling me away from the truth of what happened. I let myself fall. I want to fall. I want to be submerged in the black and forget what happened.

Chapter 20

A ticklish feeling draws a line along my nose. I knock the finger that's causing it away. The sensation runs all the way down to my queasy stomach.

I roll onto my side on the sofa, aiming for the basin Jonny left on the floor. It's just mucus that dribbles out of my mouth, but my stomach decides that's not enough and keeps thrusting to empty its contents with painful spasms.

'Where were you?' Susan asks as I retch noisily over the basin.

She's sitting, cross-legged, like Buddha, on the floor behind the basin, dressed in the baggy T-shirt she wears at night.

When my stomach finally stops acting like it's an alien trying to break out of me, I wipe my mouth with the back of my hand and sit up. The room spins. 'I need the loo.'

Her eyes are alert following my movement and her lips press together hanging on to something exciting that she's eager to say even though she can see I'm not well.

I leave her in the living room and walk upstairs without saying any more.

In my head, I woke on the tarmac and every horrible detail

that followed last night is back in my mind. My hand slides up the stair rail as I climb. My legs still feel like breakable twigs.

Uncle Charlie's snores drive like drills through the walls on the landing and throb through my head.

I open and shut the bathroom door carefully. I don't want to wake him and Mum.

When I pull down my shorts and knickers and sit on the toilet, there are bruises on my thighs and streaks of blood in the discharge in my pants. I don't remember Jay gripping my thighs, but the bruises are the shape of fingertips. I don't remember him pulling down my clothes either, though.

I can still feel Jonny pulling them back up.

My back and bottom are sore; my fingertips run over the scabs covering the grazes from the tarmac. Memories hover in my head with a dreamlike haze. They are distant. I don't want to connect with them and make them real. I'm going to shove the whole memory in a cupboard and shut it away. But I ache inside and out, and the ache whispers constantly that it was real.

I don't cry. I think I should be crying. I cried last night, in front of Jonny. But today my mind is stunned. I don't know what to do. Nothing. Nothing will make it not have happened. I need to be strong. Be rubber. Bounce back. I can't let Jay know he hurt me. I must brush it off like a fly on my shoulder; that's another of Uncle Charlie's phrases. It was just sex. Mum does it all the time.

'Sex happens in loving relationships.' 'It's nice when two people love each other.' That's what a teacher said in sex education lessons in the first year we were at senior school, when we went.

Love. The word appears in my mind in a visual form, a neon sign, spinning and glowing.

It had happened to me. Sex. It had happened and no love had been involved. It was just his penis pushing into me. It wasn't love. Just an action.

I feel as if I have invisible ink inside me. His mark has rubbed off on me and I want to get in the bath and scrub it off. But I can't. Susan is waiting downstairs. I must be strong. Like rubber bouncing. I have to brush the memory off me like a nasty, horrible, bluebottle fly.

I swallow against a pain in my throat, get up off the toilet and pull up the clothes that I want to rip to pieces.

I put the toilet lid down quietly and push the handle to flush the toilet, hoping the noise won't wake Mum and Uncle Charlie.

I scrub at my teeth with the toothbrush, hate exploding in my head, cleaning my teeth as if it will clean Jay off every part of me. Then I go to our bedroom, push off my shorts and knickers, pull my T-shirt over my hand, throw them all on the small pile of dirty clothes and stamp on them as if they are on fire – as if they are the fly and I can squash it. I kick them all under the single bed that Susan and I share. I won't wear them again. When no one else is around I'll throw them in the bin.

I still feel dirty inside when I take clean knickers, a T-shirt, and my faded jeans out from the drawers we share. The jeans were given to Mum by someone at the food bank. They took pity on her daughters with their tired too-short clothes. I wobble as I put one foot then the other in the legs. These are too long. The hems are turned up. They're women's jeans.

But I am a woman now.

I drag the T-shirt over my head, wishing that Mum could afford to buy us bras for our breasts that are large enough to sway all the time. I know boys notice our breasts; I've seen Jonny look at and touch Susan's. I pull on the jeans one leg at a time and roll up the hems a couple more times so my calves are bare.

Has Jay looked at my breasts? Had he thought about doing what he did before last night? Had he planned it? He had pulled back the ring on every can of cider I'd drunk and handed the can to me. He had kept passing me the bottle of vodka we'd shared. He'd urged me to take a deep pull and breathe the cannabis into my lungs, and he had given me a pill. But I don't remember Jay or Wayne taking pills.

Susan wasn't there. I can see the space in the bicycle shed where she and Jonny were standing, and they aren't there.

I'd forgotten about the little white pill he'd called ecstasy; I'd been so drunk and high by then. But now I see it in his palm. His palm had been dark; it was after sunset. I'd let him tip it from his palm into mine, and then I'd taken it and he'd given me the bottle of vodka to wash it down. We'd been talking, me, Wayne, and Jay. They had made me laugh, and I had not wanted to go home when Susan left. I was having fun.

I don't remember Wayne leaving or anything else until I woke on the tarmac.

But I don't want to remember. I have to forget it. I hurry out of our room and run downstairs, my bare feet quiet even

112

though I am rushing. I don't feel sick anymore. I'm empty. Hollow. Dead like a zombie.

'You took your time,' Susan gets up off the sofa and comes to the stairs. She's taken the kitchen bowl away. I can see she's washed it up and it's back in the sink. Her expression still speaks of excitement, but her voice is accusing.

'I wanted to change.' She should know what happened. She should know without me having to say a word. She should be able to see my memories and hear what I've said in my mind. She should feel every emotion I feel. It used to be like that. Until Jonny broke our connection.

My hand grips the scarred paint of the wobbly newel post – everything in this house is falling apart. Susan takes hold of my wrist and pulls my hand off the post. 'I want to tell you something. Come and sit down.'

She pulls me down the last two stairs and across our little living room to the sofa.

We sit down facing one another, like we used to when we were smaller. We haven't sat together in this way for a long time.

There are so many words trapped behind my lips but I don't speak them. I can't speak them; they are too horrible to say.

She reaches for the green plastic pouch of Uncle Charlie's tobacco that's on the arm beside her. Pulls out the pack of white papers, takes one, and starts rolling a cigarette. She hands the first skinny cigarette to me then rolls another.

Her hands are shaking. Her nerves are buzzing with exhilaration. I can see she is feeling like we used to when she would challenge me to do a dare.

She lights her cigarette, hands me the lighter, puts the pouch of tobacco back on the arm of the sofa and draws her knee up onto the sofa in front of her, displaying a long bare leg. She is still dressed in her T-shirt and knickers.

My knees and thighs press together, my legs bending up and my arms wrapping around them so I can hug myself.

She takes a long drag from the cigarette. Whatever she's done, she's holding it back.

She breathes out smoke, exhaling upwards so the smoke doesn't blow in my face.

The pulse at the base of her neck, just above her collar bone, flickers quickly.

When her head lowers, her blue eyes look at me – we have dramatic eyes because our eyelashes are so long and dark. Mum says we inherited our eyes from our vanishing dad. Eyes that are the same, down to every single fleck in the variation of the blue.

'We did it. Last night. Jonny and I. We did it.'

I try to swallow something that's pulsing in my throat; my heart has come up into my throat to choke me. 'Where?' The question stumbles out because I have to say something, and I don't know what to say.

'In the park. Under the trees,' she carries on. 'It was romantic. I could see the stars between the branches.' Jonny did that with her ... then he had come back and helped me.

'Jay did it to me,' I say. I can't hold it in when she's talking about this. I want her to know, to understand that I can't hear this.

'No.' She smiles, wide-eyed. Excited. She thinks I feel the

same as she does. 'We lost our virginity on the same night. That's amazing. It feels weird, doesn't it? It's strange, but good. I didn't know what to do but Jonny told me.'

Her hand waves her cigarette around, her movements rushing with excessive energy. Her body language is open, excited but comfortable.

I wish for the sofa we had in Swindon with the dip that would have embraced me. My arm that's holding my legs tightens, holding me together before I fall apart. I breathe in through the cigarette.

'What about Jay?' she says. 'What was he like? Jonny was gentle. Nice. But Jonny is always nice. I didn't know there was anything like that going on between you and Jay.'

There wasn't. There isn't. I can't reply. I take another drag from the cigarette. The roll-up trembles on my lips. I think every muscle in my body is trembling. I imagine the aftershock of an earthquake is like this, everything shaking, but Susan doesn't see it.

The lit end of the cigarette glows and catches into flame because I'm smoking it too fast. I blow the flame out, and just hold the cigarette for a moment. But I need the nicotine, I need something in my bloodstream to take this shaky feeling away.

'I like that it just happened,' Susan goes on, not waiting for me to answer her.

I don't want her to wait. I can't answer her. I nod at times, as she tells me how great it felt.

Slugs, spiders, and snakes crawl across my skin.

I stub out the short dog-end of the cigarette then reach

out, asking for the pack of tobacco to roll another. I want cannabis, but we don't have any.

'Jonny's body feels good. He made me tremble. I felt it from the inside out ...'

I want to slap her. To silence her. Press my hand down on her mouth to stop her talking. To stop her breathing.

She is putting Jonny in my mind. I feel him carrying me home and touching my hair when I lay on the sofa. But he'd done that with her just before that.

She rolls another cigarette and doesn't stop talking. Jonny. Jonny. Jonny.

I want to stub my cigarette out on her face. I have never fallen out with Susan. We don't argue or fight. But today. Today, I want her to just know what I feel. To reach out to me and take my hand and tell me that she knows, and that it's going to be okay. But she just keeps talking about Jonny and about how great sex is and how we are both women now, both grown up.

I don't want to grow up.

Chapter 21

A knock hits the wooden board covering the top half of the front door, where one of our short-lived uncles had broken the glass panel.

I unravel from my crossed-legs position, stand on the sofa, and move the yellow nicotine-stained net curtain so I can look out and see who is there. We haven't moved from the sofa since I woke Sarah this morning. I'm still not dressed. It's Sunday; we have no one to hide from, and Mum and Uncle Charlie haven't got up. But sometimes they stay in bed all day at the weekend, depending on how much they drank the night before.

'It's Jonny.' I wave through the window before climbing over the sofa arm to open the door.

My insides have become cold ice-cream and quivering jelly. I love him. It's different from loving Sarah. She is a part of me. We just are. We have been together since we were a single egg in Mum's womb. We are holding hands in her scan picture. Sarah is more like another limb than a loved one. Like a kidney or a lung that I can't live without. But Jonny ... He has possession of my heart. It's in his hands and he is holding it like a china pot so he won't break it.

Now I understand why people talk about heartbreak. If he dropped my heart it would shatter into a million pieces.

As soon as the door is open my arms fly around his neck as I leap over the door step to be caught by his hug. I expect him to squeeze me tight like he normally does and kiss my lips, but he doesn't; he uses the hug to move me back into the house and puts me on my feet.

'Calm down,' he says quietly.

Why? Because Sarah is watching? No. I don't feel calm. I feel anything but calm. He has unlocked a secret and I love that secret. Every moment of it is playing in my head like a film on repeat, replayed and replayed. The first intense touch between my legs. My first touch as he pressed my hand over his jeans, and then it had all unravelled into something ridiculously amazing.

I am a woman.

Jonny's hands pull my arms away from his neck, untying himself from my hug and when he is free he walks around me. His eyes focus on Sarah. 'You okay?' It's said in a casual way, but something in the words pulls at something in my head. Or maybe it's the way he's looking at her. It's not a hello look. He's looking for something from her.

'Yes.' She tosses the pouch of tobacco at him, offering it, even though it's Uncle Charlie's and we've smoked nearly all of it. Uncle Charlie will be angry when he comes down.

Jonny catches the pouch.

'Have you got any cannabis?' Sarah asks.

He shakes his head. Then he looks at me and smiles.

I love his smile. Everything about Jonny's face is perfectly aligned. When we lie down on the grass together, or on his bed when we go to his house, I like drawing shapes on his face with my fingertip. Drawing along the profile of his nose and his lips, and around his eyes and jaw.

'Why are you here?' I ask. He never comes to the house. Last night was the first time he walked me home. It was also the first time Sarah hadn't walked home with me.

Jonny and I had gone for a walk on our own. She'd said she was going to go home but she wasn't here when I got in. She had stayed with Jay and Wayne.

'I came to see how you're feeling,' he says.

I grin at him, sharing the secret we have.

He looks at Sarah. He must know I've told Sarah. Maybe that's what he's looking for, to see if she's upset with him for doing it with me.

His dark-brown eyebrows lift at her, as if he is asking her if she knows.

Her eyebrows lift too, and her lips twitch but it's not really a smile; she reaches out to take the tobacco back off him. Her hand is shaking. But she must be wondering if he knows about Jay.

She and Jay had surprised me, but it must be hard for her because I have Jonny and she's on her own. We always do things at the same time, from getting our vaccinations to earning our one hundred metres swimming badge – we've lost our virginity on the same day now.

He looks back at me. 'I'm not working so do you want to go and get something to eat?'

'Yes.'

He looks at Sarah. His expression asks her if she wants to come.

'Yes, please,' she answers him then looks at me. 'If that's okay?'

'Yes,' I say, but I think, *no*. I want to be on my own with Jonny today. I want to talk to him about last night. To talk about what comes next. He hasn't said it, but he is my boyfriend.

Sarah annoys me while we walk into the town centre. She is quiet. As if she's sulking. And it means he keeps talking to her, to try to make her talk.

We go into a café. I choose a table by the window. Jonny and I sit on the window side. He orders a bacon roll, so I order a bacon roll, then he orders one more for Sarah and a pot of tea that will be large enough for all of us.

Sarah's eyes look over my shoulder, staring out through the window. Maybe because I am talking too much to Jonny. But no one's telling her she can't talk and Jonny keeps stopping our conversation to prod her to join in.

I want to say, *let her sulk, like Mum would*. But he won't do that. He's nice. I've never known a man be nice like Jonny. Unless I count Dave from social services. But he was being paid to be nice to us. The woman who is our social-worker now is an old cow. She only comes round to try to force us to go to school. She threatens Mum all the time.

Uncle Charlie says the threats are bollocks; they'll never take Mum to court. She doesn't have any money to pay a fine and they won't put her in prison.

I shuffle closer to Jonny on the cushioned bench, my thigh pressing up against the denim covering his thigh, and I think about the shape of him hidden under his clothes.

When we're in the park, Jonny pulls me onto his lap on the roundabout, or draws me in front of him to stand between his legs if we are standing up. I want him to put his arm around me and pull me closer now.

He doesn't. His elbows and forearms are on the table, and his hands are playing with the little packets of sugar in the sugar bowl in a distracted way.

'Let's take a picture.' A picture of the day after I became a woman. It had been dark last night and I hadn't thought about it. But now I think about it, I really want to remember it.

The disposable cameras Mum and Uncle Charlie bought us for our thirteenth birthday are a novelty for us. The cameras were probably stolen. But we'd both got one and we don't care where they came from. It's the best present we've had.

I take the flimsy plastic camera out of Mum's old handbag that she gave me and look at Sarah. 'Will you take a picture?' I don't want her in it.

As I hand over the camera, Jonny straightens up, wraps an arm around my shoulders and pulls me close so my head rests against his neck. I smile at the camera. Posing.

Click.

The moment is preserved forever. The day after I had sex with Jonny for the first time. The day I'm no longer a virgin. Uncle Charlie said he will pay for the film to be developed.

I smile at Jonny as I tuck the camera back in my bag. He smiles at me too.

'Do you fancy hitchhiking to Buscot?' he speaks to me, then glances at Sarah, including her in the invitation. 'We could swim in the weir pool.'

'I'd love that,' I say, trying to exclude her. 'It'll be nice to be somewhere different.' It's a beautiful day. The sky is a super blue. There isn't a single cloud out there.

Buscot is only thirty minutes away. It's a small village on the Thames. We've never been there.

Jonny and I will be able to go anywhere soon. He's learning to drive. He's using his wages for lessons and he's saving to buy a car. Then I'll have a boyfriend with a car and we'll be able to go to lots of places.

'Are you going to ask Wayne and Jay to come?' I ask.

'No.' He looks at Sarah. 'I think the three of us should enjoy the day on our own.'

Sarah nods. Why would she nod at that? There's something in her eyes, though, words and emotions I can't read. 'Don't you want Jay to go?' I ask. I don't understand what's going on with her today; we always understand each other. First, she lets Jay have sex with her, out of nowhere, and now she doesn't want to see him.

She shakes her head quickly, and the colour in her skin drops away, underneath her tan, making her a pale washed-out white.

'Are you okay? Is your hangover still bad?' She isn't being normal.

She nods but she doesn't look at me; her gaze reaches over my shoulder again, through the window into the street.

Jonny is watching her. Staring.

122

Chapter 22

2019

*A serious traffic accident yesterday at around
five o'clock in the evening, on the road between Keswick
and Cockermouth, took the life of a Cumbrian woman.
A second woman is in the care of Carlisle Hospital,
in a critical condition. It is believed the car swerved
off the road to avoid an oncoming vehicle.
The police are calling for witnesses.*

Jonny closes the paper, fighting with the folds that don't want to turn back. In the end he throws the creased copy of the edition of *The Cumbrian Bugle* on the coffee table.

'Just a few short paragraphs in the local paper; that's all Lucy is worth. Where is the driver of the other car? Where's the desire to find them? If she was a missing child there would be a search party, but Susan is dead and Lucy is in intensive care fighting for her life because of a reckless driver and it's just a cold fact. They don't give a shit. They haven't done anything to find the driver.' A sharp sigh slips in and out of his lungs.

His breath has a lingering smell of cigarettes. He gave up ten years ago, but he began again in the face of this. I don't blame him. It's hard.

I put the lid back on the shallow box of Susan's belongings that the police had given me as her next of kin and put the box on the table. It doesn't contain much: her car key, purse, phone. At some point we will have to clear out her flat but I can't face that yet.

My heartbeat is so hard it rushes all the way to the end of my fingertips with every pulse. The horror of this, the panic and fear, will not leave. Susan has gone. And Lucy ...

'Reporters record the naked reality and see nothing else. One dead. One alive. That's their news.' He stands up and his shaking hand lifts to comb through his hair. 'My mind and my stomach are in turmoil.'

'Mine too.' I've lost my sister and Lucy is in a coma. We had argued when we parted. I said I hated her. But I did hate Susan. Everything was always Susan's fault.

My mouth is dry. I'm terrified. Half my head is empty. I'm no longer a twin. Just me. But I keep trying to hear her; my mind constantly searching for her, as if she will speak if I listen hard enough. She must be in the room in spirit, but I don't feel her.

I wish Lucy would wake up. She has to come back to us. She shouldn't have even been in that car.

Jonny's fingers comb his fringe back again, his fingers lingering in his hair as his head leans back. I know fears for Lucy are tumbling through his mind too; they have been for every single minute since the police came here to tell us there had been an accident.

For the last twenty-four hours our lives have centred on the hospital's warren of hallways. We will go back in a minute. We only came home to change clothes. But I've made him sit down and drink a cup of tea. He smoked two cigarettes in the time it took me to make the tea, blowing the smoke out of the kitchen door into the garden. He bought a packet at the hospital and he's been smoking every time we've had to leave Lucy.

He hasn't begun processing the fact that Susan is dead. But maybe that's a good thing. I can't talk about it yet. I want to manage it alone for a while. My thoughts are split between Lucy and the body I was asked to identify in the hospital morgue. It must have been obvious to them as soon as they drew back the sheet that I would say, 'It is Susan.' But the body was no longer identical to me; it was imperfect, bruised, and cut in the car accident.

The car had rolled down a hill, through woodland. They had been crushed inside. Sandwiched in a metal skeleton. The fire brigade had cut them out. They'd been too late to help Susan. She died before they were able to get her out.

Lucy is bruised and her face has more than a dozen cuts. But the only broken bones are her ribs. It's her head that took the worst of the battering. Her brain is injured – the most delicate and necessary organ.

A doctor told us he has no idea what her mind will be like when she comes out of the coma. *If* she comes out from the coma.

Jonny's gaze clashes with mine as his head lowers. 'I feel like one of those jellies you used to make for Luce's birthday parties when she was a child. Do you remember? You made a green rabbit one year. I can't think straight; I can't work; I need to be with her.'

'I know.' I touch his leg. 'It doesn't matter, they can carry on without us for a few days.' I'm living in a dream state. Detached from reality. I'm not sure who or where I am. Life has tumbled upside down.

'I don't know how you can be so calm.'

'I'm not calm, Jonny, my sister is dead and my daughter is in hospital. I am not calm. I feel as if someone has scraped everything out from the middle of me.'

'If you hadn't raced over there to start an argument ...' He leaves the fact that he thinks it's my fault unsaid this time. But he has said it four times already.

It was a horrible argument. 'We all do things we shouldn't. You included.' I get up and turn away from him to fetch a glass of water from the kitchen.

It's my fault she's gone, and that Lucy is injured. But he doesn't understand, and I can't expect him to understand, because he isn't a twin. She was a part of me. It doesn't matter what happened between us, or for how long we were separated, she was half of me. And it was my fault.

But I am still glad Susan has gone.

As I fill a glass with cold water at the kitchen sink I watch him lift up his phone as if he expects it to ring. He keeps looking at it because he's waiting for the hospital to say that

Lucy has come out of the coma or the police to say they've found the other driver.

'We should get back to the hospital.' Another sharp breath slips out of his lungs and he looks at me.

We have sat with her in the intensive care room as much as we can, only leaving when the doctors want to do some sort of test or treatment. Then I've refuelled with caffeine in the café while he's flooded his system with nicotine. We'd return after the allotted time, sit in silence, and stare at Lucy breathing through a tube that goes into her neck not her mouth. With the machines playing the rhythm of a life that has no melody.

He gets up off the sofa, pulling the cigarette packet out of his pocket and then a cigarette out of the packet. 'I'm going to have another before we drive back.' He lifts the cigarette up. 'What if she isn't herself when she regains consciousness?' he says, looking at me as he walks towards the kitchen. 'What if she's paralyzed or her brain is dead. She might not even know us.' His skin is pale and shadows hang under his eyes. The short beard defining his jaw usually gives him a sexy edge. Today it just screams of a man who hasn't bothered to look after his appearance.

'She'll be okay,' I say as he passes me. She has to be. I can't think about anything else and I've not been imaging it because anything else can't be true. I refuse any other ending.

'I only have two cigarettes left,' his voice deflates as he opens the kitchen door. 'I need to buy more.'

I drink the water as the cold air rushes in from outside.

There was a hard frost today. There was a hard frost the night the car had gone off the road.

The smoke slides back into the kitchen even though he exhales outside.

I walk over to him, reaching out a hand. 'Jonny ...'

His free hand reaches out and holds mine for a moment, but then his fingers slip free as he takes another drag from the cigarette. 'I hope they find the bastard that did this.'

Susan is in my head, her battered discoloured body.

I replace the image with a memory of Lucy's face. Of Lucy's eyes. I wish she would open her eyes.

Chapter 23

2018

As the door falls shut, I throw the keys and my handbag on the single bed, sit down, and then flop back on the bed beside them, my feet still on the floor. The mattress dips, accommodating my weight, but not really providing a comforting embrace.

It's dark outside. The skylight above me is a black mirror that reflects my lonely life.

This room replicates all the other rooms I have lived in during my adult life. They have all been prison cells in one way or another.

But at least this is just my space with everything I need in it. A bed that serves as a sofa too, a sink, and one kitchen cupboard in a corner, a shower room and toilet. I even have a chest of drawers against one wall and a bedside table with a lamp.

In comparison to the huge house that Sarah lives in it is nothing.

I hate coming back here from Sarah's big house, with all

her modern conveniences. Her dining table filled with food and conversation. She escaped the past. The stark difference between our lives pushes into my stomach with the thrust of a sharp knife every time I walk into her house or back to this building.

Envy throbs in every one of my arteries and it echoes in my veins; it's deafening at times. It's a vicious whisper in my blood. I want what she has. What they have. It should be mine. It should be me in that house. It would be mine if she hadn't run off and left me.

I feel like a wolf dressed in a fleece when I speak to her or to Jonny. Speaking about peace, forgiveness, and friendship, she sees how much those words stick in my throat. He doesn't.

It will take time, though. Nothing changes overnight. I have to make this life work. Build it up. Build a future for myself here. I will have my time. If there is any justice in the world.

My shoes fall noisily onto the floor, probably disturbing the people in the flat below mine. Then I lift my feet onto the bed, roll onto my side, pull the pillow beneath my head, and reach for my handbag. I take out my purse, in a ritual movement, open the credit card flap and take out the twisted and worn photograph of Jonny; it's marbled with thin white creases. One runs through his face, between his eyes and through his smile.

It's the only photograph I have from when we were young. It was taken the day we went to Buscot. This photograph, the memories from that day, have been my buoy for years, keeping me afloat. I sleep with it in my hand; it's a memory from a million years ago. But when there are a million things to forget, having something I want to remember is precious.

A yawn pulls at my jaw. I am tired and a little drunk from the wine Jonny poured into my glass while we ate dinner and then again, after dinner. I outstayed my welcome. I always do. But Jonny is kind; he won't let her chase me out of the house, and I was delaying leaving. This place is not a home. I've never had a home. Sarah has a home. I want a home like that and tomorrow I am going to take my next step to getting it. I need to be able to drive a car to have a life like that. They live in the middle of nowhere.

I knock on the glass in the front door of the café. It's early and the café isn't open, but in five minutes they will start to serve breakfast to the early rising walkers. Marie, Stan, and Jonny are here earlier than opening time every day to bake. Usually, I arrive half an hour later, but I wanted to be here before Sarah today. The mingling sweet and savoury smells greet me every morning when I walk in. Cakes, scones, quiches, pies, and sausage rolls are all cooling in the kitchen. I am always hungry within seconds.

Jonny walks out from the kitchen, coming to open the door. I lift a hand and wave.

His lips shift into a smile.

I can't tell if he trusts me yet. I know he doesn't see through me, but does he believe me enough to take my side over Sarah's?

He bends to release the bolt at floor level, then reaches to release the bolt at the top before he turns the lock.

Lucy is the only one of them who I know trusts me. She takes after her mother for being vocal. Takes after us. She's a free spirit. She's made up her own mind about me, and she is standing up to Sarah's rejection for me.

'Good morning,' Jonny says, gifting me with another smile. The smell of cooked sausage meat and melted cheese mingle with warm chocolate, vanilla, and sugar.

'Morning,' I answer as he holds the door open for me.

'You're early.'

'Yes, I want to ask you a favour.' *I don't think Sarah will like it, so I want to ask you while you're on your own.*

'Go on then.' He closes the door and reaches to slide the top bolt back into place.

I wait until he's looking at me. 'I want to learn to drive. I have money saved to buy an old car. Would you come and get the car with me so you can drive it home, and will you give me driving lessons? I can afford the car, the road tax and insurance, but I can't afford the lessons.'

His lips purse, his eyebrows lifting and his hands slipping into the back pockets of his trousers. He knows she'll hate it.

I wait for a no.

'I'm not sure if I could find the time. It's summer season; you know how busy we are. Why not ask Sarah?'

'Do you really think Sarah and I would be safe shut in a car for an hour? I don't think she'd want to do it.'

'It might be good for the both of you.' His hands come out of his pockets and he turns away, heading back to the kitchen.

'I'd rather it was you. You have patience, Jonny,' I say it to his back. I won't let him say no. I will pull every one of his kindness strings to get him to do this. 'Stan can manage the cooking, and Emma would be glad of any extra hours.'

Marie carries out two large plates, both of them baring delicious looking cakes that have been freshly decorated this morning and cut into segments. She catches my gaze and smiles, then looks at Jonny.

'Good morning,' I say.

I'm not sure if she'll tell tales. I haven't got the measure of Marie either. But she has Jonny's confidence; they often share speaking looks.

He doesn't return to the kitchen. Instead, he walks into what serves as an office in an old store room.

I go into the kitchen and lift a hand to acknowledge Stan. 'Good morning.' I lift my apron off a hook, wrap it around my waist and tie a bow with the ends of the cords.

I take my phone out of my pocket, touch the pad to open it with my fingerprint recognition and then follow Jonny into the office. He's looking for something in a pile of invoices. 'This is the car. What do you think?' I'd left the internet page open, so he can see the image on the sales site.

He straightens up and takes my offered phone, as I'd hoped he would. I want to keep him engaged in the conversation.

'Is it any good?' His lips purse again and one eyebrow moves with an odd play of movement as he looks up at me. 'It's an old banger. I'd get a mechanic to check it out before you buy it, just to make sure the engine isn't about to fall out of it. You don't want the thing to kill you. I've got a friend actually, one of our customers who owns the garage up the road, he might check it out for you if you ask him nicely.'

'I don't need your friend. I can check it. I've done some mechanics; I started an apprenticeship that I didn't finish so I know something about engines. I can manage an old car. If I do need a mechanic, though, there's a man called Alan in my flats who keeps asking me out for a drink. He would help. But I can't drive. I just want you to drive it home for me and then sit with me when I drive it until I pass my test?'

His lips lift into an easy smile. 'Yes. Of course, I'll help. I'll sort something out in the café.'

'May I see?' Marie makes me jump. She's standing at the door behind me. A foot away. Looking past me at Jonny looking at my phone. He hands it back to me and I hand it over. 'Oh. That's all right,' she says, as she glances at the picture of the car.

When she hands the phone back to me, I look at Jonny; his skin has taken on a light red colour, as if he's embarrassed about being caught talking about doing something for me.

When we disperse, I walk over to turn the sign on the door around to 'Open' and unlock it. Marie returns to the kitchen to bring out the rest of the day's freshly baked offerings and Jonny carries on searching for something in the office.

I smile through the glass in the door at the outside world, hiding how happy I am from everyone in the café. I am a step closer to the life I deserve.

Sarah's blue Mini drives past, travelling towards the car park as the first walkers approach along the shoreline path of the lake.

The Twins

I open the door for the two middle-aged men and greet them with a smile. 'Good morning. Perfect timing. Can I get your drinks while you're deciding on breakfast?'

'Two flat whites and two full English. No need for deciding time.'

'Then take a seat wherever you like and I'll get your breakfasts on the way.' I take the pad and pen out of the apron pocket, quickly scribble down the order, and tear off the top page to pass it to Stan in the kitchen.

'What do they want?' Marie asks as we pass each other at the counter.

'Two flat whites with breakfasts. I'll make the coffees if you take the sauces and fighting irons over.'

She smiles. Fighting irons is a phrase I introduced her and the part-time waitress, Emma, to. 'Cutlery is the more common term,' Jonny had said. But we all now use fighting irons. It's a metaphor for another reason for me.

While I'm standing by the coffee machine heating milk, Sarah walks in, jangling the doorbell.

Jonny appears from the office within a second, walking across the café to greet her. He takes hold of one of her hands and leans in to kiss her lips quickly. 'I'm going to teach Susan how to drive.' I hear him say it, even though he's speaking quietly. 'She said you wouldn't fancy doing it and I agree, so I'll need to make the time to do it somehow. But it will be good for her.' He looks over his shoulder at me. The café is small and basically empty; he will know I've heard. 'Susan, show Sarah the car you're buying.'

Well, if he'd felt any sense of guilt over offering to help me, he'd discharged it quickly. His whole manner shouts, *nothing to see here, no cheating, no secrets*.

I would have liked another secret, but at least we have one; she still doesn't know he told me about her breakdown.

'I'll finish the coffees,' Marie offers.

It's just a case of pouring the milk into the cups but I leave the metal jug of warm milk for her to use and turn to Jonny and Sarah as I delve into my apron pocket for my phone, open the webpage, and show her. 'There.'

She takes my phone and looks but her face forms an expression that says she doesn't care what car I'm buying.

I leave her looking at it and turn back to the counter, deliberately making her digest how different the knackered old wreck I am going to buy is compared to her 2016 reg Mini. There was a crossroads in our lives, a moment in time that lasted no more than a minute, when she became the one with the nice the house, the business, and the Mini, and I'd become ... the victim.

'These breakfasts are ready,' Stan says as I walk into the kitchen.

'Okay.' I reach for her apron, lift it off the peg, hang it over my forearm, and turn to pick the plates up from the hot shelf.

I smile at Sarah as I walk back out into the café, lifting my elbow to say, *I have your apron*. But I take the plates over to the customers first. Marie has given them their coffees.

'Here you are. Is there anything else I can get for you?'

'No, thank you, this is perfect,' one of the men says. As I turn away they clasp hands across the table before they pick up their knives and forks. A happy relationship.

The Twins

It's funny because I don't see those gestures in Jonny and Sarah's relationship. I see him trying to appear happy through kisses and touches that she just accepts as if they are her right, rather than welcoming them with equal expressions of love.

I take her apron to her and hold it out as she holds out my phone. Small kindnesses go a long way to nudge trust. I may not have had her happy life, but I've learned a lot about influencing people in my life.

'Thank you.' She trades with me.

Jonny has gone into the kitchen. I hear his voice in there.

My gaze lifts to her eyes that are exactly like mine. 'Sarah ...' When I'm with her I feel as if I am narrating myself in the third-person. I am still not over the oddness of seeing her again, of seeing me in her and how alike we are after all these years. We might have been different in many ways, but she is still the exact copy of me. Or I am the copy of her. Susan and Sarah. Sarah and Susan.

'Do you think about the past very often?' I ask her. 'About when we were younger?' I'm still not sure if she has really forgotten what happened in London. Really, I don't trust her any more than she trusts me.

But perhaps if she regrets things she has tried to forge—

'Since you arrived, yes. Far too much. But I don't want to. The past is the past. I thought we agreed that?'

The front door opens and the doorbell jingles, announcing the arrival of more customers.

She turns away from me. 'Good morning.'

I think, if the past was today, she would do the same things again.

137

Chapter 24

1985

We are walking through the long grass on the verge of the main road, kicking up the seeds from numerous dandelion clocks. Jonny is in the front, a metre ahead of Susan. His arm is raised, reaching out towards the passing traffic and his thumb protrudes from a fisted hand.

As a car passes, the driver toots the horn for two short blasts, then the left-hand indicator flashes on and off. The car slows and stops ten metres ahead of us.

'Come on.' Jonny glances back at us, then breaks into a run towards the car.

Susan and I run behind him.

He pulls the car's passenger door open, leans in, and says, 'Thanks mate,' before twisting around and dropping onto the front seat.

Susan opens the back door on the passenger's side, climbs in and then slides over the seat so I can get in beside her. I pull the door shut.

There are empty crisp packets and chocolate wrappers in

139

the footwell of the car, as well as mud and leaves.

'We're going to Buscot,' Jonny says to the man in the driver's seat. 'Can you take us all the way there?'

'Yes, sure. I'm on my way to Faringdon; I'm going past it.'

'Thanks.'

The driver's hair is really short and a mixture of brown and grey, but every strand looks neatly ordered, freshly cut; it tapers into his neck and brushes the top of a pale blue checked shirt collar.

I feel strange. I can see things. But I feel like if I were to reach out to touch things I wouldn't be able to. I'm walking around in another world, on another planet, in someone else's life. Balanced on stilts. Dressed in an astronaut's uniform. I'm behind unbreakable glass or a one-way mirror like the ones in police dramas, watching, when no one knows I'm here.

The driver's eyes look at me and Susan through the rear-view mirror. He has brown eyes and his hair is receding on either side of his forehead, above his temples, where there is another sprinkling of grey hair.

His head turns for a second as he glances at Jonny. 'What's your names? Why are you going to Buscot?' The rhythmic click of his indicator ticks as he looks over his right shoulder, preparing to pull out and drive on.

'I'm Jonny, and they're Susan and Sarah. We're just going to hang out there for the day.'

As we travel, I watch the driver through the mirror while he talks to Jonny. There's a prickly sensation in my spine. I don't like the driver. I don't trust him. Susan and I are good judges of men's characters because of all the uncles passing through our lives. I knew from the beginning I didn't like Jay, but he's Jonny's friend so I'd pushed the feeling aside.

Jonny laughs about something the driver said.

He isn't nervous about being in a stranger's car but I watch the road signs at every turning, trying to tell if the driver is going in the right direction. I can't tell. But I do know I don't trust Jonny's judgement any longer.

Uncle Harry slips into my mind. Mum is a bad judge of men. But now I know what sex really is, I realise what it means. She's had sex with all the men we call uncles.

The moment when Uncle Harry had sat on me and hit me, still naked from getting out of her bed, forms an echo in my brain, and the memories of that and last night tangle up. Jay's weight on me, and Uncle's Harry's face distorted with anger. Jay's dark shadow. Uncle Harry's fringe cut at an awful short angle. His fist hitting me. I can smell garlic in the car. The garlic I smelt on Jay last night.

I don't want to remember any of these things

As the car takes another turn following a sign for Lechlade, I start wrapping up each thought, mentally enclosing it, to stop it from coming back. I shove each thought into a box, fold down the lid and tape the box up. Then I find a cupboard to open in my head and hide them in a dark place, where I won't ever look again.

The field beside the weir pool at Buscot is a little like a beach. We went to a real beach once. We went to Weston-super-Mare years ago with Mum and Uncle Rick – a man who was only in our lives and Mum's bed for about two weeks.

She had let him do that to her and leave almost as soon as he'd arrived.

Jonny leads us across the field of cut grass towards the river bank.

It's the atmosphere not the appearance of the place that is the same as the beach had been. It's noisy and busy. There are picnic tables where families are eating and a group of young people have lit a disposable foil barbeque.

As we walk past the young people, smoke drifts in front us. It smells of the burgers and sausages they're cooking.

My stomach makes a growling sound. I hadn't felt like eating in the café earlier. I haven't eaten since early last night. I'm empty but I'm not hungry.

A family are playing frisbee in one corner of the field with a jumping tan and white Jack Russell.

Jonny stops a couple of metres away from the river bank and faces Susan and me. 'Shall we leave our stuff here? We can see it from the water.'

'Yes,' Susan agrees. She is smiling at him, in that adoring way she does.

Jonny pulls his T-shirt out from the waistband of his jeans, lifts it up over his chest, and raises it over his head. 'Are you going to get undressed?' he says to us as he strips his T-shirt off his arms and drops it on the grass. 'I'm getting in the water.'

I sit down next to his T-shirt as Susan drops the handbag she uses to make her look older on the grass. She releases the button at the waist of her shorts. 'I'll stay with your stuff,' I say. 'I don't want to swim.'

'Are you sure?' Jonny asks.

'Yes.'

He doesn't argue against my decision.

One of Susan's trainers flops down beside his T-shirt as Jonny's belt buckle jangles. The sound stirs nausea through my stomach. I stare at the people already in the water, and those playing in the waterfall from the weir on the other side of the area of river that has been dammed and reformed into a small lake.

Jonny takes off his trainers and jeans. Susan removes her shorts.

'Are you sure you'll be okay here?' he asks me when they're ready to go in the water. He's wearing boxer shorts; she is wearing her knickers and T-shirt.

'Yes.' I nod. I don't want to take off my clothes and expose the bruising on my thighs.

Susan clasps his hand and pulls him. He lets her draw him away, but he takes his hand out of hers when they reach the water and dives into the lake, forming a perfect muscular arrow. Susan jumps in, tucking up her knees and bombing the water near where he has risen to the surface.

I watch them swim across the lake to the weir, side by side, talking as they swim.

Lots of people are standing on the stone barrier of the weir on the other side, playing and shouting as the water cascades over the upper level. Jonny reaches the weir first. I see him haul his body out of the water in an athletic movement. Then he turns and take Susan's hand to help her and pull her out. It's years since we swam with the class at school. She's probably exhausted.

As they mess around in the flow of water over there, I take off my trainers and lie down on the grass. My eyes close so I'm not staring at the sun. I slide my T-shirt up beneath my breasts and let the sun warm and tan me.

The sunshine makes my closed eyelids blood-red as I listen to all the happy human and animal sounds around me. Laughter. Excited barks from the dogs. Birdsong flowing from the hedgerow at the edge of the field and from an oak tree further along the bank. Bees buzzing around me, harvesting nectar from the clover in the short grass.

'Hey! Come in the water!'

My eyes open and I lift onto my elbows to look for Jonny.

He's further along, pulling himself out of the water onto a wide branch of the oak tree that overhangs the water, his biceps bunching and his abs working.

The last thing I need to see today is Jonny, my sister's boyfriend, in just his wet underwear.

I shut my eyes and lie back down.

A few moments later, water sprinkles across my face from what I guess is a flick of Jonny's fingers. 'Come in the water. It's really cool, and you must be hot.'

I open my eyes again, looking upwards and facing the outline of the bulge in his wet black boxer shorts. A bulge that I fully understand the mechanics of now. I close my eyes again. That is a thought I scrub out with a scratchy rubber eraser, leaving only a grey smudge in my memory.

'Are you okay?' His voice is lower, in height and sound, as he squats down next to me.

'No.'

He drops to an upright kneel, his buttocks resting on the backs of his heels. 'I'm sorry. I told Jay he's a dickhead this morning.'

I breathe in and out, trying to keep my mind steady and Jay in his box. I tie it up tighter. I wrap tape around it over and over. 'I don't want to talk about it, Jonny.'

'Okay. Then we won't talk about it.' He turns to sit on the grass, his knees bent up. His hair is dripping. It's a darker brown now it's wet.

'Where's Susan?'

'Racing some kids out there. Do you want a roll-up?'

'Yes.'

I sit up as he takes the pouch of tobacco out of the back pocket of his jeans.

The first cigarette he rolls, he gives to me, and he hands me the lighter before he rolls a cigarette for himself.

'Sorry,' he says after he's lit his cigarette. 'I can't not talk about it. I can't forget it. My mum used to be with this man who would hit her and then force her ...' His head turns, and he looks at me. 'Men like that should be castrated.'

The thrust of the statement drags a giggle from my throat. But then I take a drag from the cigarette. It had been wrong to laugh.

Does Susan know his mother was assaulted?

'Our mum had to go into a refuge,' I say. To tell him that, even though I'd laughed, I do understand. He doesn't say, *I know*. I don't know if Susan has told him that. 'Did your mum?'

'In the end.' He looks at the water, his eyes obviously searching for Susan. 'After he nearly killed her and knocked me out when I tried to stop him.'

'He hit you too?'

He nods. 'All the time.'

'Uncle Harry hit me. But that wasn't when we went into the refuge. That was because of Uncle Will.'

He looks at me. 'You've been unlucky with uncles.'

'They aren't real uncles.'

'I know, Sarah.'

We're silent for a moment as we draw in the smoke from the cigarettes.

'I don't let bad things win,' he says suddenly. 'I use them. I use them to make me stronger. I'm going to make Mum proud. I'm going to make something of myself. Wayne and Jay are happy on the dole. They don't care what they do, or what they become. I care.'

I look at him as he looks at Susan in the water. His dark eyelashes look longer wet. 'I care too,' I say. 'I don't want to be like Mum.' I think I only just started to care about not being like Mum. I think being like Mum would be the worst thing that can happen.

His head turns and his eyes look into mine and something passes between us. An agreement. It's the same way that things pass between Susan and me without a need for words. In this moment he understands me, and I understand him, in a way other people can't.

The Twins

'Jonny.' Susan staggers up out of the water at a shallow point along the muddy bank, water dripping from her body and hair. Her white pants are transparent and her T-shirt clings to her small breasts. 'Come back in the water.'

She thinks we're women now but she doesn't look like a woman physically. She still looks like a girl.

We are feral wolf cubs who have been thrown out into the world, like babies thrown into a river to teach them to swim, and we've grown up too fast. I can't turn back time. I can't grow up slower. I want to. I want to walk up to a clock that has hands and wind them back several years. Or at least until before last night.

Jonny glances at me, smiles, and stubs out his cigarette, crushing it in the grass. 'Are you sure you don't want to come?'

I nod. 'I'm happy here.' Listening to happy sounds and pretending I live in a happy world.

Chapter 25

2019

Jonny closes the door as the two police officers walk away from the house.

They came to the house to tell us that the driver of the other car has come forward.

He's said her car was on the wrong side of the road. Susan's car swerved off the road on the corner, not because of him. He had stopped, but it was a narrow road, so he'd driven to a safer place and then called 999. He was the caller, he just hadn't said at the time that he'd had any involvement because he hadn't. Through his eyes, he'd just driven around the corner and watched a car drive off the edge of the road.

'It's most likely that the car skidded on ice,' Detective Inspector Jenny Watts had said. 'It may be difficult to determine a cause beyond that but we have asked the forensics team to look at Miss Tagney's car to check if there are any signs of a collision.'

'The car collided with a hundred trees didn't it? How are they going to be able to tell?' Jonny had asked.

'There might be traces of paint. There are no signs of a collision on the witness's car,' had been her answer.

Jonny's head bows and his forehead presses against the front door as his hand hangs from the handle, his body looking defeated now they've gone.

I know why. The anger derived from his fear for Lucy had a target when there was a missing driver. He wants someone to blame.

Me ...

My fingers surround his forearm, offering comfort. Whether another driver was involved or not, it doesn't make any difference for Lucy. She's still fighting for her life.

He turns in a way that forces my hand to let go and his hazel eyes look at me.

His eyes aren't pretty today. Sometimes they're gold but today they lack lustre, and the whites of his eyes are a mesh of red, like red net curtains.

I think he's going to say something but he doesn't; he moves, walking around me, shutting me out of his thoughts. He keeps doing it because he's dealing with his fear and sorrow over Lucy by not discussing it. It is a weight he is determined to bear alone, even though we are both carrying it.

Last night when I tried to talk about things, he said, 'I can't be your crutch. Just leave me alone. Or I'll need one too.'

Am I really being too needy? My sister is dead, and Lucy is my daughter too. Shouldn't we be consoling one another?

But neither of us know if Lucy will be all right, so his view is that there can't be any consolation. 'Just let me cope with this,' he said.

Isn't it more normal to tell each other I love you, and hold one another? That would be a comfort for me.

I follow him into the kitchen. If he won't say it to me then I will say it to him.

He moves the dirty cups we and the police officers had drunk from to the sink and starts rinsing them out.

I walk up behind him, wrap my arms about his middle and press my cheek against his shoulder. 'I love you. Lucy will be all right. It will be all right.'

'I hope so,' he answers.

I am sure his anger will turn on me now because he thinks our argument placed them on that road that night.

My hands slide free because the gesture has become awkward with no physical response from him.

He breathes out heavily as he puts the cups on the drainer and picks up a tea towel. 'I'm going to have a cigarette then we'll go and see Luce.'

I nod. It hurts that at a time when we should need each other the most, he doesn't want me.

Chapter 26

2018

'Y
ou should put this cake on the menu.' Susan has looked something up on her phone. She holds her phone out, screen first, showing Jonny.

I presume there's a recipe on the screen.

'Almond and lemon. Interesting.' His lips purse and his eyebrows lift for a second, expressing that he is mentally debating it as an option. 'Have you tried it?'

'A friend recommended it. It's something different. I thought you could try it.'

A friend ... That's the first I've heard of a friend. She's with us every waking hour. When does she see this friend? I wish she would take herself off and visit this friend.

'What do you say to the idea of almond and lemon, Sarah?' Jonny calls across the café.

I'm clearing tables in the opposite corner to where Jonny and his groupie are. It is always Marie, me, or Emma serving.

I put the last lot of cups I'd picked up on the tray, the stack of china rattling, then turn, my face screwing up with distaste as if I'd just eaten a bitter lemon. 'I don't think almond and lemon would be my thing.'

'It's vegan, and gluten and lactose free. You need more things for people who need or want alternatives.'

Every step she takes into my territory annoys me but she keeps finding ways to take more steps. We gave her a job here, but she's not a business partner – just a waitress. When she stops talking and actually works. She has no reason to make recommendations about what we sell. She's already in my house, at my dinner table, nearly every evening because Jonny takes her on a driving lesson after work and feels sorry for her because she has no one to go home to, so he brings the stray home every night.

'But she's turning her life around ...' he keeps saying as if that is a reason to do everything for everyone. I don't mind that she is in a good place. I'm glad she is in a good place, but I wish her good place was somewhere else. Not here, where she is threatening my life.

I don't acknowledge that she's spoken. I answer Jonny. 'If anything, I would say orange and almond is better. It's a classic match.'

He nods. 'Maybe. I'll think about it and look at some new recipes with Stan.' He looks at Susan. 'You're right, we should serve more options for vegans and people who have allergies.'

We should ... *We* should ... She is not a part of *we*. We, the owners of this café, are Jonny and me.

I pick up the tray with a desire to hurl it across the room at her. At them. Her and Jonny. They're getting friendlier and friendlier since the driving lessons began. They behave as if they're the ones who are married the way they talk all day. Chatter. Chatter. Chatter. He treats her as if she's a part of our family. Our relationship. He has forgiven her. He trusts her now.

She's just flattering him. Manipulating him. When I'm not angry it makes me laugh. Jonny falling all over her feet is funny. She is so obviously flirting and making herself appear desirable. I've said that to him. His answer was a shrug that dismisses the whole idea of that as unimportant.

As I walk across the room with the full tray, I smile at them both, sarcastically, although I don't think they see that. I twist to squeeze past Susan to get into the kitchen. Jonny moves out of the way of the tray and it's Jonny who is working, refilling the chiller cabinet; she's just talking. Keeping Jonny hanging around on her hook, waiting for the next word to fall out of his mouth so she'll have another chance to flatter him.

I take the tray into the kitchen.

'Sarah,' she calls a minute or so later.

'Yes,' I call out from the kitchen, shouting over the top of the noise of the running water as I rinse off the china to put it in the dishwasher. I answer her innocently, as if I have not been mentally throwing all this crockery and cutlery at her. I'm glad she doesn't know what I think and feel anymore. My mind is free to think what I like.

'Are you still going out with Lucy for a drink on Saturday night?'

'Yes.' This time my answer carries more meaning. What's coming next? I turn off the tap and walk out of the kitchen, drying my hands on a tea-towel. 'Yes,' I say again, as our gazes clash over the chilling cabinet.

'Good. She asked me to join you. She thought it would be fun if we have a girls' night.'

My teeth clench against a desire to swear. Lucy and I have girls' nights. Mother and daughter nights that don't need an additional member. I want to go out with my daughter on my own. It's rare that I have a chance to have a good conversation with Lucy since she moved in with her boyfriend, Michael.

Accusations thrust to the tip of my tongue. But what would I accuse her of? Being nice to my daughter?

'Great.' *No. You can't go. I'll tell Lucy to un-invite you.*

I turn away, go back into the kitchen, and start loading the dishwasher noisily. Jonny will know that I am annoyed. I felt his eyes looking at my back as I returned to the kitchen.

His decision to trust her is causing problems for us, because I'm struggling to keep my trust in him.

She laughs loudly in the other room making a point of the fact that I am angry and she is happy. It feels as if she is laughing at me.

Narcissist!

But I shouldn't think that; we are identical twins so if she is a narcissist then I am too. But my tendencies are more psychopathic – I have less and less empathy for her.

A humour-fuelled smile catches at the corners of my lips. Maybe I am viciously self-centred sometimes, but sometimes that is justified.

Later, when I unlock the café door to go, it's to leave Jonny behind again. 'Goodbye,' he says as he holds the door. He leans forward to receive my kiss and our lips touch for scarcely a tenth of a second, then he pulls away. 'I'll see you later.' He's doing a stock take and food order tonight, but he's still giving Susan a driving lesson afterwards.

Susan waves from beyond the counter.

I give him one last smile before I turn away.

He shuts the door and his hand lifts to say a final goodbye before he bends down to throw the bottom bolt. Susan walks across the café towards him.

I should not be jealous. I have never had a reason to doubt him. But as I walk to the car I see her hand rest on his shoulder as she says something. I want to be able to trust him, even though I don't trust her. How, though? How, when they are becoming so close?

***

The bedroom door opens. The light in the hall goes out. Jonny's footsteps fall lightly across to the ensuite. The light clicks on in there and the ensuite door shuts.

I roll over and look at the alarm clock on his side of the bed. I'm wide awake. The red numbers say 2:14. I've been looking at the numbers on the clock every few minutes for two hours.

2:14am!

My mind is boiling, stewing on the possibilities that might have led to him coming home so late. I'm bubbling like a pressure cooker.

Angry images are rampaging through my mind, crafting the accusations I am going to scream, and what I might do with a kitchen knife to certain parts of his body. But I don't want to kill him, I want to kill her.

The tap runs. He brushes his teeth. The tap continues running, along with splashing sounds, as if he's putting a hand or a flannel under the water and then washing himself. Probably washing the toothpaste off his chin. But maybe he is washing her smell off his body.

For every thought that claims he must be innocent there's another in my head that's certain he is guilty. But I don't want to be a crazed jealous bitch. Jonny has always, always been loyal to me. I don't want to believe what this implies.

But if he doesn't get into bed quickly my volcano is going to erupt. I can't keep myself calm forever, and I want to sound sensible and diplomatic. I've been mentally pinning myself to the bed, to stop myself tossing his clothes out of the window onto the front drive for the last hour.

The ensuite door opens. The light goes out.

I don't move or speak.

His quiet steps come across the room, accompanied by the jingle of the buckle of his belt.

I guess he has undressed in the ensuite, because the jingle stops in the region of the chair near his side of the bed, where I imagine his pile of clothes are left. A second later the duvet lifts on that side and he gets into bed cautiously.

He thinks I'm asleep. Or maybe he hopes that's true. Hopes he's got away with this.

The bed shakes slightly as he lies down.

A memory floods my mind. Susan and I had shared cheap mattresses as children, mattresses that meant when we were in bed there was a dip in the middle that we rolled into so we always ended up huddled together, usually spooning.

He lies facing me. His breath brushing over my face.

'You're late,' I say into the pitch black. I feel and hear him breathing, but I can't see him.

His breath catches, like a scratch on a vinyl record. I surprised him. His body stiffens too. He's wary of what I will say. 'We were talking. I didn't realise how late it was.' His tone and the stiffness in his body drip with false excuses.

'Catching up on old times ...' I mock, my voice bitter in flavour. I can't help myself.

'Sarah, it's late. I want to sleep,' his voice warns that he doesn't want to argue.

Jonny the conflict hater never argues. If he can't turn around and walk away he hides from it with silence. It's hard to argue with silence.

'You made it this late,' I whisper across the pillow. Speaking into the darkness. Not having to look into the gold in his hazel eyes makes this easier. 'Why do you have to spend so much time with her?'

His sigh sweeps over my cheek. 'She's your sister. She lives on her own. She doesn't have any friends here. Being considerate is the right thing to do.'

'It's every night, Jonny. I never see you alone anymore.' I sound like a whiny teenager. Jealousy never sounds nice. It doesn't empower, it undermines. But how do I stop the feeling?

'She moved here to find you, to get to know you again, she can't do that if you don't speak. Give her more of a chance.'

Stop presenting her side. My husband should be on my side.

I picture us lying here in the early morning light, in the afterglow of love. Me looking at Jonny's beautiful face that has matured but never lost that art-like quality. Whispering from pillow to pillow. I want our pillow talk to be like that again, to be about how much we love each other.

I feel as if Susan is lying in the middle of us. I don't feel loved. 'You're meant to be on my side,' I speak the accusation.

'I'm not taking sides.'

'Why not? I'm your wife.'

'You aren't giving her a chance. That's all she's asking for. It's not about sides. She's not trying to be your competition. There shouldn't be sides.'

'I didn't ask her to come here. I don't want her here. Why should I give her a chance? All she does is flirt with you. Have you succumbed to it?'

'Stop it. And she doesn't flirt.'

'Don't act innocent. You aren't stupid. You know she flirts and you know how much time you're spending with her. It's not normal.'

'She's just being nice. She wants to be liked. That's all. And I'm being kind.'

'And you like her.'

'I don't know what that's supposed to mean from the tone of your voice. But yes, I do like her. So does Lucy.'

I hate her. 'I want a part of your life left for me. Don't drive with her tomorrow, or bring her home for dinner. You can lock up the café and walk away. She's like a stray cat that follows you home every night.'

His arm moves and his hand touches my shoulder then

his body moves towards me and his lips kiss where they land in the dark on the edge of my temple. 'Go to sleep, Sarah.' His breath is warm and a little alcoholic. 'Don't make this into something it isn't.'

I touch his waist and move closer to him, into his embrace as his arm falls around my shoulders and mine slips around his middle.

Then please don't make it become something that I need to be afraid of. Please don't hurt me.

Chapter 27

1985

A light knock taps on the wooden panel that replaced the glass in the front door.

I glance at the clock. Seven. It's Jonny. He said he would come here and collect us.

Us. Not me.

I think he's doing that because we're something different since last night. But he's including Sarah in everything and I wish he wouldn't.

For the last hour, I've been imagining what it would be like to be an only child. If I were just me, I would say to Jonny, *let's not go out, let's stay here and go up to my room. Let's get into bed.*

I want to be alone with him. To talk about last night. To kiss. But he doesn't seem to care. We've been with Sarah all day. Would she understand if I told her we want to be alone for a little while?

I open the door. Behind me, Sarah gets up off the sofa.

She's been quiet all day. I've told her everything about me and Jonny but she hasn't said anything about her and Jay having sex. If I were her I would want Jay to come here too. Maybe she's annoyed that he hasn't tried to see her. She let him have sex with her last night and he's ignored her all day. Maybe she's angry. But if she's angry, why hasn't she told me?

'Are you ready to go out?' Jonny asks, staying outside, standing on the door step.

I glance over my shoulder at Sarah. 'Yes. We're ready.'

Mum and Uncle Charlie have already gone out. They weren't here when we came back from Buscot. We haven't seen them today, but that's normal for our family. No one greets us when we come home, and no one says goodbye.

Jonny looks beyond me. I follow his gaze to Sarah. She hasn't moved forward; she's standing in the middle of the room looking at Jonny.

'Jay isn't coming out,' he says. 'He won't be in the park again. Is that okay?'

She blushes a deep scarlet red. We never normally blush.

'Why?' I look at Jonny. Jay had sex with her, why doesn't he want to see her?

Jonny doesn't answer me. He's still looking at Sarah. My gaze, and my head, turn from one to the other. What is he telling her?

She doesn't look upset. Just embarrassed. 'I'm sorry,' I say. Although I don't know what I'm saying sorry for. It's Jay who should be here saying sorry. I just feel as if that's the thing to say. I walk over and hug her, leaving Jonny at the door. Her arms wrap around me in return but her body is stiff, not relaxed and welcoming.

I want to ask her if she's upset or angry. But not in front of Jonny.

When I let go of her I hold her hand and squeeze it and pull her towards the door.

I'd feel terrible if Jonny had ignored me today and then said he'd never see me again. She must feel horrible. To do that and then be rejected like that.

Her hand pulls out of mine as I step outside. She follows and treads on the grass to walk around Jonny.

'You okay?' Jonny asks her as I lock the door.

She doesn't answer.

My loyalties are torn as we walk down the path. I want to hold Jonny's hand but Susan is beside us and she's miserable. I slot my arm through hers and walk with her. She doesn't talk as we walk to the park.

When we meet up with Wayne at the swings, the boys act as if Jay never existed. Nothing is different except that he isn't here and no one mentions him.

While Jonny rolls a joint, I catch hold of Sarah's arm and pull her aside, leading her over to the roundabout as if we're just going to mess around. 'Did you really like Jay?' I ask. I feel as if I'm saying a word that carries a curse because his name has not been said all evening. But I think Jonny knows something she hasn't told me.

'No,' she answers in a quiet voice.

I let go of her arm. 'Then why did you do it?'

She shakes her head. 'I don't want to talk about it.' Her expression shuts me off as much as her words. 'I've forgotten about it now.' Her eyes turn away from me in the second before her body does too. Then she walks back to the boys. 'Can I have a drag of that?' she calls over to Wayne as he takes the joint from Jonny.

Jonny's gaze reaches to her first. Then it reaches further, to me. I lift my hands, palm up, as well as my eyebrows in a gesture that expresses my lack of understanding. Sarah and I tell each other everything. Always. I don't understand why she's not talking about this.

Jonny's lips lift in a shallow smile, as if he's telling me not to worry about it.

I love him. I can't be sad today. I won't be. I just want to be happy because I have Jonny. When I reach him, I wrap my arms around his middle and tilt up my face to receive his kiss. He kisses me properly, his hands in my hair, as Sarah and Wayne talk and smoke the joint.

When Sarah and I are in bed later, we lie facing one another, lying close. It's a warm night, so she's kicked the duvet onto the floor. She's still quiet. Jonny walked us home and she went up to bed while Jonny and I kissed for a while downstairs.

He hadn't wanted to have sex because Sarah was up here.

I know she's awake – I can tell from her breathing – but she hasn't spoken since I came into the room.

'Are you okay?' I whisper to her. 'Are you sad?'

'I don't want to talk.' Her breath smells of toothpaste.

'Okay. But we should talk about it.' You don't need to talk to Jonny. I can see them, sitting on the river bank this afternoon. Whatever she told him she must have told him then because I'm sure he knows why she's sad.

Her hair brushes on the pillow as she nods in the limited light creeping through our thin curtains.

She rolls over, then, turning her back on me.

Chapter 28

It's Saturday. The town centre is full of people who have come to buy from the farmers' market. People who can afford artisan cheeses, chutneys, organic meat, and vegetables. These people don't live on tins of baked beans and cornflakes.

Susan and I come here because when the stalls are busy, people are distracted, and we steal something nice, like a jar of honey. It's easy to hide something under a jumper that's hung over an arm or slip something in a pocket.

My gaze rolls over the people who fill the street on either side of the stalls. We've never tried to pick wallets out of back pockets, or purses from bags, but I imagine that in a crowd like this we could do it. Maybe we should do it just for fun one day. Like we used to do dares for fun. I need a distraction.

There's a ginger head among the people at the other end of the market square. The colour screams like a siren. The crown of ginger hair moves through the crowd about twenty metres ahead of us. It's short, bright, ginger hair that is far too familiar.

It's Jay.

I can't see his face or his body, just the top of his head, but I know it's Jay.

My feet stop, sticking on the pavement, as heavy as the stone slabs. I can't walk on.

Susan carries on. She is six paces ahead, lost in the river of people, before she realises I've stopped. She turns back, letting people bump into her. As people dodge around and between us, I see, rather than hear, her say, 'What?'

I open my mouth but my throat is so dry I can't even swallow and no answer comes out. I can't talk. I can feel Jay on me and in me; I smell the garlic on his breath. The sunny day is now a dark night and the tarmac is unforgiving and painful beneath me. The air and blood have drained out of my body.

'You're white as a ghost. What's wrong?' Susan is beside me, holding my arm. I don't remember her walking back.

'I … I …' I can't talk. My head is a muddle.

The people beyond Susan separate a little, moving in a way that gives me a glimpse of Jay's face. But it's not Jay. No, it is him, but he doesn't look the same. His face is badly bruised around one eye, and his jaw is swollen on the same side around his lip.

He's been hit. By hard, heavy punches. I can see that. I feel that, because it happened to me once. Someone attacked him.

His bruises must throb with excruciating pain. I know how it feels. Those sorts of bruises go all the way to the bone. Maybe his attacker had even broken his jaw. I hope he broke his jaw.

I bet Jonny did it.

For me.

The Twins

I bet Jonny did it to get him back for what he did to me. It's revenge. Justice.

There's a small piece of paper folded up in a tiny square, hidden inside a sock, tucked inside my pillowcase at home. A note to me from Jonny. He gave it to me on the Sunday, the day after we hitchhiked to Buscot. His neat writing says:

Don't worry. Jay won't come anywhere near you again.
I promise. I've sorted it.

Now I understand those words. Jay has been sorted.

Every time we've gone to the park this week, I have been afraid. I've looked around, constantly nervous of Jay walking over from any direction. Feeling sick all the time because I've been scared he'll turn up. But now I know Jay won't ever come back to the park.

I breathe and realise I haven't taken a breath for ages. I breathe again and realise that I feel as if I can breathe forever. I'm glad Jay is hurt. Relief swells up inside me as the crowd swallows him up again. I've being trying to trust Jonny's words, but now I really believe them. Jay won't be back. Just like Uncle Harry never came back.

Jonny had sorted it.

When I see Jonny later, I'll say thank you.

'Sarah. Come on.' Susan pulls on my arm.

I step forward and realise I can move.

I don't have many chances to speak to Jonny alone. That's why he gave me the note, because he knows I'm not talking about what happened and I wouldn't want him to raise it in front of Susan. But he wanted me to know that I would be safe and so he wrote it down and gave me the note the second night after I was raped.

I want to tell Jonny that I know what he has done. But he's not in the park when we take our stolen jar of honey there and eat it by dipping our fingers into the jar and licking them clean because he's working. Wayne joins us after an hour.

I see Jonny first when he walks across the grass in the park because Susan is swinging and she's up in the air. He walks with long strides, his arms hanging loose at his sides, his body tall and confident.

I want to run to him and say thank you. I want to wrap him up in a hug and tell him I love him just as much as Susan does. He's saved me. He's helped. He's more than kind. He's like a hero.

Susan spots him. 'Jonny!' she squeals with excitement, letting go of the chains that the swing seat hangs from and using the energy of the swing's movement forward to leap off. She runs towards him at full pelt and when she reaches him she jumps at him, wrapping her arms around his neck and her legs around his waist. His hands hold her thighs as they kiss, and he walks several paces with her feet off the ground. A few steps away from us, her feet slip back down to the ground and they let go of one another.

'Hi,' I say.

'All right?' he says carelessly, without any meaning.

'Yes,' I answer, my voice full of meaning.

He looks at Wayne and smiles as his hand hangs onto Susan's.

My heart is aching, and the ache spreads out into my blood, into my muscles and bones. I wish I was Susan.

I watch Jonny all evening. The way he speaks, the way he moves and holds Susan. The way he smokes his cigarettes. The way his smiles lift and fall, and one eyebrow twitches with his expressions. I listen to the depth and variance in his pitch as he talks and the music in his laughter.

My contribution to the conversation is minimal. I am too busy observing and thinking.

What had it felt like? To hit Jay.

What had Jonny said when he'd done it?

What would it feel like to dish out revenge like that? Relief? I can picture myself hitting him, like Uncle Harry had hit me. Sitting on him and hitting him.

I wish I had been the one who had hit him.

I think I would have liked the feeling of causing him pain.

The words I want to say to Jonny, and the questions I want to ask him, build up in my mouth, packing themselves up behind my closed lips. The memory of him slipping the note into my hand whispers constantly in my mind. A moment of private knowledge. He'd held my hand to pull me up off a swing. I thought he'd done it so I wouldn't lose my balance but the piece of paper had been in his palm and he'd left it in my palm when his hand had let go. He'd been waiting for that moment, and he'd kept that moment secret from Susan and Wayne. That note, what he'd done to Jay and what happened that night, are our secrets to keep.

Wayne is talking, telling Jonny about his new mechanic apprenticeship. They're sitting on different swings, a metre apart. Susan is sitting on Jonny's lap and I am a metre away on another swing on the other side of Jonny.

It's strange that he knows something so personal and private about me, while Susan sits on his lap.

She leans into his shoulder.

He wrote his phone number on his note, and told me:

> *Call me if you need to talk. Susan will tell you*
> *I'm a good listener, and I have a phone in my*
> *room so you can call any time.*

The toes of my trainers push the swing seat back and forth slightly, stirring up the dusty mud.

'I need the loo,' Susan says, getting up off Jonny's lap. His hand slides over her bottom as she turns and looks at me. She's expecting me to say I'll walk over to the public toilets with her. I don't want to.

'I'll go with you,' Wayne stands up, leaving the swing rocking behind him. 'I've got some money; we can go over the road and buy some cider from the shop if you like?'

Susan looks at Jonny for his agreement. But he hasn't got up off the swing. He doesn't. He just nods at her. Maybe he knows I want to talk. 'See you in a bit, then,' he adds, looking at Susan then Wayne.

'See you in a bit.' She comes back to him then leans down and kisses him; it's one of their long kisses. I've not been kissed by anyone. I don't know what that feels like. I wish I did. I wish I knew what it felt like to kiss Jonny. No one else. It looks nice.

As they walk away, he watches.

Susan glances back and waves. His hand lets go of the chain that holds the swing and he waves too. Then he looks at me. 'Do you want a cigarette?'

'Yes please.'

He takes a packet of tobacco out of his pocket, opens it, and takes out a paper. He begins rolling a cigarette.

'I saw Jay today,' I blurt out.

'Did you?' He nearly drops the packet of tobacco as his gaze rushes over to me. 'He didn't do anything?'

'No.' I shake my head to confirm it. 'He wasn't anywhere near me. It was in the town centre.'

'And ...' he prods, as he carries on rolling the cigarette, his eyes on me. He lifts the skinny roll-up to his tongue, licks the paper and rolls the end over so it sticks. He reaches out to hand it to me, his eyebrows lifting, his expression asking again, *and ...?*

I take the roll-up. 'I saw what you did. Thank you.'

A blush darkens his skin.

I take the lighter out of my pocket and light my cigarette as he starts rolling another. His blush fades.

'Like I told you the other day,' he says. 'I don't like men like that. He needed to know what he did was wrong so he doesn't do it again.'

'I think you taught him that.'

I swing a little, using my feet and legs to move the swing backwards and forwards, the cigarette dangling between my fingers. Now I can speak I don't know what to say. *I love you.* 'Thank you,' I say again. 'I feel better now I've seen him.'

'Good. I told him not to come near here, or wherever you are, and if he goes anywhere near you I said I'd kill him.'

I stop the swing abruptly, pressing the soles of my trainers into the ground as the seat of the swing bashes into the backs of my thighs. 'What did it feel like, when you hit him?'

'Good.' He smiles. 'It felt like I was hitting every man who abuses women. My dad. Your uncle …' His smile pops up and then falls away again. 'I just want you to feel safe.'

'I do feel safe now.'

'Good,' he says again. Then he puts his roll-up between his lips and lights it.

'Would you mind if I ring you later? When Susan's asleep. I have nightmares.'

'You can ring me any time. That's why I gave you my number. I know my Mum has nightmares still.'

A stupid tear escapes one of my eyes because he is being so nice. I swipe it off my cheek with the heel of a hand and take a drag from the cigarette.

'How much have you told, Susan?'

'Not much. I told you, I don't want to remember. If I ring you, I want you to talk to me about something else. About things that will make me forget it.'

'Deal,' he says with another smile.

'But I can't call you,' I suddenly remember. 'It would show up on the phone bill and Uncle Charlie pays it. He had the phone put in.'

His smile lifts higher and he shrugs a little. 'Then I'll call you.'

'The phone would ring and wake everyone.'

His smile drops. 'What if I say I'll ring you at one-thirty tonight. You can wait by the phone. I'll just let it ring once then put it down so if you don't answer it won't disturb the others.'

I smile now. 'Okay.'

'Jonny!' Our gazes are pulled away from one another to the distance where Susan is yelling and waving at him. Wayne isn't with her. She hadn't gone to the shop. She must have gone to the loo, then turned back and left him to go to the shop on his own.

I don't want to stay here with just them. It's a sudden feeling. I can't stay here and watch him hold and kiss her.

I climb off the swing, drawing his attention back to me. 'I'll go and meet Wayne. I can help him carry the cider.' He doesn't need help but I can't stay here.

I don't give Jonny a chance to reply, I walk away from him in the same moment that Susan starts running towards him.

Chapter 29

Moonlight is seeping through the thin curtains, letting light into the living room so I can see clearly now my eyes have adjusted to the lower levels of light.

'I'd hate sharing my bed,' Jonny says on the other end of the phone. 'If I had to share a single bed the other person would end up on the floor.' Jonny laughs in a low, tired-sounding pitch.

I smile into the phone receiver as if he can see. I'm holding the phone receiver tight, pressing one end to my ear and the other close to my mouth so I can whisper. I don't want anyone to hear me. Us. I don't want anyone to hear us talking. That's why Jonny and I talk in the middle of the night.

These night-time whispered conversations are another secret now.

At one-twenty every night I roll out of bed carefully so I won't disturb Susan, creep out of our room and downstairs, and sit on the bottom stair with the phone in my hand, waiting for his call. He calls at one-thirty.

When Jonny rings, I pick the receiver up to stop the bell making anything more than a slight blip of sound.

Mostly he talks and I listen as the fingers of my free hand play with the curly cable leading from the receiver to the phone.

I love listening to his voice and his laugh in the darkness. In secret.

'What music are you listening too?' I can hear it playing quietly in the background.

'INXS. *Listen like thieves.*'

I picture him in his bedroom, lying on the bed. I've been in his bedroom once, with Susan. I walked around looking at everything while they'd sat on the bed, preserving everything in my memory so I can imagine him in his room when we talk.

His narrow black phone is in there. It's attached to a long cable that comes under his bedroom door. The phone could be screwed to a wall but he carries it around while he talks. I hear him moving, pacing sometimes. Sitting at other times. Lying on his bed and lying on the floor.

He has a cassette player in his bedroom with a radio. It's that that's playing the INXS album. There is a stack of single records and cassette tapes on the floor near his tape player. His mum's record player is downstairs.

He has shelves with stuff on them too, things he's collected since he was a child. He even has some silly little toys from cereal boxes.

His mum isn't wealthy, but he's earned money himself for years. He had a paper round from the age of seven. Then washed plates and glasses in a pub. Now he's learning to be a chef. He wants his own restaurant. I want that for him too.

I admire, Jonny. He's been trying to persuade me to do an apprenticeship too.

I haven't told him I love him.

We don't talk about what I feel or what he feels. But I think he thinks of me like a sister.

We just chat and he makes me laugh in a breathy whisper into the phone. He makes me feel better. Happy.

'Stop talking, let me listen to your music.'

The music becomes louder. I know he's lifted the receiver and has held it towards the cassette player. I smile as I listen to the song. I like it. He sings to it. Not into the phone, the phone is still held towards the music, he's just singing along. I like it when he does that. But then, I like everything Jonny does and likes. He's a good man and he has good taste.

'Like it?' he says when he puts the receiver back to this mouth.

'Yes.'

'What's your favourite INXS song?'

Our conversations flow like this. They travel all over the place for half an hour, and then he says. 'I should get to sleep. We'd better say goodnight.'

Our goodnights are warm and friendly, but that's all. 'Speak tomorrow,' he always says just before he ends the call.

I creep up the stairs, walking on the balls of my feet, to get back to our room and back into bed with Susan. Then every night I lie there wondering what she would say if she knew about Jonny and me talking on the phone. He's not being unfaithful to her, just kind to me. It's just conversation. He still kisses her in the park, and they go off sometimes and leave me with Wayne.

But when he comes back, he always looks at me, his eyes saying, *are you okay?* Even if his lips don't say it.

Sometimes he winks at me too, over Susan's shoulder.

It doesn't make me feel guilty. He is hers in the day, but he's mine at night.

'Sarah. Sarah,' Susan shakes my shoulder as her urgent whisper travels into my sleepy mind.

I don't want to wake up. I'm tired.

'Sarah. I'm bleeding.' Panic and fear ring through the quietness of her voice. 'I'm bleeding between my legs.' Her eyes look into mine desperately seeking help.

I see the blood dripping down her thigh and onto her calf.

'There's blood on the sheets. Is it because I had sex with Jonny? We had sex tonight. Do you think he hurt me?'

'I don't know. Did it hurt?' I rub a knuckle over one eye as I sit up. My hand touches the wet patch of blood in the bed.

'No.' She turns away her fingers pressing between her legs, trying to stop the flow as she leaves the room. 'I need toilet paper. Do you think I should go to the hospital?'

'Mum bleeds.' I remember as my mind wakes up. 'Mum bleeds,' I say again in a louder whisper so it will reach her in the bathroom. A memory swings back into my head like an opening door. I get up and follow her. 'Women bleed every month. Don't you remember? They told us at school years ago that girls start to bleed every month when they grow up.'

I join her in the bathroom then close and lock the door. She's sitting on the toilet with her knickers at her ankles. Her knickers have a scarlet stain in the middle.

'It's called a period,' I tell her as I sit on the edge of the bath. 'Mum has things to stop it, like a cork. They're in that cupboard.' I nod towards the cupboard by the sink.

Susan must be bleeding because she's a woman now. Because she's having sex with Jonny.

I get up and open the cupboard with my finger in the hole where the doorknob used to be. There's a box of yellow things called tampons in there. 'Here.' I pull one out of the box and give it to her.

'How do I use it?'

I hold out the box so she can look at the pictures on the back. 'You put it inside and push it up.'

She is crying. There are drying streaks from earlier tears on her cheeks too. She's doesn't look like a woman. She looks like a scared child.

I put the box back. 'Here,' I take the paper parcel off her, open it and hand the contraption back to her.

She lifts up, squatting, so she can put the thing inside her. I see the blood in the water in the toilet bowl. It is a lot of blood.

'Did Jonny hurt you?' I ask again.

'No,' she shakes her head.

After that, we sit in the living room downstairs because she has stomach ache and can't go back to sleep. We chain smoke, mostly in silence, watching television and not talking about what's happened – or about how Susan's body must have changed to make that happen. Is it because she's had sex? All I remember is the teacher saying that it happens when girls get older.

What about my body? Has it changed because of Jay?

I don't know if I'm ready to be a woman like that. I don't want to bleed like that. I'm happy as I am. I don't want to grow up anymore.

Chapter 30

2019

'Amazing grace! How sweet the sound, That saved a wretch like me ...'

The melody of the hymn resembles a mashup of strangled cats and howling dogs. The few of us here are singing merely to fill the room with noise, our voices choked by grief.

My voice drops out.

It isn't just Jonny and me who are still in shock from the first sight of the coffin in the hearse. For some reason it had suddenly made her death real. Marie, Emma, and Stan, and the sprinkling of nosey neighbours from Susan's block of flats, have stuttered their way through the hymns and prayers.

The atmosphere in the small room is thick with a lack of understanding over the cruelty of fate.

We closed the café today so everyone could come.

It's strange to think that in the context of time, it's only a moment ago that Stan, Marie, and Emma said goodnight to Susan as she walked out through the door of the café for the last time. Now, she's in that coffin.

But Jonny and I know that in between her leaving the café that day and the car dropping off the edge of the road, there was that terrible argument. An argument during which the past was dredged up in a vicious net of destruction. Jonny and I are living with the weight of that net tied around our necks.

The coffin is on the stand in front of us, in front of a short red curtain. Her body. The face I had seen in the morgue, now painted to represent a false expression of peace. 'Blood changes colour when people die,' they'd told me in the morgue. 'It's the oxygen that makes it red. People turn blue-green when the oxygen leaves their blood.' But the mortician has painted her skin pink again. We were shown the body at the funeral parlour yesterday. I'd watched Jonny. Trying to judge what he saw.

A river of memories flows through my mind, tumbling over a waterfall and crashing into one another. I see her smile and hear her laughter. We were so close as children; we had laughed together all the time. But I feel detached from those images. My emotions feel as if I've had a local anaesthetic injection to numb the pain.

We, me and her, had been arguing for so many months leading up to this. I had wanted to be rid of her and now she's gone. Forever. Jonny's right: mourning her makes me a hypocrite. But I do feel regret and so what does that make me? Two-faced?

But I know so much more about her than anyone here. She was not the person that these people saw. She was a fake. She lied to them.

The Twins

I never thought I would miss her. But now she's gone, and I can't do anything to unite us again, I do miss her. But even though I know that in my mind, still the emotions in my body are a dense, murky unfeeling fog. My heart feels as solid as volcanic rock; no tears are waiting to fall. Everyone else has a tissue in their hand. Even Stan.

Marie's voice breaks apart with a sob as the hymn comes to an end, putting the throats and ears about the room out of their misery.

But I was alone for years without her around anyway. Why is it different now that there really is just me? Because I'm genuinely alone on the earth? Because there's no carbon copy to be found somewhere? When we were apart, I always felt her presence. Like a spirit even though she was alive.

I wish I could feel her like that now. It was oddly comforting. Even if she were here to haunt me. But she isn't. She's just cold, lifeless matter in that box and there is nothing more. I think if she were haunting me, this remorse would ease. If she were cursing me, then maybe I would not curse myself for hurting Lucy too.

The minister, clothed in black and white ankle-length robes, speaks with an open bible balanced in one hand, waving his other hand around expressively.

The minister is a man the crematorium frequently use. He has no relationship with the family. None of us are church-goers. But Susan had not made a will to dictate her ending, and who knows whether or not God exists. So, as her next of kin, I chose to give her body a religious send off and a chance on the other side.

When we were young we would have laughed over the vicar's exuberant praise of a woman he didn't know.

Jonny's hand reaches for me and his fingers close about mine, uniting us in guilt and grief. It's a rare gesture of affection. I have not received many from him since the accident. He's locked himself up tight because Jonny doesn't have a heart of stone. His heart is more like a marshmallow. It's soft but weak. I see that now. I hadn't seen it before. He isn't coping. He isn't giving out affection because he isn't strong enough to receive it either. Anything and everything distresses him.

He does need someone to be a crutch. But he won't let me be that. I irritate him, I think. The way I'm coping with my grief and guilt annoys him. But I'm not sure how he expects me to behave.

I look at him and smile, even though he isn't looking at me. My heart stretches out in his direction. We will come out the other side of this. Lucy will recover. She has to. When she's well, we'll be close again.

'Please kneel and join me in saying the Lord's prayer.' The vicar's gaze passes over the small number of us in the large room.

The nosey neighbours on the other side of the aisle sink down, descending in a flow of movement that travels to Stan, Emma, and Marie behind us.

Jonny looks at me.

We don't kneel. We bow our heads as his fingers work their way between mine, lacing us tightly together. Perhaps there is a God, because I feel my silent wishes answered. The guilt and grief will go away if we are okay, and everything will be all right then.

The vicar's orator voice recites the words with the rhythm I learned in primary school and have never repeated since. I say them now. 'And forgive us our sins ...' My words seem louder because the room is virtually empty.

Jonny's hazel-gold eyes look at me as I speak. I let everything bad that is in my head go. I let her go. 'As we forgive those who sin against us ...'

'Amen,' is the only part of the prayer that he speaks. But it is enough. That one word makes me feel forgiven.

'Please stand,' the vicar requests.

Everyone rises like a swelling wave in the sea.

It's time to say goodbye. I feel able to do it now.

There are more words. More rhythms of religious verse and then the short curtain behind the coffin slides open automatically and the coffin begin its journey towards the fire. Susan begins her journey towards the fire.

My fingernails press into the skin on Jonny's hand. Clinging. He is all I need.

The coffin moves slowly through the hole in the wall, until it passes entirely over the threshold, then the curtain closes.

The short red curtain hangs still, back in place, denying that there was ever a coffin, that beyond it there was ever a person.

I take a breath in the same moment that Jonny does. It's as if we've both been holding our breath until this moment.

Susan has gone.

Chapter 31

1985

Mum's laughter is throaty and cracked and it ends with a cough. 'You two,' she says. As if that phrase explains her laugh.

We are sitting on the sofa, Susan and I. She's lying back against me and I'm holding her while we watch TV. Her stomach hurts and she feels sick.

'Can I have a cup of tea, Mum? With sugar,' Susan asks as Mum walks across the living room towards the kitchen. 'I've got tummy ache.'

Mum stops and turns around, clutching her short dressing gown across her middle. 'So that's why your sister is hugging you like you used to hug each other when you were three. What's the magic word?'

Susan sits up, pulling free from my arms, as Mum walks into the kitchen area. 'It's *please*. I've got a period. I used one of your things.'

Mum stops and looks back. 'Have you?'

'Yes.'

She looks at me. 'And you?'

No. I shake my head.

'You'll be soon after her. You two do everything together. I bet you'll be on soon.'

'On?'

'On your period. That's what people say. You come on and go off.' She looks at Susan and I see her thinking, thinking about what she has and hasn't said. She's remembered now that she's never told us about periods. 'It lasts for about a week. But don't use all my things. They're expensive.'

'I've got to use something, Mum, I was dripping blood.'

'Then you'll have to stay in. I'll have the two of you to buy things for as well as me and I'm not asking your Uncle Charlie to buy those.' She turns away and walks into the kitchen.

'Can I have a cup of tea?' Susan shouts after her. 'Please?'

'You can. If you make it yourself,' Mum shouts back.

'I'll make it for you,' I say, getting up off the sofa.

The kettle clicks on as I walk into the kitchen. Mum is making herself tea and rolling a cigarette. She looks at me. 'Which one are you?'

'Sarah.'

'You're the one that's not bleeding.'

'Yes.'

'It's nothing to be afraid of,' she says as I line the mugs up on the side, then reach for the pot of teabags. I take the teabags out and put one in every cup as she lights her cigarette.

She offers me the packet. She knows we smoke. She doesn't argue with us about it. She doesn't really care what we do, as long as we don't annoy her.

The Twins

I roll a cigarette as the kettle begins to steam. The sound of the water inside it changes, getting quieter as it boils.

She pours the water. I put the cigarette down and get the milk from the fridge. I tip the milk in, take out the teabags with a teaspoon and drop them in the sink.

She picks up the cigarette I rolled. 'I'll take this for your Uncle Charlie,' she slips it into her dressing gown pocket. 'You can roll another.' She picks up two mugs and carries them away.

I put three sugars in Susan's mug, roll two cigarettes, and take the mugs and the cigarettes into the living room. 'At least because it's the school holidays we don't have to go out of the house today,' I say.

She nods as she reaches for the mug of tea. 'Jonny doesn't finish work until eight tonight. But I'll ring his mum and ask her to tell him he can come here if he wants to.'

Susan and I are still curled up on the sofa when Uncle Charlie comes downstairs, dressed in his jeans and T-shirt to go to work. Mum isn't with him. Her bed had been squeaking for a little while before he came down, in the rhythm that I hate.

I had held onto Susan's shoulders, crushing her against me like a shield while they did that in the room above us.

'You on the rag?' Uncle Charlie says, looking at Susan.

Mum has told him about Susan.

Susan smiles but she doesn't answer. She said her stomach ache is like cramp. It's too painful for her to want to talk or move.

'Poor love,' Uncle Charlie walks over and pats her on the

189

head. 'Bit of a shock, was it? Did you think your guts were spilling out?'

We ignore him.

He makes another cup of tea and drinks it sitting on the door step, leaving the door open behind him, basking in the early sunshine. Then he goes to work.

Susan and I stay on the sofa. We don't get dressed or eat when Mum gets up to eat lunch; Susan says she feels too sick to eat. Mum leaves the house to go to the pub after lunch. She says that Uncle Charlie is meeting her there.

We're still on the sofa watching TV in just T-shirts and pants when Jonny knocks on the door just after half-past eight.

She opens the door as I go upstairs to put my jeans on. When I come back down Jonny has taken my place. She's leaning against him and he's stroking his fingers through her hair.

Susan's gaze lifts to me as I walk downstairs. 'Would you roll a joint?' she asks. 'Jonny said it might help with the pain.'

His gaze lifts from the TV to me and he smiles. 'Hi.'

'Hi.'

There are never any clues about our late-night conversations when he speaks to me in front of Susan.

Jonny's hand delves behind Susan's back, into his pocket and he pulls out his tobacco. I know the cannabis resin will be in that. I walk over to take it from him.

When we share the joint I sit on the floor beside them, leaning back against the sofa so Susan can pass the joint down to me and I can pass it back up to Jonny. We spend the whole evening like that until it's midnight.

Just after midnight, Jonny kisses the top of Susan's head. 'I'm going to go.'

I look at him, getting up, getting out of the way, wanting to say, *will you call?* But there's no opportunity to ask as Susan moves out of his way and gets up off the sofa so he can get up.

He picks up the packet of tobacco and shoves it into the pocket of his jeans. He smiles at me but then looks at Susan before I have a chance to smile back.

They kiss, and I stand there awkwardly.

'Goodbye,' she walks to the door with him as she says it.

He opens the door.

The sky is pitch black above the street lights.

He looks back, just at Susan, not at me. Today all his concern is saved up for Susan. Pity. That's what I see it as suddenly. Pity.

He has pitied me for weeks, because of Jay, and now he pities Susan because she is in pain.

Pity is a horrible thing. I don't want to feel pitied. It means that the person giving pity thinks the other person lacks something that they have. It makes the pitied person inferior.

When he's standing on the step outside, they kiss again. Her arms hang around his neck, resting on his shoulders as his hands hold her waist and his head is angled, so I can tell their mouths are open and his tongue is in her mouth.

I don't like him anymore. It's instant. I don't want to be pitied. I feel as if he's been patting me like a dog to be calmed.

'I'm going to bed,' I say to Susan; she doesn't hear.

I walk upstairs as they stay at the door, their foreheads pressed together whispering to each other.

I am awake at one-thirty when the phone does a half-ring. I'm not sitting on the stairs. I'm in bed lying next to Susan. I don't need to be pitied. I am strong. Feral. Let him pity Susan because she is bleeding. I can look after myself.

***

'You bleeding yet?' is the first thing Mum says when she comes downstairs in the morning and sees Susan and me on the sofa in the same position we were in the day before. She's looking at me.

I shake my head.

Even when Susan stopped bleeding, whenever Mum saw us for the first time in the day, she would say to us both, because she didn't know which one of us I was, 'Have you started bleeding, Sarah?' She'd wait then, until one of us said no.

The answer is always no.

She's still asking the question when Susan starts bleeding again, four weeks after the first time.

Jonny comes to the house again that night.

We haven't spoken on the phone since the last time Susan bled. He rang the phone for three nights, then he stopped ringing. We have not spoken about it. When we're in the park, if Susan goes to the loo or the shop then I go so that Jonny and I are never left alone, and I talk to Wayne more now. He's okay. He makes me laugh most nights. I like his stories about work. He told me they sent him to the supplier to order striped paint to spray a car. Of course, the shop didn't sell striped paint; they'd been teasing him and he'd fallen for it.

I don't want to stay in tonight and sit indoors with Jonny and Susan while they snuggle up and he pets her and pities her.

'I'm going out,' I say as he sits on the sofa.

'Where?' Susan asks, frowning at me as if it's a crazy idea.

'To the park. Wayne will be there.'

'He's gone to the pub,' Jonny answers.

'Then I'll go to the pub. Where is he?'

'At The Three Lions,' Jonny answers. 'But are you going to be okay on your own?'

'I can walk along the road,' I jab, as I turn to the door. 'I don't have to stay here. I can do whatever I want.'

'Is she okay?' I hear Jonny say to Susan as I close the door.

'Yes, she's okay.'

Susan's going to want to stay in tomorrow if her tummy is still hurting, but we can't because of school. Mum had another warning letter from the council the first week of term. They said if we don't go to school this month then they'll prosecute and send her a court date.

I walk quickly, aware of everyone walking on the other side of the street, or behind me. It's cold. Officially it's autumn. I wish I'd put a coat on. I walk faster.

We'll need to find somewhere warmer to hide than the park soon. We usually go to the public toilets in the winter and sit on the sink unit, but they're smelly.

Mum might be in The Three Lions. She goes in different pubs but I know she mostly drinks in The Duke of Wellington.

A man's quick footsteps walk behind me. As he gets close

he makes me nervous. I try to walk faster than him, but I can't. He passes me.

Most people aren't rapists or murders. But the fear makes me start running anyway, and I run as fast as I can the rest of the way to the pub.

I'm nervous when my hand pushes on the cold brass plaque at the edge of the pub door. The door is heavy; for a moment I think it's locked when it doesn't give but when I push it harder the door opens. I am the daredevil, I remind myself as I walk in.

The room isn't busy and my entrance is obvious; some of the people sitting on barstools look over at me, through the mist of tobacco smoke.

The door falls shut behind me, committing me. I swallow, daring myself to carry on into the room and act as if I have a right to be here. I can see Wayne at the furthest end of the bar. He is talking.

'Hello, love, which one are you?' A man shouts from a corner. I can't see him properly; he's hidden by someone sitting in front of him, but I think he shouted at me and I know the voice. He was probably an uncle at some time.

I don't answer. I ignore him and everyone else except Wayne.

Wayne is leaning on the bar, with a pint glass braced in one hand. He's talking to other people at the bar. People his age and older.

'Hello.' I wave but he doesn't notice me. 'Hello,' I say again as I walk closer, awkwardness accompanying me as a long dragging cloak.

He still hasn't noticed me.

'Hello.' His head finally turns when I am a foot away and I say it nearly in his ear. 'Jonny told me you were here. Will you buy me a drink?'

He acts differently. He doesn't smile a welcome and his body doesn't turn. He doesn't even say anything straight off.

'I know she's not eighteen, mate, so don't even ask me for it,' the man behind the bar says. He has a pile of blond curly hair that falls onto his forehead and hides one eye.

Wayne looks from me to the man. 'Give her a Pepsi. She can have that; she's sixteen.'

I'm not sixteen, but I'm not going to say it because maybe there's a rule that I can't even drink Pepsi in a pub unless I'm sixteen.

I spend my night standing beside Wayne with a glass of watery Pepsi that came from a spout not a bottle or a can. I make it last hours while he talks to the people I don't know. They are people who don't want to know me either. They don't talk to me; they talk around me and past me.

When one of them goes off to use the toilet, Wayne leans over a little, speaking to me aside from the rest of the conversation. 'I work with these guys,' he says in a low voice.

I nod.

When the pub closes at eleven, Wayne walks me home. Keeping me company. He is being polite. It isn't pity. He has no reason to pity me. It's nice of him to do it. His hands press into his jeans pockets as he walks. My arms swing beside me. He is my friend. That's all.

When we reach the house, I say, 'Do you want to come in for a cup of tea or coffee?'

'Don't know.' His answer is non-committing but he follows me along the path to the door, his gaze darting around, taking in the look of the house and the street we live in.

I take the key out of my pocket, open the door and step in. Jonny and Susan are lying on the sofa. She's squashed up against him and his arm is around her. He scrabbles to get up when Wayne comes in behind me. 'Hi,' he says to Wayne, not me.

'Are you going back?' Wayne asks him, his hands remaining in his pockets.

'Yes. Sure. If you're walking back.' Jonny climbs over Susan to get up.

She sits up behind him, while he puts his trainers on. He looks at me. 'You okay?'

'Yes.' I had a nice night.

He looks at Wayne as if he wants Wayne to agree with my answer. Wayne doesn't say anything.

Jonny leans down and kisses Susan on the lips, his fingers spreading in her hair and holding her head still. When he straightens up, she gets up and follows him to the door.

Wayne steps outside first. Jonny and Susan kiss again, before Jonny steps outside. Susan closes the door on him. As soon as she has shut it, she looks at me. 'Are you into Wayne now?'

The question is like a lance that stabs right into my heart. I don't need a boy. I don't want one. 'No.' I turn away. 'I'm going to bed.'

'Sarah?' Mum asks, when she finds me downstairs on my own in the morning, eating toast on the sofa. Susan has stayed in bed. She said if anyone comes from the school, or social services, we'll tell them how sick she is.

'Yes,' I answer, I can't be bothered to lie, although lying to Mum is always funny. She never knows the truth.

'Have you started bleeding?'

'No.'

'I think you should be by now,' she says as she crosses the room to get to the kitchen.

Uncle Charlie isn't here. He went to work over an hour ago.

I carry on watching the TV eating my toast as she makes tea in the kitchen and lights a cigarette. The smoke drifts back into the living room.

She comes back with her mug of tea held by the handle in one hand while the cigarette dangles in between her fingers in the other hand. 'Charlie reckons you're pregnant,' she says as she sits on the chair opposite where I'm sitting on the sofa. 'Have you got a boyfriend?'

I shake my head, not taking my eyes off the TV. Sex. Sex leads to babies. I remember that from our first-year sex education too.

'Have you had sex with anyone?'

It takes a moment to force my head to shake.

'It's just with you and her, everything comes together. You smiled for the first time on the same day. You crawled and walked on the same day. You said the same first word on the same day. You've grown at the same rate in the same way. I don't see why you wouldn't start bleeding on the same day, or at least nearly the same day.'

I don't answer her. It's because Susan is having sex and I am not.

But I had done it once.

Was once enough to have periods? Or to get pregnant?

'Are you sure you're not pregnant?' Mum says. 'Because I'll fucking kill you if you are.'

'I'm not pregnant,' I thrust the words at her. 'I don't even have a boyfriend.'

Chapter 32

2019

My hand shakes as my thumb touches the red phone icon to end the call.

'What is it?' Jonny is beside me. He leans closer, as if he's looking for the caller identification. He must have heard the level of surprised emotion in my voice when I took the call.

I turn and look at him. 'She's awake. Lucy is awake.' I slide the phone into my back pocket.

'Really ...?' The colour drains from his skin, leaving him white. 'We need to go.' He turns towards the door of the café, his hand reaching into his pocket for the car key. 'How is she? What did they say? Can she speak?'

'They didn't say and I didn't think to ask. But she's alive, Jonny. She's breathing on her own.' I pull the end of a cord to untie my apron and turn towards the kitchen to go and hang the apron up.

'Marie,' Jonny calls across the café, disturbing customers. She's serving at a table in the far corner. 'Lucy is awake, we're going.' The urgency in his voice is taut with the tug of war between hope and fear that we have been fighting for weeks.

She nods, accepting responsibility for the café with that one call. She has more help, though. We hired a fresh-from-school eighteen-year-old, who is helping her and Emma because of all the hours we've been spending at the hospital. But since the funeral, we've been working in the morning and going to the hospital in the afternoon.

'We're leaving,' I say to Stan as I walk into the kitchen. 'Lucy's woken up.' But I don't know if she is rational. If she is herself or only half-alive and unable to control her mind and body. I should have asked.

When I leave the kitchen, Jonny is outside the door of the little office.

'Your coat.' He presses it into my hand.

He has his coat too, and his phone gripped in his other hand as he turns and walks ahead of me towards the front door, racing to get to Lucy.

Will the injury have altered her?

Will it alter us?

If she is ill – unable to move – what will we do?

'Come on, Sarah.' Jonny urges me to hurry as he holds the door.

Jonny pushes open the door of Lucy's intensive care room and holds it for me with a forgotten hand that hangs behind him as he looks towards the bed. A nurse told us that Lucy seems fine.

'Mum.' Lucy's eyes look at me not Jonny, and her hand lifts

off the bed, reaching out to me. She is fine. Even the cuts and bruises on her face have healed in the weeks she has been lying here. She is fine.

Jonny lets the door fall shut and walks to the other side of the bed from me. 'Luce.' Tears crack his voice and I see them glisten on his cheeks.

'Dad.'

He wipes the back of his hand over his cheeks then takes hold of her hand that has the cannula fixed in the back of it.

I take the hand that was offered to me and kiss the back of it. It smells medical – sterile and chemical.

Jonny leans down and kisses her forehead, his fringe falling forward. 'Luce.' His tears drip on her cheek. Her hair is lank and greasy because it hasn't been washed in all the weeks she has been lying here. It's darker too; I can't see that hint of red in it anymore.

'Don't cry, Dad, you'll make me cry.' Her voice is croaky. It has that roughened just-woken-up sound exaggerated by weeks of lack of use.

Lucy's fingers wrap around mine, holding me. 'Hello,' I say. 'Do you feel ill?'

She nods. 'A little. The nurse said she thinks I feel sick because of the medicine not the injury. But I have a headache too.'

'You took a heck of a thump on the head, Luce. Have they told you how long you've been out cold?'

'Yes.'

I stroke a hand over her hair, brushing it back for her and catch Jonny's gaze. He smiles. The largest smile I have seen on his lips in all these weeks. Emotion wells up like a boiling kettle spewing steam. I have my family. I had begun to fear that this moment would never happen.

'Do you remember anything about the accident?' Jonny asks.

She shakes her head.

'Have they told you anything?' he adds.

'That I was in a car that came off the road.'

He nods at her. Leave him to say this. I don't want to. 'Susan was in the car with you. She died.'

She doesn't make a sound but her eyes close and tears run from the outer corners into her hair and onto the hospital's greying pillowcase.

I have been in a place like this before – sitting beside a hospital bed in an emergency room. The memory suddenly fills my head. The machines had broken to a single flat sound, dropping from a steady beat to a ringing noise. When Mum died. Fate had finished Mum off in a bed like this.

But Lucy is alive. She has survived.

Her eyes open. The bluest flecks in her irises catch the electric light and the tears make her eyes liquid. 'I want to go home. Is Michael coming?'

'I rang him before we left the café. He had to pack up at work then he was coming,' Jonny says. 'I need to ring your nanna too, now I know you're okay.'

I hadn't thought about ringing Michael, or considered Jonny's mother. He's been speaking to her most nights to let her know there's been no change.

'You'll stay with us, won't you?' Jonny says. 'You should live with us for a while at least. One of us can stay at home and look after you until you're safely back on your feet. Michael will need to work.'

'If Michael can stay too.'

He nods without looking at me for agreement, a smile kicking up one corner of his lips. 'But your mum and I will be running around after you. He won't get a look in. You scared us.'

She looks at me and I see memories flood through the back of her eyes.

Her fingers curl further around mine. 'I'm sorry, Mum.'

'For what?' *For getting in the car? For being on Susan's side?*

'I'm sorry you've lost Susan.'

When Mum died we'd not even realised she was going until she had gone. We'd been sitting beside the bed arguing over something and not realising how dramatically our lives were about to change.

I lean closer to Lucy and kiss her cheek.

Jonny lifts Lucy's hand and kisses the back of it, beside the cannula.

Her eyes stay on me. 'Everything will be okay,' I say. 'We will always be here for you.'

'Do you remember getting in the car with Susan?' Jonny asks.

She shakes her head.

'Do you remember the argument?' I ask.

'No. What argument?'

'Forget about it. It doesn't matter now anyway,' Jonny finishes. 'All that matters is you're alive.'

She lets go of my arm and rolls towards Jonny, reaching up as he leans down to thread an arm behind her shoulders and pull her close. She holds him with both arms. 'Dad.' His name is a sob.

'It's okay, sweetheart,' he answers as he rocks her slightly as if she's a small child.

There's a strange detached sensation that tingles through my nerves. I feel as if I'm sitting up high in the corner of the room watching all of us acting out a scene in a play. I'm in the audience. High above them, on the upper balcony. Like a queen on a throne orchestrating all of this. I'm the one who will pull us through it and make everything better. I've seen how weak Jonny can be, now, and I know I am stronger. I will get us through this. The wounds of this will heel. I know.

We stay with Lucy all afternoon, even though she spends most of it sleeping or talking to Michael when she's awake. Jonny sits beside her, clinging on to her hand and staring at her face, watching her breathe when she's sleeping and watching her talk when she's awake. I stand at the end of the bed watching Jonny. Michael took my seat when I went out to the toilet and he hasn't offered to give it back. He's also claimed Lucy's hand on that side.

When a doctor comes in, she doesn't ask us to leave. She just looks at the notes, the machines, and the drip going into the cannula on the back of Lucy's hand. Lucy doesn't wake.

'Good news, isn't it?' the doctor says.

I nod.

'Yes,' Jonny answers.

'Yes. Thank God,' Michael says.

'She seems absolutely fine,' the doctor adds. 'No harm done really.'

'She can't remember anything about the day of the accident, though,' Jonny says.

'Amnesia is very common when there's been such a significant brain injury. She's lucky she's only lost some short-term memory. It could be a lot worse. Other than that, her brain is in good working order. I think it's more about the mind protecting itself, though, when people can't remember that day. The brain's just closing off a horrible memory it doesn't want to go back to.'

'Yes,' Jonny agrees, his gaze moving to me. He doesn't say anything else.

Jonny is the one who lifts a few spoonfuls of soup to her mouth at teatime but she doesn't have the energy or the appetite to eat much.

'If you tell us what you'd like to eat, I'll bring it in tomorrow,' I say. 'It might make you feel hungrier.'

She nods as her head rests back against the pillow. 'You know what I like—' she smiles at me.

'Prawn sandwiches, made with fresh brown bread,' Jonny finishes for her, smiling too. 'I'll go into the café and make you a round, sweetheart.'

'Just like you used to,' she says. She looks at Michael. 'Dad used to take me to the café before school and he'd pack my lunch box. I always had the best lunch in the school.'

'I'll find a My Little Pony lunchbox for you,' Jonny teases.

Michael laughs. The smile has not shifted off his face since he came into the room.

I want to prise him loose with a crowbar. I want to get close to her.

Chapter 33

1985

When Jonny comes around to sit and watch TV with Susan in the evening, I take my coat off the hook and go out. But I don't go to the pub. I walk to the big superstore on the edge of town. It's dark by the time I get there, and it's quiet because it's a Monday evening.

Mum scared me, talking about pregnancy. I could be pregnant. Jay had sex with me and I could have his child in me. I have felt it all day. Like a little alien growing in me. It's as if she planted a seed in my head. It's rooted and growing.

The security guard is standing by the doors. I won't be able to steal the pregnancy test if it's tagged because it will set the alarm off when I walk out.

I find the kits in the chemist's aisle, on the bottom shelf, near the condoms.

I squat down, pretending to read the back of the packet, then shove it up the sleeve of my navy anorak. The packing doesn't have a security tag.

I've seen these tests advertised on the TV but I don't know what to do with one.

When I walk back to the front of the shop, the security guard is leaning on the scanning machine near the exit, shouting a conversation with the woman behind the tobacco counter. His eyes track me as I walk towards the door. He'll wonder why I haven't bought anything.

I turn to walk along behind the tills to the toilets. Maybe he'll think I really came in to use the toilets.

No one else is in the toilets. I lock myself in one of the toilet cubicles and slide the packet out of my sleeve to read it properly. If I stay in here long enough I can pretend I have a bad tummy. If the guard stops me when I come out, I'll pretend I might throw up on him as a reason to get away.

I thought I might have to use the pregnancy test inside me, but it says I should wee on it.

I might as well use it now, then I can leave it in here and the guard won't find any evidence even if he does stop me.

The plastic coating comes off the box easily, and inside the box is a long flat plastic thing, with a lid. Under the lid is the stick I'm supposed to put into the flow when I wee.

I take my jeans and pants down, sit on the toilet, put the plastic thing in between my legs, then wee.

A piece of paper inside the packet has pictures of what means no and what means yes. One blue line in a window in the plastic is no, two blue lines are yes. It says it takes a couple of minutes to show the results.

The Twins

I don't get up off the loo. I stay seated holding the thing and looking at the little window where the line will show.

The door into the toilets outside the cubicle opens. Someone wearing clicking high-heels comes in. There's a thump. I imagine a heavy handbag put on the shelf where the sinks are. Then there's a plastic rattle that I think is a bag of make-up opening. There's a moment of quiet before a little smacking pop that might be lips parting after lipstick has been applied. Then the woman's high-heels clack into the cubicle next to mine.

Her wee sounds like a tap turned on full, and her clothes rustle with a static sound as she pulls them up, as if she's wearing tights, then the toilet flushes.

I look down at the pregnancy test as the bolt slides open in her toilet. Her door bangs shut behind her.

Two lines.

The tap turns on outside.

There are two blue lines in the little window. I look at the piece of paper. The picture definitely shows two blue lines for yes.

But, no. It's wrong. It's got to be wrong.

I shake the whole plastic thing, as if shaking it will make the second line disappear. It doesn't. It's still there. Staring at me. Two lines. Yes.

No.

I pull my jeans up, zip the fly, and secure the button quickly. I flush the toilet then open the cubicle. I throw the plastic thing and its packaging in the bin and leave the toilets. But I don't walk out of Tesco. I find the tills that have a wider gap for wheelchairs, the ones that haven't been closed off completely, so I can walk back through the gap between the barriers into the shop. I go back to the chemist's aisle. Back to the pregnancy tests. I lean down, snatch another one from the bottom shelf and shove it inside my coat, holding it in place with my left arm as I walk back to the toilets.

I don't even look to see if the security guard is watching.

I use the same cubicle. I undo my jeans and push them and my pants to my knees, then I sit on the toilet and open the packet. But I can't wee. I don't need to go.

I sit there for ages, waiting. No one comes in.

Finally, after about twenty minutes a tiny little bit of wee trickles out onto the stick.

It's going to be no. The first one must have been wrong. I stare at the little window, waiting.

One blue line comes through in a stronger darker blue colour.

It's no. I exhale as if I've been holding my breath for an hour. But then the second line gets darker too. The two lines become darker and darker. Clearer and clearer. Yes.

Shit. It's yes.

I feel sick. I feel as if there's vomit stuck at the back of my throat.

I can't have a baby. *I'll fucking kill you if you are.* Mum's words punch through my thoughts. I can't look after a baby. I don't want one. I don't want to be like her.

I get up, do up my jeans, open the toilet door, throw the test and the packaging in the bin and walk out of the toilet.

The security guard speaks as I walk past him and the exit door slides open. I don't answer. I walk through the door and keep walking. I don't even know where I'm going. To Susan. No. She's with Jonny.

To who then? No one. I have no one else to go to.

I am walking around with Jay's baby inside me. He put it there without asking me. He put himself inside me and left a baby there without asking me. I don't want it.

I walk for ages until I find myself in the playground in the park. As I sit on a swing, illuminated by the single electric light in the far corner, it starts raining. The sky spits down on me. I hold the scratchy chains of the swing, kick off from the ground and lean back, stretching out my legs, and I swing as high as I can, as if reaching as high as I can go will get me away from here. I don't want a baby.

The rain becomes heavier. It pelts down on me. My hood has fallen back as I swing, but I don't care. The rain can soak me. Maybe it will wash the baby out. Or make me ill with a cold and I will die and the baby will die.

I keep swinging until the church clock on the edge of the park chimes twelve times. The twelve dongs rumble over the quiet playground. The only other sound is the creaking of the hinges of the swing.

If I'm not going to die, then I have to go home. I don't stop the swing with my feet, I just let go of the chains and let myself fly off at the highest point, the motion of the swing launching me into the air. I land on my feet with a hard jolt. Maybe that will shake the baby out.

I pull my hood up as I walk home but my hair and my jeans are already soaking, and the rain is so heavy it's soaked through my coat anyway.

When I get home I use my key to open the door. The light is turned off in the living room but Jonny and Susan are still in there, lying on the sofa together and the TV is on. It's twenty past twelve. Mum and Uncle Charlie must have come in and seen them on the sofa. I know his hand had been on her breast beneath her T-shirt because of the way her T-shirt is lying. He'd moved his hand when I opened the door.

Susan strains her head back to look at me. 'You're late.'

I don't answer. I turn my back on them as I take off my coat.

'You're wet,' Susan says.

'It's raining,' I answer.

'Was Wayne all right?' Jonny asks.

'Mmm.' My voice is not committal. He'll speak to Wayne at some point and Wayne might tell him I wasn't at the pub. I toe off my damp trainers.

'You okay?' Jonny leans up on an elbow.

'Yes.' I answer, my voice flat. I don't want a baby. I walk across the room, trying to walk away from the truth. 'I'm going to bed.' I run up the stairs as if I can run away from the baby.

When I get undressed upstairs my hands shake, and when I use the bathroom, while I'm cleaning my teeth I retch and then I'm sick in the toilet.

When I lie in bed I hear them talking downstairs, and up here in the room next to me, where Mum and Uncle Charlie are, the bed creaks in a steady creepy rhythm. My palm and fingers feel around on my stomach. I don't feel anything. But

I know something has been pushed into me. I don't want it in my stomach.

It's one o'clock when Susan comes up to get into bed. She doesn't put the light on.

I move over to make room for her to get in.

'My pillow is wet, where your hair was touching it,' she complains.

I don't say anything. But the words are there, in my head, in my mouth. I turn to say them. *I'm pregnant.*

'Jonny's moving to London,' she says before I can speak. 'He's asked me to go too. He has a job in a restaurant there, as an apprentice chef. He said he can learn better there. It's his eighteenth birthday this weekend. His Mum is going to take us out for dinner and then he's going to London.'

'You can't go,' I say back. 'You're too young. Mum will tell the police to look for you.'

'Mum doesn't care.'

'Social services will.'

'He said you can come too if you want to. He's going to rent a room in a house, but he said you could sleep on the floor.'

That's nice of him to offer me a floor because he would pity me if he left me behind. 'I don't want to go, and you can't go. We're only thirteen. It's illegal.'

'I'm going to run away. Lots of kids run away to London. And I don't care about doing something illegal.'

I don't say any more. Let her think she can run away to London. I turn over, turning my back on her. But her hand slips around my middle and she holds me like Jonny had been holding her downstairs. I'm cold and she is warm.

I think about the alien thing in my stomach as I hear her breathing change when she falls asleep.

What can I do to get rid of it?

A desire to be sick wakes me. It's like a horrible tickle in the back of my throat, a bitter taste and an ache in the glands in my neck. I swallow, fighting the sensation but it doesn't want to be fought. I scrabble over Susan to get out of bed as sick lurches from my stomach up my throat and into my mouth. I press my hand over my mouth as I run to the bathroom. I don't shut the door, just drop to my knees and lean over the open toilet. Uncle Charlie must have left the seat up in the night. I throw up into the bowl over and over until it's painful to keep retching.

'Have you got cramps?' Susan is at the door behind me. 'Are you bleeding?'

'Uh huh,' my groan of acknowledgement reverberates in the toilet. Let her think that. I don't have to tell her the baby is there. I am not going to keep it. It is going to be gone. I kneel up, resting my bum on my heels and reach for the toilet paper to wipe my mouth.

'Do you want a cup of tea?' Susan asks.

I nod. I just want something that will make this go away, and tea won't do it.

When Mum gets up, she looks at Susan curled into one corner of the sofa and me at the other end. 'Are you both bleeding?' she says into the space in between us.

'Yes,' we both answer.

It's easy to pretend. I have flushed one of Mum's things down the loo. The paper wrapper stayed bobbing on the surface.

A sharp knock hits the door at nine-thirty. It strikes the wooden panel in an oddly hard way five times. Uncle Charlie is out and Mum is back in bed. We don't move.

The knock strikes another three times. Harder than before.

Susan kneels up on the sofa and turns to look through the net curtain. Someone is on the outside looking in, trying to see through the nicotine-stained netting.

'There's a police car,' Susan says, dropping down on the sofa. I duck down too.

'Did they see you?'

'I don't think so,' she whispers, and then presses a finger against her lips.

'It's social services.' Mum's on the stairs, looking down at us. 'Stay quiet.'

I can hear talking outside, near the window.

'Are they in there?'

'Can you see anyone?'

The knock hits the door harder than ever saying, *let me in.*

I wonder if the police will kick the door in if we don't answer.

'If you're in there, open up,' a man says.

'Miss Tagney!' The woman who is our social worker calls through the wooden board. 'Susan? Sarah?'

I look up at Mum, asking without words if she's going to answer. She doesn't move from the top of the stairs where she's trying to stay out of sight.

They knock on and off for ten minutes, then a letter drops through the letter box, and a few minutes later we hear car doors closing. Finally we hear their cars drive away.

'They've gone,' Mum says as she walks downstairs. 'But you girls better stay out of sight.' She's still wearing her short dressing gown that falls to the top of her thighs. It droops open at the chest and displays the curve of her breast.

She walks over to the door and picks up the letter they pushed through the letter box. Her finger slips under the edge of the fold and tears it open.

'What is it?' Susan asks, kneeling up on the sofa and looking over Mum's arm.

Mum turns away so Susan can't see and walks across the room into the kitchen. The bin flicks open, the dented metal lid clanging as it hits the wall.

We both get off the sofa and walk into the kitchen. 'What was it, Mum?' I say. It involves us.

'A court summons. You girls are going to have to start going to school, you know.'

'We're ill,' Susan says.

'You're not ill every day,' she snaps back as she reaches for a bottle of whiskey Uncle Charlie has left on the side by the kettle. She unscrews the cap and drinks straight from the bottle.

I'll fucking kill you if you are. Would I end up in prison if the police found out about my baby? Or would Mum?

Susan and I stay on the sofa all day. The police and the woman from social services don't come back.

When Uncle Charlie comes home, he has a white plastic

bag of newspaper-wrapped, delicious-smelling parcels, full of fish and chips. He tells us five times while we're eating that we have to go to school the next day because we're getting Mum into trouble. Then he and Mum go out to the pub.

'See, I told you we had to run away,' Susan says as soon as Uncle Charlie shuts the door.

I press a finger to my lips. They might hear her.

'Well you stay and go to school, then. But I'm going with Jonny.'

I don't answer. I get up off the sofa and go upstairs to put some clothes on. Susan doesn't want to go out but I do. Jonny's coming here and I don't want to be alone with them, making stupid fairy-tale plans about London.

When Jonny knocks, my hand is on the door ready to open it. He's earlier than normal.

I pull the door open and move out of his way to let him walk past me and come in.

His gaze lifts to my face. 'Where are you going? To meet Wayne? You didn't see him last night. Where did you go?'

'To the park.'

'On your own?' There's a note of doubt in his voice that says it's wrong for me to go to the park on my own.

'On my own,' I say as I step outside. I pull the door shut behind me, forcing him out of the way and then I turn and run, making sure Jonny and his pity won't follow. He doesn't any way. Today he is focused on Susan.

I know where I'm going tonight. I'm going to the library. It's open until eight o'clock. I want to look at the books and find out how to get rid of a baby.

The door of the library is automatic; it opens as I walk up to it. It's completely still and calm inside. There are six or seven people in there. They are all quiet, either looking along the shelves or reading on chairs or at desks. I don't want to ask so it takes me ages to find the books on pregnancy. They are with books that talk about good parenting. They have pictures that show what the baby looks like inside me, how it grows, and how it will be born. None of the text says how to get rid of a baby if you don't want it.

'Are you all right, love?' I jump when a woman speaks and drop the book with a picture of the baby at this stage. It looks like a lizard. Just like in the *Alien* film. 'Have you found what you're looking for?' The woman is next to me with a ponytail and bright red circular glasses that perch on the bridge of her nose. She was behind the desk when I walked in. 'We're closing in a minute. Do you want to take that book with you?'

I shake my head then pick the book up, straighten a page that bent when it fell on the floor, close it and put it back on the shelf.

'Is there anything else you want?'

Help me get rid of my baby. 'No. Thank you,' I turn away. I don't know where to go now. I don't want to go home.

It isn't raining tonight but it's colder and when I walk outside a cold breeze sweeps at me.

All I can see in my mind is that little lizard thing. I don't want it inside me. It's Jay's, not mine. He should have it.

The light is on inside the scarlet telephone box on the corner. The light draws me closer. I can see an A4 poster stuck on the back by the phone box through the window. Big black letters say:

SAMARITANS
We support anyone who needs help.
Whatever you're going through, talk to us now.
Call us. Freephone.

I pull the cold metal lip of the door handle and open the heavy door.

The Samaritans telephone number is printed on the poster. It's free to call.

Whatever you're going through, talk to us now.

I need someone to help me.

The stone floor inside the telephone box stinks of urine and the smell is overwhelming when the door falls shut but I pick up the heavy grey receiver. A single pitch monotonous tone drones from the receiver. I press my finger into the hole and turn the dial for zero first. The dial is stiff. Eight. Zero. Zero. My heart pulses quickly as I dial each number and then the dial twists back around. I don't know what to say if they answer.

It rings at their end, then there's a moment of silence before it rings again. 'Hello, this is James. You've reached the Samaritans, how can I help?'

He has a voice that sounds like someone I should know. A friend. It reminds me of our old social worker, Dave. 'Hi.'

'Do you want to tell me your name?'

'Sarah.'

'You sound young, Sarah, what age are you?'

'Thirteen.'

I press the receiver tight to my ear, as if it will keep the conversation private, because it's echoing in this small box.

'What do you want to talk about? Anything in particular, or do you just need some company?'

'I'm pregnant.' The words spill out. They've been trapped behind my lips for hours. 'I was raped by a friend and I'm pregnant and I want to get rid of the baby. I don't know how. Will you tell me how?'

There's a quick breath. That's all I hear that tells me he's surprised. 'Can you talk to your mum or dad, Sarah?'

'No. She'll be angry, and I don't have a dad.'

'Isn't there anyone else you can talk to?'

'No.'

'Well don't worry. You have me. Do you want to talk about what happened?'

'No.' I shake my head even though he can't see. 'Can you tell me how to get rid of the baby?'

'You want an abortion?'

'What's that?'

'It's the name of the procedure used to end a pregnancy.'

'Yes. I want to do that.'

'Give yourself some time to think about it properly, Sarah.' I hear the movement of paper at his end, office sounds. 'Abortion is a big decision, especially when you're thirteen.'

'I don't want his baby in me.'

'I've found somewhere that might help. The British Pregnancy Advisory Service supports under-sixteens. Where do you live, Sarah?'

I don't want to say, in case he tells the police or social services.

'Just give me a county if you like.'

'Gloucestershire.'

'There's a clinic, a place to go, in Swindon. Do you think you can get there? Speak to them on the phone first and they can talk to you about your situation and discuss what's involved better than I can. But you'll need to go to Swindon, if you choose to go ahead with that.'

'There are buses to Swindon from here.'

'The clinic is open now. I could make the call for you and let them talk to you, if you want me to?'

'Yes, please.' I will have to steal the money from Uncle Charlie's wallet to get to Swindon, but I will get there.

Chapter 34

2019

'Come in, come in. Get in the warm.' Jonny holds the door wide with one hand and the small holdall of Lucy's belongings in his other.

Later on, when she's settled in, Michael is going to collect more of her belongings from their flat so that she can stay here for as long as she wants to.

I want her to stay here forever, tucked tightly under a mother's wing.

'Sit down,' I order, pointing at the sofa. 'I'll get you a drink. What would you like?'

She obeys my order because I know she's exhausted herself just getting out of the car and walking in. I see her fingers moving the fabric on the sleeve of Michael's coat where she's gripping his arm tighter. 'Hot chocolate, with all the extras. The way you used to make it for me after school at the café, Mum.'

'I'll have to pop down to the café and get some whipped cream and marshmallows, then,' Jonny says as he puts her bag down beneath the coats. 'I'll go now. Any other treats you want?'

'A slice of one of Stan's delicious bacon and tomato quiches for my lunch.'

He comes across the room as Lucy drops onto the sofa, leans down, and kisses the top of her head, then brushes a hand over her hair. 'Not my quiche?'

'Sorry, Dad, Stan's are better. I used to love it when you brought a leftover quiche home for tea.'

'He's making my recipe, remember,' his fingers mess up her hair. Then he looks at me. 'Do you want anything?'

'We could do with milk.'

'Can I make myself a coffee?' Michael asks me.

'Milk, cream, and marshmallows.' Jonny lifts a hand, the keys rattling as he takes them out of his pocket. 'See you later,' he says as he opens the door and leaves.

'I'll put the kettle on so you can make your coffee,' I say to Michael.

I walk over to join them on the sofa once the kettle is boiling and sit on the left side of Lucy. Michael is sitting at her right. 'While you're waiting for your hot chocolate, what do you want to do?'

'Shall we put a boxset on?' Michael suggests to Lucy.

I didn't ask you.

'Good idea.' Lucy reaches to the coffee table to pick up the TV controls and Michael gets up to make his coffee. They spend the next ten minutes scanning through what's on offer and debating what to watch.

When he sits back down, she leans into him. As we watch the TV, his fingers stroke through her hair.

I curl up my legs at the other end of the sofa, holding my ankles. I feel awkward. I want to hold her.

She's asleep when Jonny comes through the door an hour later. I look over at him as he shuts the door quietly. Now Lucy is home and Jonny is happy, there is such a sense of family in this house; it's as if it has a heartbeat in the walls. But I wish Michael wasn't here. He's spoiling things. He is not part of our family.

'If you're staying tonight you need to fetch your things,' Jonny says to Michael in a quiet voice as he walks to the kitchen.

Michael cautiously starts unravelling himself from Lucy, moving himself out from under her and replacing himself with a cushion.

'I'll go back to the flat now and bring our stuff over,' he answers, walking towards the door.

I watch Lucy, my hand longing to reach out and hold the arch of her foot that is stretched out towards me. But if I touch her, I might wake her.

'If she wakes up, tell her I won't be long,' Michael adds.

'Okay. Don't worry, we'll look after her until you get back,' Jonny says.

They share a smile in the moment before Michael reaches up to take his coat off the hook, as if they're sharing some sort of male code.

I get up off the sofa and walk over to the kitchen as Michael puts his coat on.

Jonny picks the kettle up, looking at me. 'Do you want a drink?'

I shake my head.

'Goodbye,' Michael says. Jonny and I look over as he reaches to open the door.

'See you soon,' Jonny responds.

Michael opens the door and closes it behind him quietly.

I look at Jonny. 'No. What I want is for Michael to stay away.'

'Why?' Jonny's voice is challenging but physically he just turns to run the tap and fill the kettle.

'Because I want to be the one cuddling Lucy.' I thrust the jealous confession at him in a breathy whisper, so I won't wake her.

The sound wakes Lucy anyway.

She sits up in a sudden sharp movement, looking over the back of the sofa at us.

'Do you want your hot chocolate?' Jonny says.

'Yes, please. Thanks, Dad. Where's Michael?'

'Gone to fetch the things for your stay.'

'Okay.'

Jonny opens a cupboard and takes out the grater for the chocolate.

Lucy gets up, leaving the third episode of *Stranger Things* playing on the TV.

'Lucy, you should sit back down,' I say. Her figure is so willowy because she's lost weight in the hospital; it makes her look fragile. 'We can snuggle for a little while.'

'I'll be okay sitting at the breakfast bar. I want to talk to Dad.'

I have no control over her. She isn't a child to be directed by me. I can't make her do anything. Anxiety breaches the barriers I've trapped it behind for weeks and floods me with a tsunami-size wave. I can't control any of this.

'Mum?' Lucy is close as the world turns black. 'It's okay, Mum. I'm okay.' She holds me, stroking my back.

'Here.' It becomes Jonny's strength holding me, and he hands me a tissue to wipe the tears from my eyes and nose. With his hand under my elbow I take a couple of steps until I reach one of the chairs at the breakfast bar.

'Use this.'

Lucy has taken the paper bag full of mushrooms out from the fridge, tipped them out on the side and is now holding the brown paper bag out towards me.

'Thank you, sorry.' I apologise to Lucy. Then I press the bag to my mouth and breathe into it. Jonny's hand rubs over my back as Lucy sits down.

'Count to ten on each breath,' he says.

I do that. One. Two. Three ...

I want us to be like this always, pulling together and helping one another - with no Michael. Jonny stays close until the milk boils over and sizzles on the hot plate.

'It's just ...' I say, I take the bag away from my mouth and look at Lucy. 'I've waited for you to come home, and now ... I don't know ... I just feel emotional.'

'It's okay.' She leans across the breakfast bar and strokes my hand as if she is the mother. 'I understand.'

I sniff away the tears then blow my nose in the tissue Jonny had given me. He glances over with concern in his eyes as he mops up the spilt milk.

It's going to be okay. We are a family. The three of us. This is going to knit us back together and repair everything.

When the doorbell rings, Lucy almost jumps off the sofa to get to the door but she moves too fast, stops, and catches hold of the back of the sofa.

'I'll let him in.' Jonny gets up off the chair near her and walks around her. 'Sit back down.'

Michael brings the cold in with him as he comes through the door, even though Jonny closes it quickly.

'All right, babe?' He calls over at Lucy as he puts two small cases down just inside the door.

'Dinner will be ready in half an hour; we were waiting for you,' Jonny says over his shoulder as he walks to the kitchen.

Michael unzips his coat and hangs it up, wipes his boots on the coir mat, then unlaces them and takes them off. His eyes reach across the room to Lucy; he is smiling at her too, his cheeks red from the cold wind that's blowing outside. Her eyes are focused on him too.

She is hijacked again. She won't want to sit with me now. I get up off the sofa.

Michael's socks brush over the wooden floor as he crosses the room, his arms open. She kneels up on the sofa and opens her arms to receive the embrace he offers and they kiss as if Jonny and I aren't in the same room.

I feel awkward. Jonny is in the kitchen cooking and I'm just standing beside the sofa without a purpose, but I don't seem to be able to move.

She breaks the embrace. 'Dad's cooking fried chicken and sweet potato chips.'

'Cool.' He holds her hand as he walks around the sofa and then she shuffles up, so she sits in the middle of the sofa and he sits at the end. She snuggles into him then and his arm wraps around her, holding her away from me.

'I'm glad I've got you safe and sound,' he whispers to Lucy, but not quietly enough for me not to hear.

'What's that, Mum?' Lucy points at the cardboard box that's under the coffee table as her back leisurely rests against Michael's chest. She looks too comfortable.

'It's Susan's belongings that the police gave me, and a few things I kept from her flat.'

'Can I look?' She surges into movement, like a crest breaking on a wave, suddenly coming to life as she reaches for the box. 'Maybe there's something I could keep to remember her by.'

'Here.' Michael moves too, leaning down to get the box for her.

I haven't even agreed to her looking at it.

She turns around, her legs sliding off the sofa and hanging down so she's sitting straight and can hold the box on her lap. Michael places it there.

Lucy's fingers lift the lid. 'Is this all that's left? Just this little box?' The fluid in her eyes catches the electric light, glinting. The tears spill over and drop, forming spots on the cardboard lid.

'Yes. Just this.'

She turns the lid upside down and discards it on the sofa beside her, where I was sitting.

Lying on top of the contents is the picture.

'Dad.' Lucy looks over her shoulder. 'There's a picture of you with her when you were young.' She lifts it up, showing it to him, even though he's too far away in the kitchen to see.

He walks out of the kitchen, though. I haven't shown it to him. He didn't know the picture was here.

He squints a little as he crosses the room, trying to see it. He doesn't walk around the sofa but leans down and reaches across the back to take it out of Lucy's fingers. His eyebrows lift and his lips stiffen in the opposite of a smile as he looks at it properly.

'Is that when you were dating her?' Lucy asks. She might not remember the argument, but she has remembered other things.

'Yes,' his voice is hard and dismissive. 'That was a long time ago.' He gives her back the picture, then turns away as if it has no meaning at all. But he has his secrets to keep from her too. She doesn't remember anything about the day Susan died and neither of us wants her to.

Lucy puts the picture on the coffee table, not back in the box, then starts rummaging through the other items inside it.

Chapter 35

1985

I sit on the concrete kerb at the edge of the pavement, just up the road from our house, like Susan and I used to do years ago in the summer after school. But tonight it's dark and cold, and the kerb feels damp even though it hasn't rained tonight. I don't want to go into the house while Jonny is there,

The woman at the abortion clinic was kind. She has promised me they will help but I still have to get there.

My hands hold my ankles. I'm curling over into a ball the way I am sitting, trying to be as small and unnoticeable as possible. I'm not wearing socks; there weren't any clean ones and my trainers are wet because I stood in a puddle.

The babies in the pictures in the books were curled up like this.

The visions in my head twist between the little alien lizard and a full-size baby that would have to come out through where Jay had put it in.

I don't want it in me. But I have to wait until next Saturday to see the woman and then I have to wait again until they will do it.

I just want it out.

Mum's figure is painted as a ghoulish silhouette in the intermittent street lights when she comes stumbling along the pavement on the other side of the street. She's leaning on Uncle Charlie. He is just as wobbly. She doesn't see me hunched over on the pavement in the shadows between the street lights further along.

When she steps off the pavement to cross over, she falls down onto the road laughing, trying to grab for Uncle Charlie's arm as she drops to her knees. He reaches out but their hands don't collide. She ends up on all fours, laughing, then she falls sideways and lies in a puddle on the road.

'Come on, you silly cow.' Uncle Charlie leans down to help her up and nearly pitches forward himself.

They are drunk. As drunk as I was the night Jay did what he did. I am not drunk or high tonight. I see life as clearly as if I'm looking at it through a microscope. Mum looks stupid. She is embarrassing, lying there laughing, her clothes all wet and dirty.

Uncle Charlie holds her elbow and manages to haul her up, dragging her off the floor. They stumble three paces to the side as they cross the road, going backwards not forwards and then Mum falls, dropping away from Uncle Charlie's hand and landing on her bottom with a splash in the same puddle he has just pulled her out of.

This is my mother. She made me. I was a little lizard inside her once, when she was fifteen. Susan and I were lizards, and then we became big babies that she squeezed out. I don't want to do that. I don't want to be her.

Uncle Charlie pulls her up again. 'Stop messing about,' he says as he hangs onto her waist and pulls her towards the house and front door. It's a slow progression but they reach the door, he opens the lock with the key, and shoves her inside.

I imagine Jonny and Susan in there on the sofa, breaking apart. They would have been kissing.

If Susan goes to London, what will I do?

I rock back and forth, my fingertips trying to reach for the tops of my thumbs around my ankles as my chin presses onto the bony tops of my knees. There's nowhere to go except school.

I keep waiting outside. Waiting for Jonny to go.

Maybe I'll tell Susan tonight? She could come with me on Saturday. Maybe she'd stop talking about running away if I told her?

Our front door opens and Jonny steps out. He and Susan are captured in the bright beam of a street light, illuminated like a couple in a film as they kiss with arms wrapped around one another, and hands sliding over each other, in a way that they don't kiss in front of me.

I stay hidden in my dark spot, hiding in plain view if either of them were to look.

But Jonny is going to walk the other way, the same way Mum came from. I don't think he will look.

They mess around, talking and kissing, taking ages. Then finally he walks off and raises a hand to wave goodbye.

Susan doesn't close the door until he's walked around the corner at the end of the road.

I get up and rub the grit from the pavement off the back of my jeans.

The key is in the front pocket of my jeans, and the words I want to tell Susan are piled up on my tongue.

She is in the living room. 'Hello, I'm—'

'Jonny passed his driving test.' She gets up off the sofa, bubbling with excitement again, words flowing.

'I didn't know he'd taken it.' But I knew he had been learning. I unzip my coat.

'His mum's bought him a car for his birthday. He's going to pick me up tomorrow and take me to the restaurant with his mum.'

'I didn't think his mum had any money,' I say as I slip off my coat.

'She's been saving for him ever since he was born. She gave him a thousand pounds to buy a car, tax it and insure it. Do you want a cigarette?'

'No. I'm going to bed.' I don't want to tell her how terrible things are for me, when for her ...

Above us, Mum's bed squeaks in the horrible rhythm.

I can't speak about it. The words won't come now. They have slid back down my throat to my stomach and they are making me feel sick again.

I toe off my trainers as Susan rolls a cigarette from a packet of tobacco that Jonny must have left for her. She has everything. All I have is a little lizard in my stomach living off my blood.

My feet, heart, and head all drag as I walk upstairs, like I'm pulling a dozen large chains.

Grunts and groans strain from Mum's room along with the squeaks of the mattress springs and the creaks of the bed's wooden slats as I get changed. I remember to open another one of Mum's things in the bathroom and flush it down the toilet before I go to bed.

When I get into bed the noises from Mum's room have stopped.

Sarah comes upstairs soon after me. She doesn't put the light on but changes in the dark, uses the toilet, and I hear her tear open one of Mum's things and use that. Then she comes back into the bedroom, lifts the duvet, and gets into bed next to me. I don't move. I pretend I'm asleep already. But I can't sleep because all I can feel is the lizard.

Chapter 36

Social services and the police don't knock on the door. All I hear is them forcing Uncle Charlie and the door out of the way. It's eight-thirty in the morning. We are still in bed. The noise wakes us as Uncle Charlie shouts and Mum shouts. It's Friday. We hadn't expected them to come on a Friday.

'Where are the girls, Miss Tagney?' A strange man's voice says.

'You're not taking them away!' Mum shouts.

'Calm down, Jackie.' Uncle Charlie's deep, rough voice, orders. 'If you get all worked up then they'll take them. Let them take control and get those girls into school. They won't do a thing we say.'

'That's all we want to do, Miss Tagney,' I hear the social worker woman's posh voice lift over everyone else's.

The next thing I hear is footsteps on the stairs.

'Shit,' Susan's voice is breathy with the sound of panic. 'They can't take us. I won't be able to see Jonny. We won't be able to go to London.' She's out of bed and pulling on her jeans.

I roll, turn, and grab my jeans off the floor as the footsteps – more than one set – climb higher up the stairs.

When the social worker knocks on our bedroom door and calls, 'Sarah. Susan. Come along, we're going to get you to school today,' I'm zipping up my jeans and Susan is pulling a sweatshirt over her head.

'Shit,' Susan says again.

'Can I come in?' the woman says.

'We're coming.' I open the door.

'Hello, girls.' The social worker is a larger sized woman but she always looks pretty because she wears bright neck-scarves, uses a lot of make-up and has painted fingernails. She fills up the space of the doorframe. Her gaze runs over us, looking up and down, assessing our appearance, judging our worn second-hand clothing. 'I've come to take you to school today. We're going with your mum to talk to the headmistress and draw up a plan to help you improve your attendance.' She looks at our jeans again. 'Have you got uniforms to wear?'

'We have,' I answer. We can't run. There's nowhere to run to unless we jump out the window into the front garden. But our uniforms are old and the blouses and cardigans are short in the sleeves.

'Get yourselves ready!' Uncle Charlie shouts from downstairs. 'The game's up, girls!'

'Shut up! You're not our dad!' Susan shouts back.

'No one's your dad!' Uncle Charlie shouts back. 'But I'm the one that pays for your food and the TV you watch so you better be nice and do what you're told!'

Susan makes a face in the direction of the door.

I've already turned to the chest of drawers with the broken runners to find our school clothes.

The Twins

I feel like we've been arrested when we leave the house. A policewoman opens the back door of her police car and waits as we get in. But the social worker, who asks us to call her Doreen, says a dozen times we aren't in trouble. Mum is, though. She's told to get in another car, behind the one that we are sitting in with Doreen.

What will they do if they find out I'm pregnant? Will they take me away from here? I don't want to live anywhere else.

We don't see Mum at the school. The headmistress welcomes us as though we're new, telling us what a lovely place her school is, as if that will persuade us to come every day. Then we're taken to a classroom by another member of staff.

When we went to school before we were in a class of people who stayed in the same group, but the teacher explains that we will be moving around different classes with different groups of children with the same ability as us in the different subjects. It means we will be with different children to those we knew in our first year here.

It's horrible walking into a class of boys and girls we don't know. They look at us as we walk in. They're working around benches in a science lab and they have plastic goggles on. They stare as the teacher shows Susan and me where to sit. It makes us feel like their experiment. These children don't like us. Their eyes, their stares, say they think we're odd.

What would they think if they knew I was walking around with a little lizard inside me?

When the lunch bell rings, everyone picks up their books, puts them in their bags and rushes for the door, trying to push themselves through the crowd to be one of the first out

239

through the narrow classroom door. 'Slow down,' the teacher shouts.

Susan and I look at each other. We know what we're going to do. We leave the classroom last, and at the bottom of the stairs we use the fire door to leave the building, then we cross the carpark, throw our virtually empty, torn, and mud-stained, school bags over the fence, then climb the fence and run away.

We run to the park, as if Jonny and Wayne will be waiting there. They aren't there; they're working. It starts to rain so we sit under the canopy of a great big horse-chestnut tree, watching the prickly green cases drop and split open as they hit the ground, revealing the glowing amber conkers. I feel like a child again for the whole afternoon, sitting on the ground talking. But then we have to go home because Jonny is picking Susan up in his car at seven-thirty and taking her out with his mum. Then I remember I am not a child and I have a lizard inside me.

Chapter 37

Jonny leans across the stained black fabric covering the passenger seat of his red Ford Escort, pulling the door leaver to open the door for me. I step down off the pavement. I'm not walking easily because I put on a pair of Mum's high heels for the night. Sarah and I have practiced walking around in them in Mum's bedroom before, but wearing them outside on the uneven pavement makes it harder to walk.

I pull the car door wider so I can get in.

'Hello,' he says.

'Hello.' I'm breathless with excitement. This is so grown up.

'You look beautiful.'

'Thank you.' I try to slide sexily into the seat, but it's hard in Mum's short black dress because it's so tight around my thighs. It slides right up every time I move. I took everything of Mum's after she went out with Uncle Charlie, and painted my nails red with her nail varnish and used her red lipstick.

'Put your seatbelt on. I don't want to lose my licence. I only just got it.'

As I turn to catch hold of the metal end of the seatbelt I see myself in the small mirror embedded in the visor. For a moment I don't recognise myself. I look like a proper woman in the mirror. Like Mum. Mum's black eyeliner is thick under my eyes, her mascara has lengthened my eyelashes and the charcoal grey and powder blue eyeshadow makes my eyes look huge.

I smile nervously at Jonny as I pull the seatbelt across me and plug it in.

His palm reaches over and rests on my knee for a second, before it moves to the gear stick.

I'm a little scared about spending a whole evening with his mum. I've met her before, but only in passing. She's not like our mum; she really loves Jonny.

'Was Sarah all right tonight?' he says as he looks through the window at the wing mirror outside the car and flicks on the indicator.

I look at the mirror in the sun visor. Nothing is behind us. 'Yes. But I think she's jealous. She sat on the bed watching me the whole time I was getting ready, but she didn't help me. I asked her to paint my nails, but she said she didn't feel like it.'

'Maybe she's still feeling ill.' He presses the pedals, moving the gear stick, and the car rolls off as smoothly as a sledge on ice.

'Maybe.'

'Or maybe she's changing her mind about coming with us. She knows she would be welcome, doesn't she?'

'Yes, I told her.' I have, but I don't think it would be a good idea to have her sleeping on the floor in the room with us. I just don't want to leave her with Mum either.

'Did you tell your mum today?'

'Yes.' *No.* I have to keep him away from the house when Mum is there, until Sunday, in case he says anything to her. We're leaving on Sunday. It's not a long time to keep a secret. 'It's cold. Can you put the heater on?' I ask.

'It doesn't work. Sorry. There's always some disadvantage to a cheap car. How did your mum take it? Is she okay about you moving out?'

'She can't make me stay here. I don't care what she thinks.' It's so easy to lie to Jonny because lies make him happy and I just want him to be happy, and to stay with me. He believes me because he is nice. He doesn't lie.

His hand lifts off the gear stick and touches my knee again, before lifting to the steering wheel.

I look over and watch him drive. He's looking at the road. My boyfriend. We will have our own place in London on Sunday.

'Is your mum meeting us at the restaurant?'

'No. She wasn't ready when I left home. We're going home to pick her up.'

'Oh.'

'She got a bit upset earlier. It's a big deal for her, me moving away. I told her I'm not moving to Mars; I'll come back and see her.'

I haven't thought about coming back. I don't want to come back. I can't. Sarah says the police will look for us. I don't think they will find us in London, but they will find us if he comes back.

I chew my lip then remember I'm wearing lipstick and look

243

in the mirror. I've messed my lipstick up; it's on my teeth now. I press my lips together then part them and rub the vivid red lipstick off my teeth with a fingertip.

'Are you nervous?' he asks.

'A little bit.'

'It will be difficult leaving Sarah.'

I nod and bite a pinch of skin on the inside of my mouth to stop the tears from coming. It will be. But I will leave Sarah if it means I can have him.

His hand touches my knee again as he pulls up at the crossroads at the end of the road. My hand lies over his and I hold it until he has to use the gearstick to pull away.

When we reach his house, he looks at me as the car stops and he pulls the handbrake on. 'Do you mind sitting in the back so Mum can sit in the front seat?'

'Okay.'

The car only has two doors so I have to open the door, get out, and then Jonny shows me how to move a lever so the front seat will lean forward. It's hard to climb over the seat into the back in Mum's tight black dress and heels. As I climb, the dress slides right up and shows off my washed-out-grey knickers. After I sit down I pull the hem back down, while Jonny flips the seat back into place.

He leaves me in the car and walks up the path to meet his mum at the front door.

'Hello, Susan,' she says to me as he holds the car door open for her to get in.

'Hello, Mrs Moorell.'

'You look lovely dear.'

'Thank you.'

She is nice like Jonny.

'I suppose you're equally excited and nervous about London, like Jonny?' she says as she sits down. Jonny closes the door.

'Yes. But mostly I'm excited.'

Chapter 38

2019

The doorbell rings. Jonny and I are sitting on one side of the dining table and Lucy and Michael on the other. We've all just picked up spoons to tuck into the key lime pie Jonny has brought home from the café for our pudding.

I'm nervous of the doorbell ringing when no one is expected. I don't like unexpected callers.

'Who's that?' Lucy's voice doesn't really ask a question, but moans in a tone that says, *go away whoever you are*, echoing my sentiments.

The doorbell rings again.

Jonny's spoon chimes on the edge of the pudding bowl as he drops it and gets up, sliding the chair back on the wooden floor.

As he walks across the room, Lucy and Michael take their first mouthfuls of the dessert; my attention is still on the door.

The doorbell rings again before Jonny reaches the door.

He wipes his mouth on the back of his hand in the moment before he opens it.

'Mr Moorell,' a woman says.

'Hello. Come in,' Jonny says to the man and woman standing on the outside doormat.

Detective Inspector Jenny Watts and her colleague Detective Inspector Matt Witherstone step into the house.

Jonny closes the door behind them, shutting out the cold night. 'Sorry to interrupt your meal.' She glances our way. 'We'd like to speak to you, if we may?'

'About the accident?' Jonny asks as he ushers them further into the room with a raised hand.

'Yes,' DI Witherstone answers.

'We've just finished dinner. It's no trouble,' Jonny glances at all of us at the table, then looks back at the police. 'Take your coats off. Do you want a cup of tea? And there's a slice of key lime pie if you want it?'

'Tea would be nice,' DI Witherstone says.

'I'll make it.' I get up as Jonny takes DI Watts' old-fashioned trench coat. I think she wears it to make her look more like a police officer. She looks very young and too pretty to be an inspector. 'Sugar? Milk?' Why have they come? 'Is there some news?' I ask as I walk to the kitchen. 'If you've come thinking Lucy might fill in some details, she doesn't remember anything,' I add, before they have time to reply.

'Hello, Miss Moorell.' DI Watts looks beyond me, ignoring everything I've said, and smiles at Lucy. 'It's good to see you recovered.'

'Thank you,' Lucy leaves her spoon in her bowl and gets

up from the table. 'Have you come to talk to me? Shall we sit on the sofa? What do you want to ask?'

As Jonny hangs up DI Witherstone's coat, Matt pulls a small black notebook from the inside pocket of his dark grey suit jacket and a short pencil from a rubber band around the pad. When he flips the small book open, the inspector's gaze catches mine as I walk to the kitchen.

It feels like a threat.

When I pick the kettle up, my hands shake and it takes me a moment to get the lid off so I can fill the kettle with water.

No one speaks until the kettle is on its stand and I've pressed the switch down to start it heating.

Lucy and Jonny sit down on the sofa with Michael between them. The police detectives sit in the chairs that are at an angle either end of the sofa. DI Watts perches on the edge of the seat, looking at Jonny, Michael, and Lucy, who have positioned themselves in a row to be shot at like metal ducks on a fairground stand.

I lift mugs out of the cupboard. 'Does anyone else want tea?'

'Please,' Jonny and DI Watts answer.

'Two sugars and milk for me, please, Mrs Moorell,' DI Witherstone says. 'Jenny likes hers black and straight up.'

I drop tea bags into the mugs.

'I bet it's good to be home again,' DI Watts says to Lucy with a wide smile.

'It's good to have her home,' Michael wraps an arm around her shoulders and pulls her against him.

'Is the other driver to blame after all?' Jonny asks.

'No. We've had the forensic results back from the car and we want to talk you through the findings but we'll wait until Mrs Moorell joins us.'

Chapter 39

2018

I push the toaster-handle down to start the bread cooking. Jonny is sitting at the breakfast bar with an empty bowl in front of him typing something into his phone. A text. He doesn't have Facebook, Twitter or Instagram. I've watched him progress the conversation for the last twenty minutes while I made and drank my tea, and he's not mentioned who he's messaging or what he's messaging about. It feels strange. Secretive.

But we've been talking less and less over the last few months. We don't talk much, and we don't have sex at all, but he hasn't even seemed to notice. The last four times I've been the one to instigate it and he just went along with it. I won't embarrass myself again by being the first to break. He should want to have sex with me after a month of starvation.

I walk over to him, lean down, kiss the back of his neck and run a hand appreciatively from his shoulder down to his chest, my palm sliding over his T-shirt, unable to help myself from prodding.

He unfurls from his position hunched over his phone.
I see the words:

I really need to talk to you. You can't ignore this.

His thumb taps the phone a couple of times until the screen
is black, then he puts it down flat on the breakfast bar in a
very precise movement that looks like a rejection of something
in his typed conversation. He slides off the barstool. 'I'm going
up to clean my teeth then I'll head off.'

A clunk from the toaster announces my toast is done, and
the crisped browned bread pops up, filing the room with a
delicious smell that denies the bitter undertones in the atmosphere between Jonny and me. 'If you give me ten minutes,' I
say, as my hand slides off his shoulder. 'I'll come with you.'

'No.' The rejection is firm and absolute. 'There's no need
for you to hurry; eat your toast.' He tries to sugar the rejection a little, but he doesn't give me time to disagree. He flees
the kitchen quickly.

He knows I have lingering anger over his late-night adven-
turing so maybe he thinks I want to argue and I am just
disguising it. Or maybe he is fleeing from my touch.

Coward, I want to call after him.

Instead, I pick up his phone and press the button to open
it up again. A picture he took years ago of Lucy on her prom
night appears on the screen with the clock counting down
the time I have left before he comes back. I know his passcode.

My thumb types 196172 and the phone's screen flares into
life.

The Twins

I open his text history.

The last text stream showing is Susan's. I open it up looking for the words, *I really need to talk to you. You can't ignore this.*

His last sent text, says,

Yes, that's okay.

What's okay?

The text below talks about the date she has for her driving test. She's asking if he will drive with her to the test centre but her text and his reply were sent yesterday, not this morning.

There's no recent text in his phone about not ignoring something.

Did he delete a conversation when he was tapping at the screen? If he did then why? If he felt he had to delete the conversation then it must be something he wanted to keep secret. Something he shouldn't have been saying then. Or shouldn't have been doing.

What is he doing?

Jonny doesn't stay out late or keep secrets; he's always been reliable. He's a good man, a good husband. People are jealous of our marriage. But since Susan's return into our lives, Jonny is different and he's doing all sorts of things he never used to do.

I scan down more of their texts. Mostly they're about her driving. But occasionally there's a random conversation about something she's seen or done and told him about. Via text? She sees him every day at the café; they spend a few hours together while she's driving every week and then she comes here.

I put his phone down.

I don't care what he says. I'm going to travel into work with him today, and every day, from now on, and I will sit in the back while she's having her lessons when the café is closed. If they have nothing to hide they won't care.

I leave the toast to grow cold in the toaster.

'I'll come with you,' I say as I walk into the bathroom to use the mirror in the same moment he turns to walk out. 'I just need to do my make-up. I can be with you in a minute.'

He doesn't answer.

I know, without knowing, that he doesn't want me to go with him. But he doesn't say it.

When I walk outside and lock the front door behind me, ten minutes after him, he's sitting in his Range Rover. The engine is running and the fumes from the exhaust are condensing into a billowing fog that spreads out in the cold air.

The handle of the passenger door is cold. I pull it, so the door opens. His hands are on the wheel and the gear stick, and his expression is stiff not welcoming. A short sigh escapes as I climb into the seat. 'Thank you for waiting.' *I know you didn't want to. But I don't know why.*

What has happened to my Jonny? I'm starting to feel as if I don't know him anymore. But what if I never really knew him, and Susan has brought back the real Jonny?

Chapter 40

1985

Uncle Charlie's wallet is left where it always is, by his bottle of whisky in the kitchen. His wages are paid in cash so there's always money in his wallet. When I open it, I see a stack of notes packed in there but I just take one crisp twenty-pound note. He won't notice a twenty is missing. He never notices.

A noise pulls my attention to the front door but it's nothing, just a car door slamming. I had thought it might be Susan coming home. She didn't come home last night and must have stayed with Jonny. I saw them in my head, an imagined view, lying on his bed listening to music. Or lying under the sheets and doing things to each other.

I shove the twenty-pound note into the front pocket of my jeans.

I'm ready to go.

My whole body is trembly as I leave the house and shut the door. My legs feel as wobbly as Bambi at the start of the film. I push that thought out of my head. I don't want to think about a newly born Bambi. My child is never going to be born. It makes me think about my baby looking like a baby with hands and feet and eyes that would look at me. I don't want to see it like that. It's just a lizard now.

Every time I see that horrible lizard thing in my head, nausea grabs at the back of my throat.

I swallow about twenty times to make the nausea go away as I walk along the road.

No one knows where I'm going. I haven't told anyone. If the bus crashes, or I'm kidnapped, or get lost in Swindon, they will wonder why I was there.

It is cold this morning. My breath mists in the air as I walk quickly. It is a little foggy too, and the moisture in the fog is clinging onto the cobwebs making the world look eerie.

I walk into the town centre to catch the bus. Other passengers slowly gather around me. Old people who look like they're going to Swindon to do some shopping, and a couple of other young people who look like they are going to work. They won't be able to guess that I'm going to find out how to get a baby out of me.

I wish I was one of the other young people standing here. I wish I had a job and I was going to work.

Another young woman walks up and starts talking to one of the others. They laugh within a minute of starting their conversation.

I wish I had friends. Proper friends, like they seem to be. I had thought Jonny, Wayne … and Jay … were my friends, but even Jonny and Wayne aren't friends like that. They don't sound that pleased to see me, or excited about talking to me.

Maybe when Susan goes to London, I will go to school. I might make friends at school. Friends like these two. Then I can get a Saturday job and we can travel to work together on the bus. I don't want to be feral anymore. I want to be like Jonny. I want to have things, to feel safe, to be able to look after myself with money and do what I want to do.

The red bus draws up a minute before it's due to leave and the door folds open to let me in. The driver complains about changing my twenty-pound note but he does and I walk along the bus and sit by the window three seats from the back.

The bus's route winds its way through pretty little villages and countryside. The girls, the friends, keep talking. One old woman reads a book while the man beside her reads a paper. A young man at the front of the bus is listening to music through earphones that are attached to a Walkman.

I look out through the window, watching the houses, the people, and the countryside we pass. It makes me think about Buscot. Buscot is a nice place. Maybe when I grow up I will move somewhere like that. Where people always smile and are happy. Where no one shouts, and no one pretends to be your friend and rapes you. Where friends are proper friends like the two girls on the other side of the bus.

Swindon is a big town. The bus takes ages to get to the middle, and the bus station is huge, and busy and noisy. I follow the other people who have got off the bus and let them lead me out of the bus station.

The woman I'd spoken to on the phone told me where to go and how to get there but when I walk out of the tunnel from the bus station into a paved street full of people and shops the space is overwhelming. There are four different entrances and exits. I can't remember which one to take.

There's a map on a stand a few paces away. I walk over and look at that. I remember the name of the street I'm looking for.

It takes more than half an hour to find the right street, the building, and the entrance. My heart pumps with the rhythm of a snare-drum beat as I push the door open three minutes late for my appointment.

'I'm sorry,' I say to a woman who is sitting behind a desk with a sign saying *reception* above her head. 'I'm late.' My words are breathless from rushing, and from fear.

'And what's your name, dear?' She looks into my eyes as the door closes behind me on a delayed mechanism. She's looking at just my eyes, as if she's trying to avoid looking at my clothes or my age, as if she's trying not to judge me.

I feel safer in here. 'Sarah Tagney.'

'Hello, Sarah—'

'Am I too late?'

'No. The doctor you are seeing is Penny Shaw. She will be with you in a moment. But before you go in I need you to fill in this form. Just to give us your information. We need your date of birth, your doctor's details and your next of kin.' She slides a piece of paper towards me and holds out a black biro.

'But the woman said on the phone you don't tell my doctor. I don't want my mum to know.'

'Don't worry. This is just for emergencies. We aren't going to tell anyone that you've come in to talk to us. You don't need to worry, love. I promise.'

I take the pen from her hand and start writing my name

in the first box on the form. When I sit down to fill the rest of the form in and wait for the doctor to call me, I have a desire to reach for Susan's hand. I need her today. But she is in bed with Jonny. She is like Mum.

I don't think I am like Mum. I want to be more than I am. Like Jonny … Susan isn't like Jonny.

'Sarah Tagney.' The woman who has called my name is standing in an open doorway. She doesn't look very old.

I stand.

'I'll take your form back,' the receptionist says, standing up and reaching out a hand to take it.

'This way, just through here,' the other woman says. 'No need to look worried. We'll look after you.' She directs me with a hand and holds the door for me so I can walk through into an office.

'May I call you Sarah?' she asks as she shuts the door.

'Ye-es.' The reply stutters from my dry lips.

'Sit down.'

I sit in a chair with orange upholstery.

'Would you like a cup of water?'

I nod.

She turns to a water dispenser in the corner, fills a little cardboard cone for me and brings it over. The water in the cardboard cone is really cold. It's refreshing. I drink it all as the doctor sits down.

'Now then, can you tell me why you're here?'

I tell her everything, through tears and sobs, and she presses a box of tissues into my hand so I can dab the dampness off my cheeks.

259

'You do know, Sarah, that what this young man did to you is rape? It is illegal. If you would like to, you can speak to the police. We have contacts with people who can speak to the police with you so you won't feel alone.'

'No.' My hand and the tissue drop to my lap. 'I don't want to tell the police. I just want to get rid of the baby.' And forget.

'And that's fine. That's exactly why you're here and why I'm here to help. But I need to talk you through everything to make sure you think things over properly so you won't regret your decision.'

'I won't regret it.'

She breathes out quickly. 'Let me tell you about the procedure then, so you'll know what you'll be letting yourself in for. If you can attend next week you will still be in the time-frame to take medication so there'll be no need for surgery. You will be given tablets to take and within two to five hours you will begin to lose the child. Usually within one or two days the abortion will be complete. There will be considerable bleeding and discomfort as you pass the pregnancy tissue, which will include blood clots. Once the pregnancy has passed, the bleeding will become less but it may continue for another day or two. Do you understand?'

I nod.

'Are you able to come in next Saturday? I know you don't want to tell your mother or the father, but were you told on the phone that you must be accompanied by someone who is eighteen who can be responsible for seeing that you get home safely? Someone who can stay with you for twenty-four hours after that too?'

I hadn't been told.

'If it's a woman they can come into the treatment room with you, but men are asked to wait outside in the waiting room.' She points towards the door into the reception area.

I only know one person who is eighteen who will help me, even if it is out of pity. I also know he won't say anything to anyone.

'Are you able to bring someone with you next week?'

'Yes.'

'Then would you like me to book you in?'

'Yes.' My fingers tighten around the tissue I'm holding. I want it done sooner.

'Okay then, Sarah, I need you to read through this and sign to give your consent.' She pushes a form across her desk and marks a cross by the box where she wants me to sign.

The form tells me all about the risks. It tells me that the medication might cause complications, that in the worst case I may bleed to death. I sign it. I don't care.

She gives me a small stack of leaflets to take away. Leaflets about what will happen. Leaflets for support to talk to counsellors. Leaflets on the risk of the medication and what symptoms I should be aware of in case I have a bad reaction.

When I return to the town centre I throw the leaflets in the bin before I reach the bus station. I don't want anyone else to see them. The only person I will tell is Jonny, and only because I have to persuade him to bring me back.

It isn't until I walk through the door of our bedroom at home that I remember Jonny isn't going to be here next Saturday. He and Susan will be in London.

Susan's shoving her knickers into a small holdall that she must have borrowed from Jonny. The holdall is already packed full of most of the clothes that she owns.

She stops and looks at me as I walk further into the room. 'Where have you been?'

'Into town ...' The next words hover like a butterfly resting on my tongue. I want to say—

'Last night was amazing.' She doesn't wait for me to find the words I am struggling to speak. She launches into her own story. 'Jonny's mum paid for me to eat prawn cocktail, steak and chips and a chocolate sundae for pudding. She was the one who said it would be okay for me to stay over if I wanted to.'

I went to speak to someone about an abortion. 'Are you staying at Jonny's tonight?'

'No, he's packing too. I said I'll spend the evening with you. He's going to pick me up at ten tomorrow.'

I sit down on the bed, watching her turn to pull some socks out of the drawer. I'm confused. My mind is a distance away from all of this. We used to be so close. Wolf cubs hiding from the world. It's so strange to be in the same room but feel completely separate from her. We were so close that we were like conjoined twins – physically as well as mentally attached. But Jonny has surgically separated us. She doesn't need me anymore. She won't be anywhere near me ever again after tomorrow if I don't go with her. She can't come home.

We might look identical, but we aren't the same. I know it now. We want different things. I want a normal life. I want money. I want a house that feels like a home. That feels safe. She ... she just wants Jonny. She's like Mum. I'm not.

Chapter 41

2018

My fingers tackle the tangled green wire of Christmas fairy lights with an angry tug that expresses my impatience, not with the lights but with my life. It is the 1st of December and Susan is still here. Six months was the bargain, and at the end of six months she said I could tell her to go away if I wanted to. The problem is that it's Jonny who's not upholding the bargain, not her. Jonny likes her. Lucy likes her. Everyone working in the café likes her. Our customers like her. No one but me wants her to go, and so Jonny has banned me from telling her to get lost.

I thread the plug through a loop of wire that releases the last knot in the fairy-lights, step on the chair, reach over, and begin dressing the tree. Jonny and I bought the tree this morning and put it up in the corner of the café half an hour ago. It smells deliciously of Christmas. I know the fresh tree-smell never lasts, but when I'm dressing it, it feels so luxurious to have a woodland smell inside the cafe. I've always been a little over the top with Christmas, because we didn't celebrate

Christmas as children. Every year I try to make up for all the Christmases I missed out on.

The café is closed and the room is quiet. It's dark outside, it's cloudy and pitch black down here by the lake where there are no street lights. Stan and Jonny are in the kitchen; they are doing some baking to fill the food cabinets with mince pies, gingerbread, *stollen* and fruit cakes. That's what people want with their tea and coffee this time of year. The winter spices and orange-peel smells drift from the kitchen to mingle with the aroma of evergreen leaves.

Susan is not here. That's why I said to Jonny I'd stay back and decorate while he and Stan bake, because I don't want her here while I decorate the tree

We have not discussed what will happen to her at Christmas but I'm waiting for Jonny to make the horrendous choice of inviting her to our house for Christmas dinner. Lucy isn't even going to be with us. For the first year she's going to Michael's, and Jonny's mum has chosen to stay with a friend.

I think my patience will finally crack right down the middle if Susan invades our Christmas day.

When the lights are wrapped around the branches, I take my phone out from the back pocket of my denim skirt, open up the music app and press play on my Christmas playlist. I lean down, plug the lights into the electric socket and turn them on. They'll sparkle and help me decide where to place the baubles.

This feels like a moment of escape from her.

It's rare that I get moments to just be me these days. But strangely, I have always felt I was living the best ever

Christmases for both of us. It doesn't mean I want her here, though.

I sift through the box of tissue-paper-wrapped glass baubles and take out all the baubles decorated with gold. They dangle from ribbons that hang over my fingers. I pick them off one at a time and hang them on the tree just so. Everything in its perfect place and in perfect order. Exactly where I want it to be. Everything feels under control for a couple of hours while the café fills with yummy baking smells.

'Do you fancy eating a little bit of the profits? I have a mince pie for you,' Jonny says in the same moment I step down from the chair after placing the angel on the top. I step back and look at my work, pleased with the overall effect, expecting Jonny to walk up behind me, wrap an arm about my middle, pull me back against him, and press a kiss on my neck or my hair.

'Here.' He always brings me a mince pie when he's made them, but this time it's different.

I turn around to accept the small plate he's holding. It's the most unemotional gesture imaginable. 'Thank you.'

There are two mince pies on the plate. When I take the plate, he takes one of the mince pies. We both look at the sparkling tree as we eat, looking at the lights glittering back in the reflection in the windows. My phone plays 'Last Christmas'.

This year ... I have no idea what Christmas day will bring, but I don't bring up the subject of Susan. I don't want to give him a reason to say, *let's invite her*.

Chapter 42

2019

I carry the full mugs of tea that I've made for DI Watts and DI Witherstone into the living room. When Jonny sees me coming he rushes up from his seat on the sofa, twisting around the arm to go and fetch the other mugs.

I put their mugs down on the coffee table and take the seat Jonny left vacant. There's enough space on the four-seater sofa for us all to squeeze in and I want to be beside Lucy.

Michael's arm is still around her but I hold her hand, lifting it out of her lap and onto mine. I slide along a couple of inches, squeezing up against Lucy so Jonny can sit.

'What is it, then?' Jonny says to the detectives. 'What's new?'

DI Witherstone looks down at his black book as if that's going to tell him what he should say.

DI Watts opens her mouth to speak. 'While much of the car is significantly damaged, the engine is fairly intact ... but there's something strange.'

DI Witherstone's head lifts and his gaze runs across us one

way, then comes back the other. When his gaze reaches me for the second time, I smile. He is expecting some sort of reaction to the next words.

'There is an incision in the brake fluid reservoir.' They're both staring at us, looking for the tiniest change in our expressions.

'Is that really strange, though?' Michael's voice cuts through a silence that seems minutes long when it was probably a tenth of a second. 'If the car was badly damaged couldn't it have happened when it rolled down the hill? Maybe it was punctured by a branch.'

'Possibly,' DI Watts answers, looking along the row of us again. Then her gaze narrows on Lucy. 'Do you remember if there was a fault with the brakes?'

'No,' Lucy answers immediately. 'I told you. I don't remember anything at all. I don't even remember getting up that morning.'

The woman's eyes turn to Jonny – because of course it would be the man who would know about the brakes. 'But there was this argument just before the accident ...'

Is she asking him if he did something to the car? What does she expect him to say?

'I'm sorry,' he leans back further, his face shifting into an ugly expression that shows every one of the lines that are becoming wrinkles. He looks like a stuffed prune. 'Are you asking me if I decided to kill my daughter and sister-in-law in the middle of a heated argument?' His eyebrows quirk up. 'By ringing a mechanic and getting him to pop over and tamper with the car? That's a bit far-fetched isn't it? I shouted.

I was angry. But I had no desire to kill anyone. I've been through hell over this.'

He leans forward, his elbow knocking against mine as his hands move to his knees. He's not shocked anymore. He's angry. 'I can't believe you're asking this.'

'It's crazy,' Lucy adds, sliding forward on the sofa too, slipping free from Michael's hold. 'No one would have done it deliberately.'

DI Watts lifts a hand to calm things as DI Witherstone scribbles in his little book. I want to ask him what he has seen in their denials as something worth writing down.

'We're just doing our job, Mr Moorell. The car came off the road. There are no skid marks, which implies Susan Tagney did not have a chance to – or was unable to – use the brakes. A failure of the braking system may have caused the accident.'

'Then ask the mechanic who serviced and MOT'd the car if he checked the brakes. Don't come here accusing me of nearly killing my daughter and achieving it with my sister-in-law. That's absurd!'

DI Witherstone stops writing, leans forward, picks up the mug I put on the coffee table for him and takes a sip of tea. He knows he's about to be asked to leave, and he was the one who had asked for the tea; he must be thirsty. His brown eyes look at me as he puts the mug down.

I nod at him and slide forward on the sofa too. 'I think you should go. This is Lucy's first night home. She doesn't remember anything, and we certainly had nothing to do with the accident. We can't help you make sense of this.' My voice is calm. I feel calm. I have Jonny and Lucy with me.

Jonny shakes his head and his eyelids droop a little, calling the whole thing absurd in his expression.

'Okay, we'll head off.' DI Watts gets up as she speaks. She hasn't even had one sip of her tea. 'But, Lucy'—she looks at her—'if you remember anything, then please call us.'

'I will. But no one can have wanted to kill us. It must have been due to the trees, or something else happened.'

DI Watts takes a wallet out from her trouser pocket. DI Witherstone reaches out for his mug and takes a couple of large gulps of the hot tea as DI Watts withdraws a business card and leans down to pass it to Lucy.

As DI Watts straightens up, DI Witherstone leaves the mug on the table and stands, folding his notebook with a snap that says the interview is over.

Jonny stands, his movement stiff with restrained anger. Michael also stands, in a way that implies he's playing Lucy's guard dog. An over-protective alpha male club forming.

'We didn't mean to cause any distress,' DI Watts says as she walks across the room with DI Witherstone, Jonny and Michael rounding on them from either end of the sofa, herding them out like sheepdogs.

'As you came here to ask those stupid questions, I think you did,' Michael says.

DI Witherstone throws Michael a warning look with slanted eyebrows and deep furrows in his forehead.

Jonny takes their coats off the hooks and hands them over roughly. Michael opens the door, making it clear they are not welcome to stay long enough to put their coats on.

'That was bizarre,' Michael says when he shuts the door on them.

'It has to be an accident,' Lucy says. 'When was Susan's car last serviced, Dad? Do you know?'

He walks back into the room, rubbing his forehead with his fingertips as if he has a headache. 'I don't know. When she bought it, I suppose. But she told me once she knew her way around an engine.'

'You should text them and tell them the name of the guy who did the MOT.' Michael sits down beside Lucy and pulls her close.

'It will be on the government's data systems,' Jonny answers. 'The mechanics have to register it.'

Lucy's eyes are on Jonny as he walks around the sofa.

'Please tell me you don't believe I could do something like that, Luce?' he says.

'What? No! Why would I?'

'It's just the way you were looking at me.' He leans down and picks up the cigarette packet and the lighter he left on the coffee table earlier. He hasn't smoked in the hours since we brought her home.

'I was thinking about what they said. I can't imagine it being deliberate. Do you think someone really tried to kill her?' She looks at me.

I shake my head. 'No. As your dad said, it's absurd.'

Chapter 43

1985

My feet are cold when I creep across the frayed carpet to get out of our room. Susan's quiet breathing sets the pace of my steps. The bedroom door creaks as I hold the handle down and pull it open. I glance back. Susan's outline under the covers doesn't move, and there's no noise from Mum's room.

I pull the door open wide enough for me to walk out – quickly, so the creak will be short. Then I slip through the gap and pull the door closed with a second short creak.

My steps are cautious as I walk along the landing, avoiding the places that make a noise. I learned them all when I used to speak to Jonny on the phone. The landing is darker than anywhere else because there's no window. The only light comes from the bathroom window because that door is open. But I know my way by running my fingertips along the wall until the wall comes to an end, and then I know I've reached the top of the staircase.

My hand fumbles around, looking for the bannister, and when I find it my toes search for the edge of the top step, then

I slide my heel forward, down over the edge and onto the top step. The next three steps I need to navigate by feel alone, but then the streetlight breaking through the living room curtains begins to illuminate the stairs and I can see things.

The navigation of the last few steps is quick, easy.

I pick up the phone but I don't take it to the stairs. I sit on the far end of the sofa, near the front door. As far away from Susan as I can be.

Jonny's number is written into my mind. Even though I was never the one who rang I've read the note he wrote it in a hundred times.

The buttons on the phone descend with a tune of beeping sounds. Then there's a click, and then it rings. It rings and then it echoes. It rings and echoes.

A noise descends from upstairs, through the ceiling, Mum or Uncle Charlie moving in her bed.

'Hello?' Jonny answers.

'Hello.' Now I hear his voice I don't know how to say what I need to tell him. But the words have been circling in my head for hours.

'Susan ...' I hear him moving; it's in the catch in his breath. 'What is it?' I imagine that he has sat up on his bed.

'It's not Susan.'

'Sarah?' His voice lifts to a higher tone. 'Why are you ringing? Are you okay?'

'No.'

He doesn't ask for an explanation and my words have dried up and swelled on my tongue as if I'd eaten a dozen dry crackers.

'Tell me,' he says in a quieter voice. A sensitive voice. The sort of voice he had used just after Jay had—

'I'm pregnant.'

'What?' He has heard. He just can't believe it.

I don't repeat it. 'I'm having an abortion.'

'How?'

'They giv—'

'I don't mean that, Sarah. I know how. I mean where?'

'There's a place in Swindon. It's booked for next Saturday, but you have to come with me.'

'I'll be in London.'

'I know but I need to go with someone who's eighteen and I don't have anyone else to ask.'

I hear the air slide out of his lungs. 'Okay. I'll come. But why are you only telling me now? How long have you and Susan known?'

'Susan doesn't know. I don't want her to know.'

'Why not?' There is less pity in his voice now.

'Because every time I try to build up the courage to talk about it, all she talks about is you and running away.'

'Then what about your mum? You should tell someone else.'

A quiet strange laugh pushes its way out of my mouth. 'No. She'd be angry and I'd end up in care.'

'You don't have to worry about social services anymore. You're sixteen now, you—'

'We're not sixteen. We're thirteen.' I shove the words at him through the phone receiver. 'I'm thirteen and I'm pregnant.'

'What the fuck?' The answer is a quick punch back that

isn't quiet. 'No. You're sixteen. Susan said so. It was your birthday at the beginning of the summer.'

'It was our thirteenth birthday at the beginning of the summer. She lied.'

'But Jay ... Shit. You're serious, aren't you? You're thirteen.'

'Yes. You will help me, won't you, Jonny?'

There's a pause as he breathes in a deep breath. 'Yes.' His breath has changed the tempo of his voice. 'But what do these people say about you being thirteen?'

'They'll keep it a secret as long as an adult comes with me and will take me home and look after me.'

There's another long slide of breath. 'You should have spoken to the police about Jay.'

'No. I was drinking.'

'They wouldn't care about that, Sarah. You could go to the police now. You're pregnant. That's your evidence.'

'No. I just want the baby out. I want to forget about it. That's all.'

'You know what this means.' His words hold a different tone again, a sudden note of realisation. 'I could go to prison too. It's illegal, and Susan and I ...'

'I told her that she can't run away with you.'

'We aren't running away. We're just moving to ...' He's thinking as he speaks. I hear it in the words. 'I'm just moving to London and I asked her to come. I thought she was sixteen. It would be kidnap, though, wouldn't it? Oh shit. The police would look for her.'

'I told her that. She said you could lose yourselves in London.'

'I don't want to be lost. I want to be successful. Sarah, why didn't you tell me this before? Why did you go along with this lie?'

'I never said I was sixteen. I didn't know you thought that until the other night when Wayne told someone in the pub I was sixteen.'

'I'm sorry,' he says suddenly.

'For what?' I bite down on my tongue.

'For having anything to do with you two. If I'd realised how old Susan was I wouldn't have kept seeing you. Then what happened with Jay ... I'm sorry. What he did was wrong but I don't think he knew you were thirteen.'

'Don't tell him I'm pregnant.'

'I won't. I don't speak to him anyway.'

'But you'll help me.'

'Yes.' His voice has lost its energy. 'I'll come back home next weekend. What time?'

'I need to be in Swindon by nine o'clock.'

'I'll drive back Friday night and pick you up at eight o'clock in the morning.'

'Thank you, Jonny.' I put the receiver down on the stand and put the phone back. I'm shaky and queasy inside. He will do what he said, but Susan can't run away with him anymore.

I walk through the dark at the top of the stairs, imagining Jonny with the light on in his room, sitting up on his bed, his plans for tomorrow exploding in his head.

Susan rolls over when I lift the duvet to slide back into bed.

'Where were you?' she asks, her voice low and quiet, full of the sound of sleep.

'I just went to the toilet.' I should tell her. I should warn her that Jonny knows she lied. I can't. I don't want a fight now. I just want to sleep and make this all go away.

Her breaths stroke across my cheek as she falls asleep.

I can't sleep. I know what will happen tomorrow.

Sarah is still asleep when I wake. I have to climb over her to get out of bed. She doesn't wake.

I left the clothes I'm wearing today on top of the bag Jonny leant me. They're the best clothes I own: my jeans, a long-sleeved T-shirt, and a loose black jumper. My knickers are the best that I own too; they have pink lace along the top and the colour hasn't faded or greyed in the wash.

I strip off the T-shirt and knickers I wore to bed and put them into the holdall to wash when we're in London. The room is cold; it makes all the tiny hairs on my skin lift up.

I don't want to sit on the bed and wake Sarah so I continue with the acrobatics to get my jeans on then pull on the rest of my clothes in a hurry.

A car engine starts up outside. I push the curtain back and look through the net. It jerks along the string it's hanging from so I can watch the street. It's not Jonny's car.

I turn to the chest of drawers and use Mum's eyeliner, mascara, and lipstick that I took from her make-up bag the other day. After I've used them I throw them into the holdall.

Balancing on one foot at a time again, I pull on one sock then the other, and lastly I push my feet into my trainers, crushing down the backs and then unhooking them from under my heel with a fingertip. Sarah has not woken.

The Twins

My hands hang at my sides; my palms are sweaty, even though it's cold.

I can't take my eyes off Sarah.

Now the day I'm leaving is here, I wish she would come. It's going to be hard not having her with me. I've told her we'll write. That I'll find an address where she can write to me safely. I said I would ring her sometimes too. But just for a few minutes in case the police try to track my calls like they do on the TV.

We have always been a two. We have always been we. I don't think I can ever just be me, even when we're miles apart. I will always know that the other half of me is here.

A movement in the street outside pulls my attention and gaze to the street, to Jonny's car drawing to a halt. His exhaust is spewing out misty fumes too. I can see all his things piled up in the back of the car. He has a lot more than me.

The driver's door opens.

He'd said he would wait in the car so that he doesn't wake Mum.

I turn to Sarah. This is the last minute we have together.

'Sarah.' My fingers curve around her shoulder and I shake. 'I want to say goodbye.'

Her eyes open.

I lean down and press my lips against her cheek in a quick kiss. 'I'm going.'

'Now?' Her eyes blink. They look like glass because she has just woken, all shiny and dense, like false eyes in a jar.

'Yes. Goodbye.'

Her cheek rubs on the pillow as she nods. 'Goodbye.'

She is too sleepy. She doesn't realise that this is the end. But Jonny must be standing outside the door. I can't wait. We need to get on the road and get as far away as we can before Mum realises I've gone for good.

I kiss Sarah's cheek again. Her hair smells like my hair. 'I love you,' I say then turn to pick up the holdall.

The holdall is heavy. It's small but I've packed loads into it. I sling it over my shoulder.

Sarah's eyes are still open. She's tired but she's watching me. I wave as I walk out of the door.

My footfalls are heavy as I rush along the landing and run downstairs. Mum and Uncle Charlie won't wake at this time of the morning.

The door lock is cold when I turn it and open the door. I pull my coat off the hook and my gaze crashes into Jonny's. He's right outside the door, on the step. He doesn't move out of the way. He's like a wall.

'Put the bag down.' His voice is sharp and I don't understand the expression on his face. His lips are stiff, unsmiling, and his eyes are hard.

'What's wrong?'

'Leave the bag indoors and come out and talk to me.'

'Talk?' I don't understand. What does he want to talk about before we get in the car? There will be time to talk on the way to London.

The bag slides off my shoulder, runs down my arm, and drops on the doormat.

He's frowning, and the creases in his brow lower his eyebrows, making him look like a baddy in a film. 'What's wrong?'

He moves back so I can step out. I leave the door open. I need to come back in for my bag.

A woman I've seen around here a few times before walks along the other side of the street. The police will use her as a witness when they realise we've gone. But so far she hasn't looked at us.

Jonny turns his back on me. He hasn't taken my hand. He walks in front of me towards the car.

'What is it?'

He still doesn't answer me.

He walks as far as the car then stops and turns and his arms cross over his chest as he leans back against the passenger door of the car. He has set up a wall again to stop me from getting into the car. Why is he angry?

A warm sensation runs from my tingling palms all the way up my body into my cheeks. I must be blushing.

'You lied to me,' he says.

'When?' I've told him lots of lies. I don't know what he thinks he knows.

'When I first met you and for every day since. Sixteen, you said. That's what you told me. Your age, Susan. You're thirteen.' His eyebrows lift to punctuate the statement with an exclamation.

I can't say no. He knows for certain. 'Who told you?'

'I could be put in prison for having sex with you.' His voice is low so his words won't carry but they hold his anger just as well as if he's shouting.

'We love each other—'

'I wouldn't have done that if I'd known your age. I'd have

281

walked away after you gave me a cigarette that first day and never spoken to you again.'

I swallow. My throat is tight. 'Jonny. You love me. Age doesn't mean anything.' My hands curl into fists then open and close again.

'Taking you to London would be kidnap. Until you're sixteen it means everything. You're crazy.' His arms unravel from their folded, protective position and one forefinger taps the side of his head then falls. 'You're just a child.'

'Aren't you going to take me with you?'

'No. Of course I'm not.'

The tears run onto my eyelashes and the moist mascara makes my eyelashes stick together as I blink. There will be streams of black mascara on my cheeks. 'But you love me.'

'I did.' He leans towards me spitting his words at my face. 'I don't now. Not now I know you lied. The girl I loved doesn't exist.' Some of his spit hits my lips.

When he leans back, I wipe the sleeve of my jumper over my cheeks and lips. 'I don't like you either. I lied when I said I loved you.'

He turns away from me to walk around the back end of his rusty old Ford Fiesta. It isn't even a cool car.

'The problem with you, Susan, is that all you really care about is yourself. You lied to get what you wanted; you didn't care about how that might hurt me. Or your sister.' He throws the last words across the top of the car at me.

'Sarah ...' *What does Sarah have to do with it?* 'Did Sarah tell you?'

He opens the car door. He's going to go and just leave me here.

'Did Sarah tell you?' I shout.

He doesn't answer. He gets in the car. But who else could have told him?

I slap a hand on the roof of the car. When had she told him though? How? He hadn't known yesterday.

I thump the side of my fist against the passenger window as the car starts. All her walks lately ... Where did she go? I kick the tyre as the gears grind. All her going out alone and disappearing.

'Ahhhhh!' As he drives off without me, my scream is pulled along by the motion of the car that's left me behind in this horrible life.

There is a solid pole through the middle of me. It stills me, pinning me here. I can't move or think or ... I love him. I let him do things and I had done things ... I thought we would be together forever. I thought he would marry me.

Anger simmers in my heart and my head. Bubbling. No. It's chewing at me. Gnawing like a rat. My fists curl tight as I walk back to the house. Sarah is there. I see her at the window, a human shadow looking through the net curtain.

I hate her. The emotion surges into me. 'I hate you!' I yell as I push the door out of my way and charge in at her. 'I hate you! You bitch! You told him!' I slap, hit, pull at her T-shirt and her hair, and punch as I growl and scream. *Bitch. Bitch. Bitch.* 'Why couldn't you just be happy for me?'

'What the hell is going on down there?' Uncle Charlie's voice booms through the ceiling and his feet bang on the floor as he runs.

I don't stop hitting her as she tries to defend herself slapping my hands away from her face and screaming back at me.

I grip her neck, like Uncle Harry did.

Uncle Charlie's smack sets off fireworks in my head as it hits my temple. The force of it knocks me off Sarah, off the sofa and onto the floor, like a dying fly with my arms and legs splayed, still reaching and kicking.

'What is this about?' Mum is on the stairs. 'You two never fight.'

'She took Jonny away from me!' I yell at Mum, as if Mum can bring him back. As if she can put everything back into its right place.

'This is about boys ...' Mum's voice is accusing. She says it as if Jonny is nothing special.

'It would be, wouldn't it,' Uncle Charlie says. 'Bloody kids. Fucking boys.'

'She took him,' I say again, as if they can't have heard me the first time. She's taken my life away. 'He loved me!' I say it to her.

Her lip is bleeding. She wipes it on her arm as she turns to sit on the sofa and pulls her T-shirt down over her stomach. 'It isn't my fault you lied.'

She had told him!

She is my other half. We are the same. We do everything together. She chose to stay behind and now she's made me stay with her. We aren't sisters any more. We are shattered. I don't care about her.

'Bitch,' I throw at her as I turn, get up, and pick up my bag. I'll get out of this house somehow.

Chapter 44

2018

'Thanks for picking me up, Jonny,' Susan says as she slides into the rear seat behind him, then pulls the door shut with a thump.

'It's not a problem,' he says. 'I'm happy to play chauffeur to my women.'

'You liar, Dad. You used to moan like mad when I was a teenager and wanted a lift.' Lucy's voice comes from the seat behind me.

'That was a bit different, Luce, love. That was every Saturday and Sunday and three nights in between. I don't mind doing the occasional Saturday.'

'Well, I appreciate it.' I reach out and lay a hand on his firm denim-covered thigh, and I leave my hand there as he drives, sliding it up near his groin so he can use the gear stick. He doesn't react. But I'm not touching him for his reaction; I am touching him to get Susan's. To let her know that he is mine.

Her driving test is just after Christmas, the first Friday after the New Year. He told me he's having the afternoon off to take her. I hope she passes because then they won't have an excuse to keep seeing each other alone. My sitting in the car with them had lasted one day. They'd not complained, just talked and laughed as if I wasn't there. I didn't go again. Watching the interaction and feeling so distant from it had only made me more jealous. But today, I'm in the front seat next to him.

'Which pub am I taking you all to?' Jonny asks as he turns the Range Rover out onto the main road, the indicator ticking.

'The George' Lucy calls. The night is hers. She planned it for us and then added Susan onto the invite list.

I am not looking forward to this at all. But I wasn't going to back down and hand over my mother-daughter time to Susan as if I don't care.

Drops of rain fall onto the windscreen. Jonny turns the wipers on, but the rain isn't very heavy; the wipers screech back and forth because the windscreen is too dry.

It's a ten-minute drive from Susan's block of flats into Keswick town centre. The strings of Christmas lights that were turned on in November twinkle at us, catching the glistening pavements that are damp from an earlier, heavier rainfall.

He pulls into the carpark at the back of the pub, but he doesn't park. He drives as close to the back door as he can, so even though the rain is light we won't get wet.

He slides the gearstick into neutral, pulls on the handbrake and then his hand moves to hold onto mine as he looks over his shoulder. He looks at Lucy, but he can't really see Susan because she is behind him. 'Have a good time.'

'We will,' Susan and Lucy answer him.

As they get out he leans towards me, and I lean towards him, our lips touch in a quick kiss but it feels more like an automated gesture, not a thing of meaning. 'I love you,' I say as the doors close in the back.

'I love you too,' he answers. The sincerity and warmth in his voice tells me he still means it, but a tone of voice is easy to have learned by heart and to mimic. Even a parrot can say *I love you*.

My hand pulls free from his. I open the door and get out. Lucy and Susan are running through the puddles from the earlier rain to get into the pub.

It's windy too, tonight; it sweeps around and shakes the trees at the edge of the carpark. I rush for the back door.

Jonny's Range Rover drives away.

My lifeline has gone. He won't be able to throw me any rubber rings to pull me out of this if the night becomes a figurative storm.

Lucy holds the pub door open until I join her there. I smile. I haven't complained to her about her inviting Susan. I don't want to fall out with her. That would just play into Susan's hands. I'm calling truce tonight, for Lucy's sake. A timeout.

'Shall we sit in the window seat?' Lucy suggests as we enter the bar.

Susan doesn't answer, just walks ahead, towards it. Leading the way. I catch Lucy's gaze and we share a smile that speaks the thousands of *I love yous* that we have said to each during her life. There is nothing automated in the emotions that Lucy and I share. It only makes it more obvious that something is wrong between Jonny and me, though.

'I'll buy,' I say turning to the bar. 'Can you find out what Susan wants to drink?'

'Oh, she'll have a pint of that gold something ale. She always has that first.'

The words hit me in the chest and strike all the air out of my lungs. *Always*. The word is a kick. How many times have they been out together? But then, they both live in Keswick and I've told Lucy not to talk about Susan when she's with me. I can't complain that I don't know how often they speak, or what they talk about when they do speak.

It feels as if she's slowly taking over my life, day by day creeping further in like fog obscuring everything that has previously been mine.

'What do you want to drink, Lucy?'

'Gin and tonic. Do you want any help carrying?'

'No, I'll manage.'

She and Susan take off their coats and settle themselves in the window seat, similar silhouettes against the black night beyond the window.

'Hello, love, what can I get you?' the barman asks.

'A pint of the Golden Fox, a large glass of merlot and a gin and tonic, please.'

Their voices, just as similar as their looks, begin a to and fro behind me.

I wait, balanced on one thin stiletto heel, my other foot moving behind my leg nervously.

Everything takes so long to pour when I want him to hurry.

This is ridiculous. I should not feel nervous about spending time with my daughter.

I carry Susan's pint and Lucy's gin and tonic over to the table, then return to pay and collect the glass of red wine.

'Thanks,' I say as I turn away from the bar.

They are side by side on the window seat. I can sit next to Lucy but that would leave us sitting in an awkward row, like the three monkeys. See no evil, hear no evil, speak no evil. I draw out the wooden chair opposite them. It scrapes on the old scared pub floorboards. I put down the red wine, take my coat off, hang it over the back of the chair, and sit down, with a sense that I'm facing the voice of evil, and there is no hiding from it because she is sitting beside my daughter.

'Thanks, Mum,' Lucy says as she picks up her glass and the ice rattles.

'Yes, thanks,' Susan says, with no sincerity in her voice. She drinks from her pint, leaving her top lip shining with foam. Her tongue slips out and licks it off. She catches me watching and looks into my eyes. The same eyes that I see in the mirror stare back at me. 'Lucy keeps asking me how Jonny ended up with you. I haven't told her yet. That's your story. I don't know all of it ...' Her words drop away as though she expects me to fill in the details on her dotted line.

I take a sip of wine.

'I've told her you took him away from me.'

I'm not going to be allowed one moment to have a nice easy conversation with my daughter about her life then. 'I did not take him away. He left. He moved to London. Neither of us was involved in that. How's Michael?' I say to Lucy.

'Good,' she answers. 'But I do want to know why Dad went out with Susan and then you.'

'Have you asked him?'

'Yes, but you know Dad. He just shrugs things off. He said it was too long ago to be worth talking about.'

'I agree with him.' I look at Susan and dare her to disagree. If I tell the story, she will not come out looking good. But I don't want to tell the story, because other things happened in my life at that time that I don't want to remember.

Until now, in front of Jonny and Lucy she has smiled and lied. She seems to be in a different mood tonight, a mood for telling truths that should remain unspoken. Susan's gaze meets mine and her fixed expression tells me that she thinks she's in some sort of a wrestling match with me.

'Has your mother ever told you that she nearly killed someone,' she says. The vicious words are spoken in a matter-of-fact voice but they are a threat thrown towards me. She's not looking at Lucy. 'She doesn't seem the type to be a murderer, does she? But then how do you ever see things like that?'

My whole body stiffens as if I've been dropped into ice. 'Susan.' She knows why I did that. I did it to save her. But Lucy won't understand. She will never be able to imagine what our lives were like then. I don't want to her to imagine it. She's only known security and love; that's all I want her to know.

'That was after your dad left.' She looks at Lucy, then looks back at me. 'Does he know?' Her eyes turn to Sarah again. 'After Jonny left ...' she starts saying to Lucy, beginning the story from her point of view.

I can't share it from my side without telling Lucy everything I don't want to say. 'You're showing your true colours,' I tell Susan.

All she does is smile and carry on talking.

Chapter 45

1985

Jonny arrives exactly as both hands on the clock on the living room wall point at the number eight. I'm looking through the net curtain, leaning around the sofa, trying not to wake Susan. He doesn't get out of the car or beep his horn. He just waits.

I open and close the door as quietly as I can. I'm wary of Susan. Afraid of her. She will go mad with anger if she knows Jonny is outside and that he is here for me.

I run along the path and around the car. He leans to pull the door handle, so the door is slightly open. I pull it wider and drop into the passenger seat. 'Hello. Thank you for coming.'

He revs the engine, releases the handbrake and slips the car into gear. 'How are you?'

'I'm rubbish. Susan is sad and angry with me for telling you how old we are.'

He glances over. Then looks ahead. She might have lied to him, but love does not switch off overnight. I think he still loves her. I don't know what he will say, or think, if I tell him about what she's done. But I'm not going to tell him because I know it will hurt him, and I don't want to hurt him.

'Is your job nice?'

'Yes. It's interesting. Busy. I'm learning a lot more there than I learned the place here.'

He could be unkind to me, or angry. He could blame me. He hasn't, and he doesn't. He is kind and careful of me. As he drives he talks about his week in London and lots of things - everything but what we are going to do. Then he turns the cassette tape he has in the stereo up loud and sings along to it in stupid voices, making me laugh. I don't even feel anxious until the moment he turns into the carpark of the clinic.

He walks with me to the front door, pushes it open and holds it with the palm of his hand while I walk in.

When they call out my name, I wish he could come into the room with me. But at least I know he's here.

When I am told I can go home, I return to the waiting room and I know as soon as I see him that the image of him sitting there will stay with me forever. His legs are parted, and his head is drooped down watching the movement of his hands as he taps a rolled-up magazine on his calf. A magazine I guess he has picked up and read until he is bored of it. He has waited here for me. Patient and calm.

On the way home, he says he's taking me to his mum's, and when we get there he tells me to get into his bed. His bedroom contains nothing but the furniture. Everything that made the room his has gone to London.

I sleep in his bed all afternoon while he brings me food

that I can't eat because my stomach is all twisted up in knots, and cups of tea that I throw up twice.

'I should go home,' I say when it's about ten o'clock at night.

'No. I signed a form to say I would look after you for twenty-four hours in case you're ill. You can sleep here. I'll drive you home tomorrow, before I go back to London.'

He sleeps on top of the bed covers as I sleep underneath and he holds me in the way that Susan sometimes holds me, because it's a single bed like ours and there isn't much room.

I have dreams that I should not have about him.

In the morning, we wake up looking at each other, but he moves almost immediately and gets up.

His mum is downstairs. She says, 'Hello Susan.' I don't tell her that I'm Sarah, nor does he.

He makes me a cup of tea, and she puts some toast in the toaster for me then spreads it with butter and marmalade that has thick, chewy slices of orange peel. But my stomach heaves when I try to eat, and I run upstairs to the bathroom to be sick.

As I walk back downstairs, he's in the narrow hallway, near the front door, looking at me with pity in his eyes. 'Do you want me to take you home now?'

I nod.

He turns and picks up his car keys.

On the drive back to our house I know this is going to be the last time I see him and I feel as sad as Susan. I don't want him to go. I want him to stay here. To be there to call on when I need help or pity.

When I get out of his car, outside our house, he doesn't get out. But he leans over, resting his hand on the passenger's seat. 'Goodbye,' he says.

'Goodbye. Thank you,' I answer and then I close the car door. He straightens up, looking ahead at the road. My hand shakes as I wave. What I've done is haunting me.

I don't stay to watch him drive away; he's not looking at me anyway. I turn around, crossing my fingers and hoping Susan isn't home. The door doesn't open as I walk up the path. Behind me his car drives away. If she's inside and awake, she hasn't seen him.

My arms fold across my chest, squashing my loose breasts underneath my sweat top and T-shirt as I slouch back in the squeaking red plastic chair and wait for the policewoman with a condescending voice and strict expression to come back.

Sarah and I are different now that Jonny has gone. We aren't us anymore. The change is as vivid as the days after Uncle Harry hit Sarah. Only this time I hit her because she broke my heart. We don't speak. I sleep on the sofa. She goes to school in the morning. I go out and hide from social services and the police on my own. It's boring. I don't have any friends, or a sister, or Jonny. I have nothing in the days. I have let myself get caught. I hadn't run very hard from the policeman. I don't care about anything anymore. I'm hollow in the middle, like the pumpkin shells left outside the houses in the street after Halloween with no purpose. Left outside to rot. That's what I feel like, as if Jonny has left me to rot.

The Twins

The first night after Jonny had gone, I took some money from Uncle Charlie's wallet and went to The Black Duck. The guy behind the bar didn't challenge my age. I drank from lunchtime until the evening. Then Jay came into the pub. He looked at me twice while he'd paid for his drink. I smiled. He thought I was Sarah.

He sat down next to me and we talked. He never mentioned the sex they had or anything else. He talked about me to her, and about how he doesn't like Jonny any more. He said we could be a good thing.

I let him think I was Sarah all night, even when he walked me halfway home and came on heavy against the wall of a dark alley. I let him undo my jeans and push down my knickers and I let him have sex with me. He was rough. His fingers squeezed my breast and bum and left bruises, and his teeth left marks on my neck. It wasn't nice. It wasn't like Jonny.

I told him he could piss off and go home on his own after that, and I gritted my teeth and ran home on shaking legs. But I didn't feel drunk anymore. It was horrible with Jay. No wonder Sarah hadn't liked it.

When I'd told her, though ... I went straight upstairs to tell her. She was in bed. Mum and Uncle Charlie were still out. I turned the light on to make her wake up and she sat up. Then I told her, 'I had sex with Jay.'

Her mouth dropped open like a fish, and her eyes popped wide like popcorn kernels bursting. Then she swallowed about three times as if she was drowning. 'You cow.' The cruel name was thrown quickly and quietly, and she shook her head at me as if I was mad.

'Bitch,' I spat back.

The teardrops on her cheeks had looked like diamonds in the reflection of the electric light from the bare bulb that hung down in the centre of the bedroom ceiling. She hadn't loved Jay; she hasn't seen him since they did it; she didn't have any reason to be upset.

The police caught me in the town centre today; letting myself be caught was just another way to fill a day really.

Mum and I are in a room in the police station receiving another warning about me not attending school. She's looking daggers at me while the social worker drones on about courts and fines, and how a lack of education will limit my future.

I don't care. I don't care about any of it.

'There is one option that might be better for you, Susan. You could have a tutor at home for a couple of hours a day. Should we try that?'

I sigh, without answering.

I should have said I was Sarah. I should just be Sarah. Let her take all the blame.

Chapter 46

2018

'I went a bit wild after Jonny went to London,' I say.

'You were always wild,' Sarah punctuates.

Maybe she thinks I won't tell. But then, she has no idea what I've already told Lucy. She has annoyed me too much today. Poking at me, deliberately, trying to make me say I won't come tonight. Trying to make Jonny let me down and not take me for driving lessons when my test is coming up. *She's my daughter. He's my husband.* Her body language, her voice and eyes, have been thrusting those words at me all day. They are mine too now. 'I slept around a bit.' I say it because it might make her panic, if she really does remember.

'A lot,' she answers.

I ignore her. All I see is anger, not fear. I think Jonny's right; she really has wiped out her past. I wish I could. 'I used men,' I say, slicing the words through the pleasant atmosphere in the sleepy little pub. It's like using a chopping knife to cut through a wedding cake. Music plays quietly from the speakers behind the bar – something by Aria Grande. Most of the other locals are gathered in a cluster at the far end of the bar hugging pints; the rest of the customers are spread across the tables. But it's not busy. We're a few feet away from anyone else. We came out later to avoid the dinner trade for returning tourists; they've gone home to their holiday cottages and lit their log fires for the night.

'You see,' I say to Lucy's wide eyes and raised eyebrows, 'After Jonny left I worked out how profitable men can be. Mum always knew. It was the only thing I learned from her. The amount of notes our uncles stuffed into the pot in the kitchen cupboard over the years must be thousands and by then I was old enough to understand why. She gave them a good time in bed; they helped pay for her home and her kids. I wanted money too. I've told you what little we had as kids.'

'You had sex for money?' Lucy's pretty blue eyes pop out on stalks.

'It wasn't prostitution.' *Not at that point.*

'Just like prostitution,' Sarah's words travel over the top of her wine glass before she drinks.

'As if you've never done it for money.' My accusation smashes the glass windows that try to hide her and her perfect pretend life. If she's judging me then she's judging herself, but I'm starting to believe she doesn't realise it. So I'll carry on and tell our story for her. I can't hold it back today. This is the anniversary of the day I lost my daughter and her attitude is just too grating. She's still acting as if nothing happened. I want to scream at her and smash down that façade. 'All those cute little cats are wriggling about in the bag,' I laugh at her.

All her dirty little secrets are crawling around in my head and trying to escape.

'That analogy is about a whip, not actual cats.' Her nose wrinkles as her facial muscles form a snide expression.

Even better, a whip to thrash you with. I feel nasty tonight. In the way I haven't felt nasty for years. 'I was horrible then,' I share the truth with Lucy. She should know about her mother. 'I wasn't very happy and I wasn't very nice about anything. I didn't think anything physical between people meant anything. That's the lesson your dad taught me. That physical connections have no meaning.'

'Don't paint Jonny as bad,' Sarah says.

'No ...' But the fact that he could just walk away had taught me everything. 'I sealed my heart in stone and—'

'And worked your way through every man in a three-mile radius from thirteen onwards,' Sarah snipes.

'You were thirteen when Dad left? You had sex with him when you were thirteen. But he was eighteen then? He shouldn't have—'

'He didn't know she was thirteen. She lied and that's why he left.'

So sayeth Sarah.

Lucy's eyes are not on Sarah, though, they are on me, wanting to hear more. 'What did you do?'

'Your mum went to school and I stayed at home with a tutor for two hours but the rest of the days I had to myself and I used to give men what they wanted if they gave things to me.' It feels strange to say these things, like telling a story in the third person. I am the narrator, not the participant.

J.S. Lark

'That's awful. You were just a child,' Lucy says, pity glowing in her eyes.

'Sarah's view was that I was a slut. Which was my reputation then. But we all have motivations for why we become what we are, don't we?'

'But it was Dad's fault.'

'I didn't say that.' I look at Sarah, because it was her fault Jonny went away.

She drinks her wine and looks through me. Sometimes I believe that she doesn't remember and other times I think she's just become the best liar ever, so good that she's even learned how to lie to herself.

'Every time we go out, Susan, you make me think I don't know my parents.'

'Don't be silly. You know us very well,' Sarah mediates.

'Everyone has things in their past that they would prefer others don't know,' I answer. 'Some people just have much bigger secrets than others.'

'What happened, Mum?' Lucy pushes Sarah to tell the secret, not me.

'We're in a pub,' she answers.

'No one can hear,' Lucy replies.

I lean back against the windowsill that's behind me, raising my pint to my lips and watch the disruption I created kick off.

'I thought she was being raped.' Sarah's elbows and the base of her wine glass rest on the table. 'One of Mum's boyfriends was having sex with her and I walked in on them.'

'What did you do?'

'Hit him with a glass ashtray and knocked him out,' I say.

'Oh, wow.'

'But she didn't stop there. She picked up a bottle of whisky while he was out cold, tipped it over him and threw matches at him so he caught alight like a Christmas pudding.' Laughter pulls at my throat as I remember it. In hindsight it was funny.

'You set him alight ...' Lucy's eyes are popping again.

'I thought he was raping her.'

'What happened?'

'That's when we were put into care.'

'You never said you were in care, Mum. How did you not go to prison?'

'He went to prison,' I say. 'Because I was fifteen. He got his dues. But I didn't let him burn. I smothered the fire with a wet towel. I think your mum would have let him go up in smoke.' Sarah doesn't respond; she just nurses her glass in both hands.

Lucy reaches over and holds the hand that's in my lap. 'I'm sorry you had such a difficult time.' She's angry. She believes her mother and father did the wrong thing to me. It's a shame she doesn't know it all. I think she should know it all.

My fingers wrap around her hand and I hold her. 'It's okay. It was a long time ago.'

Sarah's tongue clicks in a tut. Lucy lets go of my hand and knocks back her gin and tonic.

'I'll buy you another,' I say and drink down the last of my ale.

Lucy slides the glass towards me as I shuffle out from the

window seat. I expect her to hold Sarah's hand but she doesn't.

They talk while I'm at the bar. I imagine their conversation: Lucy the inquisitive detective firing questions and Sarah the accused fighting to defend herself. As we had done once before.

They put us in separate rooms in the police station and asked us the same questions over and over. But our stories had been the same. 'Two gin and tonics and another red wine, please,' I say as the barman comes over.

When I carry the drinks back to the table I expect Sarah to begin sharing her version of the awful stories from our past – however she interprets them now. I am prepared for that; it does not concern me. I don't have a husband and daughter to worry about.

I put her fresh glass of red wine near her half full one, then slide Lucy's and my glass along as I move back into the window seat.

Will Sarah talk about our life on the streets in London? The life she says she's forgotten? She behaves as if she has no guilt. As if she didn't leave me in that squalor and run away. I went back for her.

'Can we not talk about our childhood?' she says, trying to take control of the conversation. 'It's hardly fond memories. Tell me what you and Michael have been up to lately.' She looks at Lucy, cutting me out.

'I like hearing about your childhood,' Lucy replies. 'I should know what you went through, Mum.'

'We didn't stay in the care home for very long ...' Lucy's pretty face turns back to me, her ears pricked and her expression fixed with an intent desire to listen. Sarah has lost her interest. My stories are juicier than sterile chatter.

Jonny's mobile phone rings six, seven times, then it rings again.

'Hi.' Finally he answers.

'Hi. Have you had anything to drink?'

There's a slight pause at his end, as if it's a bad connection. 'Why?' he says after a moment.

'I want to come home now. Would you pick me up?'

'Can't you get a taxi?'

'I'd rather you came to fetch me.'

'It'll take me twenty minutes to get there.'

'I know. But it might take a taxi the same or longer and I need to talk to you. Please.' My voice cracks. It is not a request; this is a plea. The boxes where I have hidden all of my memories have been ripped open tonight, the locks kicked off and the lids scattered everywhere. My brain has been vandalised. Now I have to pick up the pieces, quickly. I remember things. Bad things. There are still things shut in the dark that I know are there, crawling around behind jet-black screens but I don't know what they look like. I just know I don't want to see them. But there are memories I can't hide from anymore.

'Okay. I'll come.'

I swipe the tears off my cheeks then realise I've wiped make-up all over my coat sleeve.

Lucy has stayed with Susan. They went to a nightclub. I can't dance as if the things Susan talked about have no consequence. She talked about our past as though it's nothing to her when it carved out our futures with brutal cuts. Every moment in our past marked me like tattoos pierced into my soul in black ink. I ran. I've been running for years, playing a game of hide and seek. But now she's caught me I can't hide anymore. There are things I need to tell Jonny before she does.

I pull my hood further forward so it covers my forehead and I wait, my arms folded over my chest, my handbag pinned under one arm. Is it possible to stand still for twenty minutes while anxiety runs riot through your nervous system?

'You all right, love? Give us a smile!' A stranger amongst a group of young men yells from the street outside the carpark.

I step back, retreating into the shadow of the porch over the back door of the pub. Hiding like the demon I feel I am tonight, there are dark voices trying to tell tales in my head, whispering about things I don't want to hear. I was admitted into a psychiatric ward after Susan and I separated. I don't remember what happened, not really. But I had heard cruel angry voices like this then.

Chapter 47

The Range Rover pulls around slowly, spitting up the rain from the tarmac behind the wheels. The headlights prevent me from seeing Jonny in the driver's seat. The Range Rover stops a few feet away. I run from the cover of the porch through the puddles to reach the sanctuary of the car. He's already leant over and pulled the door catch to open the door, so all I do is hold the handle and pull the door wide enough to get in. I close the door quickly to shut out the rain, but I can feel my coat and the skirt of my dress sliding on the leather seat, making it wet.

'What's happened?' he asks without looking at me as I pull my seatbelt on and the car rolls into motion.

If he does look at me, he won't know how hard I've been crying; he will think it's the rain that has ruined my make-up.

I open the glove box as he pulls out of the carpark and seek out the small packet of tissues in there. I pull one out and blow my nose.

Now that I'm able to tell him, I'm not sure I can.

His hands turn the steering wheel. His eyes are on the road. I'm glad the car is dark and his music is playing. I stay quiet and let him concentrate as he navigates his way through the town centre, mindful of the drunk and sober people spilling out of the bars and restaurants.

I blow my nose again as the car turns onto the road that will take us away from the centre, away from Lucy and Susan.

'Do you want to talk?' he asks, as the car leaves behind the glow of the town's last streetlight. We are illuminated only by dials on the dashboard as he turns off the main road onto the narrow road that leads home. The road is absorbed by the woods and the high dry-stone walls on either side.

Fresh tears trickle onto my cheeks. I pull another tissue out of the packet and wipe them away, blow my nose, and look at him. 'Did you ever hear what happened to Jay?'

His head turns to me, then looks back at the unpredictable road. There's always a chance of a sudden flood, or a deer jumping over a wall.

The movement had been quick. Shocked. I have not said that name in all the years we've spent together.

'No. Why would I? Did Susan keep in touch with him?'
'No.'
'Why mention it then?'
'Because if I don't tell you what happened, Susan will. And you should know. You should have known then.'

'What?' His voice is high pitched and the question kicks with concern as he steers over the dashed white line on a turn in the road.

'You should concentrate on driving.' It's wrong of me to tell him here. 'I'll tell you when we get home.'

We travel the rest of the journey with the windscreen wipers contradicting the rhythm of the Coldplay songs playing softly as his headlights illuminate the distance then drop away when a vehicle comes towards us. We pass the turning for the café and I feel the calm and peace of that lakeside idyll shatter. It can never be my little spot of calm paradise again. My hiding place has been found.

The indicator slips on. Tick. Tick. He turns onto the cul-de-sac where we live. I hear the seconds I have left of happiness tick away, single grains of sand slipping through the waist of an hour glass. This cannot continue as it has. I don't know how far Susan will go. But I am certain now that I can't trust her. She is trying to destroy everything I have. Her true colours were shown tonight.

And where is Lucy? She is with her.

Where will Jonny be tomorrow?

The car pulls up onto our drive and stops. He slides the gearstick into neutral, pulls up the handbrake and takes the key out of the ignition. Coldplay stops playing and the windscreen wipers stop moving.

'Okay?' he says.

I nod acceptance. The moment of truth can't be avoided.

He opens his car door as I do and we get out of the car into the dark and run to get out of the rain. Our breaths mist and merge when we reach the porch as he unlocks the door.

He pushes the door open and reaches inside to flick on the lights. I walk around him, shaking the rain off my coat onto the coir mat, before I undo the zip. We strip off our coats without speaking.

'Do you want a drink? Wine or a beer?' he asks, walking past me towards the kitchen.

'No thank you. I've had enough.'

I follow him, drawn in by his magnetic force. I climb onto one of the stools at the breakfast bar and watch him. He opens the fridge, takes out a bottle of lager, opens the lid with the crocodile opener on the wall and then comes towards me. 'Aren't you going to tell me?'

'I was waiting for you to sit down.'

He doesn't walk around the breakfast bar to sit next to me; he sits facing me on the other side of bar, the bottle still in his hand. 'What happened?'

A deep breath pulls right to the bottom of my lungs. I search for the courage and strength to say it or stall for a second longer. 'I lied to you. I'm sorry.'

His forehead fills with wrinkle lines as he frowns. 'How?'

'I didn't tell you I had a child.'

'What do you mean? You had an abortion.'

'No.'

His head shakes. 'I took you to Swindon. You came to my house. I stayed with you. You were sick.'

I close my eyes and breathe away the hurt that presses through me. I don't remember any of that. When had he done that? But I do remember that I couldn't go through with the abortion. 'I pretended,' I say, and I look at him. 'I couldn't do it in the end, and when my daughter was born then I was glad. She looked perfect. Beautiful. She was perfect, Jonny.' I don't ask him to fill in any of the gaps that he remembers and I don't. I would rather leave what is left in the dark there.

I'm afraid to remember anything more. I remember too much already.

His mouth is open. The frown has gone, and his raised eyebrows touch the few strands of hair that fall forward on his brow. 'Where is she?'

'I gave her up for adoption. She made a childless family happy, and they will have made her happy. I hope.'

'But you don't know? She's never been in touch?'

'No.'

He shakes his head then drinks from the lager bottle. His Adam's apple is moving. When the bottle lowers, he says, 'Why not tell me this before?'

I think he'd just taken a drink to buy himself some time to think this through. 'Because there's more, and because I didn't tell you when we ran away from London and then there never seemed a right time.

'What else?'

I take another long breath, wishing I had said yes to a drink to buy myself time too, and wishing I had turned on the TV or some music to create a distraction with another source of sound. But the only sound is my voice. 'Susan was pregnant too. She had a baby too.'

'What?' The base of the bottle hits the slate surface with a hard clunk.

'I don't know ... She didn't know if it was yours. If *she* was yours.'

He leans back in the seat, a breath sucking into his lungs. 'A daughter. Oh my God.' His eyes are wide and his eyebrows are high. 'Are you saying I might have another daughter?'

'Maybe. But officially she's Jay's.'

'Jay's?' The pitch of his voice is deep. Not just shocked but angry.

'When I was six months pregnant it couldn't be hidden anymore and social services became involved. That's when Susan said she was pregnant too. The condom split the Friday night before you left, but on the Sunday she had sex with Jay to hurt me. She doesn't know who the father is. But she didn't want you to go to jail so she said it was Jay's; he'd already been charged for having sex with me. He didn't argue because he'd had sex with her.'

He shakes his head. His free hand slides down over his face then lifts and combs back his hair. 'Why didn't Susan contact me?' His hand falls palm up. 'She knew my mother would tell me. Either one of you could have told my mother. I would have wanted to know if the child was mine.'

'Because you would have been sent to prison. It was better that Jay claimed her.' I don't remember the details. I don't remember so many things. The blank gaps in my mind make the memories a patchwork of moments that still keep secrets. I have locked so much away. I don't remember Jonny taking me anywhere. But I know I had a child and Susan had a child. 'She had a girl too, and she was adopted too.'

'If she wants to find her father she won't even know that it might be me.'

There is no answer to that. It's the truth. He leans back, his free hand dropping on his thigh and he drinks more of the lager then looks at the ceiling as if there is an answer up there.

'I'm sorry. I should have told you before. But there's nothing you could have done.'

His gaze comes back to me. 'I could have put my name forward to one of those lost relative agencies.'

'We don't even know her name. It would have changed when she was adopted.'

'No. That's rubbish. They would have some sort of record. I'll find out. I'll put my name forward. She might look like Luce. Have you thought about that?'

'She might.' I nod. Susan's daughter had dark brown hair. But my child, my daughter had bright auburn hair.

'Lucy has two sisters then.' Something shifts in his eyes as he realises.

'She has one sister. I don't know about the other girl.'

'Does Lucy know? Has Susan told her?' He leans on the slate top of the breakfast bar, his forearm spread along it.

'No. But I think Susan will tell her at some point. That's why I wanted to tell you. Do you want to tell Lucy or do you want me to? She should hear it from us. Susan told her how old we were.'

'She'll think I'm some sort of paedophile.' His hand slides over his hair.

'She won't. You were young too.'

'This is a mess.' He sighs and leans back again.

I realise I haven't moved. I have been as still as a statue preserved in one position. 'I'm sorry.'

He drinks more beer. His mouth opens and he sighs as his head bows. Then his head lifts and he looks at me. 'I'm angry, but I shouldn't be. You were both thirteen. You shouldn't have been pregnant, or having to handle giving up babies. It must have been horrible for you. For her too. I'm the one who's sorry. I'm sorry I put you in that position.'

The statement is pure Jonny. Kind. Considerate. But something about the tone in his voice rings hollow. He might say that, but I don't believe it's what he feels. He's still angry. Hurt. Betrayed. He left Susan because she lied to him.

'I'm going to bed,' I say as I slide off the tall chair.

'I'll stay up for a while. I couldn't sleep even if I wanted to.'

'I am sorry,' I say again before I walk away.

He doesn't reply.

Chapter 48

Zzzzz. Zzzzzzz. Zzzzzzzzz. The sound wakes me from an alcoholic mind-curdled sleep. It's the door buzzer for my flat. No one rings it. No one visits me. It must be someone using a random flat number.

Zzzzzzzz. The buzzer sounds angry.

Zzzzzzzzzz. Whoever it is they're lifting their finger off then putting it straight back on to be deliberately annoying.

My eyes open to see the clock. 4:12.

Who does this at four o'clock in the morning? A drunk.

Zzzzz.

'Go away.' I say it as if the person can hear me from my bed, two floors above the front door from the inside of the building.

Zzzzzzzzzzzzzzzzzzzzzzzzzzzzzz.

'Shut the fuck up!' Someone shouts out of a window from the flat next to mine.

'I waannt to speeek to Susan! I Knnno shheee's in thurr!'

It's Jonny. My brain clears of alcohol as quickly as if someone threw a bucket of water over my head. He sounds as if he's smashed out of his mind. 'Jonny!' I call even as I

313

scramble to get out of my bed and get to the window. The latch on the metal window frame is stiff and cold. I jerk it open and push the window wide enough to stick my head out. 'Jonny. I'll buzz you in and come down. Wait in the hall.'

His Range Rover is parked at an angle on the pavement in front of the flats. The idiot drove here drunk. At 4am.

I scrabble around in the case that serves as a wardrobe and find some leggings to pull on. Then I pull a sweatshirt over my head as I walk to the door. I press the button to let him in.

My bare feet race down the two flights of stairs, rushing over the dirty carpet with the rubber treads on the edge of each step. 'Jonny,' I say as I break through the door from the staircase and see him. 'What on earth are you doing here?'

He's sitting on the floor, slumped back against the far wall, and the stubble on his cheeks is glistening with tears. 'What's happened?' *Why have you come to me?*

I kneel, facing him, resting a hand on one of his knees as I reach out and stroke back a few loose strands of his hair off his forehead.

A pained noise breaks from the back of his throat like a wave in an ocean of grief.

'What's happened?'

His bloodshot eyes focus on me. 'Yooo hadd my dauughhterrr.' The accusation churns out of his mouth and spreads around me in a threatening mist.

'Yooo didn'tt tell me.'

She's told him. I didn't think she would. But now she's told him about that, what about everything else that I know she's kept a secret and denies remembering so believably.

314

'Come on, you drunk. You can't drive home and I can't drive you home so you'll have to sleep it off here and somehow I am going to have to get you upstairs.'

'I cannn't stay heeere.'

'You don't have a choice. Come on.'

I am shorter than him by seven inches and skinny, but I'm no weakling. I hold his forearm and his upper arm, my fingers reaching beneath his armpit, and pull hard. He doesn't budge.

'You're going to have to help me.'

I pull again, and this time his other hand pushes back against the wall and he tries to stand as I pull. He moves, swaying away from me, but I pull him back and haul him up onto his feet then slot his arm around my neck. All his weight falls on me, but I manage to stay upright.

It takes more than thirty minutes to get us both up to my flat because we keep taking nearly as many dangerous steps backwards down the stairs as we do forwards.

When I reach my front door, I lean his shoulder against the wall while I unlock it. He falls into the small space that I call mine, nearly smashing his forehead on the corner of the bed and ends up on his side, on the floor.

I step over him and push his legs out of the way so I can close the door.

Now he's inside, he can stay on the floor. It won't kill him to spend the rest of the night there.

The only light in the room comes from the numbers on the alarm clock by the bed.

I step over him again to reach the bed. His breathing is

heavy but rhythmic. I think he's passed out. Let him sleep it off. We can talk when he's sober.

Why did she tell him? Because I've succeeded in stirring her up and making her run from the woods? I was like a thrasher in the undergrowth tonight, chasing the pheasant out into the open to be shot.

There's a sound behind me. The basest of human sounds. He is vomiting on my carpet.

'Jonny.' I switch on the bedside lamp and turn back.

There's a bowl in the sink in the small kitchen area. I get it, turn him over to his other side and leave his head resting in it so he's sick into it. Then I set about cleaning up the mess he's made. 'Cheers to old times,' I say to the filthy carpet.

When he stops retching I wash out the bowl, put it in the kitchen sink and wipe a flannel over his face and hair. Then I leave him on the floor to sleep.

Chapter 49

My hand reaches out, searching Jonny's side of the bed. He isn't there. The sheet is cool and smooth. It doesn't feel as if he's been here at all in the night. The clock on his side of the bed says 5:33am.

I roll over, throwing the duvet cover off me and get up. I don't look for my slippers or night gown, even though the house is cold because the heating hasn't come on yet. 'Jonny?' I shout so my voice will carry through the walls. 'Jonny?'

The bedroom door is closed. I don't remember closing it. Did he come to the room and shut the door at some point in the night?

I open it and walk out into the hall.

'Jonny?' My call echoes along the short corridor and breaks out into the open-plan living space at the end. The electric downlights that speckle the ceiling like random freckles are still on.

There's no reply. 'Jonny?' The wooden floor that's warm when the underfloor heating kicks in is cold under my bare feet, it's too early. 'Jonny, are you here?'

Maybe he's sleeping on the sofa. I stop shouting in case

he is. If he fell asleep late it would be cruel to wake him now.

'Jonny ...?' I say in a quieter, more tentative voice as I near the back of the sofa. There's an empty bottle of whisky on the coffee table. The screw cap from the bottle is discarded beside the empty glass, bent at the edges so it can never be screwed back on.

I lean over the sofa, expecting to see him there where he falls asleep in the evenings when he's exhausted by a hard day at work. The sofa cushions are empty.

I turn around, still expecting to see him, perhaps in the far corner of the kitchen where I just haven't noticed him before. Or by the front door. He's not here.

The bathroom.

I rush back along the hall. Maybe he fell asleep in there. Or what if he fell and knocked himself unconscious on the side of the toilet if he was drunk? 'Jonny?' The handle gives way and the door swings open. He's not in here.

Upstairs.

We don't use the rooms built under the eaves of what had been a bungalow; they were always Lucy's territory. They still feel like that even now she isn't here. I can't imagine him going up there. But what if ...

'Jonny! Jonny!' I am screaming now as I run up the narrow staircase opposite the kitchen. The staircase folds back on itself. 'Jonny!' There's no reply. No response. The house feels as if it's laughing at me as I open the doors of Lucy's bedroom and her dressing room, now empty beyond a few clothes she wants to keep but will never wear again – her prom dress, her child-sized Snow White costume. I open the bathroom door last. No Jonny.

I turn back and run downstairs to the living room. In my mind I'm already running outside to find him but I'm not dressed. I run to the front window, twist open the wooden blinds and look out at the drive. It's still raining and pitch-black. But in the light from the house I can see that his Range Rover is not on the drive.

Where's my phone?

The handbag I used last night is on the shoe rack by the front door. I unzip it and pull out my phone and ring him.

He doesn't answer; it just keeps ringing. Eight. Nine. Ten rings.

Why doesn't he have his phone set to take messages?

I end the call and ring again. I do that fifteen times but he doesn't answer. My insides are being scraped out with paint striper. Jonny. I ring again and let it ring twenty or more times.

He's not going to answer. A weight is hanging from my neck, a millstone that is strangling me, shutting off my windpipe.

Come home darling. Please. Where are you?
Please just let me know you're all right. Please.

My thumbs key in the message and I touch send. It disappears into an ether of silence.

Nothing.

Nothing.

Nothing.

* * *

I wake up. It's 5:59am. There's another buzzing sound but this time it's more like a whisper. An insistent whisper that keeps going, on and off, in the same way the door buzzer had earlier. But this is—

A phone.

Jonny's phone.

The sound is coming from the pocket of his jacket.

I turn the lamp on.

He's out cold still. He isn't going to answer. I bet it's Sarah. But perhaps it's Lucy?

I crawl over the bed so I don't need to clamber over him, lean down and pull the mobile out of his pocket. It vibrates again. Sarah. Her picture is on his screen. It could be a picture of me. I press the off button on the side of the phone and switch it off completely, then let the phone drop on the floor near him. Sarah will figure out that he's not going to make it into work today and it will do her some good to feel a little fear while she stands at the top of the castle walls of her perfect life. She thought I wouldn't find her. I have. She thought I couldn't break down her family's defences. I have. She and Jonny are not as solid as she tells everyone they are.

I crawl back up the bed and roll myself up in the duvet. I'm cold even though I'm still wearing the leggings and sweat-shirt.

The minute I close my eyes the darkness drags me down into a zombie-like sleep. When I drink, the drugs I take for my depression tend to make my mind heavy like this. I'm not meant to drink with the drugs. But I do.

* * *

It is 6:54am when I look for Lucy's name in my contacts and ring her.

'Hi, Mum. Do you realise what time it is?'

'Is Dad there?'

'No, why?'

'He's not here, Lucy. He went out last night and drove when he was drunk, and I don't know where he is. He's not answering his phone.'

'Mum. Why would he take the car when he's been drinking?' I imagine her sitting upright in her bed now. Her voice is high and panicking.

'I don't know.' The full stop of my sentence is a sobbing sound. I'm so tired. Terrified. Twisted up in a tangle of emotion. 'I don't know where he's gone.'

'Do you want me to ring the hospitals?'

'No, because what if he's fine and we tell the police he's been driving while he's drunk and he loses his licence? Maybe he's just sleeping it off somewhere.'

'Maybe. Shall I get in the car and go looking for him?'

'No. He could be anywhere.'

My fingers rub at my temple, pushing hard and trying to wake my mind up as if somewhere in my head I do know where he is.

'What should I do then, Mum?'

'I don't know. I hoped he might be with you. I ... It doesn't matter. We'll wait a couple more hours. Then if he doesn't come home I'll call the hospital.'

'Mum ... are you all right? Did something happen?'

She knew Susan had upset me last night, but she'd stayed with Susan.

'Dad and I argued.'

'Why? What did you say?' Of course she assumes the fault lies with me. Susan is turning her against me.

'He'll tell you when we find him.' I press the icon to end the call. I can't talk about that now.

Tears run from my nose in sticky trails as much as from my eyes. It's over. Everything. It's broken now. I always knew she would break it. I hid because I knew she would break this.

Chapter 50

When I wake up, Jonny is sitting on the floor, with his legs bent up and slightly parted and his back against the door. He's looking at me. He's been watching me sleep. It reminds me of the night I spent with him before I lost him to London. I don't move at all, just look back at him.

'Did you have a good time with my daughter last night?' he says.

I pull the pillow further under my head which elevates my view of him slightly, but I don't move from my side. 'Yes. Why?'

'She has two sisters, doesn't she?' His skin is sickly pale. He isn't well – more than hungover. The alcohol is probably still a poison running through his blood and his liver. 'Sarah told me you both have children. Is your daughter mine?'

'I don't know. Perhaps.' I play along with this conversation, as I keep playing along with all of Sarah's games, because I want to see where this will all come to an end. On which sister will the ball of the roulette wheel stop.

'Sarah said she might be mine or she might be Jay's.'

My ear rubs the pillow as I give him a single nod of confirmation. 'Might is the crucial word, Jonny.'

'Are you registered with agencies to try and find her?'

'I am. I want to find my daughter someday. But she might not want to find me.'

His head presses back against the painted wood of the door and he looks up. His whole manner expresses exhaustion.

'Do you remember last night?' I ask, as I sit up and pull the covers around me.

'No.'

I hug my legs through the covers. 'You drove here, you idiot.'

'I was disturbed. Confused.'

'By the time you got to me you could hardly walk or talk. I don't know how the hell you didn't crash the car.'

He doesn't answer.

'Sarah rang you about a million times. I switched your phone off.'

He twists to pull the phone out of his coat pocket. He'd put it away without switching it on. 'I don't know what to say to you.' His eyes focus on his phone as the screen flares into life. Then his lips twist in an odd halfway expression of judgement about something on his screen.

'Thank you for not sending me to prison ...?' I suggest. 'It isn't all bad, Jonny.'

He looks up at me. 'I would rather have known I had a daughter.'

No. That's not true. I know what prison is like. 'But perhaps you don't have a daughter.'

'I'll never know now, will I?' He looks down as his thumbs type something into his phone. A message for Sarah. She won't like him being here. She won't believe he was passed out on my floor all night. I don't care.

'No. But it doesn't matter. As long as she's had a good life.'

'How can we know if she has? She might have been given to awful parents.'

'I like to think she's had a very good life. Much better than mine.' I don't really want to talk to him about this. I turn, throw the covers off, and get out of bed. 'Will you ask Sarah to collect you? You must be too drunk to drive still. I'm going to get ready for work. She can drop me there to save me catching the bus.'

'That's it then. That's all you have to say about this.'

I stop moving and look at him. 'Yes.' My shoulders lift in a shrug. 'There's nothing else to say.'

'You can be a heartless cow sometimes.'

'Can I?' No. If I was heartless I would not be standing here with my lips sealed on a lie that would smash your family to pieces.

I sort out some clean clothes from my suitcase while he carries on a typed conversation on his phone. Then I take the clothes into the bathroom to change.

'Hello.' His voice breaches the thin bathroom door. He's rung someone now. I assume it's Sarah. 'Yes. I know. I know. Yes. Can you come and get me? How long will you be? Okay. I will. No. That's fine. Okay. Thank you.'

It's not Sarah who comes to pick us up; it's Lucy. I imagine Sarah is in a state because Lucy's face carries a look that says she's walked into an obnoxious smell. 'Dad,' she says when he walks outside; his name is a rebuke.

'Thank you for coming,' he answers, with no explanation for his presence here, and no apology for his stupid behaviour.

His car is left abandoned half on the road, and half on the pavement and verge.

She drops me off at the café. They don't get out of the car, and their goodbyes are terse.

I cut some deep fractures into this family last night. 'Goodbye,' I close the car door on them but it doesn't quite shut. As I open and shut the door again, Lucy is saying, 'Mum said you have something to tell me ...'

'Not now, Luce, it's not the time.'

Then when is? That will probably be my choice.

I close the door harder the second time.

Chapter 51

The Jonny who walks through the front door is pale and tired, nervous and cowed. His shoulders slump, his cheeks are flushed, and his body looks weighted down.

I could explode and shout and make a scene about him spending the night with Susan. Or about him taking the Range Rover when he was drunk. I don't because I'm pleased to see him home safe.

'Jonny.' I rush at him, wrap my arms around him, and hold on. 'I thought you were dead in a ditch somewhere.'

'I'll put some coffee on.' Lucy shuts the door and walks around us.

We're not behaving like her parents today but Jonny needs me more than she does.

His arms fold around me, enveloping me in a way that only his body can, embracing me as firmly as I hold him.

'I'm sorry.' The words are warmth seeping through my hair to my scalp as his prickly cheek presses against my head. 'I shouldn't have driven. Hide the car keys if I'm drinking when you go to bed next time.'

'We won't let it happen again.' If Susan thinks she's broken us, she hasn't.

He cries into my hair in a way I've never known Jonny to cry. It's noisy and ugly.

We don't move from our position by the door, clinging to each other, until Lucy shouts, 'Coffee's ready.'

We break apart as she carries two steaming mugs out of the kitchen. She walks across the room ahead of us and puts them down on the coffee table in front of the sofa.

She straightens up and moves out of the way. 'I'll go in and do a shift at the café for you.' She says. 'You should both stay here.'

'Thank you,' Jonny answers.

'And you should have a shower, Dad. You stink of alcohol and vomit.' After she's thrust that parting shot at him, she walks away, towards the door, to leave.

'Thank you for helping, Lucy,' I call after her.

'You're welcome. And, Dad, whenever you feel like telling me what was so bad you had to melt down, I'll be waiting to listen.'

He doesn't answer.

She opens the door, walks out, and closes it behind her.

I collapse on the sofa beside him. His arm lifts and embraces me. I lean into him the way I used to when we were younger, my palm resting over his sweater, on his stomach. 'I love you.'

'I think we should take a break. We should go away for Christmas. Let's go on holiday somewhere warm. We need a holiday. We need some time together. Just us.'

'I'd like that.'

The Twins

'We'll look for somewhere later. The others can manage at the café for a fortnight. It's not that busy with Emma in to help through the holiday too, and Lucy can take Susan into Kendal for her driving test.'

I nod against his chest. I don't care about how. I just want to be alone with him and away from her.

We drink our coffee in silence. But the silence is different. It's okay. It's not threatening. It's safe and companionable.

Later, when Jonny's in the shower, I pick up my phone and see a message from Susan. It says.

We need to talk.

She's right. We all do. She pushed her rook across the chess board of our lives last night and called check. Now I've moved and called check back. Maybe this is check mate? I hope it's the end of her game.

Okay, but not until after Christmas. We're going away.
I'll message when we get back.

My thumb thumps the send icon.
The phone vibrates less than a second later.

Okay.

I hear Jonny's phone vibrate after that. It's in the pocket of his coat. I walk over and take the phone out. It's her. I can see the message on the screen without unlocking the phone.

J.S. Lark

Sarah said you're going away.
What about my driving lessons and the test?

I feel like answering for him. I type in his security code to do it, but the phone doesn't unlock. I type it again. Then again. It's not my typing. He's changed the code.

I shove his phone back into his coat pocket and leave it – and my concerns – there. We're going away together. I don't need to worry about her.

Chapter 52

2019

I can't sleep. I've lain here for hours, staring into the darkness and listening to Jonny breathing in the quietness. A barn owl screeches from somewhere in the garden.

Lucy and Michael are upstairs, sharing the double bed in her childhood bedroom. She went to bed at eight o'clock with Michael. Noises, a mixture from the television and their conversation, drifted down the stairs for an hour or more afterwards; they did not go straight to sleep. It had been a choice to spend her evening with him, not us.

I had been wrong. I'd thought everything would be normal if Lucy recovered. When I sat in the car today, on the way home, while I watched her smiling at Michael in the rear-view mirror, I saw our family in my head – Jonny, me and Lucy – standing together, holding hands, united by survival. A family who would put each other first to get through anything. But Lucy is putting Michael first and Jonny is no different with me.

Jonny's attention has focused on Lucy's wants and needs

all day, ignoring me, when she doesn't even need him because she wants Michael's attention not ours. I feel isolated still.

Sometimes it feels as though Jonny doesn't see me. I'm in a room with him, standing beside him, even speaking to him, but his eyes and his mind are elsewhere, absorbed in thoughts which don't include me.

I thought it would be different tonight. I thought he would want to have sex when we came to bed, or at least to hold me. To release the pent-up emotion and celebrate our daughter coming home.

'Don't.' Was all he said when I rolled onto my side and rested a hand on his stomach. I had only moved my hand down an inch towards his boxer shorts.

I want an intimate relationship, a physical connection. I don't want a barren marriage. Is it because of me? Or is it still Susan's fault?

He sighs in his sleep and turns to his side, rolling away from me.

Voices, good and bad, a devil and an angel, fight in my head. Susan and me. She says this is my fault. I say it's hers. It's not her spirit talking, just my own mind that cannot let her go. But it feels as though she died for nothing. Her death has not changed anything.

Why am I not good enough?

Chapter 53

When DI Watts and DI Witherstone push the café door open and set off the bell, I am in the middle of cutting a new carrot and walnut cake with cream cheese icing into our standard size slices. Jonny is sitting at a table with Lucy and Michael in the far corner of the café. This is her first excursion out of doors. These police officers seem to like destroying the first memories of her recovery.

'Hello!' I call over. Jonny hasn't noticed them. I leave the knife on the plate beside the cake and walk out from behind the glass food cabinet. 'How can I help you?' I hope they will keep this low key; there are several local customers in here. We wouldn't want nasty rumours spreading around the village.

Jonny has seen them now. He stands up, his posture stiffening. He doesn't like them. He's angry and critical about everything they've done in their investigation.

'Can we have a quick word with you both?' DI Watts looks from me to Jonny.

'Here?' I ask, which is stupid because they are here, so of course here.

'If you can spare a moment, it won't take long. We were passing and we thought we'd call in rather than bother you later at home.'

'Is everything okay?' Jonny asks as he nears us. 'Would you like a drink? Coffee, tea, or something cold? On the house.' He's keeping his voice low.

Though he may be angry under the surface, fortunately he's cooler and calmer than me, remembering to offer them drinks so they will look like customers and not disturb anything.

Jonny glances at Marie as she moves around us to take an order. 'Marie, please will you get whatever DI Watts and DI Witherstone want? Thank you.'

'Tea will do, for both of us,' DI Witherstone says.

Jonny leads them towards a vacant table a few feet away from Lucy, drawing the police officers away from our customers too. Lucy is watching.

DI Witherstone moves ahead and pulls out a chair for me. I sit, and he sits beside me, forcing Jonny to the other side of the table. DI Watts walks causally around to sit beside Jonny. It feels as though they manoeuvred us deliberately. Why? What have they come to find out?

'We need to ask a couple more questions.'

'Have you discovered any non-ridiculous evidence?' Jonny says.

They ignore his comment with immobile expressions.

'Ask away,' Jonny adds, his voice dry and accepting. Not approving. He leans forward and rests his elbows and his forearms on the table, facing DI Witherstone like a boxer in a pre-match confrontation.

'Are you aware of Miss Tagney's past?'

'I'm her sister. We have the same past.' The words burst in a sudden explosion from my lips. But I must remember not to rush my answers. These people are detectives; they will read words in my expressions and meaning between every other word. I must think before I speak.

DI Watts's eyes search mine for something. 'I am speaking particularly about the last fifteen years. Do you know where Miss Tagney was during these years?'

'No,' Jonny and I answer in the same moment. I look at him. His gaze has shifted to DI Watts and his eyes are expecting her to tell us.

'I presume you know,' I say. I think they had deliberately not added the detail of what she had done into the question to obtain a reaction.

'Yes. We know.' There's a pause for some sort of effect, or to achieve a reaction from us.

And ... I want to prod with a poking finger. *Tell me what you know.*

DI Watts makes us wait for what feels like three or four minutes but is probably just a few seconds. I feel as though I can hear a clock ticking.

'Susan Tagney served a prison sentence for manslaughter. She was released in March 2017 and spent a year on probation in Birmingham. She left Birmingham when her probation period came to an end and moved here.'

Jonny leans back in his chair and his lips part as he absorbs a shocked breath. 'She killed someone?'

'Yes, Mr Moorell.'

Jonny looks at me as DI Witherstone scribbles something in his little black book. 'She didn't find us earlier then, because she couldn't look for us until last year.'

Is DI Witherstone writing something about Jonny or about me?

I move forward on my chair and rest my forearms on the table, feeling a tingle in my skin that suggests I'm blushing a vivid red. 'Who was involved? I mean, who did she hurt?'

'Tea,' Marie announces. Jonny's gaze lifts to her and he smiles a thank you.

'Thank you,' the detectives say, leaning back so Marie can put the tray down and offload the teapots, cups and saucers, milk jug, and sugar bowl. Nothing more is said until she's finished the task and has walked away.

'Miss Tagney stabbed her boyfriend with a kitchen knife,' DI Witherstone says in a flat voice as he reaches out and picks up one of the small teapots.

'Her boyfriend who was also her drug dealer and her pimp,' DI Watts adds.

Jonny shakes his head. 'Do you know what happened? I mean, why?' Jonny asks in a quiet voice. I don't know if the pitch is because he's thinking about the customers again, or if he's still shocked.

'There was an altercation. He assaulted her and she retaliated.' The narration progresses in a male voice as the story is passed to DI Witherstone, accompanied by the sound of tea pouring as he fills DI Watts's cup. 'The evidence corroborated her statement. He had hit her several times and his hand was around her neck at the point that she picked up the knife.' He puts down one teapot, lifts the second, and fills his own cup.

Jonny shakes his head. 'Isn't that self-defence?'

I think so too.

'Unnecessary force. She stabbed him ten times,' DI Witherstone says.

Jonny breathes out then covers his mouth with his palm for a moment before his hand drops.

'You look pale, Mrs Moorell ... Do you want my cup of tea?' DI Witherstone asks as he lifts the milk jug.

I shake my head. I thought I was blushing. 'No. Thank you.'

'Why did you want to tell us this?' Jonny asks.

'Because it might be a reason for someone to want to kill her. You said you didn't know anyone who might want to harm her, as if there was no possible reason.'

'We don't know anyone,' Jonny pushes back. 'We didn't know about her prison sentence. We haven't had any contact with her for years until she showed up here without any explanation a few months ago.'

'Did you ask her for an explanation?' DI Watts looks at me for the answer.

'No. Because I didn't like her. I didn't want to know her reasons for coming. All I wanted was for her to go.'

'Could it be someone connected with the pimp?' Jonny asks.

DI Witherstone shrugs as he drops sugar lumps into his tea. The spoon scratches around the china for a moment.

The bell on the door interrupts us. Jonny looks from one to the other of them as he gets up, sliding back his chair.

'Well, I doubt anything I can tell you will be of help, so, if you don't mind, I'm going to get back to work.'

'I should be working too. There are tables that need clearing,' I say. 'I'll leave you to finish your tea.' I stand, sliding my chair away, and turn my back on them.

Jonny is not greeting the customers; he's gone into the kitchen. He's gone outside to smoke a cigarette. Jonny's answer to every problem now is to have a cigarette.

I walk over to the customers who are stamping mud off their walking boots. 'Hello. If you choose a table, we'll be with you in a moment.' I go back to slicing the cake and leave Marie to respond when they're ready to order.

DI Witherstone and DI Watts stay at the table, drinking tea, for twenty minutes. Discussing something. Us?

I wait tables, smiling, and talking as though nothing is amiss, but my heart is stone in my chest, my throat is dry, my brain is jelly, and I have no idea how I'm standing on the twigs I have for legs.

When they get up to leave, Marie walks over to clear the table. I lift a hand acknowledging their departure as DI Witherstone opens the door. I wait, holding my poise for as long as it takes them to walk along the path by the lake and move out of sight, then my smile falls and my teeth grit, closing down on the storm surge of emotion in my head. I remember things. There are visions. Moments. Seconds of memory. I see her, and I see me. In a squalid dirty place. There is pain and confusion in my mind – not today, it is a memory from then. I see men too. One particular man, and others.

I turn and walk out of the cafe towards the cupboard that disguises itself as an office.

I open the office door and close it behind me then collapse into the office chair that's wedged in the tiny space between the desk and the shelves. The room disappears amongst the tears. Horrible memories fly through my head, so terrifying that I labelled them unreal. Imagined. Dreamed in nightmares and never thought.

But they are real. The memories are disgusting. I let myself become her, *that* woman. I want to have a bath and scrub my skin until it's sore. I want to scratch all the memories out of my head and off my body.

The door opens, and Jonny comes in; his eyes are all for me. 'I'm sorry. Do you remember? I mean, do you remember where she lived?'

'Yes.' His kindness brings more tears and a sob breaks out of my throat as he squats down on his haunches in front of the chair. One hand holds mine and his thumb strokes across the tender places on the back of my hand as he reaches for the tissues on the desk, grasps a handful out of the box, and hands them to me.

I wipe the bunched-up tissues under my nose.

His hand strokes the hair that has escaped my ponytail and tucks it behind my ear. 'How much do you remember? Has it brought everything back?'

'No. Just snippets. It's like flashes. I don't want to remember, Jonny. But do you think we should tell Lucy about Susan?' My hand shakes in his. I'm afraid of what I see. All the fear of that time is in me, even though I can't remember the details.

Something runs around in my mind, pushing all the memories away, shutting them back into boxes.

'That's up to you.'

'What if she finds out and we haven't told her? The police might say something to her.'

'Then that's about Susan, not you. But if you want to tell her about you, then tell her.'

'I don't want to talk about it.'

'I know.'

I close my eyes; I can't hold his gaze. His eyes are too honest.

'It's okay.' He pulls my head to his shoulder and his arms surround me as he kneels on the floor helping me to balance in the dodgy little chair. 'It's okay.'

When I met him in London I was sixteen and Susan and I were living on the streets. Our job was to beg, steal, or bed. We were both heroin addicts.

I remember telling him how awful things were, pouring out that horrible truth. That I was doing things I didn't want to do. He helped me clean the drug out of my system. He looked after me, and we had planned to leave London together.

His hand strokes over my hair. I remember the days I lay in his bed going through the withdrawal. He stroked my hair like this for hours. It's a hypnotising feeling even now. He hasn't touched me like this since the accident. It feels good to have his attention again. To have all of his attention on me and not to have to share it with Lucy, or the café. 'I think I want to tell Lucy.' If I tell her everything then perhaps empathy will pull them both back to me.

Chapter 54

I smile at Lucy as I join her on the sofa. She's tucked up under a blanket, even though a fire is raging in the log burner. Jonny started the fire going for her before he left for work so the house would be warm all day. It's just the two of us at home. Michael has gone to work too. I took the day off.

Lucy turns and slides across the sofa towards me. I lift my arm and lay it around her shoulders as she rests her head against my breast and tucks the blanket in around her, settling in.

I'm going to tell the ugliest truths about the past today. That's why I've taken the day off work.

Jonny was wonderful last night. Last night was wonderful. He held me all through the night, kissed my forehead and drew circles on my bare arm as we talked. I wanted to ask about sex. To ask him why we aren't having it and if we could start again. I didn't because I didn't want to ruin what felt like precious hours.

But perhaps tonight ...

I kiss the hair on the crown of Lucy's head. I'm scared. I

don't want to tell this story. But it needs to be told. I want her to hear it from me and not the police. She should know

'I have something to tell you,' I stroke her fringe off her brow. 'I want to talk to you about our conversation with the police yesterday.'

She sits up, turning to face me, her knees curling up and her arm resting on them.

'Susan was in prison before she came here.'

'She didn't tell me that.'

'No. She wouldn't have wanted to. She went to prison for stabbing a man who fed her heroin and sold her to men.'

'What?! She said things were bad and she told me some horrible stories but she never said they were that bad. Wouldn't it be considered self-defence if she was escaping all that?'

'Yes. But, she stabbed him ten times, not once. I'm not sure it could be called self-defence.'

'But was she defending herself?'

'Yes, she was. They said she retaliated when she was hit.' Our gazes hold. I have to tell her. 'I used heroin too. Before ... I was an addict when I met your father for the second time.'

'No.' Her voice and her whole expression drops in a way that tries to deny my words. But why would she ever believe such a thing about her own mother?

'Yes.' I admit it to myself as much as her. 'Susan started it. She started everything bad in our lives. She chose the wrong man to play with in London.'

'Really?'

'That's the main reason I didn't want her here. I don't want to remember that part of my life.'

'What happened?'

A log explodes in the burner, smashing sparks against the glass door, like a firework explosion. We both look and I think we both wonder if it's a warning to me not to say this.

I look back at Lucy. The movement of my head draws her gaze back to me. 'We met some boys when we were in the care home. As usual, they were older. All the boys that Susan found were older. And, like always, she picked one of them first and I was left to endure whichever one of them was interested in me. But when she fell out with that boy, he made her life, *our* lives, hell and she decided we should run away.'

'I thought you weren't as close after Dad left. Why would you go along with her?'

'We were close again in the care home. We only had each other to rely on. The past was forgotten and we trusted one another again. There was no one else to trust.' A cracked laugh escapes my throat. 'We used to pretend we were one another in the care home. Everyone was confused. But Susan didn't tell you why I hit the man I thought was attacking her. He had tried to touch me when Susan wasn't there. He touched me over my clothes and then pushed his hand into my jeans, and he only stopped when I slapped him. I knew afterwards, after I'd seen him with Susan, that he thought I was Susan and that I was just playing around. When I hit him with the ashtray, I thought he was attacking her too.'

'Why didn't you tell me that before?'

'Because it's horrible. But the police know all of this, and they might say something. So I want to be the one who tells you.'

'But, Mum, I'm no—'

'Please. Let me finish. When we ran away from the children's home, we hitchhiked to London. We were naïve. Susan had this beautiful vision of how we could live out the last couple of months until we were sixteen then we would find jobs. But we didn't know anyone there. We had nowhere to stay and no money to buy anything. At least in care we'd had an allowance. Susan's way of paying for things was to trade sex for money but she couldn't control that in London. She traded with the wrong man.

'Chris was clever. He pretended he had fallen for her; he asked us to come and live in his flat. He gave us food, alcohol, and drugs. Cannabis first and then when we were stoned he injected us with heroin. We weren't given a choice. He wanted us to be addicts so he would be in control. He wanted us to need him.

'He hadn't fallen for Susan; he'd seen a business opportunity. The novelty value of two for one. Underage twins were a rare luxury. Men paid.' I don't even know when the tears started to run, but my cheeks are wet. Lucy will never be able to imagine the reality and I don't want her to be able to. I wipe my cheeks with the heel of my hand and the cuff of my jumper.

She moves the blanket off her lap and gets up. 'Do you want a cup of tea?'

'Yes please.' She is kind like her father. I should never have doubted her reaction. I wipe my face again, then wipe my hand on my leggings.

She comes back with a box of tissues and drops it in my lap, then goes away again to make the tea.

'You're still meant to be resting. I should be making tea for you.' My words follow her back towards the kitchen.

'I'm meant to be doing a little more each day to build up my strength.' Her back is to me. I think this tea break is for her too. To gain some time to adjust to the knowledge that her mother had been a prostitute as a young teenager. It's not a thing anyone wants to know. Or do.

I yank out a tissue, blow my nose, and hold the crushed paper in my fist as the kettle boils in the kitchen. The memories are there. Vivid things that have woken me up through the years, covered in sweat for a fear I haven't understood. I remember the counselling, but the psychological wounds of that life won't heal. I've tried to cover them with plasters, but they're festering sores. I could vomit; the nausea presses at the back of my throat.

'Here you are, Mum.' She puts a mug down for me then sits down facing me again, her knees bent up and her mug embraced in two hands.

'Can I tell you the rest?' I say, pulling out another tissue.

She nods as I blow my nose and keep the second tissue crushed in the same hand.

'He made us go to houses and places he had arranged and sold us to more than one man at a time, and sold us several times a day. If we didn't go he would hit us. Our lives were not our own.'

'How did you meet Dad then?'

'It was luck, Lucy, or fate. I don't know. Just an accidental meeting. We were in the same place at the same time. But he was so kind. He wanted to help. He helped me. But ...' Her sweet, beautiful pale blue eyes, so like mine and Susan's, look their horror at me, the pupils large. I want to tell her everything. But I can't do that. I shake my head as I speak the last words that I'm going to say. 'Susan stayed there.' Lie. It's a lie. But I can't admit the truth; it would destroy the whole family. It will never be known.

'That's awful, Mum.' She leans sideways and puts her mug on the table, then moves forward onto her knees and wraps her arms tightly around me in the same way Jonny did last night. 'I'm sorry you had to go through that.'

I hold on tight, as if I am falling.

But she pulls away in a sudden movement. It feels as if she's ripped herself free from me, like a plaster tearing off my skin. 'How did you meet Dad on a street if this man kept you locked up?'

'He didn't lock us up. I said he controlled us. He controlled us through fear and an addiction to heroin. We were allowed to leave his flat, but the need for heroin brought us back. In the end, you don't take heroin for the release of the rush, you take it just to be well enough to live.' I hold her hands in mine and press them together, pinning her here with me so she won't run from me.

Concern cuts through her beauty and furrows her forehead, drawing her eyebrows into a slight vee. 'But you left Susan there ...'

'Not by choice. I went back for her.'

'And Dad helped you get away?'

'That was the plan. He had a job to come to, here in Cumbria. He was going to take us both with him.'

She hasn't taken her hands out of mine.

She breathes slowly, controlling her breaths, perhaps controlling her thoughts. Her head shakes fractionally. She is shocked. 'I don't know what to say, Mum. Susan said your lives were awful, but I didn't understand ... I thought you should have told me. I see now why you didn't. I'm sorry.'

I pull her forward and wrap my arms around her, holding her tightly as she holds me.

Neither of us says anything else. We don't need to. It doesn't matter. Susan has gone. Everything will be all right. Jonny and I are strong again, and Lucy and I are close.

Chapter 55

The Bluetooth speakers are shouting out Taylor Swift's album *Reputation*, playing the song 'I Did Something Bad', as I dance, skating over the wooden floor like Hugh Grant in *Love Actually*. I'm wearing a pale pink shirt that I took out of Jonny's wardrobe and the sexiest set of bra and knickers – virtually a thong – that I could find in Sarah's top drawer beside the bed, matched with a pair of her little woolly bed socks.

I perform a victorious, self-celebratory spin that brings me to where my glass of wine is standing on the mantelpiece. I drink down the last few mouthfuls, then lick away the ruby-red dribble from the edge of the glass, pick up the bottle, and fill the glass again.

'To me!' I shout out to the speakers as I lift the glass high in a toast. I'm excited. I feel as if everything that happened in the past will be rectified by the future. It had a reason, a purpose, if this becomes the truth. I take another drink then put the glass down and dance again. Laughing. Smiling. I don't think I've ever been so happy. This house is beautiful. It has everything.

I feel a little like I had as a child, when I'd used Mum's make-up, only today I'm dressed up in Sarah's make-up and clothes. When I looked through her wardrobe it felt as if her shoes should be several sizes too big, like Mum's were. Of course, they fit me perfectly. Cinderella's slippers. Dozens of them.

All her clothes fit me perfectly, and the house, and her car and her daughter and her husband. Laughter breaks from my throat. Drunk laughter. Out-of-breath laughter.

The underfloor heating is warm. It's luxurious, this house - this life. It should be my turn to enjoy it. She's had her share of it.

'Don't Blame Me' plays out from the speakers. I spin, drop to my knees, wave my arms around to the song, and roll to my back as the wine flows in my blood. At the end of the song I'm still on my back, on the floor, laughing up into the air.

The stupid old chiming clock they have on one wall, that fits in with nothing else in the house, dings out twelve out-of-tune little ringing thuds.

I should go to bed soon. I have to be at the café by seven-thirty in the morning. With Jonny and Sarah away, the place is reliant on the rest of us and I do want to keep their little money spinner going. Marie said Boxing Day always brings in lots of walkers; if the weather is sunny people want to walk off all they ate on Christmas Day.

I stay on the floor and sing along to 'Delicate' then get up and pick up the glass of wine as 'Look What You Made Me Do' begins. I toast to every chorus and shout out the words of the song.

I finish off the wine in the glass when the song ends and press the icon on my phone to stop the music playing. It's time to crawl into their big cosy bed and sleep on their soft Egyptian-cotton covered pillows. I've been sleeping in their bed like a starfish trying to use it all. Like Goldilocks, I'm making the most of everything I have here in the week they're all away. No one knows I'm here. I stole the key from Lucy when she left her handbag with me in the club the other week. I thought she might notice that it was gone, but she obviously hasn't, or hasn't said anything to Sarah and Jonny. They hadn't changed the locks.

I let myself in and there is no chance of anyone discovering me here. They are in Tenerife for another week and Lucy is in Slough with Michael's family this week. I have this house and this life to myself while Lucy, Sarah, and Jonny are all far far away.

It's fun living out Sarah's life. Stealing it for a week. I don't have her husband, but I have everything else, and he will come.

My head is a little fuzzy from the wine and my walk to the bedroom takes a little detour against a wall as I stumble. I hum the song 'I Did Something Bad', then break into quiet singing as I make my way to their bedroom. The slippery socks are now a hindrance to my stability.

I turn off the switch that controls all the lights in the open-plan area and open one of the scarce doors in this house, reaching to turn on the light in the bedroom. But I don't need to turn on the light. There's a blue light circling around the bedroom walls and reflecting on the white ceiling. My eyes follow the light around. I know the colour. Police blue.

What are they doing here?

Has someone told them I'm here?

My feet don't feel a part of my wine-pickled body, but I get them and me over to the bedroom window, or they get me there, one way or the other. I pull the blind out a couple of millimetres so I can look through a gap.

A police car is on the drive, and there's one police officer in a black uniform illuminated by the automatic light on the wall near the garage. He's standing with his hands on his hips, looking at the living room windows.

Well, I'm the sister and the sister-in-law of the owners. You can do your worst mate. I have a reason to be here and a key; you can't accuse me of breaking in. I haven't broken anything. Yet ... I smile and pull at the cords of the annoying blind to raise it so I can reach the window latch. When he sees me, I wave, and then open the window to speak.

'Hello!' I shout out. 'Can I help you?' He's only a few feet away from the ground floor bedroom.

He lifts the brim of his hat a little then resettles it on his forehead as he walks forward. 'Yes. Sorry to bother you late at night. A neighbour reported seeing someone in the house and the residents thought you were on holiday.' His expression implies that he's recognised me, but he thinks I'm Sarah.

'Yes, It's my sister's house. I'm housesitting.' He can probably hear the alcohol in my voice, but I'm not drunk like

Jonny was the other week and there's no crime in having a drink in the privacy of your own home.

He's just outside the window.

'Susan,' he says, and nods.

I remember his face. He comes into the café in plain clothes; he's a walker when he's not working. He comes in for an early breakfast sometimes. 'Hello, Mr Reynolds.'

'So, everything's fine ...?' he says with a note of caution as if he's not sure.

'Yes. Everything's fine.'

'Okay.' He nods, obviously deciding that there's nothing to investigate.

'Thank you for coming out,' I say. 'I'd rather you did check if someone has seen or heard something.'

'You're welcome, Susan. I'll probably see you in the café on Sunday morning.'

'Yes. See you then.' I pull the window closed as he turns away, and wind down the blind.

Now I'm going to have to come up with a reason for being in the house if he says something to Emma, Marie, or Stan, or Jonny and Sarah when they come home.

I'll think of something. I'm too tired to think of something tonight, though. It's a shame I couldn't just tell him I'm Sarah. If the police stopped me in the car I planned to tell them I'm Sarah. I hadn't thought about them knowing she is away.

I'll have to get a taxi to the café tomorrow. I've been parking her car a little down the road and walking the rest of the way, just so Marie and the others don't see me driving it.

Chapter 56

2019

I turn the key in the lock, push the door open, and reach inside to turn on the lights. Warm air sweeps out, carrying that lovely welcoming feeling of being home. Holidays are wonderful, but home is always the place I want to be in the end.

I hold the door open for Jonny to carry the suitcases in.

We had a good break. We'd needed some time to be us and we'd found it. For the last few months we've let ourselves become submerged by the café and Susan's nonsense. It all feels so far away from us now.

We spent hours talking, laughing over nothing, and our sex life developed a new spark. We agreed on the flight out that we would shut everything else out for two weeks and focus on ourselves and our happiness. I feel as if we got to know each other again.

We share a smile before I close the door, then he walks past me, carrying the cases to the bedroom.

'Do you want a cup of coffee or tea?' I call after him as he disappears around the corner.

'Tea please,' he calls back.

I pick up all the post that's scattered on the coir mat and start looking through the envelops as I walk over to the kitchen. I don't open anything, just drop the pile of white envelops and junk mail on the dark slate of the breakfast bar.

I tip the old water out of the kettle, refill it, and switch it on to start heating. Then I open the cupboard to take out the mugs.

There's something different about the mug cupboard. My hand hovers without picking one up. I always turn the handles of the mugs to the right so the artwork on the sides shows. Two of the mugs are straight. The handles point towards me. The whole front row of mugs is not quite right; they are all askew, twisted in slightly different angles. Why? I wouldn't have left them like that and Jonny wouldn't have either. Even Lucy follows my habit because she grew up with it. It's a small thing, but I like certain things just so, and Jonny and Lucy are too used to me complaining if the cupboard doesn't look right.

Maybe Lucy did it to annoy me, or for a joke. If so, it isn't funny.

I take out the two cups with handles pointing towards me and put them in the sink to be washed, choose two others to use, and reposition those left in there before I close the cupboard door.

I open the tea caddy and release the aroma of the ground tea. Tea is not as satisfying a smell as coffee; it's like a sweet wine compared to dry wine, the coffee smell being sweeter to the senses. My fingers reach into the china caddy. They have to reach further to find a teabag than I think they should.

Is it mad to think someone has taken teabags while we were away? But I'm sure I refilled the caddy before we left.

Am I going mad?

Did I imagine refilling it?

I put teabags into the mugs and put the lid back on. Then I can't resist the urge: I open the cutlery drawer looking for things that have moved. Nothing looks odd.

The kettle is boiling but I don't make the tea. I open the china cupboard. The plates are stacked in the same way they always are.

Nothing else in the kitchen looks different.

My gaze reaches into the living room. It's minimalist; there isn't much in there to move. But there is a bronze figurine on the mantlepiece, a seated naked woman. She has been moved. I think. Steam spews from the kettle and it switches itself off as I leave the kitchen and walk over to the mantlepiece. She's only moved slightly; the foot that stretches out the farthest is facing more towards the sofa. It's no more than about five millimetres out of line but I'm sure she's been moved. Deliberately or accidentally? I turn her back.

My eyes study the whole the room. Is there anything else? I can't see anything else. But what about somewhere else?

I walk along the hall towards the bedroom as Jonny comes out of it. 'Something's happened,' I say, my arm knocking against his as we pass.

'What do you mean?' He turns back and follows me.

'There's something wrong.' I walk on and into the bedroom.

'Sarah?'

The bedside lamp on his side of the bed has moved two centimetres to the left. I put the lamps exactly in the middle of the square cupboards; his is off centre. 'Did you move the lamp?' I look back at him as I point.

One of his hands is holding the door frame. He shakes his head. 'What's happened?' His voice is laboured. It has been energetic and interested every time we talked while we were away. He doesn't really want to know what I think has happened.

I walk over and pull open both the doors of my wardrobe. Lots of things have moved, my dresses are not in the right order and my shoes are muddled up. The jumpers on the shelf have been moved around. They are messy, chaotic. I shut the wardrobe.

Jonny's hand falls off the doorframe and he walks into the room. 'What is it?' Perhaps now he can see that this is more than nothing. It's serious.

I turn to my drawers and open the top drawer. My underwear and the bits and pieces I keep in there are so muddled it looks as if someone has turned everything upside down and then just pushed it flat.

Who would come into the house look at things and move things and take nothing other than teabags? I look at Jonny. 'Look at your clothes.'

'Why?'

'Just look. See if anything's been moved.'

'What do you mean?' His voice is confused, but he's walking across the room; he isn't waiting for my explanation or to be persuaded. He opens the wardrobe doors.

'Have your clothes been moved?'

'Perhaps.' He's still looking.

My arms fold over my chest and I hold on to my elbows. She has invaded this space absolutely while we were gone. 'I think she was here.'

He looks at me. 'She?'

'Susan.' I thrust the name at him. We haven't spoken her name for two weeks. It's a bloody curse.

His expression changes. The Jonny I spent the last week with has gone. He's frowning at me, angry with me, as if *I* am creating a problem. She's causing another argument, ruining our lives again. We've been back for less than half an hour.

'How could she have got in?' His voice sounds tired and disbelieving but something in his mind believes it because he walks over to window casement and reaches around the back of the blind to check the window is locked. It is.

I pull my phone out from the back pocket of my jeans and open contacts.

'What are you doing?' Jonny asks.

'Ringing Lucy to check no one else has her key.'

'I'll make the tea.' He walks past me but his body moves stiffly. With anger I think. But I don't think he believes it's Susan. Before we left he was tired of the arguments and lies, he'd said that. But he must understand why I'm angry about this.

Lucy's phone rings. I sit down on the bed, my legs wobbling.

'Hi, Mum. Are you home? Did you have a good holiday?'

'Yes,' my answer is swift and blunt. 'Did you give your key to the house to anyone?'

359

'Your house key ...? No. Why?'

'Because someone's been in here. Will you look and see if you have it please?' My hand rests on the pillow beside me. The pillowcase has a just washed feel. I didn't change the bedding before we left. I didn't have time that morning. I'd wanted to do it, but Jonny was in a rush to avoid the traffic. The pillowcase is white, and so similar to the other set that anyone who doesn't know they are different might think they were the same, but the piping at the edges is a slightly different width. The duvet cover is from the clean set too. Someone changed the bedding while we were away. Susan.

'Mum.' Lucy's voice pushes through the phone, interrupting the anger racing around my mind. 'The key is missing. It isn't on my set of keys.'

'When did you last see it?' My stomach is empty; there's a pit inside me, an empty black coal shaft.

'I don't know. I haven't had to use it for ages.'

'What about Michael?'

'Michael wouldn't use your key. Michael,' she calls, shouting away from the phone. 'Have you seen Mum and Dad's key anywhere?' It would stand out; it still has a small blue-haired Troll keyring that she had as a child attached to it.

'No, babe,' he answers from a distance away.

'When did you last see Susan?' my voice is rigid.

'Why? Do you think Susan took it? Why would she?'

'Because why would anyone else? Nothing is missing but lots of things have been moved. Who else would break in here and not take anything?'

'Why would she do that?'

'I don't know, Lucy, you tell me.' My thumb taps the red image of an old-style handset to end the call. Enough. I can't stand her taking Susan's side.

I close my eyes and flop back on the bed. I haven't been home for five minutes and she has destroyed my family again. Again!

The phone vibrates in my hand. I lift it and turn my head to look at the caller information. Lucy smiles at me in a round frame – a picture I took of her in a restaurant when I thought she was looking particularly pretty.

I don't answer. I don't want to be told that I'm wrong, or that I shouldn't be so quick to judge, or that I should forgive and forget.

I don't want Susan here anymore.

I sit up, stand up, and slide the phone into my back pocket. It vibrates again.

'I don't want her here anymore,' I shout out so my words will reach out into the hall and along to the kitchen. 'Jonny. I've had enough. I don't want her here.' I leave the room in a storm. Storm Sarah is going to blow in from the north and wreak havoc.

I look at my watch. It's seven forty-two. The café is closed. She'll be at home.

Storm Sarah sweeps along the hall. My coat is still in the Range Rover.

'I'm going to go to Susan's,' I say to Jonny as I pass the kitchen.

He lifts a hand as if he is ordering me to stop. 'Why?' I hear a teaspoon go down on the worksurface. 'What are you going to do?' He walks after me, like debris swept along on my tidal wave as I turn the corner to reach the front door.

'She took Lucy's key. I'm going to get it back and ask her why she was in our home.'

'Stop it, Sarah. Please.'

I do stop and look back, held by the plea in his voice. 'Tell me you didn't give her that key?'

'Of course I didn't give her a key.'

He shakes his head and his expression displays disgust. He's insulted by me asking. We didn't speak about my suspicions while we were away. About his deleted texts and his changed password. I wanted to forget, and I thought he did too. But what if I'm right. 'Are you sure?'

'Don't be stupid.' He turns away, to return to the kitchen.

I don't know whether to believe him. I don't know, and I should know. I can't believe him because of her. If she isn't here I won't doubt him anymore and we can be us every day.

I turn and pull my keys off the hook near the door. The key ring rattles because it hits the door as I turn the lock and open it.

'Sarah,' Jonny shouts from the kitchen. He didn't believe I would go. 'Sarah!'

I slam the door shut. It's cold; my breath immediately mists in the air. There's a layer of sparkling ice on the drive, and on the grass beside it.

I press the key fob to unlock the Mini. The car is cold inside, but it's been sitting here for two weeks. It needs a run. The leather seat presses the cold into my thighs as I pull the door shut in the same moment that Jonny pulls the front door open.

I push down the door lock my hand is shaking. It takes two attempts to get the key into the ignition. By the time it's in he's slapping his palm on the window.

'Get out. Don't be stupid. Leave it for now.'

'No,' I shout back through the glass. 'I have to stop this.' I'm not going to let her ruin my life.

I start the engine and turn the electric heaters on for the front and back windows to melt the ice. He slaps the window again. I don't wait for the windows to clear but start reversing, blind.

'Sarah! Sarah!' Jonny yells outside the car.

I turn the wipers on to try to clear the ice quicker.

The anger's pumping to the tip of my fingers and it's clenched in my teeth. I grip the steering wheel as if the car is my weapon. If she were standing behind the car, I would reverse into her. Strike! One hundred points for one of twins.

I drive slowly to the junction, blasting the windscreen with the air con on high to help clear it, and wait at the junction until the windows are clear, wiping the inside with the sleeve of my jumper.

I'm not concentrating on the road as I navigate the narrow lanes. I leave my headlights on full and glare them at another driver on a bend; they turn up their lights deliberately to blind me in retaliation.

The anger is so sharp I can't concentrate. I don't care. I just want to get to Susan. I will explode when I do get there. Lightning and thunder. Tornado and flood.

Another car travels towards me. I don't attempt to slow, but nor does the other driver hidden behind their headlights. I feel as if we pass only inches apart. I don't care. This anger is invincible. I will get to her flat no matter how badly I drive. Or how badly anyone drives at me. Because justice has to prevail. She is not going to ruin my life. I'm going to make her go. I want my husband and daughter back.

A tyre catches on a patch of black ice and the car swerves on a sharp corner. I steer into the slide. The car reaches an area of the road surface with more grip.

The torrent of my anger is powering this car not the petrol in the tank.

***

Zzzzzzzzzzzzz.

The lipstick moves away from my lip as my hand lowers. The angry door buzzer sound fills the room. 'Jonny's home,' I say aloud in a mocking psycho-killer voice. It's only half a joke because it definitely isn't Lucy's quick little buzz to say she's downstairs and waiting for me to come out. We're celebrating my graduation as a legally qualified driver tonight.

Zzzzzzzzzzzzzzzzzzzzzzzzzzzzzzzzzzzzzzz.

The finger presses constantly with no relief.

Zzzzzzzzzzzzzzzzzzzzzzzzzzzzzzzzzzzzzzzzzzz.

Jonny and Sarah have come home today, but would one of them really come straight here to have a go at me?

I twist down the lipstick and slip the lid over it, refusing to rush to the beck and call of the buzzer.

Zzzzzzzzzzzzzzzzzzzzzzzzzzzzzzzzzzzzzzzzzzzzzzz.

Whoever it is – and I'm sure it is either Jonny or Sarah

– is not here in a happy mood. They have not come for a nice chat.

Zzzzzzzzzzzzzzzzzzzzzzzzzzzzzzzzzzzzzzzzzzzzzzzzzzzzzzzzzzzzzzz.

But they don't sound as if they will go away if I ignore them.

A sigh of acceptance slips out as I walk over to end the torment of my doorbell. I'm dressed in jeans and a sparkly jumper, made up and ready to go out. Lucy will be here in about five minutes.

I press the speak button on the intercom. 'Hello? Who is it?'

'Let me in.' The voice threatens. Sarah is trying to bully her way in, in a thuggish way. *Hand over your home and your life.*

'Hello, Sarah, did you have a lovely holiday? How can I help?'

'Just let me in.' Her voice bristles like a hedgehog.

'I'll come down.' I'm going down in a minute anyway. I don't want her up here shouting at me.

I smile as I slip my feet into the heels I stole from her house and pick her key up off the top of the bedside table. I slip it into my handbag to keep it safe until I can put it into Lucy's handbag later. Sarah's spare keys are still in my handbag too. I've kept them as a useful memento. I had a nice holiday in her house and it seems as though my aim to disrupt her life has been successful again.

'I Did Something Bad.' Taylor's song starts singing in my mind.

I run downstairs smiling. Happy. I can drive. I can be

independent and even more disruptive from now on. I can be anywhere, anytime. I haven't worked out everything I'll do with that freedom, but it's going to work to my benefit in one way or another.

When I open the door, I smile at her as if she will be thrilled to see me, and wave through the glass.

Her hand is on the door handle waiting to pull or push it open, to break through and attack. Her teeth sink into her upper lip as I approach. The frown line between her eyebrows is deep. But I've caught her out; she had not expected me to arrive downstairs in her clothes and coat. Shock has knocked the anger out of her. I see her expression change.

'Hello.' I press the lock release and open the door to step out, not to let her in.

She isn't dressed for the outdoors. She's in her jeans, a sweatshirt, and trainers; she is pale and cold and surprised by what she's looking at. 'You've been in my house.'

I imagine that when she left home, she had come here to yell that accusation at me, but the fact I am wearing her clothes means she's just stating the obvious and instead the accusation falls like a feather not a stone.

'Yes. I wanted to see what it's like being you.' There's no reason to lie. No one else is here.

Her anger explodes into flames, I see it in her eyes, sparking like fireworks as her teeth grit and the muscles in her jaw flare. 'Get out of my life!' Her palm shoves at my shoulder, knocking me back against the glass door.

'No.' I don't straighten up. I lean back so she will have nowhere else to push me to.

'Why won't you go away? You're not wanted here.' Her voice is high and it carries in the cold air like the mist in her breath. Other people in the flats will hear her.

'Lucy wants me,' I speak quietly.

'She isn't yours.' The words spit from her lips and the spittle that accompanies them sprinkles across my face. 'Nothing I have is yours! *I* made this life! It's *mine*! Go away and leave us alone!'

Has she remembered? 'But there's room for me too.' I don't really want room. I want it all. 'And maybe, after all this time, this life is bored of you and it wants me.'

Her expression shifts, her anger building. She knows when I said *this* and *it* I meant Jonny. I mean Jonny. I know in the end he will want me not her.

'Please,' she says, desperation slipping into her voice. 'Just go away. You're destroying everything.' Her arms flail, waving around pointlessly to express her words.

She has no control. That is what she is displaying. That I am in control now.

Laughter slips out of my throat – quiet, sarcastic laughter that is perhaps a little manic. Ha. Ha. Ha. Ha. I can laugh at her now. Years of counselling has left me able to laugh at her as I ruin her life and watch it burn around her - just like Rome.

A car on the road slows down, its indicator flashing. It reverses into a place behind Sarah's blue Mini.

Sarah's hand slaps the side of my head.

The slap is sharp and instantly sore and stinging like a burn.

I hold up a hand to defend myself from the next slap.

367

'Mum! Mum!' Lucy screams as she gets out of the car. She shuts the door and runs up the icy path that a workman from the housing association spread with gravel an hour ago. She comes to help me.

I am still pinned against the door. Sarah's hand slaps again. I twist so she hits my hair.

'Mum! Mum!' Lucy is closer, but not close enough to stop Sarah.

I don't fight back. I don't need to fight back in anger. I spent years in prison; I know that staying calm, thinking, gives you the edge. Today or tomorrow, sense not strength is the winner. You learn patience by the bucket load in prison.

'Mum!' Lucy pulls Sarah's arm, pulls her a step away. 'What are you doing?'

'She took your key. She's trying to take you.' Sarah's accusations ring with madness.

What would she do if I just told Lucy now that I was her. If I just said it and became her. How could she defend herself? How would anyone even know the truth?

You're mad, I could say. You think you're me, but you're mad. I'm wearing her clothes. I could twist this around.

'Mum.' Lucy's voice quietens. 'Please. Susan isn't trying to take me, or anything.'

I straighten, standing on my high heels, her high heels, not leaning on the door. I want to break into applause for Lucy for standing up for me. But she's wrong. I *am* going to take everything. I've made up my mind. *Everything*.

'You don't understand.' She pulls her arm free from Lucy's and turns to face her. 'She wants your father. She wants my

368

life. She wants you because she had a child and she gave her up for adoption and now she thinks you can be hers.'

Another car races along the road, then slows. The tyres screech. It's the Range Rover. Jonny.

'And now all the family is here,' I mock. See. I am in control. They have all come to me. I am their circus ringmaster. The orchestra's conductor.

'Don't listen to her, Luce!' Jonny shouts as he leaps out of his car.

The zookeeper.

He leaves the driver's door hanging dangerously wide, on the road side of the Range Rover, and runs up the path, desperate to end this conversation. The soles of his shoes crunch on the gravel. 'What has she said?'

'I haven't said anything about her sister,' I shout past Lucy, calling it out into the night. Throwing a black-eyed toad into this cauldron, into this potion of discontent. The world has been told now. The truth is out. He thought Sarah didn't remember anything, but she remembered that.

'Sister?' Lucy's gaze turns to me. 'What do you mean?'

I smile and look past her, directing her question to Jonny.

'What does Susan mean?' she looks at him. 'Is that why you behaved so stupidly before Christmas?' Lucy's questions delve around in the family's bag of horrid history. She was kept out of it for years. I was trapped inside.

His eyes look past Lucy and accuse me of betrayal. 'She should know she might have a sister,' I say. 'I'll tell you,' I say to her. He won't. 'When I was thirteen, I fell pregnant ...' I leave the truth in the air.

'When you were thirteen?' Her voice accuses me. But then she looks at Jonny. 'When she was thirteen ... she had your baby?'

'I didn't know, Luce.' His hands lift, placating, trying to calm the conflict in a very Jonny way.

Avoider. Runaway. Run away.

'She was thirteen ...' Lucy hisses the words at him in a whisper of shock.

'She was adopted,' I say. 'But she might be your sister.'

'Might,' Sarah repeats, throwing the word at me, along with more spittle. 'She also might be Jay's. She might not be Lucy's sister.'

'She might not, but we'll never know,' I answer.

Jonny reaches out and touches Lucy's arm. She pulls away.

I'm leaving them with nothing. But, when you invade a city, you have to knock it down if you want to rebuild. Who are you Sarah, Romulus or Remus?

'Dad ...' Lucy's voice becomes a whisper. He was her hero. But heroes don't impregnate thirteen-year-old girls.

'It's true that he didn't know,' I say, tipping in more toads. 'He'd gone by then.'

'Bitch,' Jonny casts across his wife and daughter. 'Why say that? You know why I left. I left because you lied about your age and I found out.'

'She was thirteen, Dad ... If I'd done that at thirteen ... you'd ...' Lucy's voice wavers between accusation and doubt. 'How will I know if I have a sister?'

'We don't know,' Jonny says. 'I don't know. Don't you think I want to know? I didn't even know she might exist until the other night. I'm going to try and find her, Luce. I've already sent my name off to an agency to see if I can.'

Lucy shakes her head at him. Her judgement is made.

I look past her, speaking with my eyes and hoping he will understand. 'Lucy had to know,' I say aloud. 'It's time she knew.'

'And I should have known when you were pregnant,' he shouts. 'So this shouldn't have been a surprise to anyone.' His hands lift and fall. He looks at Sarah and Lucy. 'Come home. Come back and talk about this at home.' When Lucy and Sarah don't move he turns away. 'I'm going home.'

Would it be wrong of me now to say to Lucy, *aren't we going to celebrate?* 'It wasn't my fault,' I say. 'I fell in love with your dad.' I smile at Sarah as I say the words to Lucy.

'I know,' Lucy answers to me. 'I'm sure it wasn't your fault.'

Sarah looks at me. She thinks she's found some control. She thinks she can go and take Lucy with her.

She can't. 'Lucy should know everything,' I say. I'm still not sure if Sarah remembers everything. Even now nothing in her expression tells me.

Jonny is striding away from us, as determined to leave as he was energetic about arriving. He hasn't heard what I said. I'd like him to stay so I can tell him the truth too. I feel like breaking everything tonight. But for now, I let him go.

'What else should I know, Mum?' Lucy is afraid of the truth now. Scared of how bad this might be.

'You do have a sister,' Sarah says. 'I had a baby at thirteen too. Come on. Come home with me. Let me explain it.'

'You ...' Lucy is caught in the crossfire tonight, walking through a minefield of truths and lies. It is not over.

'Come away, Lucy,' Sarah pulls on Lucy's arm, grasping at her coat. 'Come away.' The urgency in her voice pulls harder than her hand. Perhaps she does remember everything.

I don't say anything. I let Sarah pull Lucy.

None of this is real, I want to shout at her. I laugh again, but quietly, as my arms fold over my chest. I watch them. It's cold. Even the trees have started to catch the frost.

Chapter 57

1989

'Susan.' I tap on the door. I don't want to knock hard and draw attention from anyone living in the flats around us. 'Susan. It's me.' My knuckles tap repeatedly. 'Susan. It's Sarah. Susan.'

The sticky bolt mechanism scrapes back on the other side of the door.

'Susan.' I whisper again.

The bolt sounds as if it's stuck and she's trying to jiggle it a little to free it and get it to slide back so I can open the door.

I'm scared even though I know Chris isn't here. My palms are sweating.

If Chris was here the bolt would be loose and he would be in the room, lounging on the two-seater sofa, taking the whole space up with his dirty trainers on the arm.

'Susan.' She hasn't answered but I'm sure it's her.

I waited outside until Chris had left, tucked behind the kebab shop's industrial bin. I watched him walk along the pavement, hands in his pockets, walking with a swagger as if he rules the space around him. He doesn't rule London, but he rules us. He runs a dictatorship in Flat 17.

'Susan.' She opens the door an inch and peers through the gap. Then she opens the door wider.

The flat we share is shadowy. The curtains are closed. It's dirty. The carpet is gritty. It's never vacuumed. Chris doesn't own a vacuum or a washing machine. The whole place stinks. He makes enough money to keep the flat and us clean, but he doesn't bother.

'Susan?'

'Mmm.' She retreats to the sofa, sitting in the far corner, leaving me to close the door.

She's not really conscious. There's a used syringe on the floor beside her and the rubber band she uses is still on her arm. She has taken heroin this morning, not long ago.

My heart. My blood. They jump at the memory, wanting to follow where she's led. Everything in me craves that feeling. There's a pressure at the back of my throat that's as strong as the need to drink water when I'm thirsty.

But my body is clean. My blood is as clean as it was the day I was born. And my head. I can hear things and smell things and taste … Jonny bought me fish and chips last night. We ate the meal from paper wrapping, leaning on the stones of the embankment wall alongside the River Thames. My nostrils were full of the smell of salt, vinegar, and crispy batter, and my mouth with the succulent flavour of the batter's crispness and the soft flesh of the fish. I want that. I want that a million times over and a million times more than I want heroin. It can sing to me, playing siren, and hold its arms out to me as much as it wants. I am not going back to it. I'm not.

'Susan.' I kneel on the floor. The grit in the carpet presses into my knees through the new jeans Jonny bought me.

'Mmm.'

'Come on. I need you to stand.' My hand surrounds her thin arm; my fingertips can touch my thumb.

I am this thin too. Jonny is horrified by how thin and sick I look. I saw tears in his eyes when I started shaking while we were sitting in the café, even though it's summer. 'I just need a fix,' I told him and his eyes had glazed with a sparkling fluid. He promised to help me. I thought he was going to buy heroin but he took me to his home and stayed with me, day and night for four days. He called into work sick while the world flew through my head in random, strange visions. Pink sheep, green cows, and blue birds. I remember.

'Where have you been?' she says, as I take the band I don't want her to use again off her arm.

It's been two weeks and three days since I last saw her. 'With Jonny.'

'Chris wants to see you.' Her speech slurs the words, letting the letters smash into each other.

'Did you hear what I said? I was with Jonny.'

'He'll make you work twice as hard.'

'Susan.' My hands embrace her cheeks and I turn her face so she's looking at me. 'I was with Jonny. Remember? Jonny. He's still in London.'

'Jonny ...' Her eyes look into mine.

'Yes. I stayed with him. I'm clean. He's moving. He's going

up north. To a place called Cumbria. He's taking us with him.'

'Jonny.' Her gaze sharpens, her focus closing in on my lips.

'Yes. Come on. We need to get out of here.'

'My Jonny?'

'Yes.' Only, he's not hers anymore.

'Come on.'

Her hands move; she pushes me away then pushes herself up to get on to her feet. 'Where is he? Is he here?'

'No. He's working in a restaurant in Southwark. He's there now. But I know where he lives; we can go there and wait until he finishes work.'

When she stands, she's wobbly on her feet. It'll be another hour before she's stronger, then another four until the heroin begins to withdraw from her blood again.

Her palms press against my cheeks and she stares into my eyes, looking for something. Pink sheep, green cows, or blue birds. 'You smell nice.'

'I had a shower at Jonny's.' I've had about fifteen showers at Jonny's, and every single time I stand under the water for what seems like hours because the warm water and the soap on my skin and the shampoo in my hair feel so nice.

'Chris will find us.'

'He won't. Jonny's leaving tomorrow. He won't find us.'

'Look ...' Her hands drop away from my face and she lifts her T-shirt to show me dark bruises spread around her ribs. They are boot shaped. She's been kicked.

I told Jonny I had to come back. He'd persuaded me to stay.

'Why go back and risk never getting away again?' he'd said. 'Get clean. Get clean and then you can go back and get her. If you're clean you can get her out and then we'll help her.'

He wanted me to ring the police but I told him the police don't listen to junkies. They don't believe us. We are unbelievable.

'Come on.' I take hold of one of her hands and pull her as I stand up.

'Chris makes me work double. Double men.'

She lets me pull her towards the door.

'What did Jonny say about my baby? Did you tell him about my baby?'

'No. You can tell him if you want to.'

'I want to see him so badly. I've always wanted to see him.'

'You will now. If we hurry.'

'Has he missed me?' She stops still suddenly, pulling back against my tugging hand. 'Is he sorry he left me with a baby.'

'He doesn't know about the baby, does he? But he's sorry we ended up here. That's why he wants to help us. Come on.' I tug her into movement again and with the other hand open the door.

'Does he talk about me?'

'Yes. Come on.'

'But he helped you and you didn't come back.'

'I told you I was too ill until now. Come on, or Chris will be back.' I pull her out of the room, leaving the door open. I don't want to waste any more unnecessary seconds. I have no idea how long Chris will be gone.

Chapter 58

2019

Iwatch Sarah and Lucy. Sarah's voice flows with a hurried need to explain, to console.

Lucy stops on the kerb as Sarah walks around the Mini. Sarah talks across the top of the car as the lights flash when the locks release.

I have successfully pushed them apart. But how do I take the final step and have her life?

Sarah opens the driver's door and the lights inside the car flare so I can see her clearly. Sarah closes the door and waves a hand. Lucy turns towards her car. The car's inside light goes out as Lucy walks away. A second later the engine stutters but it doesn't start. Lucy turns back and watches, halfway to her car. Sarah tries the engine again, and again. Lucy walks back.

Sarah hits the wheel with the palm of her hand, silhouetted by the streetlight on the other side of the road. I walk forward, with slow steps, over the grit that has been spread on the pavement; it grinds under the soles of my high heels and makes the walk, in these shoes, nearly as treacherous as if it was ice.

I know what's wrong. I didn't refill the tank with petrol and she hadn't checked the level when she raced over here in a rage.

Sarah opens the car door. The internal light turns on. Lucy has walked around the car to the driver's door. 'Mum ...' she says as Sarah gets out.

'It's out of petrol.' Sarah's gaze turns to me, sending me a look across the top of the car as I walk closer. She knows I've driven her car; the knowledge is in her expression, the accusation in the bitter twist of her lips.

If she speaks the accusation I will hurl the truth back. Like a hand grenade it will explode in her lap right in the heart of her family. I am tired of being quiet, of being nice. I feel like being evil tonight. If she pushes me too much, I will be.

'Come with me,' Lucy says. 'I'll drive you home. We'll sort it out tomorrow.'

Yet again, the flotsam and jetsam of their storms are washed up outside my flat, metal carcases left like whale bones on the sand. I might just find a key out of my handbag and there might just be a scratch along the side of the Mini in the morning. I also still have her spare car key in my bag. I could hide her car.

They walk towards Lucy's car. I'm still walking towards them, watching them as if they are here to entertain me.

Lucy's keys are in her car. She hadn't taken them out of the ignition when she ran up the path to intervene in the argument. I know what will happen; the image of the next moment is in my head as if I have a crystal ball and can see the future.

Lucy reaches for the driver's door handle of her old Vauxhall as I reach the end of the path. She pulls the handle but the door doesn't open. Sarah takes the last step and reaches for the passenger's door handle. Lucy pulls the driver's handle again. The door doesn't budge. 'Oh no.' She looks over the roof of the car at Sarah. 'I've locked myself out.' The car had locked itself with the keys inside it. Her hand moves to her coat pocket. 'I'll call Michael; he can bring my spare key over.'

'You can use my car, Sarah.' I step forward, look down, and open the handbag that's hanging from a long shoulder strap at my side. At the same time, Lucy uses her phone, lifting it to her ear. 'Then you can get home to Jonny,' I keep talking, my heart jumping into a heavy thump against my ribs. 'Rather than wait for Michael to bring Lucy's spare key,' I say as I pull my car key out and hold it out towards her.

What choice does she have? There's no way for her to get home without waiting for someone else to help. I shake the keys, remembering the keys that belong to her in my bag.

I have something else in my bag. It's a wicked thought. But I'm in a wicked mood. The little devil is shouting on my shoulder. *If she takes my car …*

'I'll call a taxi.'

'They'll all be busy in this weather. Just use my car.' I reach out further, offering the keys. *Go on. Take them.*

'I'm not insured to drive your car.'

'You are. Jonny told me the car insurance you have allows you to drive any car when you have the driver's permission.

He told me to take out the same insurance that you have so I can borrow his Range Rover if my car ever breaks down.'

My imagination is out of the starting blocks and it's running in a sprint. *If she takes my car …*

I throw the keys. Instinctively she catches them.

'Open it. I just need to put some windscreen wash in.' The windows all need scraping off too; the car is covered in a layer of ice.

I can't move fast. The pavement is slippy and my shoes have no grip. I steady myself with a hand on the roof of the car. The cold from the metal pushes through my woollen gloves all the way to my skin and the thin bones in my fingers

She presses the key and the side lights flash as the locks release. I walk ahead of her and step out into the road to open the boot and get the windscreen wash.

'Hi, Michael,' Lucy says behind us. 'I've locked myself out of the car. Can you bring the spare key over? It's freezing.'

'You can stay in the flat until he gets here!' I shout to Lucy as I pull out the bottle of blue screen-wash. I don't think Lucy is listening to me. 'If you get in the car, Sarah, you can open the bonnet for me.'

She steps off the pavement and we pass as I turn back carrying the screen wash, leaving the boot open.

'Oh, okay. No,' Lucy is saying as Sarah opens the door, while I walk around the other side of the car.

'Don't worry. No. Honestly,' Lucy says, her voice carrying in a mist.

Sarah sits down in the car and a moment later the bonnet pops up a few millimetres.

With the screen wash hanging from one hand. I slide my fingers under the bonnet to move the catch back and lift the bonnet. I balance the windscreen-wash bottle on the engine as I move the strut and slot it into place to hold the bonnet up.

'No honestly. Yes, I know.'

I lean over, leaving the windscreen-wash bottle where I had put it as I reach into my open handbag that's lodged between my hip and the front of the car. The streetlight illuminates the engine. The white plastic brake fluid container is at the back, I can see it clearly. My fingertips find the handle of the small sharp knife in my handbag. I carry the knife because it makes me feel safe. Tonight, I take it out because I want my life back.

The knife has a comfortable grip, that is why I had chosen this knife to put in my handbag, it's easy to hold. I reach across the engine, angling the knife down towards the base of the container and thrust the tip. The blade is sharp enough to cut through human flesh, it slips through the plastic, and immediately I twist it, opening the wound.

'Yes. Don't worry honest. No don't send a taxi. I'll get home okay. I love you too.' Lucy is ending her call, but I don't really hear her.

'Mum!' Lucy's shout pulls at my attention as I withdraw the knife. I lean back putting the knife into my bag and reach to unscrew the cap of the windscreen-wash bottle.

'Mum,' Lucy's voice is closer and it has dropped in pitch. She's behind the boot.

The passenger side window slides down as Lucy walks around to it. 'What is it?'

'Michael's had a drink; he can't come. Can you drop me at home?'

The windscreen wash glugs out of the bottle and into the holder, spilling over the edges and running down over the engine parts.

'Come home and stay with us tonight,' Sarah says. 'You can talk to your dad. He needs to talk to you. He really didn't know, Lucy.'

The blue liquid spills over the mouth of the screen-wash holder. I lift the bottle and screw the lid back on.

'He had sex with Susan when she was thirteen. It's wrong.'

'It was wrong. He knows that. But he didn't know how old we were.'

'Didn't you tell him?'

'Not soon enough.'

My heart pulses hard as I step away from the engine, release the strut, and let the bonnet drop. A heavy metallic thump rings out as the bonnet hits the car. 'Turn the engine on,' I call towards Sarah. 'Get the car warmed up and the heater blowing on the windscreen. The scraper is in the passenger door.'

Lucy is still standing near the passenger door. She bends down to open it.

Sarah puts the key in the ignition and starts the engine.

There's no going back. I've done it. *If she takes the car …* It's in the hands of fate. I don't know what will happen.

'I'll scrape the windscreen off.' Lucy walks around, crossing paths with me as I carry the now half full bottle of screen wash back to the boot.

'I'll scrape the back window. I can use my bank card,' I say.

A moment ago we were all at war. Now we are working together to send Sarah on her way.

As I slam the boot I see Sarah lean over to turn the heater up.

Lucy takes the scraper out from the pocket in the door and closes it. While I dig out my purse and pull out my debit card.

When I look down to put my purse back in my bag the tip of the knife is sticking out. My hand shakes as I push the knife down.

Lucy has moved to the windscreen.

I lean across the back window and scrape thin lines, breaking up the layer of ice crystals with the bank card.

Sarah didn't take a handbag out of her car; she can't have brought one with her. She has nothing with her that is hers other than her clothes and her keys. I scrape the ice off in horizontal lines.

I didn't think before I used the knife. Now I'm trying to predict what will happen. If the brakes fail, what could point it back to me?

'Shall I finish the back window? It's quicker with this. You do the side windows,' Lucy says.

I move to the back door on the driver's side.

Sarah winds down the driver's window. 'Lucy, are you going to come home with me?'

'Yes, I'll come.' Lucy taps the scraper against her thigh, knocking off the loose ice as she walks around to the passenger side rear window.

I look at her as her words sink in. 'You're going ...? I hoped ...'

What do I hope? Lucy is the only one who knows it's Sarah in my car.

I open the rear door behind Sarah and reach into the backseat. Something inside has taken control tonight, a sensation that just wants everything to be over and done. The devil on my shoulder. It's my turn to be happy.

I drop my bank card into the footwell, take the purse out of my bag and drop that on the floor as my other hand picks up a duster off the back seat and throws it into the front. 'There's a rag here if you need to wipe the windscreen on the inside.'

'I'll call you tomorrow,' Lucy says as I straighten up and move out of the car.

'Okay.' *You go. You can leave me like they did.*

I walk around the back of the car as Lucy opens the passenger door and gets in. I pass through the smoke and condensation billowing out from the exhaust to reach the pavement. My hands shake and I fold my arms over my chest and tuck them underneath, as if it's only because of the cold when it's really to stop my hands shaking. The bag hanging from my shoulder is light now the purse is in the car. If anyone found her keys, would they test them, or would they assume they were mine? But who would they give all of my possessions to? Her.

I watch them leave, standing on the pavement, with my arms held over my chest, dressed in Sarah's coat and high heels. Lucy looks back and lifts a hand to wave as they drive along the icy road with the break system secretly leaking.

It's not until they're ten metres along the road and the indicator light flashes to say they're turning onto the main road that I realise I need to follow. If fate plays its hand, I need to be at her house. I need to be where she should be.

But I don't have a car.

My gaze reaches along the street, searching for a solution.

If I am her from this moment, and her car is here ... I need to move it. I need to move me too.

Alan's white transit van is parked further along the road. He's a mechanic. He might have a can of petrol for emergencies.

My hand grips my bag to stop it rocking against my hip as I try to hurry back along the unsafe path to get to the door. These stupid shoes. I should have worn boots in this weather. I look along the buzzers. Flat 24. I press the button beside the sign for Flat 24 so it will ring once.

'Hi.'

'Hello. It's Susan, from Flat 15. Can you help me with something? My car's run out of petrol.'

'That was silly, love. It's not the weather to get stuck out on the roads.'

'Have you got any, or can you take me to a garage to get some?'

'You're lucky. I have a full can. I'll come down. Be with you in a minute.'

Every minute feels like an hour as I wait for him to come through the door from the stairs into the hall.

'Hello,' he acknowledges as he opens the outer door, bringing a sweep of warm air out with him. 'It's freezing out here; you should have waited inside.'

I can see he was all set for a night in. He's dressed quickly to come out and help me. His blond hair looks messed up by the tight neck of the thick black jumper he's pulled on in a rush and he's wearing boots with jogging bottoms that cling to his muscular thighs but he hasn't bothered to tie the laces.

'Where's your car?' His arms cross and his hands rub at either arm, fending off the cold. The keys that hang from one hand jingle.

'I'm in a rental. My car's in the garage. It's there.' I point at Sarah's Mini.

'Were you off somewhere nice?'

'I'm going out with my niece.'

'You take off the petrol cap and I'll get the can. Cor, it's freezing out here.' He rubs his hands together as he walks on, his shoulders rising in a muscular rejection of the cold air.

I turn away from him, slip, and nearly fall but he grasps my arm and holds me up. 'Steady, love.'

'Thank you.' I carry on to the car as he heads off towards his van. I look down, my fingers rummaging at the bottom of my handbag for her spare keys. I can't catch hold of them with my gloves on and shaking hands so I pull the glove off my right hand.

My thumb catches on the tip of the knife.

When I take out the key, I suck the dark ball of blood off the tip of my thumb.

I unlock the car then open the cap of the petrol tank while he unlocks the side door of the van and reaches in to take out the petrol can. He comes over to car with the can in his hand.

I'm sucking on my thumb as he joins me. 'Cut yourself?'
'Yes.'

Every single muscle in my body is trembling with the need to hurry, and the need not to show it. I hide my hands in the pockets of Sarah's coat.

The petrol glugs into the tank with the same sound the screen wash had made as it flowed into the engine of my car.

Maybe in a different lifetime, if I had no past, I could have liked this man. But I can't change the past. Or the future.

What will happen? What will happen?

In my head, the knife is in my hand and I can feel the resistance of the plastic as I push the blade. But then I feel the grip of a different knife; it sinks into human flesh again and again. Chris's body was soft; his stomach had received the blade easily, but in his chest the knife had hit a dead end, a rib bone. My mind had been lost in the repetition, then I'd revelled in it. I stabbed the knife into him long after he stopped fighting. To have the power to hurt him had fulfilled something I hadn't understood. The police were right; it had been more than self-defence. But none of the counsellors in the prison system had helped me understand why I found it so enjoyable to kill. He had deserved it, though. It had been defensive in the beginning. But this time it's different. She's my sister. If she does die …

And Lucy. I hadn't wanted to hurt Lucy. Just Sarah. Just … Susan. The evil twin is always Susan. It's Susan who led us into trouble. Susan who met Jonny, and Jay. It's Susan who was fooled by a drug dealer. It's Susan who killed.

My shaking muscles jerk my shoulders.

'You're cold. You should get in the car, love.'

After this I have to get to the garage and fill up, before I can even start to drive to their house. My house. I have to think of it as my house.

I'd thrown my bank card into my car, but I have my phone. I can buy petrol if I spend less than £30. My stomach is churning like a washing machine.

What have I done? What have I done?

Snap. He closes the latch on the petrol tank. 'That should get you to the petrol station up the road.'

'Thank you. I owe you.'

'You're welcome. You have a good night, and if you want to repay me with a drink any time, just say.'

I smile, dismissing the invitation. 'Thank you,' I say again. 'Goodnight.' I open the driver's door and get in, letting the urgency that's sprinting inside me spill out.

I might have killed her, and I have to carry on with this otherwise I will be back in prison, and I will still be Susan, still be alone. If the car crashes, I need to be in her house. Everything she has is just a tank of petrol away.

I suck more blood from my thumb, slip the key into the ignition, and start the engine. At least the windows haven't had time to freeze over.

I drive off, but my mind is not present; it's in that horrid dark kitchen with Chris. The dirty beige vinyl on the floor is covered with a flood of glistening red blood. The police showed me pictures of my bloody footprints and handprints all over the house. They looked like the handprint paintings children do.

Chris's hand had held his side after I stabbed him the first time, and the shock kept him still as I stabbed him a second time. He'd never imagined I would hurt him, even though he had hurt me every day for years.

Why would I not choose to hurt him?

An eye for an eye.

A life for a life.

He deserved to die. I had never told a counsellor that.

And Susan ... If she dies, her past can die with her.

I deserve to have Sarah's life. I'm the one who suffered the life of the evil twin. I want to be the good twin.

But I don't want to think about the blood.

As I drive to the junction, the devil sits on one of my shoulders whispering while the angel on the other is shouting.

She's my sister.

But look what she's done.

I turn left towards the petrol station.

The shaking worsens. I tremble from the inside out as my mind is thrown around in a wrestling match. I need to think. What if Jonny's at the house? He knows what I'm wearing.

What if she is there? What if they haven't crashed?

What about Lucy? What about Lucy?

Where are they now?

I drive onto the forecourt of the petrol station and get out of the car feeling just like the me who, unaware that she was covered in blood, stepped out into the street. But this time there's no blood on my hands. No one can see what I did. My gaze spots the CCTV camera. I lift the hood of Sarah's coat over my head. I rub my hands together, trying to stop the shaking then struggle to open the petrol cap. It moves free in the end.

I can't pay at the pump without a bank card. I press the button on the pump's screen to pay at the kiosk.

Life is normal here. There are a dozen pumps, and cars are coming and going. Everyone and everything around me normal; there is no blood, nothing is broken.

I lift the petrol nozzle and slide it into the car.

The knife slips into the plastic.

The petrol throbs from the pump into the car.

Chris's blood leaks in pulses.

For the first time in years, I want heroin. I want to escape these thoughts and stop the shaking.

The pump's handle rattles as my hand shakes, struggling to get it back in the fitting.

I want heroin so I don't have to think about what I've done.

But she made me do it.

She made me.

It's her fault. It's Susan's fault. It's always Susan's fault. She's the evil twin.

I bite my lip hard as I walk across the forecourt to the kiosk to pay.

I feel everyone's eyes follow me but when I look at the other pumps no one is looking at me.

I take my phone out of my bag and open the payment app. The man in the kiosk stares at my hand as I hold out my phone. He's staring because I am shaking so much but it's cold.

'I don't need the receipt,' I say as soon as the payment is registered as approved.

I ran away when I stabbed Chris, but not far. I had nowhere to run to. A police car pulled up beside me just three streets away. I would have run to her if she had been anywhere close.

When I sit in the car and close the door, I feel as though people can't see me anymore, and if they can't see me, they can't know.

I start the engine.

There are three different routes to get to their house. My house. I don't know if I'm taking the same one she did. But possibly not. I doubt she would have taken a detour via the petrol station.

As I drive along, my eyes scan every opening where a car might have gone off the road. I don't see any signs of an accident, or my car. But the night is black; I can't see beyond the reach of the headlights.

It becomes like a dream. I feel as if I will see her when I arrive.

But I'm nearly at the house and there's no sign of my car.

What if she is there?

I don't know what I will say if she's there. Or if Jonny is there.

That I am returning her car, that's what I will say. *Hi, I'm just returning your car, so I can have mine back.* If Jonny's there I will have to tell him, *she took my car, I'm bringing hers back.* If she's there then I will have to find an excuse not to go home ... because I can't risk taking my car.

I am Sarah. My mind starts chanting as I drive nearer and nearer her house.

I am Sarah.

'I am Sarah, the good twin,' I say aloud. I am. I always was, and I haven't been allowed to be Sarah for so long.

There are no cars on the drive. She isn't home, and nor is Jonny.

I park the Mini where she does, pull on the handbrake, turn off the engine, open the door and get out.

I am Sarah.

The soles of these silly high heels slip on the ice on their drive. I have to navigate it slowly.

How long will I have before Jonny gets home?

Will she come home?

What do I say if she comes home after I'm in the house?

Just get in the house.

I slide the key into the lock and open up her life. My life now, no more pretending.

The house is lit. They left the downlights on in the living area.

My shaking hand drops the key as I close the door. I pick the door key up and hang it and the spare car key I used on the keyholder, hiding them in plain sight as if they had never disappeared.

Hurry. The devil pushes. The throb of adrenaline rushes through my body, drowning out anything the angel says in my other ear. I need to change my clothes. I need to change before Jonny gets here. He saw what I was wearing at the flat. I need to be wearing something else. I strip off her coat and hang it on the hooks by the door where it had come from, kick off her heels, and pick them up.

I run around the corner, past the kitchen and into the hall to their bedroom.

Their suitcases are in there, unopened, left on the floor beside the bed. Her wardrobe doors and the top drawer of her chest are open.

I put the shoes back into their place in her wardrobe.

She often changes clothes after work. She wears black leggings and hoodie tops in the evenings. Perhaps he will just assume that I changed to be comfortable and think nothing else.

I strip off everything except her underwear, push the used clothes into the washing basket, find her casual clothes and put them on. I close the drawer and the wardrobe and catch sight of myself in the mirror. I don't look like her. I'm wearing the make-up *I* wear. She wasn't wearing make-up. She wears hardly any even when she does. I've been watching every detail of how she dresses and lives. I know how to be her.

Me. I am going to be me.

But I have to look like her.

I run to the ensuite bathroom, my feet bare on the warm wood floor. There are make-up remover wipes in the cupboard under the sink. The first two are dry because the packet has been unused for so long. I use Jonny's shaving mirror as I rub my closed eyes with the damp cloth, wiping the eyeshadow and mascara off, then removing lipstick, and the skin-tone foundation.

I can't put the wipes in the bin. Jonny might see them. I take them to kitchen, wrap them in kitchen towel and put them in the bin in there.

Then there's nothing to do but wait.

I don't know what I can say now if they come through the front door together ... Lucy, Sarah, and Jonny.

I wait near the door, sitting on the floor in the space beside the coats, their walking boots, and umbrellas, my back pushed up against the wall, my knees bent up tight and my arms wrapped around my legs. The whole house is silent until the oil-fired boiler for their heating and hot water switches itself on in the kitchen; it runs for ten minutes then turns itself off again. A moment later, the clock on the mantelpiece chimes nine times.

My forehead rests on top of my knees.

I am held on pause.

The long hand on their clock has moved just over another half an hour around the clock when a key slides into the lock.

As the door opens, I scrabble up from the floor. Jonny. 'Hello ...' *What's happened? What do you know?*

'Hello.' He doesn't look at me. He looks everywhere but at me. His eyes appear to deliberately avoid me. They pass over the room, looking at everything and nothing as he takes off his coat.

I touch his jacket. 'Where have you been?' His leather coat is warm.

'I needed to think.' He turns his back on me as he hangs his coat up. 'How's Lucy?' He looks at me now.

'She ... Lucy ... She went out with Susan. She isn't happy.'

'I didn't want her to know that.'

'I'm ...' *sure.* 'I ...' Now I have you I don't know what to say.

The Twins

'Are you okay?'

'No.' The answer rushes out of me, everything that has been paused rolls back into play. 'No.' I fall into him, my arms reaching around his middle and my cheek pressing against his shoulder. His jumper is warm and soft. He must have had the heater turned up to full in the car. His arms fall onto my shoulders but his body remains stiff. It's as if I'm trying to hold a statue not a man.

I need him. I want all the years that have passed to go away. I wish I could wake up to find all those years are nothing but a dream. That I just *am* Sarah.

He holds me rigidly for a few minutes until I choose to move back.

'You win,' he says. 'I agree, your sister is a bitch. I'm going to tell her she can't work at the café tomorrow.'

My eyes catch sight of my painted toenails. I don't know if Sarah painted her toenails. I haven't put my hair up either.

'I need a beer. Do you want one?' He walks around me .

'Yes please.'

When we sit down in front of the TV, I feel as if I'm still waiting for him. He doesn't talk. He stares at the images on the TV but I don't think he's watching them, or listening to the programme. We are at either ends of the four-seater sofa, and I don't know if that's normal but he doesn't seem to want me to move closer. But he doesn't know it's me beside him. I move my legs up onto the seat and hold a leg as I stare at the TV too, until he says he is going to bed.

He doesn't know that it's me beside him as we clean our teeth at the his-and-hers sinks, or that it's me who undresses in the bedroom at the same time he does. He doesn't know it's me getting into his king-sized bed. He doesn't know.

And Sarah hasn't come home.

Something rings with an old-fashioned ringtone. In my dreams I wake up in 1985 and it's Jonny ringing on the phone downstairs.

Then I wake up in 2019.

The red numbers on the alarm clock glow. 3:12.

The ringing has stopped. The phone is on my side of the bed but it wasn't that.

Jonny's bedside light turns on.

The ringing chimes again.

'What is it?' my voice croaks. The last time I looked at the clock it had been just after two. In the dark my mind has been spitting memories at me, memories of Chris's pulsing blood and images of fluid dripping down through the parts of a car engine.

'Someone's at the door.' Jonny straightens up, moving the duvet back and sitting at the edge of the bed. He rubs a hand over his face. I think it took him a long time to get to sleep too. His body had felt as stiff in the bed as it had when I'd held him earlier.

The doorbell chimes again. Now I recognise the sound.

He stands up and walks over to where he left his clothes and pulls on his jeans as the doorbell rings another chime.

I get out of bed and pick up the leggings I wore earlier. I pull them on as he comes across to go out into the hall. His hand rubs over his face again. 'This is something bad,' he says in a low voice as he passes me.

I follow. We're both barefoot and he is shirtless. He presses the light switch in the hall so all the lights turn on in the open-plan part of the house. Whoever is outside now knows we've heard them. His footfalls are quick and heavy. Mine are light. I walk on my toes as though, because I am silent, my secrets will be kept.

He reaches out to turn the lock and open the door. I stand behind him.

Two uniformed policewomen are outside. Their breath is a mist as the cold air and the warm air from the house cross over.

'Hello. Is it Mr Moorell?' The woman who is closest looks at him and then looks around him at me. 'Mrs Moorell?' Her voice is gentle, tentative.

'Y-yes,' Jonny replies.

'May we come in? I'm afraid we have some bad news.'

Bad news. The car. Every muscle in my body trembles.

Jonny steps back, moving out of their way to let them through the door.

'I suggest you both sit down,' the woman says.

'What is it?' Jonny asks without moving towards the sofa or a chair. 'Has someone broken into the café?'

'No, Mr Moorell,' the second woman says. 'Your daughter, and your sister, Mrs Moorell, have been involved in a serious road accident.'

My stomach heaves. I clench my teeth and swallow back the taste of bile as I press a palm over my mouth. It's happened. But Lucy too ...

'But they're all right?' Jonny's voice rises in pitch, disbelieving. 'Where's Luce? Where are they?' He moves, starting to walk around the first police woman as if he will see them outside.

Her hand lifts and stops him. 'Miss Moorell is in Carlisle hospital, in intensive care. We can drive you to the hospital now, if you would like us to?'

Jonny's skin has become white as paper.

'But Miss Tagney, Mrs Moorell'—the other police woman has very blue eyes and they look at me as if she can see who I am—'passed away at the scene. I am very sorry.'

Very sorry … I feel … lost. Empty. Alone. 'Where is she?' I don't know why I ask.

'At the morgue in the hospital. You will need to formally identify her, but the car involved was registered to Susan Tagney and her personal possessions were inside the car. We have every reason to believe that it is Miss Tagney.'

She believes it.

Jonny's eyes focus on me. 'Do you need to sit down?'

'I don't know.' I'm not sure of anything.

'We need to see Luce. She needs us.' He looks at the police-women. 'I'll get dressed. We'll leave soon.'

She nods but he's turned away without waiting for her response, or mine.

'The identification can wait until tomorrow, Mrs Moorell,' the policewoman says. 'Someone will call you tomorrow to discuss it.'

I nod. I'm numb. Hollow. Like dead wood.

I've got what I wanted. But now … the price.

The angel and the devil are here with me.

'We'll say goodnight.'

'Goodnight.' I sound like an android, an automated voice.

They turn and walk the couple of steps to the door to leave the house. One of the women reaches out to open the door, but then she looks back. 'I am sorry,' she says.

I nod.

They don't know.

She opens the door. I step forward and hold the edge of it, then close the door behind them.

I walk like a sleepwalker to the bedroom.

I am here. In her house. In her life. I am her now. No one knows but me.

This is my home.

This is my life.

Chapter 59

1989

I pull Susan along the short hall outside our flat then let go of her hand and hold her upper arm, just above her elbow, as we navigate the stairs side by side. We're not moving quickly enough; her mind is still too confused. She is disoriented. I keep urging her physically and verbally until we reach the bottom stair. The old Edwardian front door with its half-moon window in the top is ten feet away from the bottom of the stairs. The light from that small window is the only thing that illuminates the lower hall, but at this hour the sun shines directly through it, imprinting the half-moon pattern on the dirty black and terracotta floor tiles.

It's only as we cross the sun-warmed tiles that I look down and realise Susan isn't wearing shoes. There's no time to go back for them. I'll find her a pair from somewhere when we're out of this house and far enough away.

I let go of her arm to open the door. Susan leans against the wall. The lock and the handle need two hands to twist and pull the door open.

'Come on.' I take her hand again.

It's a warm, sunny day. The sky is bright blue. The sunshine makes her wince and lift a hand to shade her eyes. I don't stop moving and she doesn't even seem to notice that her feet are bare as we hurry along the street, half-running, not just walking.

'Hey! Hey!' The shout comes from behind us. Chris's shout. 'Hey! Stop!'

I glance back. I can run but Susan is in no state to run. He's about fifteen metres away on the other side of the street and he's running.

'Stop!'

Instinctively I run too and try to pull Susan with me but she's too slow. We can't both get away. It's impossible.

'Hey!' His voice is a few metres away, just waiting for a gap in the traffic so he can cross the road.

I stop and turn, pushing Susan behind me. 'Run! Get away! Run! Go and find Jonny. He's at Vanity's in Southwark. Remember it. Go!' I push her again. Pushing her on. 'I'll come later. I'll find you later.' I am clean. I'm strong enough to fight.

Our eyes meet for a moment as she understands, as she realises she has a real chance to live, and then she turns and runs as best she can with no shoes and so much heroin in her blood.

My gaze scans the street and pavement for some sort of defence as I face Chris. There are numerous people here. Lots of strangers. Londoners and tourists. Someone will help me, surely. I grasp the arm of a man. 'Please protect me from that man.' I point over the road. 'Help me.'

Chris is running between two cars; the second screeches to a halt as it nearly hits him.

His shaved head is bright red with anger. It gives the black tattoos that cover his skin a strange pink hue, and the small metal hoops in his lip and nose and the bars in his ears glint in the sunlight.

'Thanks for catching her, mate!' Chris shouts. 'Cheeky cow stole from me.' He's one metre away.

The stranger pulls his arm free from my grip and walks on as if I hadn't even asked for help.

'Help me. Please?' I look at a woman who's walking towards us, as I back away from Chris.

'Now, don't be silly,' he says to me, holding his hands up, palm out, giving me no reason to fight. No reason to try to pull away and make people realise how dangerous he is.

The woman goes around him and walks on.

I look at another man who's coming towards us. 'Please, help me?' He deliberately doesn't meet my gaze and walks past.

'Now, stop disturbing these people.' Chris's palms are still up. 'Come back to the flat and give me my money back; then you can go about your own business.' He steps closer. Close enough to grab me if he wants to.

'I didn't take anything.' I say it to the people in the street, my eyes looking for someone to be brave enough to make eye contact with me.

His hand reaches out and he catches hold of my thin arm.

I strain against him, trying to pull free. But I am thin and weak and he isn't. Just with an arm around mine he starts pulling me.

But I don't have to walk. I drop. I let my body hang in his hold. I don't have to stand.

'Get up.' It's a quiet growl because now people are looking at us. But they are looking with concern and then walking around us in a wide arc.

I won't get up. I won't go back. 'Help! Help!'

A man stops and opens his mouth as if he's going to speak. Chris looks at him and speaks first. 'She can't help it. She's autistic, mate,' he says.

The man walks on and Chris bends down and picks me up, as if I weigh nothing. He lifts me over his shoulder and holds me there with an arm across the back of my thighs, like a fireman carry. I kick his stomach with my feet and hit his back with my fists.

How can he kidnap me in a busy street? Cars and people, even a scarlet double-decker bus, pass us. No one stops. No one helps me. I remember something from school. From primary school where we read the story of Romulus and Remus. In assembly once the headmistress told a parable about the Good Samaritan. Only, before the Samaritan came everybody walks past and they don't help the wounded man. 'Help! Help me!'

'It's all right. She's autistic. Can't help it, poor lamb.' Chris shouts over my screams.

If I was in Cirencester? If I had stayed there, in the children's home? If I was in a small town and not a huge city, would a stranger stop? Would this be different? I kick, scream, and hit but I know I sound as if I'm mid-tantrum. I know what they see: a teenager and an adult.

The Twins

The door into the flats is still I open. It's so easy for him to carry me inside and close the door on the world, on hope, on my future in Cumbria with Jonny.

'Fucking bitch!' His pitch drops to mean and threatening the minute the door shuts. 'Some fucker cleaned you up, 'ain't they? Well, one out one in, and from now on the door stays shut.'

I don't stop screaming. I won't stop screaming ever. Or fighting. But no one comes out of the other flats as he carries me upstairs, as easily as if I'm no heavier than a coat over his shoulder. I push on his back and kick.

The door of the flat hangs open. He kicks it wider to carry me through. Then kicks it shut with his heel. It slams shut and in the same moment he throws me off his shoulder, his arm at the back of my knees and his other hand pulling hard on my T-shirt. I fall with no relief because I try and kick and hit at the same time. I fall like a stone. My back hits first, and the air leaves my chest in a single shocking breath, forced out of my lungs. Then my head hits something hard. The room becomes a black hole and I am falling into it, sucked away from the world.

I am alone in the room, on the bed that smells of vile human fluids. The rancid smell throws bile up into my throat. I swallow it back down. My head hurts. It throbs with a vicious pulse of pain that's so bad I can't open my eyes. My fingertips touch where the pain is and find tangled clots of hair and a long sore scab. I move my hand and force my eyes open.

The bedroom door is shut, and I am in the room alone.

I roll to my side. If Chris is out, I need to get out. I need to get to Susan and Jonny.

The room twirls in a crazy dance as I sit up. It continues to twirl as I stand up and walk to the door. I feel as though I'm walking on the moon with no gravity.

I push the door. It doesn't open. I turn the handle; it doesn't open. 'Susan,' I whisper through the wood. 'Susan.' I call her as if she might be on the other side of the door.

Of course, she doesn't answer.

What time is it? How long have I been unconscious for?

If she's with Jonny, will she be in withdrawal now? If she's in withdrawal, she won't be able to come back and save me. Maybe Jonny will send the police.

How long? How long before they send someone to help me?

I feel too ill to stay on my feet. I'm dizzy. I kneel, my hand still holding the door handle, hanging on it, as though, if I keep pulling, it will magically open. It doesn't move. Chris has locked it on the outside somehow. 'Susan! Susan!' There's no noise but the sound of my own voice. She's not here.

When will they come?

I know they will come because Jonny won't go without me. We had sex last night. On the narrow single bed in his room. It was just as I'd imagined it would have been like if we'd done it years ago, the night I spent at his house when he took me to the abortion clinic and I slept in his bed.

When my mind had been withdrawing from the heroin and lost in a delirium of delusions, occasionally in moments of sanity I saw him sitting on the floor, watching over me like a guardian angel. When the delirium passed, he moved to the bed and held me at night. Then, last night, we were lying on the bed facing each other and talking, and I had the urge to kiss him. It was the easiest, most natural thing to lean forward, reaching the three inches that separated our lips and press a kiss on his lips. He kissed me back the way I had seen him kiss Susan years ago, his tongue pushed gently into my mouth, his palm settled at my side then slid up to my breast.

No one had been gentle with me in bed.

Gentleness in a bed is heaven.

Sex with a man who is thoughtful and selfless is a bone-melting thing. My drug-clean mind felt every single touch and the internal sensation was times a thousand. Times a million. Even now I can feel him.

He wouldn't go away with Susan and leave me.

When the door in the living room opens and men's voices flow in, I'm on the floor still, with my back against the door. My new clothes don't feel clean anymore. My jeans feel as though the grit on the floor is in them, my T-shirt has blood on it, and my cheeks are sticky with smears of blood and tears. I turn, kneeling up.

Is it the police?

'Susan's in there.' It's Chris's voice. There's the sound of a bolt sliding loose but it's on the other side of the door, of this door.

There are three men with him ... Three men. They are not the police.

I know how this will go. I wish I had heroin in my blood. I want the heroin.

Chapter 60

I don't realise my feet are bare until I've walked more than half the way to Southwark from Vauxhall, but it's a hot day and the pavement is warm. I have walked and run to find Jonny. 'Vanity's. Vanity's. Vanity's. Vanity's. Vanity's.'

The people I pass stare. But I don't want to forget that name. 'Vanity's. Vanity's.' He's there. Waiting for me. 'Vanity's.' I can't forget the name.

Lots of people in London are nice. When we first came here and we lived by begging, lots of people gave us food and something to drink. But lots of people in London are also rude. They don't move out of my way. They push past me and hit me as if it's accidental when I know it's deliberate. They stare, spit, and throw insults.

I just walk and walk.

When I reach Southwark, I have no idea where to go. I grab a man's arm. 'Vanity's, where is Vanity's?'

'Leave me alone, you drunk.' He pulls his arm free.

I turn to a woman. 'Do you know where Vanity's restaurant is?'

'No, love, sorry.'

'Does anyone know where Vanity's restaurant is? My friend is there!' I shout at everyone in the street, looking around, turning around, trying to get the attention of everyone. 'Help me! Does anyone know where Vanity's restaurant is?'

A young black man dressed in a suit stops walking and he touches my shoulder. 'It's that way.' He points up the road. 'Head towards Blackfriars Bridge, but don't cross the river. It's in a street to the right of the bridge, Hopton Street.'

I hold his hand. 'Thank you. Thank you.'

'That way.' He nods in the right direction and pulls his hand out of mine then walks that way.

'That way,' I repeat and follow him. But I'm a slower walker than him.

'Blackfriars Bridge? Blackfriars Bridge?' I keep asking people as I walk on.

'Keep walking,' one woman says.

How far? I'm tired. It's a hot day, but I'm getting cold.

'Blackfriars Bridge? Vanity's? Blackfriars Bridge? Vanity's?' I look from once face to another, looking for someone to tell me exactly where to go.

The walk from Vauxhall to Southwark seemed quick; finding Blackfriars Bridge and Hopton Street seems like hours. But then I see the white metal sign with the words in black on the side of what looks like an office building. It's here. My head, and then my body turn. My gaze spins around. The restaurant isn't near the main road.

I walk along Hopton Street. There aren't many people to ask, but the restaurant must be here. Somewhere.

There's a bend in the street and when I walk around the

corner I see the restaurant on the far side. The sign above the dark glass door is black with gold lettering. The writing is a swirly style, *Vanity's*.

'Jonny.' He's here.

I cross the road and walk up to the door that opens as I reach it. A man in a black suit comes out and his hand rises, palm out, in a stop gesture. 'You're not coming in, love, sorry. Go away. We don't want any trouble.'

'But I know Jonny. Tell him I'm here. Ask him. Jonny Moorell. I need to talk to him. It's urgent.'

'He's busy in the kitchen.'

A frown pressures my forehead. 'But he'll come out for me. I know he will. He'll come and speak to me.'

The man's expression changes. 'Wait on one of the benches over there. I'll tell him you're out here but he might not be able to come.' He points; his voice isn't angry, it has a kind tone.

'Thank you.'

I walk over the road. The area he pointed at is like a tiny park with a few tall trees and black benches between them. I sit. My toes press onto the pavement as my heels tap. I see now that my feet have been leaving little trails of blood on the floor. I've cut my feet somehow. My hands hold one another in my lap and shiver. I'm tired and I ache all over; pain travels in my blood. My blood wants heroin. My body is ready for more. The last of it is draining away and my body needs more.

I hold myself, my arms crossing and holding onto either arm. The shivers are worse.

I try to concentrate on the trees, on the tall trunks and the leaves in their canopies above me swaying in a breeze. I try. I don't succeed; all I hear is my body calling for heroin.

'Come on, Jonny.' I draw my feet up onto the bench and hold my knees.

My back is hunched over. I'm almost bent double over my knees, and everyone who passes stares.

'Sarah.'

My head lifts and turns to the sound. I look at him. 'Jonny.' He's walking towards me. He's wearing black and white loose chequered trousers and a white jacket with stains on the front. His hair is different; it's longer. But I know it's him. My heart remembers him.

'What happened?' His strides are long and quick. He's beside me in a second, squatting down in front of me as I put my feet back down on the floor, unravelling from my protective dormouse-like ball.

'I got away,' I tell him.

'I wish you hadn't gone back. You've taken it haven't you?' He holds my left arm and turns it so he can see the tiny blood-coloured dot on the inside of my elbow, and the similar scars. His gaze lifts up to look into my eyes. His eyes still have that appearance of gold in the sunlight.

He just looks at me for what feels like forever. Then he shakes his head. 'You shouldn't have gone back. What about Susan?'

'I don't know. I don't know. I can't ... I don't want to think about her.' This is new. This is something new. I don't want to remember Susan and the life she had. Let me be Sarah. Let me leave Susan there, in that horrible place. I don't want to be her anymore.

'What happened?'

I lift the side of my T-shirt and show him the bruises.

'Shit.'

His eyes glisten.

'You're shaking. You're going to have to withdraw from it again.'

The need for heroin jumps out in my head and screams like a monster. 'I can't.'

He holds both my hands. 'You did it before. Only this time, you won't go back. Shall I call the police to help Susan? Is she still in that flat?'

I nod.

His thumbs are stroking over the backs of my hands. 'I'll do that. I'll call from the restaurant. What's the address?'

'Seventeen. Seventeen, Vauxhall.'

'Vauxhall Bridge Road or Vauxhall Street?'

'I don't know.' My mind is not in a state to think of things it doesn't know. 'Just a flat, with 17 on the door, in Vauxhall.'

'Sarah, the police aren't going to be able to find that.' He shakes my hands. 'They'll need more.'

'I don't know more. Please. Just help me. I need heroin.'

'No, you don't. You need to get out of London. I'll finish. I'll tell them I have to go. It's my last shift; they can't sack me. Wait here. Don't move, promise me, Sarah?' He shakes my hands.

'I promise.' I have nowhere to go but here.

His hold on my hands pulls me towards him, and his lips touch my lips quickly. All the years between the last time he kissed me and now disappear. 'I love you,' I say. *I've never stopped loving you.*

'It's a bit soon for that, Sarah. But whatever happens, I'll make sure you're okay, and we'll look for Susan.'

I nod as his hands let go of mine. I reach out to touch his hair in the instant before he straightens up; it feels the same.

'I'll be back as soon as I can. Don't move.'

My eyes follow him as he walks towards the restaurant. He doesn't go in the front door, but walks to the side. I lift my feet back up onto the black seat and wait.

He has a car when he comes back. I sit in his car in the passenger seat and he drives around the streets in Vauxhall, while I bite my lip to stop my teeth from chattering.

'Do you recognise anything?' he keeps asking.

I shake my head every time. No. I can't focus anymore. My mind is screaming for heroin. My blood hurts.

We look for ages. But I don't think we drive along the right road. I don't see the house with the flat in it.

'I feel sick, Jonny.' I'm going to be sick if we don't stop driving soon.

'Then I'll take you home and we'll get you clean again.'

I just nod, as he drives away from Vauxhall. Away from Susan.

Chapter 61

2019

The smooth white ceiling above the bed holds my gaze. The clock radio is playing. I hadn't turned it off since the alarm had set it going when Jonny got up.

He hasn't gone to work. He's in the kitchen. He said we need to talk today. I think he wants to look after me.

We kissed last night when we went to bed. We talked about Lucy, and then I leaned forward the few inches and pressed my lips against his. He answered my kiss, his lips pressing against mine, and I slid my tongue across his lips. But his hand had stayed resting at my waist, holding me gently and not seeking more. It was thoughtful of him not to press for more. I was upset and confused and ... it was kind.

I'm sure everything will be normal now. We'll be a family, now Lucy is better and—

'Tea.' He walks into the room holding two steaming mugs.

'Thank you.' I lift up onto my elbows as he puts a mug down on the bedside chest next to me. I sit up and move the pillows up behind my back.

He doesn't go to his side but instead sits down on the edge of the bed on my side, his bottom pressing against my calf. His right hand rests on his thigh, balancing the mug. He put his jeans on when he got out of bed but he is still topless and the room is warm.

'Are you okay?' I say. There's something unusual about the way he's sitting looking at his mug of tea. His shoulders are rolled forward. I can see each vertebra under his skin, when usually my eyes focus on the definitions of the muscles in his shoulders and arms.

He glances at me, his head, not his body, turning. 'Not really.'

Not really ... 'Why?' *Because you feel guilty about the child?* Jonny and his marshmallow heart.

He shakes his head. His lips are pressed together in a firm unsmiling line. 'I've thought long and hard about this, Sarah.'

My feet slide up and my arms wrap around my knees. 'About what?' I don't think I really want to know. He doesn't seem to want to say it either, and last night was so lovely after Lucy went home with Michael.

'With everything going on with Susan, and then Lucy, there's been a reason not to say anything every day.'

'Just say it, Jonny.' Something I don't want to hear is coming. I can see it in his expression. His hazel eyes have lost their generous depth.

'I want to leave.'

'Leave?' I lean back as if he's raised a hand to slap me.

'I know you'll think this is out of the blue. I know. But we've not been close for a long time, and—'

'You mean you want to leave me?'

'Yes.'

'Why? Because of Susan. Because I'm not like her.'

A frown cements the wrinkles across his forehead. 'This is nothing to do with Susan.'

'Then why? I don't understand.'

'There's someone else. I'm sorry. I—'

'Someone else? Who?'

'No one you know.'

'But last night ... I don't understand. How did you meet her? When did you meet her?'

'Eighteen months ago.'

'It's been going on all this time?'

His body language looks defeated, that hunched-over appearance, the shallowness in his eyes, and the turn down in his lips. Or is it us that defeated him? I see it now. I see what his behaviour has been telling me for weeks. He didn't love Sarah *or* Susan. He doesn't want her *or* me.

'Why?' I ask.

The handle of the mug of tea is still gripped in one of his hands and his other embraces the mug as if it's his shield. Jonny, who doesn't like conflict. He's kept this secret for a year and a half instead of saying it out loud. Instead of saying, *I don't love you anymore,* he's been creeping around.

'I can't say why. It just happened, and then, well, it's not straight forward but I've made up my mind now. I want to be with her.'

I grip my knees tighter, holding onto myself because even after what I've done, I still don't have anyone to hold onto but myself.

His hand moves, reaching out, and it touches my forearm. 'I'll always have feelings for you.'

My arm swipes out, rejecting his touch. 'No. Don't act like the good guy.' Pity. Yesterday was just about pity. I don't want to be pitied. 'Whatever feelings you have they aren't good enough.' I kick at him through the duvet cover, kicking at his hip until he gets off the bed, his tea sploshing out of the mug. I go after him, kneeling on the bed, the duvet falling out of my way. 'What do you expect me to say?' I spit the words. 'That this is okay, Jonny, you just run along and be happy? What about me? Don't I deserve happiness? I deserve loyalty and love, not this. What is wrong with you? You selfish fucking shit!' I reach over to pick up the mug he put on the bedside table for me and hurl his niceness at him. The tea goes partially over him but everywhere else too and the mug lands on the floor with a ceramic clunk.

'Sarah. Stop it.' He leans to put down his mug of tea on the same bedside table where mine had been thrown from.

'Stop it! Stop it!' I mimic, scrambling off the bed. 'What did you expect me to do? Wish you well?' I push him, my palms hitting his naked chest and I push him again and again, forcing him back across the room until I've backed him, trapped him, into the corner behind the door, between the wardrobe and the wall.

I wipe away angry tears from the corners of my eyes with the heel of my palm as I stare at him. I can't believe it.

Jonny wouldn't do this. Not the real Jonny. He's kind and selfless and ... not this.

I don't want to be the one he pities. I want to be the one he loves.

'Sarah,' he says my name in a low, quiet voice as his free hand, fingers splayed, touches my stomach as if to move me backwards.

The shouting falls out of me and leaves the horrible hollow sensation I have lived with for most of my life. 'I don't understand.' My head shakes, denying. 'Why?'

'I tried to fight it,' he says.

'Fight what? Me? Why fight me?'

His arms lift to the height of my shoulders, offering to hold me. It's the welcome I wanted from the first day I stepped into this house. I just wanted someone to want me.

I lean into him. The hair on his chest is damp with warm tea.

His hand strokes over my hair.

'When we went on holiday, I was trying to find what we lost. I wanted to be sure. I didn't choose for this to happen. But then we came back and ... I'm sorry. It isn't the same. I will always love you in some way. But the feelings are ... I just ... I don't love you like I did, and after the holiday I realised I love her more. I know it's going to be hard with the business. We'll need to work a lot of things out and—'

'Bastard!' I pull free and thump his chest, imagining a knife in my hand. Chris is in my head. I spent years living through hell to get here. To be with Jonny. Years. I've killed for this! 'Bastard!' He's supposed to be perfect. This life is meant to be perfect. He's shit too. It's all rubbish.

He catches my wrists and holds on, stopping me from

hitting him. 'This won't make me stay, Sarah. Let me clear up the tea and I'll go. You can ring Luce or someone.'

'Go where?'

'Somewhere. We can't live here together anymore.'

I can taste the salt from the tears that have run into my mouth.

He moves around me and leaves me in the room.

Memories of another room haunt me. Of a dirty, foul-smelling room.

I sit on the bed looking at the puddles of cardboard-brown tea and lick away the tears that have reached my lips.

It's over.

Everything is over.

I have no reason to live.

He comes back with a roll of kitchen towel. I say nothing as he squats down to wipe up the mess I made, unravelling pieces and tearing them off the roll. The used kitchen towel forms a snowy white mountain near him as he moves around the floor.

I have no energy. No life to live. No one to live for. I want the promise he made to me thirty years ago.

Susan. The evil one. Susan broke this before I had the chance to take back what was mine. Like everything else, she broke it.

'I'll get dressed,' he says as he rises from the squat, leaving the pile of dirty kitchen towel on the floor, and what is left on the clean roll beside it.

I'll dress too. I don't have to stay here. I'm not in prison. I'm not going to be left here and locked in. I can go anywhere.

Maybe to see Emma, Marie, and Stan in the café. I need to be with people to remind me that this is now and not then. I want to keep going and pretend that life has not just exploded in my face. Again.

I lick more tears from my lips as I move to the drawers, turning my back to him, hiding myself. I rush to avoid showing myself – putting a bra on under my nightdress, sliding my arms out of the sleeves, and fiddling around beneath the stretchy fabric. Then I take a clean T-shirt off the top of the pile in the drawer and quickly exchange it with the night dress.

I don't think he's hurrying. It doesn't sound as if he's hurrying. I glance around. He's naked. He isn't hurrying. He's behaving as if it's any other day, not the day he's just said he wants to leave.

She was his wife for years.

'I don't understand,' I say again as I pull on a pair of jeans.

'I thought you'd guessed. You know things haven't been right.' He carries on dressing, pulling clean boxer shorts on.

'I thought that was because Lucy was ill.' I take a hoodie out from the drawer.

'Our marriage started falling apart long before the accident. Things have been wrong for years.'

I slide my arms into the sleeves, lift the hoodie over my head and pull it down over my chest and stomach.

I see nothing that explains this. I want the whole thing to click back into place. I want the cogs to turn the other way and move everything back to where it should be.

'Did Susan break us?' My arms fold and my hands pinch lumps of the sweatshirt under my arms and lumps of my skin too, to stop me from crying any more tears. I can't understand this.

His eyes look at me and he shakes his head before he reaches for a clean pair of jeans. 'I'll ring you tomorrow. We need to arrange some time to talk about how we manage the café.'

'Aren't you going into the café tomorrow either?'

'I'll take the week off. It wouldn't be fair to take this into work.'

I wipe my nose on the sleeve of the hoodie. 'What about Lucy?'

'Call her if you want to. I'm going to call her later on. She'll find this difficult but she's old enough to understand that it's better for us.'

'For you,' I correct. 'I don't understand it myself.'

He just looks at me, his eyes saying nothing.

I see the Jonny who helped me recover from rape, who helped me clean the heroin out of my body, who made love to me and promised me a new life. The Jonny who came to meet me in secret to tell me not to upset his wife with the details of a past they were pretending didn't exist. I see the fantasies that kept me alive in a crack house and in prison. They were only fantasies. This is the man who left London with my sister and left me behind, enslaved.

I killed her. I want to say it. To tell him. To break his pathetic valueless heart. I killed her!

He walks past me in blue jeans and a blue jumper that hugs his body, then bends to pick up the pile of dirty kitchen towel and what's left on the roll.

I follow him, pulled along by his gravity. Unsure what to do next. What can I say to change this? There's nothing I can do. I can't turn back time. If I could turn back time ... so many things would be different now.

He puts the dirty kitchen towel in the bin and the roll on the metal holder near the sink where it belongs, leaving things tidy as if nothing is changing. I see the filthy room that was my life in the years before I ended up in prison. This place is so clean, sterile, in a way I'm starting to understand. It's nothing more than a theatre set, a pretend home.

As he walks out of the kitchen, I turn to the drawer where the cooking utensils are kept. It's a small drawer hidden inside a larger drawer. I slide both of the drawers open. The runners are smooth and silent. I take out a short, sharp pointed knife. I've used it to chop carrots and celery on a board in this kitchen. I put it into the pouch pocket at the front of the hoodie I'm wearing and slide the drawers closed on a whisper.

Jonny's keys rattle.

When I walk around the corner, he's opening the door. He's wearing his coat and boots and he's leaving.

He doesn't look back, but maybe he doesn't know I'm following. He doesn't even call out a goodbye, but maybe he thinks goodbye is not the right word, or maybe he thinks there's nothing else to say.

I have more to say.

I push one foot into a trainer then balance to lift my foot and slip the back over my heel. I do the same with the other trainer, then take the keys off the hook and pull my coat on as I walk out of the house a couple of minutes after him.

He's not been able to make a quick escape; he's scraping the ice off the windows of the Range Rover.

I pull the door shut with a hard bump. He looks. He's on the step of the passenger door, reaching over to scrape the windscreen.

The Mini's windows need scraping too.

The engine is running on the Range Rover, spewing out poisonous earth-destroying, life-destroying fumes in a cloud behind it. The Mini will do the same thing in a minute.

Jonny drops down from the step. 'Do you want me to clear off your car too?' He speaks in a voice that denies he's just told me he's going to walk out on me for good.

He promised me a future and I finally found him, and now … 'Yes. Thank you.'

When I came to Cumbria all those months ago I didn't know Susan had taken my identity. I don't know what he thought when she turned up at the place where he worked dressed in dirty clothes and drowning in heroin. He'd cleaned me up, but she'd obviously convinced him there was a reason she was dirty and high again, convinced him she was me. He thought he was living with me all these years.

'Key.' He holds out a hand, palm up. 'I'll get the heaters going; it'll shift the ice quicker.'

I throw the set of keys. He catches them and turns to the car, releasing the locks.

My hands slide into the pocket of the hoodie and one hand wraps around the handle of the knife. I feel it, that push, the pressure of the knife thrusting into something that is soft and receiving.

426

He opens the door, starts the engine running, and closes the door, leaving the windows to heat on the inside. He starts scraping them on the outside, leaning over. The blue plastic scraper cuts misty stripes through the white frost.

This is the life I wanted. This is the life I deserve. A life packed with small kindnesses and a great love. He owes me that life. But today he took happiness from me. *Again.* I feel like screaming but I stay silent, and my fingers hold onto the knife; in the kitchen I had held the knife behind my back, waiting for the moment that Chris was close enough and I was strong enough.

I wait as he walks around the car, cleaning off the windows. The cold air is heavy with the stink of petrol fumes from my car and diesel from his Range Rover.

When he finishes scraping the front passenger side window, he walks around the bonnet towards me. His lips twist into an odd sideways movement of ... regret? Sadness? I don't understand.

I can't ...

He holds his hand out, offering the key for me to take, his lips forming a grim expression that curls them down at the edges. This can't be goodbye. He can't just leave. There's the café and Lucy.

My left hand leaves the security of the hoodie and takes the key.

'I'll call you tomorrow,' he says.

'Tomorrow ...' I nod.

He turns his back to me.

The handle of the knife is in my right hand. I hold it tighter, ready to push into soft, giving flesh.

He opens the driver's door of the Range Rover and slides into the seat. He pulls the door closed, shutting himself inside the sanctuary of metal and glass.

His eyes avoid me as he looks in his rear-view mirror, then twists his shoulders to look back and reverse off the drive.

I need to follow.

He's not going anywhere. He's going *somewhere*. Years ago, I couldn't follow. But this time I'm free to follow. He can't leave me behind this time.

The Mini's engine is already running and by the time the Range Rover turns onto the road, I'm already reversing, rolling it back so I turn off the drive a second behind him. His car is at the T-junction turning onto the main road. The indicator light flicking off and on as I draw up behind him. A white BMW rolls up behind me. It also indicates to turn left.

Left. He would turn right to go to the café, and to Lucy's, but he said he wasn't going there. Where is he going? Left won't even take him to Keswick.

Will he stop if he realises I'm following him? I don't want him to stop. I want to see where he's leaving me to go to.

He doesn't stop now. He carries on along the road. I drive slower, allowing the distance between our cars to grow. Further on, this road runs up and over the top of a steep, grassy hill. It'll be easy to see him even if he's some distance ahead. Perhaps he won't look back, if I don't stay close.

The Range Rover turns numerous times, a quarter of a mile ahead, weaving its way up the twisting road that's cut into the sharp gradient of the hill. I watch it, wondering all the time if he's looked back and seen me. If he will stop. Or if he knows I'm behind and doesn't care.

His car reaches the top and goes over the brow, travelling out of sight for the first time in nineteen minutes of driving. The lake, and possibly even the café, might be visible from this high up if I look back. I don't look back. My eyes are focused on getting the Mini up, through the pass, and onto the other side of the hill so I can see him again.

Over the brow, the road descends into woodland, a mass of managed pine trees. I can't see him.

Perhaps this is why he didn't care that I was following because he knew I was too far behind and he could lose me. But he doesn't realise that I will never give up. I found him within weeks of leaving prison and came here within days of my parole ending. I will spend every hour of every day following wherever he goes if I have to.

Narrow roads that look scarcely more than farm tracks turn off the road I'm on. I keep going straight, even though my gaze stretches down every track. There's no sign of his black Range Rover. The Range Rover can go where my car can't, though. Those little roads won't have been gritted and the ice won't have melted. This is a bus route. The bus routes are the only roads the council grits. The movement of a white car that's half a mile behind me draws my eyes to the rear-view mirror for a moment.

The woodland opens out and the road wraps around the peaceful setting of a small tarn. The water reflects a blue sky and the surrounding hills, some with snowy caps. This place is full of lies: it looks idyllic but there's nothing idyllic here.

In the distance there's a cluster of white buildings with black slate rooves. It looks like an old farmhouse with barns that have been turned into holiday cottages. There's no black Range Rover on the road beyond them.

As I drive along the winding road, descending towards the buildings, they turn from the size of dollhouses into stone and mortar. They are occupied. There are cars parked around them.

Jonny either put his foot down hard on the accelerator when he went over the brow and sped along this road, or he's in one of those houses.

The narrow road becomes muddy as I near the buildings and the Mini's tyres slide. I hold the wheel firmly, turning the corner beside the buildings. On the other side of the road from the cottages there's a dry-stone wall built out of dark slate, with sharp, jutting edges.

The Range Rover.

My foot slams down on the brake pedal and the car slides. My eyes stay on his Range Rover, even as the car scrapes along the wall. When it comes to a halt I pull the handbrake on, turn off the engine, and leave the Mini in the road. 'Jonny!' I yell as I cross the road. The old farm buildings are split into a dozen different properties. 'Jonny!' I walk through the mist of my own breath onto crunching dark grey gravel that forms the parking area. The Range Rover is parked among other cars. There's no way to tell which house he's in.

'Jonny!' I scream, my lungs hurling his name into the air. 'Jonny! Come out here! I'll knock on every door if you don't!'

The first cottage in the row has the name *Briar Rose Cottage* painted on a slate plaque by the door. Someone moves a curtain aside, looking out at me.

The door of the cottage three along opens.

'Sarah.' His voice is placating, pacifying, and his hands rise as he walks out. He's already taken off his coat. He's in his blue jumper and jeans.

'Why are you here?' I ask.

'Sarah.' His hands are not reaching out to receive me; they're reaching out to hold me back. To tell me not to come any closer. 'Let's go to the café.' The door stands open behind him.

'No.' I need to know who's in that house. I walk towards the cottage, not towards him, a frown pulling at my forehead because I don't understand this.

'Jonny, you've let the cold air come in.' The voice is light, female, sweet. A moment after I hear the voice I see her.

Jonny moves, his reaching hands trying to stop me physically, as a white car pulls onto the gravel behind me. But my focus, my eyes and my mind, are on the auburn-haired woman behind him. Her hair is really bright but the colour has a natural appearance. She's much younger than me. Than *us*. I'm younger than him and she's a lot younger than us.

I push him away with a sharp shove, with both hands.

'Sarah!' his voice has a piercing pitch to it as he warns me not to walk on. But I do.

She has a baby in her arms. A child that's probably not even six months old.

I don't understand.

'Mr Moorell,' a woman's voice calls out behind me. 'Call an ambulance, and I want back up.'

'Jonny?' The woman runs out of the house towards me.

I run towards her. It's Jonny's baby, I know it is. It's his child.

There are tears on my cheeks when I collide with her. He's fake. He lied from the beginning. He lied to Susan and I killed her, my sister. Susan's not the evil one, Jonny is.

The woman's body falls hard against me. I have to catch her and the baby and hold them up.

'Mrs Moorell,' a man's voice shouts at me.

Someone grabs me from behind, a man's strength, a man's arms. I push and kick, fighting as the baby cries. I remember my baby. I remember her. I had wanted a family.

The man's grip on my wrist presses into my tendons and the feeling becomes cold steel. The pain makes me drop the knife. It falls onto the gravel with hardly any sound.

His grip on my arm and my waist drags me back, pace after pace, and I can't stop him. I can't reach his arm to bite him and my legs are dragged. 'Calm down, Miss Tagney. Jenny, I've got her! I'll put her in the car then help you!'

Jonny is on the floor with a woman near him. His jumper has a large, dark stain spreading over it and there's a red puddle around him; she's kneeling beside him and pressing her hands on him.

The man drags me to the white car. Behind my back he opens a door as the muscles in my arms scream their objection to being twisted behind me. I feel a knee in the middle of my back pushing me into the car. I fight, twisting and pulling, tearing the muscles in my shoulders, trying to break free.

'Miss Tagney.' His voice is harsh. 'I need to help the woman and the child.'

'Get off me!' I won't let another man hurt me.

The pain in my arms screams as he pushes on the back of my head and shoves me through the door into the car. I fall face down onto the backseat. He pushes my kicking legs in behind me.

Other voices rise from beyond him. People are coming out of the other houses. The door slams shut behind me. The shouts and screams outside break through into the car. The baby cries.

'Get something to stem the flow of blood!' His yell pierces through the car's glass.

I roll to the side, sit up, and hit my forehead against the window, desperately trying to break it and get out.

Chapter 62

Lucy walks across the room and sits in the chair on the opposite side of the small table. 'Hello.'

'Hello.' I smile.

She smiles too.

This is not the first time she's come here.

My arms are crossed on the table, clutching either elbow. I rock back and forth, just a little, without lifting my arms. Rocking feels good. It feels as though I have a baby in my arms. 'Where's your dad? Where's Jonny?' He hasn't come to visit me in this place they call a hospital. It's really a prison. I know it's a prison, even though they don't say it.

'He can't come, Susan.'

'I'm Sarah,' I say. I've told her before but she always calls me Susan when she visits. Probably because she thinks I'm the evil one. 'Is he at home?' I ask.

Lucy doesn't answer. She doesn't like it when I say I'm Sarah. Her eyes ice over when I say I'm Sarah. She still wants to think that her mother was Sarah. I'm the only one who knows that isn't true.

DI Watts and DI Witherstone showed me the CCTV footage

from a camera on the corner of the flats. They told me they were showing it to Lucy too. They pointed at the image of Susan as she got into my car and asked me why I leaned over the engine, under the bonnet. I answered, 'No comment.' I said, 'No comment,' to everything they asked. Even when they showed me the CCTV of me using my phone to pay at the petrol station while I was driving the Mini. I must have said, 'No comment,' thirty times. Just as the solicitor told me to. But they had taken my fingerprints and said that my fingerprints matched those of Susan Tagney. Apparently, there's one thing different about identical twins: their fingerprints. My fingerprints were recorded as Susan Tagney's in London when I murdered Chris. They charged me then for the murder of Sarah Moorell and Jonny Moorell and the attempted murder of a woman whose name I always forget. They didn't charge me for hurting Lucy, there was no evidence to say I intended to kill Lucy. I don't want to hurt Lucy. I don't want to hurt anyone. I want Jonny to come and see me.

'How have you been?'

'Good,' I say. 'And you, how are you?'

'Coping,' she says. 'Michael and I are getting married.' Her left hand slides over the table, her fingers reaching out to display a ring. It has two rubies and two diamonds.

'It's pretty.'

She nods and her hand slides back. 'We're going to get married in Rhodes. His family are going to fly out with us. I can't ...' She clears her throat with a strained cough. 'I couldn't cope with a church wedding here. There are ...' Tears stick on the mascara that coats her eyelashes.

I reach out and hold her hand. I can feel the ring under my fingers.

'I would miss Mum and Dad too much.' The tip of her right-hand index finger touches the corner of her eye as if to gather or hold in the tears without smudging her eye make-up.

She leaves a smudge of black under the corner of her eye.

Her left hand turns underneath mine and she holds my hand in a gentle grip. 'I know you don't understand.'

I nod and smile. I feel sorry for her. I feel sad because she feels sad.

They – the doctors and psychiatrists here – say I have many things. I have manic episodes, obsessive compulsive urges, and psychotic delusions. I'm not sure what any of those things are. I only know that I'm Sarah and I keep telling them that but they won't believe me.

'Jennifer sent me an invitation to the christening. Polly, my little half-sister, is going to be christened next week. I'm going to go. It's hard. I feel as if I didn't know Dad now. But she is my sister.'

I nod. Although I'm not sure what baby sister she's talking about. 'Susan's baby?'

'No. Dad's. She has lovely red hair, like Chloe's.'

'Who's Chloe?'

'You ask that every time I mention her,' she smiles. It's a look that's warm and kind. I often see Jonny in her. 'Dad's girlfriend.'

Now she's confusing me. I don't understand.

Both her hands hold mine, as if she sees my confusion. 'Chloe was adopted when she was child,' she says.

I nod as if I do understand. I like the sound of Lucy's voice. I like her talking to me.

'She's nearly nineteen years younger than Dad, did I tell you? But I suppose at their age it doesn't make a difference.'

'Susan? She wasn't nineteen years younger.'

A frown creases Lucy's forehead. I've said the wrong thing.

'My girl is red-haired,' I say, trying to recover the conversation 'Even when she was born she had lots of red hair like Jay's.'

Her lips form a solid line not a smile, just like Jonny's used to when he was thinking through something. But then she nods and smiles. Her hand lets go of mine. 'I'm sorry, I should go. Michael is waiting outside. But I just wanted to come and say hello. You know I don't hold things against you. I know it's because of what happened to you. I know you aren't well.'

'I am well.' I stand up. 'I wish people would believe me. I'm well, and I'm Sarah.'

She stands up too. 'I know.' Her hand reaches out again and this time it pats my shoulder gently. Then she looks across her shoulder to one of the men in a pale blue pyjama suit.

The man comes to join us. 'Do you want a beaker of tea, Susan?'

'Goodbye.' Lucy leans forward and kisses my cheek as her palm rubs my upper arm. Then she walks away waving.

'I'm not Susan,' I say to the man. 'I'm Sarah. But I do want a cup of tea.'

Acknowledgements

I want to say a huge thank you to the One More Chapter team, for your support and commitment. Charlotte Ledger and Emily Ruston worked with me in about four stages to turn *The Twins* into the story it has become, thank you for your acceptance of my very rough early versions and for having the vision to see what this story could be.